THE COMBINED MAZE

THE
COMBINED MAZE

BY
MAY SINCLAIR

London : HUTCHINSON & CO.
Paternoster Row   ❧   ❧   1913

THE COMBINED MAZE

I

YOU may say that there was something wrong somewhere, some mistake, from the very beginning, in his parentage, in the time and place and manner of his birth. It was in the early eighties, over a shabby chemist's shop in Wandsworth High Street, and it came of the union of Fulleymore Ransome, a little middle-aged chemist, weedy, parched, furtively inebriate, and his wife Emma, the daughter of John Randall, a draper.

They called him John Randall Fulleymore Ransome, and Ranny for short.

Ranny should have been born in lands of adventure, under the green light of a virgin forest, or on some illimitable prairie ; he should have sailed with the Vikings or fought with Cromwell's Ironsides ; or, better still, he should have run, half naked, splendidly pagan, bearing the torch of Marathon.

And yet he bore his torch.

From the very first his mother said that Ranny was that venturesome. He showed it in his ill-considered and ungovernable determination to be born, and it was hard to say which of them, Ranny or his mother, more nearly died of it. She must have been aware that there was a hitch somewhere ; for, referring again and again, as she did, to Ranny's venturesomeness, she would say, " It beats me where he gets it from."

He may have got some of it from her, for she, poor

thing, had sunk, adventurously, in one disastrous marriage, her whole stock of youth and gaiety and charm. It was Ranny's youth and charm and gaiety that made him so surprising and so unaccountable.

Circumstances were not encouraging to Ranny's youth nor to his private and particular ambition, the cultivation of a superb physique. For not only was he a little chemist's son, he was a great furniture dealer's inexpensive and utterly insignificant clerk, one of a dozen confined in a long mahogany pen where they sat at long mahogany · desks upon high mahogany stools, making invoices of chairs and tables and wardrobes and washstands and all manner of furniture. You would never have known, to see him sitting there, that John Randall Fulleymore Ransome was a leader in Section I of the London Polytechnic Gymnasium.

So far, in his way, he testified, he bore his torch. Confined as he was in a mahogany pen, born and brought up in the odour of drugs, and surrounded by every ignominious sign of disease and infirmity, his dream was yet of cleanness, of health and the splendour of physical perfection. The thing that young Ransome most loathed and abhorred was Flabbiness, and next to Flabbiness, Weediness. The years of his adolescence were one long struggle and battle against these two. He had them ever before him, and associated them, absurdly but inveterately, with a pharmaceutical chemist's occupation; of Weediness his father being the prime example; while for Flabbiness, young Mercier, his father's assistant—well, Mercier, as he said, "took the biscuit." It was horrible for young Ransome to inhabit the same house with young Mercier, because of his flabbiness.

In all cities there are many thousand Ransomes, more or less confined in mahogany cages, but John Randall Fulleymore stands for all of them. He was one of those who, in a cold twilight on a Saturday afternoon, stagger from the trampled field, hot-eyed under their wild hair, whose garments are stained from the torn grass and up-trodden earth, with here and there a rent and the white gleam of a shoulder or a thigh ; whose vivid, virile odour has a tang of earth in it. He is the image and the type of these forlorn, foredoomed young athletes, these ex-ponents of a city's desperate adolescence, these inarticu-late enthusiasts of the earth. He bursts from his pen in the evening at seven or half-past, he snatches somewhere a cup of cocoa and a sandwich, and at nine he is seen, half pagan in his "zephyr" and "shorts," sprinting like mad through the main thoroughfares. In summer some pitch, more or less perfect, waits for him in suburban playing-fields ; and the River knows him, at Battersea, at Chelsea, at Hammersmith, and at Wandsworth, the River knows him as he is, the indomitable and impassioned worshipper of the body and the earth.

And if the moon sees him sometimes haggard, panting though indomitable, though impassioned, reeling on the last lap of his last mile, and limping through Wandsworth High Street home to the house of the weedy pharma-ceutical chemist his father, if the moon sees Ransome, why, the moon is a lady and she does not tell.

If you asked him what he did it for, he would say you did it because it kept you fit, also (if you pressed him) because it kept you decent.

And to know how right he was you had only to look at him, escaped from his cage, you had only to follow his progress through the lighted streets and observe his un-bending behaviour before the salutations of the night. His fitness, combined with his decency, made him a wonder, a desire, and a despair. Slender and upright, immaculately high-collared, his thin serge suit moulded by his sheer muscular development to the semblance of perfection, Ranny was a mark for loitering feet and wandering eyes. Ranny was brown-faced and brown-haired; he had brown eyes made clear with a strain of grey, rather narrow eyes, ever so slightly tilted, narrowing still, and lengthening, as with humour, at the outer corners. There was humour in his mouth, wide but fine, that tilted slightly upwards when he spoke. There was humour even in his nose with its subtle curve, the slender length of its bridge, and its tip, wide spread and, like his mouth and eyes, slightly uptilted.

Ranny, in short, was fascinating. And at every turn his mysterious decency betrayed the promise of his charm.

It was Fred Booty, his friend and companion of the pen, who first put him in the right way, discerning in him a fine original genius for adventure.

For when Ranny's mother said he was that venture-some, she meant that he was fond, fantastically and violently fond of danger, of adventure. His cunning in this matter beat her clean—how he found the things to do he did do; the things, the frightful things he did about the house with banisters and windows, of which she knew. As for the things he found to do with bicycles on Wandsworth Common and Putney Hill they were known mainly to his Maker and Fred Booty. Booty, who could judge (being " a bit handy with a bike " himself), said of them that they were " a fair treat."

But these were the deeds of his boyhood, and in nineteen-two Ransome looked back on them with con-tempt. Follies they were; things a silly kid does; and it wasn't by those monkey-tricks that a fellow developed his physique. Booty had found Ransome in his attic one Saturday afternoon, a year ago, half stripped, and contem-plating ruefully what he conceived to be the first horrible, mushy dawn of Flabbiness in his biceps muscle. All he wanted, Booty had then declared, was a turn or two at the Poly. Gym. Then Booty took Ransome round to his place in Putney Bridge Road, and they sat on Booty's bed with their arms round each other's shoulders while Booty read aloud to Ransome from the pages of the Poly. Prospectus. Booty was a slender, agile youth with an innocent sanguine face, the face of a beardless faun, finished off with a bush of blond hair that stood up from . his forehead like a monumental flame.

He read very slowly, in a voice that had in it both an adolescent croak and an engaging Cockney tang.

" The Poly.," said Booty, " really was a club ' *where*,' " he underlined it, " ' every reasonable facil'ty shall bee offered fer the formation of a steadfast character, *and— of*—true friendships ; fer trainin' the intellec'——' "

" Int'lec' be blowed," said Ransome.

" ' *And* fer leadin' an upright unselfish life. Day by day,' " read Booty, " ' the battle of life becomes more strenuous. To succeed entyles careful preparation and stern'—stern, Ranny—' deetermination, it deemands the choice of *good friends* and the avoid'nce of those persons and things wich tend *to* lessen, instead of *to* increase the reesources of the individyool.' There, wot d'you think of *that*, Ran ? "

Ran didn't think much of it, until Booty pointed out to him, one by one, the privileges he would enjoy as a member of the Poly.

For the ridiculous yearly sum of ten-and-six (it was all he could rise to) Ransome had become a member of the Poly. Ten-and-six threw open to him every year the Poly. Gym., the Poly. Swimming Bath, and the Poly. Circulating Library. For ten-and-six he could further command the services (once a week) of the doctor attached to the Poly., and of its experienced legal adviser.

That tickled Ransome. He didn't see himself by any possibility requiring communion with that experienced man. But it tickled him, the sheer fantastic opulence and extravagance of the thing. It tickled him so much that whenever you disagreed with or offended Ransome his jest was to refer you, magnificently, to "my legal adviser."

Yes, for fantastic opulence and extravagance, Ransome had never seen anything to beat the Poly. There was no end to it, no end to the privileges you enjoyed. He positively ran amuck among his privileges, those, that is to say, offered him by the Poly. Swimming Bath and the Poly. Gym. As he said, he "fair abused 'em." But he considered that the Poly. "got home again" on his exceptionally moderate use of the Circulating Library, and his total abstention from the Bible Classes. He was not yet aware of any soul in him apart from that abounding and sufficing physical energy expressed in Fitness, nor was he violently conscious of any moral sense apart from Decency.

And Ranny despised the votaries of intellectual light ; he more than suspected them of Weediness if not of Flabbiness. Yet (as he waited for Booty in the vestibule), through much darkness and confusion and always at an immeasurable distance from him, he discerned, glory beyond glory, the things that the Poly., in its great mercy and pity, had reserved for those "queer johnnies." It made him giddy merely to look at the posters of its lectures and its classes. It gave him the headache to think of the things the fellows—fellows of a deplorable physique—and girls, too, did there. For his part, he looked forward to the day when, by a further subscription of ten-and-six, he would enroll himself as a member of the Athletic Club.

It was as if the Poly. put out feeler after feeler to draw him to itself. Only to one thing he would not be drawn. When Booty advised him to join the Poly. Ramblers he stood firm. For some shy or unfathomable reason of his own he refused to become a Poly. Rambler. When it came to the Poly. Ramblers he was adamant. It was one of those vital points at which he resisted this process of absorption in the Poly. Booty denounced his attitude as eminently anti-social—uppish, he called it.

II

ALL that winter Ransome's nights and days were regulated in a perfect order. Making statements of account for nine hours on five days of the week and four on Saturdays. Three evenings for the Poly. Gym. One for the Swimming Bath. One for sprinting. One (Saturday) for rest or relaxation after the violence of Rugger. One (Sunday) for the improvement of the mind. On Sundays he was very seldom good for anything else.

But in the spring of nineteen-two something stirred in him, something watched and waited; with a subtle agitation, a vague and delicate excitement, it exulted and aspired. The sensation, or whatever it was, had as yet no separate existence of its own. So perfect, in this spring of nineteen-two, was the harmony of Ransome's being that the pulse of the unborn thing was one with all his other pulses; it was one, indistinguishably, with the splendour of life, the madness of running, and the joy he took in his own remarkable performances on the horizontal bar. It had the effect of heightening, mysteriously and indescribably, the joy, the madness, and the splendour. And it was dominant, insistent. Like some great and unintelligible *motif* it ran ringing and sounding through the vast rhythmic tumult of physical energy.

Not for a moment did he connect it with the increasing interest that he took in the appearance of the young ladies of the Poly. Gym. He was not aware how aware he was of their coming, nor how his heart thumped and throbbed and his nerves trembled at the tramp, tramp of their feet along the floor.

For sometimes, it might be twice a year, the young men

7

and the young women of the Gymnasium met and mingled in a Grand Display.

He was fairly well used to it ; and yet he had never got over his amazement at finding that girls, those things of constitutional and predestined flabbiness, could do very nearly (though not quite) everything that he could, leaving him little besides his pre-eminence on the hori- . zontal bar. And yearly the regiment of girls who could " do things " at the Poly. increased under his very eyes. Their invasion disturbed him in his vision of their flabbiness ; it rubbed it into him, the things that they could do.

Not but what he had felt it—he had felt *them*—all about him, outside, in the streets where they jostled him, and in the world made mostly of mahogany, the world of counters and of desks, of pens where they too were herded and shut up and compelled, like him, to toil. Queer things, girls, for they seemed, incomprehensibly, to like it. Their liking it, their business-like assumption of equality, their incessant appearance (authorised, it is true, by business) at the railings of his pen, the peculiar disenchanting promiscuity of it all, preserved young Ransome in his eccentricity of indifference to their sex. In fact, if you tried to talk about sex to young Ransome (and Mercier did try) he would denounce it as " silly goat's talk," and your absorption in it as "the most mutton-headed form of Flabbiness yet out."

But that was before the Grand Display of the autumn of last year, when Winny Dymond appeared in the March Past of Section I of the Women's Gymnasium ; before he had followed Winny as she ran at top speed through all the turnings and windings of the Combined Maze.

There were about fifty of them, picked ; all attired in black stockings, in dark blue knickerbockers, and in tunics that reached to the knee, red belted and trimmed with red. Stunning, he called them ; so much so that they fair took away his breath.

That was what he said when it was all over. By that time he was ashamed to confess that, at the moment of its apparition, the March Past had been somewhat of a shock to him. He had his ideas, and he was not prepared for the uniform ; still less was he prepared for a personal encounter with such quantities of young women, all at once.

All sorts of girls, sturdy and slender girls, queer girls with lean, wiry bodies ; deceptive girls with bodies curiously plastic under the appearance of fragility ; here a young miracle of physical culture ; there a girl with the pointed breasts and flying shoulders, the limbs, the hips, the questing face that recalled some fugitive soul of the woods and mountains ; long-nosed, sallow, nervous Jewish girls ; English girls with stolid, colourless faces ; here and there a face rosy and full-blown, or a pretty tilted profile and a wonderful, elaborate head of hair. One or two of these heads positively lit up the procession with their red and gold ; gave it the splendour and beauty of a pageant.

They came on, single file and double file and four abreast, the long line doubling and turning upon itself ; all alike in the straight drop of the arms to the hips, the rise and fall of their black-stockinged legs, the arching and pointing of the feet ; all deliciously alike in their air of indestructible propriety. Here you caught one leashing an iniquitous little smile in the corners of her eyes under her lashes ; or one, aware of her proud beauty, and bearing herself because of it with the extreme of indestructible propriety.

There were no words to express young Ransome's indifference to proud beauty.

If he found something tender and absurd in the movements of all those long black stockings, it was for the sake and on account of the long black stockings worn by little Winny Dymond.

Winny Dymond was not proud, neither was she what he supposed you would call beautiful. She was not one of those conspicuous by their flaming and elaborate hair.

What he first noted in her with wonder and admiration was the absence of weediness and flabbiness. Better known, she stirred in him, as a child might, an altogether indescribable sense of tenderness and absurdity. She stood out for him simply by the fact that, of all the young ladies of the Polytechnic, she was the only one he really knew—barring Maudie Hollis, and Maudie, though she was the proud beauty of the Polytechnic, didn't count.

For Maudie was ear-marked, so to speak, as the property (when he could afford a place to put her in) of Fred Booty. Ransome would no more have dreamed of cultivating an independent acquaintance with Maudie than he would of pocketing the silver cup that Booty won in last year's Hurdle Race. It was because of Maudie, and at Booty's irresistible request, that he, the slave of friendship, had consented, unwillingly and perfunctorily at first, to become Miss Dymond's cavalier. Maudie, also at Booty's passionate appeal, had for six months shared with Winny Dymond a room off Wandsworth High Street, so that, as he put it, he might feel that she was near him ; with the desolating result that they weren't by any means, no, not by a long chalk, so near. For Maudie, out of levity or sheer exuberant kindness of the heart, had persuaded Winny Dymond to join the Polytechnic. In her proud beauty and in her affianced state she could afford to be exuberantly kind. And Booty in his vision of nearness had been counting on the long journey by night from Regent Street to Wandsworth High Street alone with Maudie, and though Miss Dymond practically effaced herself, it wasn't—with a girl of Maudie's temperament— the same thing at all. For Maudie in company was apt to be a little stiff and standoffish in her manner.

Then (one afternoon in the autumn of last year it was) Booty sounded Ransome, finding himself alone with him in the mahogany pen when the senior clerks were at their tea. "I sy," he said, "there's something I want *you* to do for me," and Ransome, in his recklessness, his magnificence, said "Right-o!"

He said afterwards that he had gathered from the expression of his friend's face that his trouble was financial, a matter of five bob, or fifteen at the very worst. And you could trust Boots to pay up any day. So that he was properly floored when Boots, in a thick, earnest voice, explained the nature of the service he required—that he, Ransome, should go with him, nightly, to a convenient corner of Oxford Street, and there collar that kid, Winny Dymond, and lug her along.

"Do you mean," asked Ransome, "walk home with her?"

Well, yes; that, Booty intimated, was about the size of it. She was a Wandsworth girl, and they'd got, he supposed, all four of them, to get there.

He was trying to carry it off, to give an air of inevitability to his preposterous proposal. But as young Ransome's face expressed his agony, Booty became almost abject in supplication. He didn't know, Ranny didn't, what it was to be situated like he, Booty, was. Booty wanted to know how he'd feel if it was him. To be gone on a girl like he was and only see her of an evenin' and then not be able to get any nearer her, because of havin' to make polite reemarks to that wretched kid she was always cartin' round. At that rate he might just as well not be engaged at all—to Maudie—better engage himself to the bloomin' kid at once. It wasn't as if he had a decent chance of being spliced for good in a year or two's time. His evenin's and his Sundays and so forth were jolly well all he'd got. It was all very well for Ransome, *he* wasn't gone on a girl, else he'd know how erritatin' it was to the nerves. And if Ranny hadn't got the spunk to stand by a pal and see him through, why then, he'd cut the Poly. and make Maudie cut it too.

To most of this Ranny was silent, for it seemed to him that Boots was mad or near it. But at that threat, so terrible to him, so terrible to the Polytechnic, so terrible to Booty and so palpable a sign of his madness, he gave in. He said it was all right, only he didn't know what on earth he was to say to her.

Booty recovered his natural airiness. "Oh," he threw it off, "you say nothing."

And for the first night or so, as far as Ransome could remember, that was what he did say.

And he wasn't really clever at collaring her, either. There was something elusive, fugitive, uncatchable about Winny Dymond. It was Booty, driven by love to that extremity, who collared Maudie and walked off with her, with a suddenness and swiftness that left them stranded and amazed. "Fair pacemakin'," Ransome called it.

And Winny struggled and strove with those little legs of hers (jolly little legs he knew they were, too, in their long black stockings), strove and struggled, as if her life depended on it, to overtake them. And it was then that Ransome felt the first pricking of that sense of tenderness and absurdity.

He felt it again, after a long silence, when, as they were going towards Wandsworth Bridge, Winny suddenly addressed him.

"You know," she said, "you needn't trouble about *me*."

"I'm not troublin'," he said. "Leastways—that is——" he hesitated and was lost.

"You are," said she with decision, "if you think you've got to see me home."

He said he thought that, considering the lateness of the hour, and the loneliness of the scene, it was better that he should accompany her.

"But I can accompany myself," said she.

He smiled at the vision of Miss Dymond accompanying herself; at eleven o'clock at night too—the idea! He smiled at it as if he saw in it something tender and absurd. He knew, of course, for he was not absolutely without experience, that girls said these things ; they said them to draw fellows on ; it was their artfulness. There was a word for it ; Ransome thought the word was cock-a-tree. But Winny Dymond didn't say those things—the least like that. She said them with the utmost gravity and determination. You might almost have thought she was offended but for the absence in her tone of any annoyance or embarrassment. Her tone, indeed, suggested serene sincerity and a sort of sympathy, the serious and compassionate consideration of his painful case. It was as if she had been aware all along of the frightful predicament he had been placed in by Fred Booty ; as if she divined and understood his anguish in it and desired to help him out. That was evidently her idea—to help him out.

And as it grew on him—her idea—it grew on him also that there was a kind of fascination about the little figure in its long dark blue coat.

She wasn't—he supposed she wasn't pretty, but he found himself agreeably affected by her. He liked the queer look of her face that began with a sort of squarishness in roundness, and ended, with a sudden startling change of intention, in a pointed chin. He liked the clear sallow and faint rose of her skin, and her mouth that might have been too large if it had not been so firm and fine. He liked, vaguely, without knowing that he liked it, the quietness of her brown eyes, and the faint, half-wondering arch above them ; and quite definitely he liked the way she parted her brown hair in the middle and smoothed it till it lay in two long low waves (just discernible under the brim of her hat) upon her forehead. He did not know that long afterwards he was never to see Winny Dymond's eyes and parted hair without some vision of strength and profound placidity and cleanness.

All he said was he supposed there was no law against

his occupying the same pavement ; and then he could
have sworn that Winny's face sent a little ghost of a
smile flitting past him through the night.

"Well, anyhow," she said, "you needn't talk to me
unless you like."

And at that he threw his head back and laughed aloud.
And quite suddenly the moon came out and stared at
them ; came bang up on their left above the river (they
were on the bridge now) out of a great cloud, a blazing
and enormous moon. It tickled him. He called her
attention to it, and said he didn't remember that he'd
ever seen such a proper whopper of a moon and with such
a shine on him. They hadn't half polished him, he said.
Anyone would think that things had all busted ; got
turned bottom side upwards, and it was the bally old sun
that was up there, grinnin' at them, through the hole
he'd made.

"The idea !" said Winny ; but she laughed at it, a
little shrill and irresistible titter of delight, always, as he
was to learn, her homage to "ideas." He had them sometimes ; they came on him all of a sudden, like that, and
he couldn't help it ; he couldn't stop them ; he got them
all the worse, all the more ungovernably, when Booty
lunged at him, as he did, with his "Dry up, you silly
blighter, you !" But that anybody should take pleasure
in his ideas, that *was* an idea, if you like, to Ransome.

They got on, after that, like a house on fire.

But only for that night. For many nights that followed
Winny proved more fugitive, more uncatchable than
ever. As often as not, when they arrived in Oxford
Street, she would be gone, fled half an hour before them,
accompanying herself all the way to Wandsworth. Once
he pursued her down Oxford Street, coming up with her
as she boarded a bus in full flight ; and they sat in it, in

gravity and silence, as strangers to each other. But nearly always she was too quick for him ; she got away. And never (he thanked Heaven for that long afterwards) never for a moment did he misunderstand her. She made that impossible for him ; impossible to forget that in her and all her shyness there was no art at all of " cock-a-tree " ; only her fixed and funny determination not " to put upon him."

And so the seeing home of Winny Dymond became a fascinating and uncertain game, fascinating because of its uncertainty ; it had all the agitation and allurement of pursuit and capture ; if she had wanted to allure and agitate him, no art of cock-a-tree could have served her better. He was determined to see Winny Dymond home.

And all the time it grew, it grew on him, that sense of tenderness and absurdity. He found it—that ineffable and poignant quality—in everything about her and in everything she did ; in the gravity of her deportment at the Poly. ; in her shy essaying of the parallel bars ; in the incredible swiftness with which she ran before him in the Maze ; in the way her hair, tied up with an immense black bow in a door-knocker plat, rose and fell for ever on her shoulders as she ran. He found it in the fact he had discovered that her companions called her by absurd and tender names ; Winky, and even Winks, they called her.

That was in the autumn of nineteen-one ; and he was finding it all over again now, in the spring of nineteen-two.

At last, he didn't know how it happened, but one night, having caught up with her after a hot chase, close by the railings of the Parish Church in Wandsworth High Street, in the very moment of parting from her he turned round and said, "Look here, Miss Dymond, you think I don't like seeing you home, don't you ? "

" To be sure I do. It must be a regular nuisance, night after night," she answered.

" Well, it isn't," he said. " I like it. But look here if you hate it——"

" Me ? "

She said it with a simple, naïf amazement.

" Yes, you."

He was almost brutal.

" But I don't. What an idea ! "

" Well, if you don't, that settles it. Don't it ? "

And it did.

III

IT was the night of the Grand Display of the spring of
nineteen-two.

To the Gymnasium of the London Polytechnic you
ascended (in nineteen-two) as to a temple by a flight of
steps, and found yourself in a great oblong room of white
walls, with white pillars supporting the gallery that ran
all round it. The railing of the gallery was of iron tracery,
painted green, with a brass balustrade. The great clean
white space, the long ropes for the trapezes which hung
from the ceiling and were looped up now to the stanchions,
the coarse canvas of the mattresses, the disciplined lines,
the tramping feet, the commanding voices of the instruc-
tors, gave a confused and dream-like suggestion of the
lower deck of a man-of-war. To-night, under the west
end of the gallery, a small platform was raised for the
Mayor of Marylebone and a score of guests. The galleries
themselves were packed with members of the Polytechnic and their friends.

The programme of the Grand Display announced as its
first item :

PARALLEL BARS

Tableau by Messrs. Booty, Tyser, Buist, Wauchope and J. R. F. Ransome

There was a murmur of surreptitious, half-ironic
applause. " Stick it, Ransome, stick it, old boy ! "

The reference was to his extraordinary attitude.

J. R. F. Ransome appeared as the apex and the crown
of a rude triangular structure whose base was formed by
the high parallel bars, flanked at each end by two bodies

C   17

(Booty and Tyser front), two supple, adolescent bodies, bent backwards like two bows. He stood head downwards on his hands that grasped and were supported by the locked arms of two solid athletes, Buist and Wauchope, themselves mounted gloriously and perilously on the straining bars.

Considered as to his arms, and the white "zephyr" and flannels that he wore, he was merely a marvellous young man balancing himself with difficulty in an unnatural posture. But his body, uptilted, poised as by a miracle in air, with the slender curve of its back, its flattened hips, its feet laid together like wings folded in the first down-rush, might have been the body of a young immortal descending with facile precipitancy to earth.

He maintained for a sensible moment his appearance of having just flown from the roof of the gymnasium. Far below, the photographer fumbled leisurely with his apparatus.

"Hurry up there!" "Stick it, Ransome!" "Half a mo!" "Stick it, Ranny, stick it!" they whispered. "Steady does it."

And Ranny stuck it. Ranny, actually, from his awful eminence, sang out "No fear!"

The flash-light immortalised his moment.

That was his way. To stick it; to see it out; to go through with the adventure alert and gay, wearing that fine smile of his, so extravagantly uplifted at the corners. "Stick it!" was the motto of his individual recklessness and of the dogged, enduring conservatism of his class. It kept him in a mahogany pen, at a mahogany desk, for forty-four hours a week, and it sustained him in his orgies of physical energy at the Poly. Gym.

Best of all, it sustained him in his daily and nightly encounters with young Mercier.

He was all the more determined to stick it by the knowledge that young Mercier was up there in the gallery looking at him. He could see him leaning over the balus-

trade and smiling at him, atrociously. He took advantage
of an interval and joined him. He was half inclined to
ask him what he meant by it.

For he was always at it. Whenever young Mercier
caught Ranny doing a sprint, he smiled, atrociously. At
Wandsworth, behind the counter, or in the little zinc-
roofed dispensing-room at the back, among the horribly
smelling materials of his craft, he smiled, remembering him.

Mercier was a black-haired, thick-set youth with heavy
features in a heavy, pasty face, a face oddly decorated by
immense and slightly prominent blue eyes, a face where
all day long the sensual dream brooded heavily. His
black eyebrows gave it a certain accent and distinction.
It was because of his dream that Leonard Mercier could
afford to smile.

He was one of those who wanted to know what Ranny
did it for. He couldn't see what fun the young goat got
out of his evenings. Not half, no, nor a quarter of what
he, Mercier, could get from one night at the Empire, or
when he took his girl to Earl's Court or the Wandsworth
Coliseum. And though up there in the gallery he had
said By Jove, and that he was blowed, and that that
young Ransome was a corker, though he boasted to three
entire strangers that that young fellow was a friend of
his, his curiosity was still unsatisfied. He still wanted to
know what the young goat did it for.

He wanted to know it now. And at his insistence
young Ransome was abashed. How could he explain to
old Eno what he did it for or what it felt like? He
couldn't explain it to himself, he had no words for it,
for that ecstasy of living, that fusion of all faculties in
one rhythm and one vibration, one continuous transport
of physical energy. Take sprinting alone. How could he
convey to Jujubes in his disgusting flabbiness any sense
of the fine madness of running, of the race of the blood
through the veins, of the hammer strokes of the heart,
of the soft pad of the feet on the highway? To Jujubes,

who went in like a cushion no matter where you prodded him, how describe the feel of a taut muscle, the mounting swell of it, the resistance and the small, almost impalpable ripple and throb under the skin ? He couldn't have described it to himself.

So he gave Jujubes his invariable casual answer. You did it because it kept you fit, and because (he let old Eno have it) it kept you decent. Old Eno would be a lot decenter if he went in for it. It would do him worlds of good.

To which old Eno replied that he thought he saw himself ! As for joining Ranny's precious old Poly., why, for all the Life you were likely to see there, you might as well be in a young ladies' boarding school. And Ransome said that that was where Jujubes ought to be. He liked young ladies. Among them (he intimated) his flabbiness might not excite remark. Girls (he pondered it) were flabby things.

Chivalry constrained him to a mental reservation: Winny Dymond and the young ladies of the Poly. Gym. excepted.

But he was glad that Mercier didn't stay to see them. Young Leonard (whose smile was growing more and more atrocious) had declared that the young ladies of the Empire ballet were a bit more in his line, and he had made off, elbowing his way through the crowded gallery and crooning " Boys of the Empire ! " as he went, while Ransome pursued him with the scornful adjuration to " Go home and take a saline draught ! "

But you couldn't shame old Eno. He triumphed and exulted in his flabbiness. For he was a Boy of the Empire. He had seen Life ; and would see more and more of it.

Ransome went down again into the hall. He removed

himself from the crowd and leaned against a pillar, in abstraction, arms folded, showing the great muscles ; a splendid figure in his white "zephyr" trimmed with crimson, with the crimson sash of leadership knotted at his side. Thus withdrawn he watched, half furtively, the performance of the Young Ladies of the Polytechnic Gymnasium.

One by one, with an air incorruptibly decorous, the Young Ladies of the Polytechnic Gymnasium hurled themselves upon the parallel bars ; they waggled themselves by their hands along them ; they swung themselves from side to side of them, and outstretched themselves between them with a foot and a hand upon each bar ; they raised their bodies, thus supported, like an arch ; they slackened them and flung themselves (with a crescendo of decorous delirium) from side to side again, and over ; alighting on their feet in a curtseying posture and with the left arm extended in a little perfunctory gesture of demonstration to an audience ; as much as to say, "There you are, and nothing could be easier ! "

Nothing could be more conventional, and more unspeakably correct. Only when Winny Dymond did it there was a difference, or it seemed so to young Ransome. Winny approached the bars with shyness and a certain earnestness and gravity of intent. She hesitated ; for a moment she was adorable in vacillation. She shook her head at the bars, she bit her lip at them ; she set her face at them in defiance ; then, with a sudden, amazing celerity, she gave a little run forward and leaped upon them ; she swung herself in perfect rhythm and motion onwards and upwards and from side to side ; she arched her sturdy but exquisitely supple· body like a bridge, flung herself over, as if in pure abandonment of joy, and lighted on her feet, curtseying correctly but with something piteous in the gesture of the outstretched arm, and upon her face an expression of great surprise and wonder

at herself, as if Winny said, not " There you are ! " but
" Here I am, and oh ! I never thought I should be ! "

And from his place by the pillar Ransome gave the little
inarticulate murmur he reserved for Winny.   It was
charged with his sense of tenderness and absurdity.

A quarter to ten.   His own performances—his wonderful performances on the horizontal bar—were over ; and
over the demonstration by F. Booty with the Indian Clubs,
where young Fred, slender and supple as a Faun, played
on his own muscles in faultless rhythm.   And now, with
an eye upon the Mayor, the order was given for the last
item on the programme :

THE COMBINED MAZE

There was a rush of energetic young men who flung
themselves upon the properties of the Gymnasium.   They
ran them, the parallel bars, the horses, the mattresses, in
under the galleries ; they uprooted the posts of the horizontal bar ; they cleared the whole of the vast oblong
space bounded by the pillars.

An attendant then appeared with a bit of chalk in his
hand ; and with the chalk he drew upon the floor certain
mystic circles, one at each corner of the oblong, one in the
centre, the heart of the Maze, and facing it two smaller
circles one at each side on a visionary line.   Seven mystic,
seven sacred circles in all did he draw, and vanished, unconscious of the sanctity and symbolism of his deed.

For he, with his bit of white chalk, had marked the
course for the great running, for the race that the young
men and the young girls run together with the racing of
the stars, for the unloosening of the holy primal energies
in a figure and a measure and a ritual old as time.

It was all very well for the instructor (blind instrument
of unspeakably mysterious forces) to pretend that he

invented it, that august figure of the seven-circled Maze ;
to explain it, as he does to the enquiring, by the analogy of
a billiard-table with its pockets.   For never yet, on any
billiard-table, was a race run and a contest waged like that
in which these young men and girls ran and contended.
Drawn up at the far end of the hall under the east gallery
in two ranks, four-breasted, the men on the one side and
the women on the other, they waited, and the leader of
each rank had a foot on a corner circle.   They waited,
marking time with their feet, first, to the thudding beat
of the bar-bell on the floor, and then to an unheard
measure, secret and restrained, the murmur of life in the
blood, the rhythm of the soundless will, the beat of the
unseen, urging energy, that gathered to intensity, desirous
of the race.

As yet the soul of it slept in their rigid bodies, their
grave, forward-looking faces, their behaviour, so exces-
sively correct.   Somebody whispered the word, and on a
sudden they let themselves go ;   they started.   Young
Tyser, breasting the wind of his own speed, his head uplifted and thrown backwards, led the men, and she with
the questing face and wide-pointing breasts of Artemis led
the girls ;   and he had young Ransome on his heels and she
Winny ;   and behind them the fourfold serried ranks
thinned and thinned out and spun themselves in two lines
of single file, two threads, one white, one dark blue, both
flecked with crimson, two threads that in their running were
wound and unwound and woven in a pattern, dark blue
and white and crimson, that ran and never paused and
never ended and was never the same.   For first, each line
was flung slantwise from the corner circle whence it had
started, and where the two met, point by point perpetually,
in the centre circle, they as it were intersected, men and
women wriggling, sliding, and darting with incredible
dexterity through each other's ranks ;   and the pattern was
a cross, a tricolor.   Then they wheeled round the circle
that was and was not their goal, and did it all over again ;

but instead of intersecting at the centre circle they struck off there at a tangent, and the pattern, blue by blue divided from white by white, and all red-flecked, was as two wide V's set point to point ; a pattern that ran away and vanished as each thread, returning, wheeled round the circle whence the other thread had started.

And all this at the top speed set by Tyser, and with the thud of the men's feet and the pad of the women's ; all this with a secret challenge and defiance of one sex to the other, with separation and estrangement, with a never-ending, baffling approach and flight, with the furtive darting of man from woman and of woman from man, whirled in their courses from each other as they met.

And now the lines doubled ; they were running two abreast, slantwise ; and as they intersected in the sacred centre circle it was with a mingling of the threads, a weaving of blue with white, and white with blue ; so that each man had in flight before him a maiden, and so that at their circles, east and west, where they wheeled they wheeled together, side by side, as the Maze flung them.   And now they were circling and serpentining up and down, and down and up, with contrary motion, in a double figure of eight ; they were winding in and out among the pillars and wheeling round the middle circles north and south, side by side, till they split there and parted and met again in the centre and were flung from it, to wheel again deliriously, double-ringed, round all the six outermost circles at once.

And now, as if they were torn from the ends of the earth by the irresistible attraction of the seventh circle, they were whirling round the centre in a double ring, a ring of young men round a ring of girls ; and then, as by some mysterious compulsion, they divided and cast themselves off in rows of two couples, man and girl by man and girl, linked with arms on each other's shoulders, eight rows in all, eight spokes that sprang from the sacred circle ringed with eight, four men and four girls, who were the felly of the wheel, all running, all revolving. Such was the magic of the Maze, and the unconscious genius of the instructor, that the pattern of the running wound and unwound and knit itself together in the supreme symbol of the great Wheel of Eight Spokes, the Wheel of Life.

And the ancient rhythmic rush and race of the worlds, and the wheeling of all stars, the swinging and dancing of all atoms, the streaming and eddying of the ancestral stuff of life was in the whirling of that living Wheel; it was one immortal motion, continuous and triumphant in the bodies of those men and maidens as they ran. And they, shop-girls and shop-boys and young clerks, slipped off their memories of the desk and counter, and a joy, an instinct, and a sense that had no memory woke in them, savage, virgin and shy; the pure and perfect joy of the young body in its own strength and speed; the instinct of the hunter of the hills and woodlands; the sense of feet padding on grass and fallen leaves, of ears pricking alert, of eyes that face the dawn on the high downs and go glancing through the coverts. And as this radiant and vehement life rose in them like a tide, their gravity and shyness and severity passed from them; here and there hair was loosened; combs were shed and nobody stopped to gather them; for frenzy seized on the young men and their arms pressed on the girls' shoulders, urging the pace faster and faster; and light, swift as their flying feet, shot from their eyes, and they laughed each to the other as they ran. So divine was now the madness of their running, so inspired the whirling of the Wheel, that the thing showed plainly as the undying, immemorial ecstasy; showed as the secret dance of magic and of mystery, taken over by the London Polytechnic, and, at the very moment when its corybantic nature most declared itself, constrained to an order and a beauty tremendous and austere.

So wise and powerful was the London Polytechnic.

For Ransome, mixed with that joy of the running, there was a joy of his own, an instinct and a sense, virgin and shy, absolved from memory. He found it, when Winny Dymond ran before him, in the slender innocent movement of her hips under her thin tunic, in the absurd flap-flapping of the door-knocker plat on her shoulders, in the glances flicked at him by the tail of her eye as she wheeled from him in the endless pursuit and capture and approach and flight, as she was parted, was flung from him and returned to him in the windings of the Maze. He found it to perfection in the pressure of each other's arms as the Maze wed them and whirled them running, locked together in the pattern of the wheel. It was not love so much as some inspired sense of comradeship, mingled inextricably with that other sense of absurdity and tenderness.

Not love, not passion, even when in the excitement of the running she swerved to the wrong side and he had to turn her with his two hands upon her waist. For it was the law of their running that, though it was one with the movement of life itself, mysteriously, while the thing lasted, it precluded passion.

IV

RANSOME left Winny Dymond at St. Ann's Terrace, and went home along the High Street. He went very slowly, as if in thought.

At the railings of the Parish Church he paused, recalling something. ,Low and square-towered, couchant in the moonlight behind its railings, the Parish Church guarded under its long flank its huddled graves.

He smiled for very Youth. It was here that he had run Winny to earth and caught her. The Parish Church had been his accomplice in that capture.

Wandsworth High Street twists and winds with the waywardness of a river. The first turn brought him to the old stone bridge over the Wandle. On the bridge before him, in the crook of the street, were the booths and stalls of the night market, lit by blazing naphtha, colour heaped on colour in a leaping, waving flare as of torches. On either side was a twisted and jagged line of houses, brown-brick, flat-fronted, eighteenth-century houses, and houses with painted fronts. Here, a tall, red-brick, modern Parade shot up the gables of its insolent façade. There, oldest of all, a yellow house stooped forward on the posts that propped it. Somewhere up in the sky a tall chimney and a cupola. All beautiful under the night, all dark or dim, with sudden flashes and pallors and gleams, lamplit and moonlit ; and all impressed upon Ransome's brain with an extraordinary vividness and importance, as if he had suddenly discovered something new about Wandsworth High Street.

What he had discovered was the blessedness of living

as he did in Wandsworth High Street within three
minutes' walk of St. Ann's Terrace.

To be sure, what with the shop and the storage for
drugs, Ransome's father's house, with Ransome and his
father and his mother and Mercier and the maid in it, was
somewhat cramped. And neither Ransome nor his father
nor his mother knew how beautiful it was, with its brown
brick front, its steep-pitched roof and the two dormer
windows looking down on the High Street like two sleepy
eyes under drooping lids. A narrow slip of a house, it
stood a foot or two back, between the wine-merchant's
and John Randall the draper's shop, and had the air of
being squeezed out of existence by them. Yet the name
of Fulleymore Ransome, in gold letters on a black ground,
and with Pharmaceutical Chemist under it in a scroll,
more than held its own beside John Randall. The
chemist's dignity was further proclaimed by the immense
bottles, three in a row (the Carboys, Mr. Ransome called
them), holding the magic liquids, a blue, a red, and a
yellow, wide-bellied at the base, and with pyramids for
stoppers. Under them, dividing the window pane, a
narrow gold band with black lettering advertised three
distinct mineral waters.

A yellow-ochre blind now screened the lower half of
that window. Drawn down unevenly and tilted at the
bottom corner, it suffered a vague glimpse of objects that
from his earliest years had never ceased to offend Ranny's
sense of the beautiful and fit.

He had not as yet considered very deeply the problems
of his life. Otherwise, in returning every night to his
father's house, it must have struck him that he was not
what you might call a free man. For his father's house
had no door except the shop-door, and it was the peculi-
arity of that shop-door that it did not admit of any latchkey. Every night young Ransome had to ring, and it
was usually Mercier, with his abominable smile, who let
him in.

To-night the door was opened cautiously on the chain, and somebody whispered, " Is that you, Ranny ? "

The chain was slipped and he entered.

A small bead of gas burned on a bracket somewhere behind the counter. The light slid, pale as water, over the glass and mahogany of the show-cases, wherein white objects appeared as confused and disconnected patches. The darkness effaced every object in the shop that was not white, with the queer effect that rows upon rows of white jars showed as if hanging on it unsupported by their shelves. Very close, turned up to him out of the darkness, was Ranny's mother's face. He kissed it.

" Where's that Mercier ? " said Ranny's mother.

" What ? Isn't he back yet ? "

" No," said Ranny's mother. " And your father's got the Headache."

By a tender and most pardonable confusion between the symptom and its cause, Ranny's mother had hit upon a phrase that made it possible for them to discuss his father's affliction without the smallest, most shadowy reference to its essential nature. For Ranny's mother, such reference would have been the last profanity, a sacrilege committed against the divinities of the hearth and of the marriage-bed. But for that phrase, Mr. Ransome's weakness must have been passed in silence as the unspeakable, incredible, unthinkable thing it was.

At the phrase, more frequent in his mother's mouth than ever, Ranny drew in his lips for a whistle ; but instead of whistling he said, " Poor old Humming-bird."

" It's one of His bad ones," said Ranny's mother.

He raised the flap of the counter and they went through. He turned up the gas so that the outlines of things asserted themselves, and the labels on the white jars gave out their secret gold. On one of these labels, Hydrarg. Amm., which had no meaning for him, Ranny fixed a fascinated gaze, thus avoiding the revelations of his mother's face.

For Ranny's mother's face showed that she had been crying.

Plump, and yet not large, her figure and her face were formed for gaiety and charm. Her little nose was uptilted like Ranny's; but something that was not gaiety but pathos had dragged down and made tremulous the corners of a mouth that had once been tilted too. A flower-like mouth, of the same tender texture as her face, a face that was once one wide-open, innocent pink flower. Now it was washed out and burnt with the courses of her tears. Worry had fretted her soft forehead into lines and twisted her eyebrows in an expression as of permanent surprise at life's handiwork. And under them her dim blue eyes, red-lidded, looked out with the same sorrow and dismay. There was nothing left of her beauty but her exuberant light-brown hair, which she dressed high on her head with a twist and a top-knot piteously reminiscent of gaiety and charm.

She laid her hand on the knob of the left-hand inner door.

" He's in the dispensin' room," she said.

Ranny turned round. His features tilted slightly, compelled by something preposterous in the vision she had evoked.

" Whatever game is he playin' there ? "

A faint flicker passed over his mother's face, as if it pleased her that he could talk in that way.

" Prescription," she said and paused between her words to let it sink into him. " Makin' it up, he is. Old Mr. Beesley's heart mixture."

" My Hat ! " said Ranny. He was impressed by the gravity of the situation.

There were all sorts of things, such as tooth-brushes, patent medicines, babies' comforters, that Ranny's father with a Headache, or Ranny himself or his mother could be trusted to dispense at a moment's notice. But the drug strophanthus, prescribed for old Mr. Beesley, was

not one of them. It was tricky stuff. He knew all about
it ; Mercier had told him. Whether it was to do Mr.
Beesley good or not would depend on the precise degree
and kind of Ranny's father's Headache.

"I've never known your father's Headache so bad as
it is to-night," said Ranny's mother. "As for makin' up
prescriptions, sufferin' as He is, He's not fit for it. He's
not fit for it, Ranny."

That was as near as she could go.

"Of course he isn't."

(They had to keep it up together.)

But Ranny's mother felt that she had gone too far.

"He ought to be in His bed——"

"Of course he ought," said Ranny tenderly.

"And He would be if it wasn't for that Mercier."

Thus subtly did she intimate that it was not his father
but Mercier whose behaviour was reprehensible.

"P'r'aps you'll go to him, Ranny ? "

"Hadn't we better wait for Mercier ? "

(Old Mr. Beesley's mixture was a case for Mercier.)

"Him ? Goodness knows when he'll be in. And it's
not likely that y'r father'll have him interferin' with him.
They're sendin' at ten past eleven, and it's five past now."

Thus and thus only did she suggest the necessity for
immediate action. Also her fear lest Mercier should find
Mr. Ransome out. As if Mercier had not found him out
long ago ; as if he hadn't warned Ranny, time and again,
of what might happen.

"All right, I'll go."

He went by the right-hand door at the back of the shop,
and down a short and exceedingly narrow passage, lined
with shallow shelves for the storage of drugs.

Another door at the end of the passage led straight into
the dispensing room outside, a long shed of corrugated

iron run up against the garden wall and lined with
honey-coloured pine. Under a wide stretch of window
was a work-table. At one end of this table was a slab
of white marble; at the other a porcelain sink fitted
with taps and sprays for hot and cold water. From the
far end of the room where the stove was came a smothered
roar of gas flames. On the unbroken inner wall were
shelves fitted with drawers of all sizes, each with its
label, and above them other shelves with row after row
of jars. Near the stove, more shelves with more and
more jars, with phials, kettles, pannikins, and pipkins.
Everywhere else shelves of medicine bottles, innumerable
medicine bottles of all sorts and sizes, giving to the honey-
coloured walls a decorative glimmer of sea-blue and sea-
green.

All this was brilliantly illuminated with gas that burned
on every bracket.

To Ransome's senses it was as if the faint, the delicate
colours of the place gave a more frightful grossness and
pungency to its smell. Dying asafœtida struggled still
with gas fumes and was pierced by another odour, a
sharp and bitter odour that he knew.

At the long table, under the hanging gaselier, in
shirt-sleeves and apron, Mr. Ransome stood. The light
fell full on his sallow baldness and its ring of iron-
grey hair; on his sallow sickly face; on his little
long, peaked nose with its peevish nostrils; even on his
thin and irritable mouth unhidden by the scanty, close-
trimmed, iron-grey moustache and beard. He was weedy
to the last degree.

Ranny came near and gazed inscrutably at this miracle
of physical unfitness. Under his gaze the pitiful and
insignificant figure bore itself as with a majesty of rectitude.

Mr. Ransome had before him a prescription, a medicine
bottle, a large bottle of distilled water, two measuring glasses
and a smaller bottle half full of a pale amber liquid. He had

been standing motionless, staring at these objects with a peculiar and intent solemnity. Now, as if challenged and challenging, he drew the smaller measuring-glass towards him with one hand. He held it to the light and moved his finger-nail slowly along the middle measuring line. Then with two hands that trembled he poured into it a part of the infusion. The liquid went tink-tinkling in a succession of little jerks. He held it to the light ; it rose a good inch above the line he had marked. He shook his head at it slowly, with an air of admonition and reproof, and poured it back into the bottle.

This process he repeated seven times, always with the same solemn intentness, the same reproving and admonitory air.

At his seventh failure he turned with the dignity of a man overmastered by outrageous circumstance.

" Mercier not in ? " he asked sternly. (You would have said it was his son Randall that he admonished and reproved.)

" Not yet," said Ranny. And as he said it he possessed himself very gently of the measuring glass and bottle. (Mr. Ransome affected not to notice this manœuvre.) " What is it ? "

" Tincture of strophanthus, sodæ bicarb., and spirits of chloroform. Just you mind how you handle it."

" Right-o ! " said Ranny.

The chemist's small iron-grey eyes were fixed on him with severity and resentment.

" How much ? " said Ranny.

" Up to three." Mr. Ransome's head was steadier than his hand.

Ranny poured the dose.

" Ac—acqua distillata—to eight ounces," said Mr. Ransome disjointedly, but with an extreme incision.

Ranny poured again, and decanted the medicine into its bottle through a funnel, corked it, tied on the capsule, labelled, addressed, wrapped and sealed it. The long-

D

drawn, subtle corners of Ranny's eyes and mouth were lifted in that irrepressible smile of his, while Mr. Ransome asserted his pharmaceutical dignity by acrimonious comment. "*Now* then! You might have club-feet instead of hands. Tha's right—mess the sealin' wax, waste the string, spoil anything you haven't got to pay for. That'll do."

Mr. Ransome took the parcel from his son's hand, turned it round and round under the gaslight, laid it down and dismissed it with a flick as of contempt for his incompetence. At that Ranny gave way and giggled.

Ten minutes later he and his mother stood in the doorway of the back parlour and watched the master's superb and solitary ascent to his bedroom on the first-floor back. It was then that Ranny, still smiling, delivered his innermost opinion.

" Queer old Humming-bird. Ain't he, Mar ? "

His mother shook her head at him. " Oh, Ranny," she said, " you shouldn't speak so disrespectful of your father."

But she kissed him for it all the same.

V

THAT was how they kept it up together.

Not that Mrs. Ransome was conscious of keeping it up, of ministering to an illusion as monstrous as it was absurd. She had married Mr. Ransome believing with a final and absolute conviction in his wisdom and his goodness. What she was keeping up, had kept up for twenty-two years, and would keep up for ever, was the attitude of her undying youth. It was its triumph over life itself.

In her youth the draper's daughter had been dazzled by Mr. Ransome, by his attainments, his position, his distinction. Fulleymore Ransome had about him the small refinement of the suburban shop-keeper, made finer by the intellectual processes that had turned him out a Pharmaceutical Chemist.

In her world of Wandsworth High Street his grave fastidious figure had stood for everything that was superior. He was superior still. He had never offered his Headache as a spectacle to the public eye. Born in secrecy and solitude it remained unseen outside the sacred circle of his home. Even there he had contrived to create around it an atmosphere of mystery. So that it was open to Mrs. Ransome to regard each Headache as an accident, a thing apart, solitary and miraculous in its occurrence. Faced with the incredible fact she found a certain gratification in the thought that Mr. Ransome's position enabled him to order the best spirit wholesale, and with a professional impunity. So inviolate was his privacy that not even the wine and spirit merchant next door could gauge the amount of his expenditure in this item.

Thus, in Mrs. Ransome's eyes, the worst Headache he had ever had could not impair his innermost integrity. Her vision of him was inspired by an innocence and sincerity that were of the substance of her soul. And in this optimism she had brought up her son.

Ranny, with his venturesomeness, had carried it a step further. For Ranny, not only did Mr. Ransome's inebriety conceal itself under the name of Headache, but in those hours when the Headache cast its intolerable gloom over the household Ranny persisted—from his childhood he had persisted—in regarding his father, perversely, as the source and fount of joy.

It was in this happy light he saw him on Sunday morning, when Mrs. Ransome came into the back parlour where he was hiding his paper, *The Pink 'Un*, behind him under the sofa cushions. She was wearing her new slaty-grey gown with the lace collar, and a head-dress that combined the decorum of the bonnet with the levity and fascination of the hat. Black it was, with a spray of damask roses and their leaves, that spring upwards from Mrs. Ransome's left ear.

" Your father's goin' to church," she said.

Ranny sat up among his cushions and said, " Oh, Lord ! That Humming-bird's a fair treat."

He took it as a supreme instance of his father's humour.

But that was not the way Mrs. Ransome meant that he should take it. Ranny's admiration implied that the Humming-bird was carrying it off, successfully, if you like, but still carrying it. Whereas what she desired him to see was that there was nothing to be carried off. Obviously there could not be, when Mr. Ransome was prepared to go to church.

For the going to church of Mr. Ransome was itself a ritual, a high religious ceremony. Hitherto he had kept himself pure for it, abstaining from all Headache over night. It was this habitual consecration of Mr. Ransome that made his last lapse so remarkable and so important, while it revealed it as fortuitous. Ranny had missed the deep logic of his mother's statement. Mr. Ransome was sidesman at the Parish Church and at no time was the Headache compatible with being sidesman.

Nothing had ever interfered with the slow pageant of Mr. Ransome's progress towards church. Outside in the passage he was lingering over his preparations. The adjustment of his tie, the brushing of his tall hat, the drawing on of the dogskin gloves he wore in his office. It was not easy for Mr. Ransome to exceed the professional dignity of his frock-coat and grey trousers, and yet every Sunday, by some miracle, he did exceed it. Each minute, irreproachable detail of his dress accentuated reiterated, the suggestion of his perpetual sobriety.

Still, there remained the memory of last night. Mrs. Ransome did not evade it, on the contrary she used it to demonstrate the indomitable power of Mr. Ransome's will.

" *I* say he ought to be layin' down," she said. " But there—He won't. You know what He is since He's been sidesman. It's my belief He'd rise up off his death-bed to hand that plate. It's his duty to go, and go He will if He drops. That's your father all over."

" That's Him," Ranny assented.

His mother looked him in the face. It was the look, familiar to Ranny on a Sunday morning, that while it reinstated Ranny's father in his rectitude, contrived subtly, insidiously, to put Ranny in the wrong.

" You're going too," his mother said.

Well, no, he wasn't exactly going. Not, that was to say, to any church in Wandsworth (he had, in fact, a pressing engagement to meet young Tyser at the first easterly signpost on Putney Common, and cycle with him to Richmond).

" It's only a spin," said Ranny, though the look on his mother's face was enough to tell him that a spin, on a Sunday, was dissipation, and he, recklessly, iniquitously spinning, a prodigal most unsuitably descended from an upright father.

And then (this happened nearly every Sunday) Ranny set himself to charm away that look from his mother's face. First of all he said she was a tip-topper, a howling swell, and asked her where *she* expected to go to in that hat, nippin' in and cuttin' all the girls out, and she a married woman and a mother ; and whether it wouldn't be fairer all round, and much more proper, if she was to wear something in the nature of a veil? Then he buttoned up her gloves over her little fat wrists and kissed her in several places where the veil ought to have been ; and when he had informed her that " the Humming-bird was a regular toff," and had dismissed them both with his blessing, standing on the doorstep of the shop, he wheeled his bicycle out into the street, mounted it and followed at the pace of a walking funeral until his parents had disappeared into the Parish Church.

Then Ranny, in his joy, set up a prolonged ringing of his bicycle bell, as it were the cry of his young soul, a shrill song of triumph and liberation and delight. And, in his own vivid phrase, he " let her rip."

Of course he was a prodigal, a wastrel, a spendthrift. Going the pace, he was, with a vengeance, like a razzling-dazzling, devil-may-care young dog.

A prodigal driven by the lust of speed, dissipating his divine energies in this fierce whirling of the wheels ; scattering his youth to the sun and his strength to the wind in the fury of riotous biking. A drunkard, mad-drunk, blind-drunk with the draught of his onrush.

That was Ranny on a Sunday morning.

He returned, at one o'clock, to a dinner of roast mutton and apple tart. Conversation was sustained, for Mercier's benefit, at the extreme pitch of politeness and precision.

It seemed to Ranny that at Sunday dinner his father reached, socially, a very high level. It seemed so to Mrs. Ransome as she bloomed and flushed in a brief return of her beauty above the mutton and the tart. She bloomed and flushed every time that Mr. Ransome did anything that proved his goodness and his wisdom. Sunday was the day in which she most believed in him ; the day set apart for her worship of him.

By what blindfolded pieties, what subterfuges, what evasions she had achieved her own private superstition was unknown, even to herself. It was by courage and the magic of personality—some evocation of her lost gaiety and charm—but above all by courage that she had contrived to impose it upon other people.

The cult of Mr. Ransome reached its height at four o'clock on this Sunday afternoon, when Ranny's Uncle John Randall (junior) and Aunt Randall dropped in to tea. Both Mr. and Mrs. Randall believed in Mr. Ransome with the fervent, immovable faith of innocence that has once for all taken an idea into its head. Long ago they had taken it into their heads that Mr. Ransome was a wise and good man. They had taken it on hearsay, on conjecture, on perpetual suggestion conveyed by Mrs. Ransome, and on the grounds—absolutely incontrovertible—that they had never heard a word to the contrary. Never, until the other day, when that young Mercier came to Wandsworth. And, as Mrs. Randall said, everybody knew what *he* was. Whatever it was that Mr. Randall had heard from young Mercier and told to Mrs. Randall, the two had agreed to hold their tongues about it, for Emmy's sake, and not to pass it on. Wild horses, Mrs. Randall said, wouldn't drag it out of her.

Not that they believed or could believe such a thing of Mr. Ransome, who had been known in Wandsworth for five-and-twenty years, before that young Mercier was so much as born. And by holding their tongues about it and not passing it on they had succeeded in dismissing from their minds, for long intervals at a time, the story they had heard about Mr. Ransome. " For, mind you," said Mr. Randall, " if it got about it would ruin him. Ruin him it would. As much as if it was true."

Long afterwards when she thought of that Sunday, and how beautifully they'd spoken of Mr. Ransome ; that Sunday when they had had tea upstairs in the best parlour on the front ; that Sunday that had been half pleasure and half pain, that strange and ominous Sunday when poor Ranny had broken out and been so wild ; long afterwards, when she thought of it, Mrs. Ransome found that tears were in her eyes.

She had no idea then that they had heard anything. Family affection was what you looked for from the Randalls, and on Sundays they showed it by a frequent dropping in to tea.

John Randall, the draper, was a fine man. A tall, erect, full-fronted man, a superb figure in a frock-coat. A man with a florid, handsome face, clean-shaved for the greater salience of his big moustache (dark, grizzled like his hair). A man with handsome eyes, prominent, slightly bloodshot, generous eyes. He might have passed for a soldier but for something that detracted, something that Ranny noticed. But even Ranny hesitated to call it flabbiness in so fine a man.

Mr. Randall had married a woman who had been even finer than himself. And she was still fine, with her black hair dressed in a prominent pompadour and her figure curbed by the tightness of her Sunday gown. Under her polished hair Mrs. Randall's face shone with a blond pallor. It had grown up gradually round her features and they, becoming more and more insignificant, were now merged in its general expression of good-will. Ranny noted with wonder this increasing simplification of his Aunt Randall's face.

She entered as if under stress, towing her large husband through the doorway, and in and out among the furniture.

The room that received them was full of furniture, walnut-wood, mid-Victorian in design, upholstered in rep which had faded from crimson to an agreeable old rose. Rep curtains over Nottingham lace hung from the two windows. There was a davenport between them, and, opposite, a cabinet with a looking-glass back in three arches. It was Mr. Ransome's social distinction that he had inherited this walnut-wood furniture. Modernity was represented by a brand-new overmantle in stained wood and bevelled glass, with little shelves displaying Japanese vases. The wall-paper turned this front parlour into a bower of gilt roses (slightly tarnished) on a greyish ground.

And as Mrs. Ransome sat at the head of the oval table in the centre you would never have known that she was the woman with red eyes, the furtive, whispering woman who had opened the door to her son Randall last night. She sat in a most correct and upright attitude, she looked at John Randall and his wife, and smiled and flushed with gladness and with pride. It took so little to make her glad and proud. She was glad that Bessie was wearing the black and white which was so becoming to her. She was glad that there was honey as well as jam for tea, and that she had not cut the cake before they came. She was proud of her teapot and of the appearance of her room. She was proud of Mr. Ransome's appearance at the table (where he sat austerely) and of her brother John Randall who looked so like a military man.

And John Randall talked ; he talked ; it was what he had come for. He had a right to talk. He was a member of the Borough Council, an important man, a man (it was said of him) with " ideas." He was a Liberal ; and so, for that matter, was Mr. Ransome. Both were of the good, safe middle class and took the good, safe, middle line.

They sat there ; the Nottingham lace curtains veiled them from the gazes of the street, but their voices, raised in discussion, could be most distinctly heard ; for the window was a little open, letting in the golden afternoon.

They sat and drank tea and abused the Tory Government. Not any one Tory Government but all Tory Governments. Mr. Ransome said that all Tory Governments were bad. Mr. Randall, aiming at precision, said he wouldn't say they were bad so much as stupid, cowardly and dishonest. Stupid, because they were incapable of the ideas the Liberals had. Cowardly, because they let the Liberals do all the fighting for ideas. Dishonest, because they stole the ideas, purloined 'em, carried them out and sneaked the credit.

And when Ranny asked if it mattered who got the credit provided they *were* carried out, Mr. Randall replied solemnly that it did matter, my boy. It mattered a great deal. Credit was everything, the nation's confidence was everything. A Government lived on credit and on nothing else. And his father told him that he hadn't understood what his uncle had been saying.

" If anybody asks *me*——" said Mr. Ransome. He interrupted himself to stare terribly at Mrs. Ransome who was sending a signal to her son and a whisper, " Have a little slice of gingercake, Ran dear."

" If anybody asks me *my* objection to a Tory Government, I'll put it for 'em," said Mr. Ransome, " in a nutshell."

" Let's have it, Fulleymore," said Mr. Randall. And Mr. Ransome let him have it—in a nutshell.

" With a Tory Government you always, sooner or later, have a war. And who," said Mr. Ransome, " *wants* war ? "

Mr. Randall bowed and made a motion of his hand towards his brother-in-law, a complicated gesture which implied destruction of all Tory Governments, homage to Mr. Ransome, and dismissal of the subject as definitively settled by him.

Mrs. Ransome seized the moment to raise her eyebrows and the teapot towards Mrs. Randall and to whisper again, surreptitiously, " Jest another little drain of tea ? "

Then Ranny, who had tilted his chair most dangerously

backwards, was heard saying something. A bit of a scrap, now and then, with other nations was, in Ranny's opinion, a jolly good thing. Kept you from gettin' Flabby. Kept you Fit.

Mr. Randall in a large, forbearing manner, dealt with Ranny. He wanted to know, whether he, Ranny, thought that the world was one almighty Poly. Gym.?

And Mr. Ransome answered, " That's precisely what he does think. Made for his amusement, the world is."

Ranny was young, and so they all treated him as if he were neither good nor wise.

And Ranny, desperately tilted backwards, looked at them all with a smile that almost confirmed his father's view of his philosophy. He was working up for his great outbreak. He could feel the laughter struggling in his throat.

" I don't say," said Mr. Ransome, ignoring his son's folly, " that I'm complaining of this Boer War in especial. If anything "— he weighed it, determined, in his rectitude, to be just even to the war—" if anything we sold more of some things."

" Now what," said Mrs. Randall, " do you sell most of in time of war ? "

" Sleepin' draughts, heart mixture, nerve tonic, stomach mixture and so forth."

" And he can tell you," said Mr. Randall, " to a month's bookin' what meddycine he'll sell."

" What's more," said the chemist, with a sinister intonation, " I can tell who'll want 'em."

" Can you reelly now ? " said Mrs. Randall. " Why, Fulleymore, you should have been a doctor. Shouldn't he, Emmy ? "

Mrs. Ransome laughed softly in her pride. " He couldn't be much more than He is. Why, He doctors half the poor people in Wandsworth. They all come to Him, whether it's toothache or bronchitis or the influenza, or a housemaid with a whitlow on her finger, and He prescribes for all. If all the doctors in Wandsworth died to-morrow some of us would be no worse off."

" Many's the doctor's bill he's saved me," said Mr. Randall.

" Yes, but it's a tryin' life for Him, sufferin' as He is in 'is own 'ealth. Never knowin' when the night-bell won't ring and He have to get up out of his warm bed. He doesn't spare Himself, I can tell you."

And on they went for another quarter of an hour, boldly asserting, delicately hinting, subtly suggesting that Mr. Ransome was a good man ; as if, Ranny reflected, anybody had ever said he wasn't. Mr. Ransome withdrew himself to his arm-chair by the fireplace, and the hymn of praise went on ; it flowed round him where he sat morose and remote ; and Ranny, in the window-seat, was silent, listening with an inscrutable intentness to the three voices that ran on. He marvelled at the way they kept it up. When his mother's light soprano broke, breathless for a moment, on a top note, Mrs. Randall's rich, guttural contralto came to its support, Mr. Randall supplying a running accompaniment of bass. And now they burst, all three of them, into anecdote and reminiscence, illustrating what they were all agreed about, that Mr. Ransome was a good man.

Nobody asked Ranny to join in ; nobody knew, nobody cared what he was thinking, least of all Mr. Ransome.

He was thinking that he had asked Fred Booty in to tea and that he had forgotten to say anything about it to his mother, and that Fred was late and that his father wouldn't like it.

He didn't. He didn't like it at all. He didn't like Fred Booty to begin with, and when the impudent young monkey arrived after the others had gone, and had to have fresh tea made for him, thus accentuating and prolonging the unpleasantly, the intolerably festive hour, Mr. Ransome felt that he had been tried to the utmost and that courtesy and forbearance had gone far enough for one Sunday. So he refused to speak when he was spoken to. He turned his back on his family and on Booty. He impressed them with his absolute and perfect disapproval.

For, as the Headache worked in Mr. Ransome, all young and gay and innocent things became abominable to him. Especially young things with spirits and appetites like his son Randall and Fred Booty. This afternoon they inspired him with a peculiar loathing and disgust. So did the malignant cheerfulness maintained by his wife. Escape no doubt was open to him. He might have left the room and sat by himself in the back parlour. But he spared them this humiliation. Outraged as he was, he would not go to the extreme length of forsaking them. He was a good man, and, as a good man, he would not be separated from his family though he loathed it. So he hung about the room where they were ; he brooded over it ; he filled it with the spirit of the Headache. Young Booty became so infected, so poisoned with this presence that his nervous system suffered, and he all but choked over his tea. Young Booty with his humour and his wit, the joy of Poly. Ramblers, sat in silence, miserably blushing, crumbling with agitated fingers the cake he dared not eat, and all the time trying not to look at Ranny.

For if he looked at Ranny he would be done for ; he would not be able to contain himself, beholding how Ranny stuck it, and what he made of it, that intolerable, that incredible Sunday afternoon ; how he saw it through ; how he got back on it and found in it his own. For, as Mr. Ransome went from gloom to gloom, Ranny's spirit soared, indomitable, and his merriment rose in him, wave on wave.

What he could make of it Booty saw in an instant when Mr. Ransome left the room at the summons of the shop-bell.

Ranny, with a smile of positive affection, watched him as he went.

" Queer old percher, ain't he ? " Ranny said.

Then he let himself go, addressing himself to Booty. " The old Porcupine may seem to you a trifle melancholy and morose. You can't see what's goin' on in his mind. You've no ideer of the glee he bottles up inside himself. Fair bubblin' and sparklin' in him, it is. Some day he'll bust out with it. I shouldn't be surprised if, at any moment now, he was to break out into song."

Booty, very hot and uncomfortable under Mrs. Ransome's eyes, affected to reprove him. " You dry up, you young rotter. Jolly lot of bottlin' up there is about you."

But there was that in Ranny which seemed as if it would never dry up. He hopped a chair seven times running, out of pure light-heartedness. The sound of the hopping brought Mr. Ransome in a fury from the shop below. He stood in the doorway, absurd as to his stature, but tremendous in the expression of the gloom that was his soul.

" What's goin' on here ? " he asked in a voice that would have thundered if it could.

" It's me," said Ranny. " Practisin'."

" I won't 'ave it then. I'll 'ave none of this leapin' and jumpin' over the shop on a Sunday afternoon. Pandemonium it is. 'Aven't you got all the week for your silly monkey-tricks ? I won't 'ave this room used, Mother, if he can't behave himself in it of a Sunday."

And he slammed the door on himself.

" On Sunday evenin'," said his son imperturbably, as if there had been no interruption, " eight-thirty to eleven, at his residence, High Street, Wandsworth, Mr. Fulleymore Ransome will give an Entertainment. Humorous Impersonations : Mr. F. Ransome. Step Dancin' : Mr. F. Ransome. Ladies are requested to remove their hats. Song : ' Put me among the Girls ' : Mr. F. Ransome——"

" For shame, Ranny," said his mother behind her pocket-handkerchief.

"—There will be a short interval for refreshment, when festivities will conclude with a performance on the French Horn : Mr. F. Ransome."

His mother laughed as she always did (relieved that he could take it that way) ; but this time, through all her laughter, he could see that there was something wrong.

And in the evening when he had returned from seeing Booty home, she told him what it was. They were alone together in the front parlour.

" Ranny," she said suddenly, " if I were you I wouldn't bring strangers in for a bit while your father's sufferin' as he is."

" Oh, I say, Mother——"

Ranny was disconcerted, for he had been going to ask her if he might bring Winny Dymond in some day.

" Well," she said, " it isn't as if He was one that could get away by Himself, like. He's always in and out."

" Yes. The old Hedgehog scuttles about pretty ubiquitous, don't he ? "

That was all he said.

But though he took it like that, he knew his mother's heart ; he knew what it had cost her to give him that pitiful hint. He was balancing himself on the arm of her chair now, and hanging over her like a lover.

He had always been more like a lover to her than a son. Mr. Ransome's transports (if he could be said to have transports) of affection were violent, with long . intermissions and most brief. Ranny had ways, soft words, cajoleries, caresses that charmed her in her secret desolation. Balancing himself on the arm of her chair, he had his face hidden in the nape of her neck, where he affected ecstasy and the sniffing in of fragrance, as if his mother were a flower.

" What do you *do ?* " said Ranny. " Do you bury yourself in violets all night, or what ? "

" Violets indeed ! Get along with you ! "

" Violets aren't in it with your neck, Mother—nor roses
neither. What did God Almighty think he was making
when he made you ? "

" Don't you dare to speak so," said his mother, smiling
secretly.

" Lord bless you ! *He* don't mind," said Ranny. " He's
not like Par."

And he plunged into her neck again and burrowed
there.

" Ranny, if you knew how you worried me, you wouldn't
do it. You reelly wouldn't. I don't know what'll come to
you, goin' on so reckless."

" It's because I love you," said Ranny, half stifled
with his burrowing. " You fair drive me mad. I could
eat you, Mother, and thrive on it."

" Get along with you ! There ! You're spoiling all
my Sunday lace."

Ranny emerged and his mother looked at him.

" Such a sight as you are. If you could see yourself,"
she said.

She raised her hand and stroked, not without tenderness, his rumpled hair.

" P'r'aps —— If you had a sweetheart, Ran, you'd
leave off makin' a fool of your old mother."

" I wouldn't leave off kissin' her," said he.

And then, suddenly, it struck him that he had never
kissed Winny. He hadn't even thought of it. He saw her
fugitive, swift-darting, rebellious rather than reluctant
under his embrace ; and at the thought he blushed,
suddenly, all over.

His mother was unaware that his kisses had become
dreamy, tentative, foreboding. She said to herself,
" When his time comes there'll be no holding him. But
he isn't one that'll be in a hurry, Ranny isn't."

She took comfort from that thought.

VI

RANNY had received his first intimation that he was not a free man. And it had come upon him with something of a shock. He had made his burst for freedom five years ago when he refused to be a Pharmaceutical Chemist in his father's shop, because he could not stand his father's ubiquity. And yet he was not free to leave his father's house ; for he did not see how, as things were going, he could leave his mother. He was not free to ask his friends there either ; not, that was to say, friends who were strangers to his father and the Headache. Above all he was not free to ask Winny Dymond. He had thought he was, but his mother had made him see that he wasn't, because of his father's Headache ; that he really ought not to expose the poor old Humming-bird to the rude criticism of people who did not know how good he was. That was what his mother, bless her ! had been trying to make him see. And if it came to exposing, if this was to be a fair sample of their Sundays, if the Humming-bird was going to take the cake for queerness, what right had he to expose little Winny ?

And would she stand it if he did ? She might come once, perhaps, but not again. The Humming-bird would be a bit too much for her.

Then how on earth, Ranny asked himself, was he going to get any further with a girl like Winny ? His acquaintance with her was bound to be a furtive and a secret thing. He loathed anything furtive and he hated secrecy. And Winny would loathe and hate them too. And she might turn on him and ask him why she was

E

to be made love to in the streets when his mother had a house and he lived in it ?

It was the first time that this idea of making love had come to him. Of course he had always supposed that he would marry some day ; but as for making love, it was his mother who had put into his head that exquisitely agitating idea.

To make love to little Winny and to marry her, if (and that was not by any means so certain) she would have him—no idea could well have agitated Ranny more. It blunted the fine razor-like edge of his appetite for Sunday supper. It obscured his interest in *The Pink 'Un*, which he had unearthed from under the sofa cushion in the back parlour, whither he had withdrawn himself to think of it. And thinking of it took away the best part of his Sunday night's sleep.

For, after all, it was impossible ; and the more you thought of it the more impossible it was. He couldn't marry. He simply couldn't afford it on a salary of eight pounds a month, which was a little under a hundred a year. He couldn't even afford it on his rise. Fellows did. But he considered it was a beastly shame of them ; yes, a beastly shame it was to go and tie a girl to you when you couldn't keep her properly, to say nothing of letting her in for having kids you couldn't keep at all. Ranny had very fixed and firm opinions about marrying ; for he had seen fellows doing it, rushing bald-headed into this tre-mendous business, for no reason but that they had got so gone on some girl they couldn't stick it without her. Ranny, in his decency, considered that that wasn't a reason ; that they ought to stick it ; that they ought to think of the girl, and that of all the beastly things you could do to her, this was the beastliest, because it tied her.

He had more than ever decided that it was so as he lay in his attic, sleepless on his narrow iron bedstead, staring up at the steep slope of the whitewashed ceiling that leaned over him, pressed on him and threatened him ; watching it glimmer and darken and glimmer again to the dawn. He had put away from him the almost tangible vision of Winny lying there, pretty as she would be, in her little white nightgown and her hair tossed over his pillow perhaps, and he vowed that for Winny's sake he would never do that thing.

As for the feeling he had unmistakably begun to have for Winny, he would have to put that away too until he could afford to produce it.

It might also be wiser, for his own sake, to give up seeing her until he could afford it ; but to this pitch of abnegation Ranny, for all his decency, couldn't rise.

Besides, he had to see her. He had to see her home.

And so he took his feeling and put it away, together with a certain sachet, scented with violets, and having a pattern of violets on a white satin ground, and the word Violet going slantwise across it in embroidery. He had bought it (from his mother) in the shop, to keep (he said) in his drawer among his handkerchiefs. And in his drawer, among his handkerchiefs, he kept it, wrapped tenderly in tissue paper. He tried hard to forget that he had really bought it to give to Winny on her birthday. He tried hard to forget his feeling, wrapped up and put away with it. But he couldn't forget it ; because every day his handkerchiefs, impregnated with the scent of violets, gave out a whiff that reminded him, and his feeling was inextricably entangled with that whiff.

It was with him as he worked in his mahogany pen at Woolridge's. All day a faint odour of violets clung to him and spread itself subtly about the counting-house, and the fellows noticed it and sniffed. And, oh, how they chaffed him. " Um-m-m. You been rolling in a bed of violets, Ranny ? " And " Oo-ooh, what price violets ! "

And "You might tell us her name, old chappie, if you *won't* give the address." Till his life was a burden to him.

So to end the nuisance he took that sachet wrapped in tissue paper, and put it in the round japanned tin box where he kept his collars, and let his collars run loose about the drawer. He shut the lid down tight on the smell and took the box and hid it in the cupboard where his boots were, where the smell couldn't possibly get out, and where the very next day his mother found it and received some enlightenment as to Ranny's state of mind. But like a wise woman she kept it to herself.

And the smell departed gradually from the region of Ranny's breast-pocket and he had peace in his pen. His fellow clerks suspected him of a casual encounter and no more. A matter too trivial for remark.

The counting-house at Woolridge's was an immense long room under the roof, lit by a row of windows on each side and a skylight in the middle. The door gave on a passage that ran the whole length of the room, dividing it in two. Right and left the space was partitioned off into pens more or less open. On Ransome's right, as he entered, was the pen for the women typists. On his left the petty cashier's pen, overlooking the women. Next came the ledger clerks, then the statement clerks ; and facing these the long desk of the checking staff. At the back of the room, right and left, were the pens of the very youngest clerks who made invoices. From their high desks they could just see the bald spot on the assistant secretary's head. He, the highest power in that hierarchy, had a special pen provided for him behind the ledger and the statement clerks, a little innermost sanctuary approached by a short passage. Surrounded entirely by glass, he could overlook the whole of his dominion, from the boys at the bottom to the grey-headed cashier and the women typists at the top.

And in between, scattered and in rows, the tops of men's heads : heads dark and fair and grizzled, all bowed over the long desks, all diminished and obscured in their effect by the heavy mahogany of their pens, by the shining brass trellis-work that screened them, by the emerald green of the hanging lampshades, by the blond lights and clear shadows of the walls, and by the everlasting streaming, drifting, and shifting of the white paper that they handled.

The whole place was full of sounds : the hard clicking of the typewriters, and under it the eternal rustling of the white papers, the scratching of pens, the thud of ledgers on desks, the hiss of their turning leaves, and the sharp smacking and slamming as they closed.

And, in the middle of that stir and motion made by hands, all those tops of heads were still, as if they took no part in it ; through the intensity of their absorption they were detached. Every now and then one of them would lift and hold up a face among those tops of heads, and it was like the sudden uncanny insurgence of an alien life.

That stillness was abhorrent to young Ransome. So was the bowing of his head, the cramping of his limbs, and his sense of imprisonment in his pen.

And all his life he would go on sitting there in that intolerable constraint. He had no hope beyond exchanging a larger pen at the bottom of the room for a smaller one at the top. He had begun at the very bottom as an invoice clerk at a pound a week. He was now a statement clerk at eight pounds a month. Working up through all his grades he would become a ledger clerk at twelve pounds a month. He might stick at that for ever, but if he had luck he might become a petty cashier at sixteen pounds. That couldn't happen before he was thirty, if then. He was bound to get his rise in the autumn. But that was no good. It wouldn't be safe, not really safe, to marry until he had become a petty cashier. To end in the petty cashier's narrow pen by the door, that was the goal and summit of his ambition.

Day in day out he worked now with desperate assiduity. He bowed his young head, he cramped his glorious limbs, he steeped his very soul in statements of account for furniture. Furniture bought with hideous continuity by lucky devils, opulent beasts, beasts that wallowed inconsiderately ; worst of all by beasts, abominable beasts who couldn't afford it and were yet about to marry and to set up house. Woolridge's offered a shameless encouragement to these. It lured them on ; it laid out its nets for them and caught and tangled them and flung them to their ruin. All over London and the provinces Woolridge's posters were displayed ; flaunting yet insidious posters where a young man and a young woman with innocent, idiotic faces were seen gazing, fascinated, into Woolridge's windows. Woolridge's artist had a wild humour that gave the show away by exaggerating the innocence and idiocy of Woolridge's victims. It appealed to Ransome by the audacity with which it had defied Woolridge's to see its point. Woolridge's itself was a perpetual tempting and solicitation. Ranny wondered how in those days he ever resisted its appeal to him to be a man and risk it and make a home for Winny.

And as the months went on he kept himself fitter than ever. He did dumb-bell practice in his bedroom. He sprinted like mad. He rowed hard on the river. He was so fit that in June (just before stocktaking) he entered for the Wandsworth Athletic Sports and won the silver cup against Fred Booty in the Hurdle Race. He was more than ever punctual at the Poly. Gym.

And sometimes, on a Sunday afternoon, he would take Winny for a bicycle ride into the country. He liked pushing her machine up all the hills ; still more he liked to help her in her first fierce charging of them, with a strong hand at the back of her waist. That was nothing to the joy of scorching on the level with linked hands. And it was best of all when they rested, sitting side by side under a birch tree on the Common, or lying in the long grass of the fields.

Thus on a Sunday afternoon in June they found themselves alone in a corner of a meadow in Southfields. All day Ransome had been overcome by a certain melancholy which Winny for some reason affected to ignore.

They had been silent for a perceptible time, Ransome lying on his back while Winny, seated beside him, gathered what daisies and buttercups were within her reach. And as he watched her sidelong, it struck him all at once that Winny's life was worse even than his own. Winny was clever and she had a berth as book-keeper in Starker's, one of the smaller drapers' shops in Oxford Street, near Woolridge's. Her position was as good as his, yet she only earned five pounds a month to his eight. And he hated to think of Winny working, anyway.

" Winny," he said suddenly, " do you like book-keeping ? "

" Of course I do," said Winny. She didn't, but she was not going to say so lest he should think that she was discontented.

" Are they—are they decent to you at Starker's ? "

" Of course they are. I would like," said Winny in her grandest manner, " to see anybody trying it on with *me*."

" Oh, well, I suppose it's all right if you like it. But I thought—perhaps—you didn't."

" You'd no business to think."

" Can't help it. Born thinkin'."

" Well—it shows how much you know. I mean to enjoy life," said Winny. " And I do enjoy it."

Ranny, lying on his back with his face turned up to the sky, said that that was a jolly sight more than he did ; that for his part he thought it a pretty rotten show.

Winny stared, for this utterance was most unlike him.

" My goodness ! Whatever in the world's wrong with you ? "

Everything, he answered gloomily, was wrong.

" What an idea ! " said Winny.

It *was* an idea, he said, if it was nothing else. At any rate it was his idea. And Winny wanted to know what made him have it.

" Oh, I dunno. There are things a fellow wants he hasn't got."

" What sort of things ? "

" All sorts."

" Well—don't think about them. Think," said Winny, " of the things you *have* got."

" What things ? "

" Why," said Winny, counting them off on her fingers, " you've got a father—and a mother—and new tyres to your bike. Good boots " (she had stuck buttercups in their laces), "and a most beautiful purple tie." (She held another buttercup under his chin.)

" It *is* a tidy tie," Ranny admitted, smiling because of the buttercups. " But me hat's a bit rocky."

" Quite a good hat," said Winny, looking at it with her little head on one side. " And you've won the silver cup for the Wandsworth Hurdle Race. What more do you want ? "

" It's what a fellow hasn't got he wants."

" Well, what haven't you got, then ? "

" Prospects," said Ranny. " I've no prospects. Not for years and years."

" No," said Winny with decision. " And didn't ought to have. Not at your age."

She had no sympathy for him and no understanding of his case.

Ranny sat up, stared about him, and sighed profoundly.

And because he could think of nothing else to say he suggested that it was time to go.

Winny sprang to her feet with a swiftness that implied that if it was to go he wanted she was more than ready to oblige him. As she mounted her bicycle, the shut firmness of her mouth, the straightness of her back, and the grip of her little hands on the handle-bars were eloquent of her determination to be gone. And her face, he noticed, was pinker than he ever remembered having seen it.

And he wondered what it was he had said.

VII

IT was after that evening that he observed a change in her, a change that he could neither account for nor define. It seemed to him that she was trying to avoid him, and that he was no longer agreeably affected by her behaviour, as he had been in the beginning by her fugitive, evasive ways. Then she had, indeed, led him a dance, but he had thoroughly enjoyed the fun of it. Now the dancing and the fun were all over. At least so he was left to gather from her manner; for the strangeness of it was that she said nothing now. There was about her a terrible stillness and reserve, and in her little face, once so tender, the suggestion of a possible hardness.

He was not aware that the stillness and reserve were in himself, nor that the hardness was in his own face as it set in his indomitable determination to stick it, and not to do the beastly thing, nor yet that there were moments when that stillness and that set look terrified Winny. Neither was he aware that Winny under all her terror had an instinct that divined him and understood.

And as the months went on he saw less and less of her. Though he was punctual at their corner in Oxford Street, he was always too late to find Winny there. He gave that up, and began to haunt the door in Starker's iron shutter at closing time. He had found out that girl clerks, what with chattering and putting on their hats and things, were always a good ten minutes later than the men. He had seen fellows (fellows from Woolridge's, some of them) hanging round the shutters of the big draperies to meet the girls. By making a dash for it from Woolridge's he could reach Starker's just in time .

to catch Winny as she came out, delicately stepping through the little door in the great iron shutter.

Evening after evening he was there and never caught her. She was off before he could get through the door in his own shutter.

Then (it was one evening in August) he saw her. He was not making a dash for it; he was strolling casually and without hope in the direction of Starker's, and he saw her walking away, arm-in-arm with another girl, a girl he had never seen before. He would have overtaken them, but that the presence of the girl deterred him.

He followed, losing them in the crowd, recovering, losing them again; then they turned northwards up a side street and were gone. He noticed that the strange girl was taller than Winny by the head and shoulders, and that she went lazily, deliberately, with sudden lingerings, and always with a curious swinging movement of her hips. He had been close upon Winny at the corner as they turned, so close that he could have touched her. He thought she had seen him, but he could not be sure. He was also aware of a large eye slued round towards him in a pretty profile that lifted itself, deep-chinned, above Winny's head. Their behaviour agitated him, but he forbore to track them further. Decency told him that that would be dishonourable.

The next evening and the next he watched the door in the iron shutter, and was too late for Winny. But the third evening he saw her standing by the door and talking to the same strange girl. The girl had her back to him, but Winny faced him. She was not aware of him at first, but, at the signal that he gave, she turned sharply and went from him, drawing the girl with her, arm-in-arm.

They disappeared northwards up the same side street as before.

That was on a Friday. On Sunday he called at St. Ann's Terrace and saw Maudie Hollis, who told him that Winny had gone up Hampstead way. No, not for good, but with a friend. She had been very much taken up lately with a friend.

" You know what she is when she's taken up," said Maudie.

He sighed unaware and Maudie answered his sigh.

" It isn't a gentleman friend."

" No ? " It was wonderful the indifference Ranny packed into that little word.

" Catch *her* ! " said Maudie.

She smiled at him as he turned away, and in the middle of his own misery it struck him that poor Maudie would have to wait many years before Booty could afford to marry her, and that already her proud beauty was a little sharpened, and a little dimmed by waiting.

On Monday he refrained from hanging round the door in Starker's iron shutter. But on Tuesday, Wednesday, and Thursday he was at his post and remained there till the door was shut almost in his face.

On Friday he was late, and he could see even in the distance the shut door.

But somebody was there, somebody was standing close up against the shutter ; somebody who moved forward a step as he came, somebody who had been waiting for him. It was not Winny. It was the tall girl.

He raised his hat in answer to the movement that was her signal, and would have passed on, but she stopped him. She stood almost in front of him so that he should not pass. And the biggest and darkest blue eyes he had ever seen arrested him with a strange bending on him of black brows.

The strange girl was saying something to him, in a voice full and yet low, a voice with a sort of thick throb in it, and in its thickness a sweet and poignant quality.

" Please," it was saying, " excuse me, you're Mr. Ransome, aren't you—Winny Dymond's friend ? "

With a " Yes " that strangled itself and became in-articulate, he admitted that he was Mr. Ransome.

The girl lowered her eyelids (deep white eyelids they were, and hung with black fringes, marvellously thick and long), she lowered them as if her own behaviour and his had made her shy.

"I'm Winny's friend, too," she said. "That's why I'm here."

And with that she looked him in the face with eyes that shot at him a clear blue out of their darkness. Her eyes, as he expressed it afterwards, were "stunners," and they were "queer"; they were the "queerest" thing about her. That was his word for their half-fascinating, half-stupefying quality.

"Are you waiting for her?" he asked.

"No. It's no good waiting for her. She's gone."

"Gone?"

"Gone home."

He rallied. "Then what are you waiting for?"

"I was waiting for you," she said, "to tell you that it's no good."

He had moved a little way out of the stream of people, so that he was now placed with his back against the shutter, and she with her shoulder to the stream. As she stood thus a man jostled her, more to attract her attention than to move her from his path. She gave a little gasp and shrank back with a movement that brought her nearer to Ransome and to his side. And as she moved there came from her, from her clothes, and from her hair, a faint odour of violets, familiar yet wonderful.

"You don't mind my speaking to you?" she said.

"No," said he, "but let's get out of this first."

He put his hand lightly on her arm to steer her through the stream. There was something about her, it may have been in her voice, or in the way she looked at him, something helpless that implored and entreated and appealed to his young manhood for protection. Her arm yielded to his touch, yet with a slight pressure that made him aware that its tissue was of an incredible softness. Somehow, for the moment while this touch and pressure lasted, he found it impossible to look at her. Some instinct held his eyes from her, as if he had been afraid.

They moved on slowly, aimlessly it seemed to Ransome ; yet steering he was steered, northwards, up the side street where he had seen her disappear with Winny. It was quiet there. He no longer touched her. He could look at her now.

He looked. And what he saw was a girl well grown and of incomparable softness. She could not have been much more than twenty, but her body was already rounded to the full flower of its youth. This body was neither tall nor slender nor particularly graceful. Yet it carried itself with an effect of tallness and slenderness and grace.

In the same way she impressed him as being well dressed. Yet she only wore a little plain black gown cut rather low, with a broad lace collar. There was a black velvet band round her waist and another on her wide black hat. And yet another and a narrower band of black velvet round her full white neck.

The face above that neck was not beautiful, for her little straight nose was a shade too blunt, her upper lip a shade too long and too flat ; her large mouth, red and sullen-sweet, a shade too unfinished at the edges. There was, moreover, a hint of fulness about the jaw and chin. But the colour and the texture of this face made almost imperceptible its flaws of structure. It was as if it had erred only through an excess of softness that made the flesh of it plastic to its blood, to the subtle flame that transfused the white of it, flushing and burning to rose-red. A flame that even in soaring knew its place ; for it sank before it could diminish the amazing blueness of her eyes ; and it had left her forehead and her eyelids to the whiteness that gave accent to eyebrows and eyelashes black as her black hair.

That was how this girl's face, that was not beautiful,

contrived to give an impression of strange beauty, fascinating and stupefying as her voice.

Her voice had begun again.

" It really isn't any good," it said.

" What isn't ? "

" Your hanging about like this. It won't help you. It won't really. You don't know Winny."

" I say, did she ask you to tell me that ? "

" Not she ! 'Tisn't likely. And if she did you don't suppose I'd let on. I'm giving you the straight tip. I'm telling you what I know about her. I'm her friend, else I couldn't do it."

" But—why ? "

" Don't ask me—How do I know ? I suppose I couldn't stand seeing you waiting outside there, night after night, all for nothing."

She drew herself up, so that she seemed to be looking down at him ; she seemed, with all her youth, to be older than he, to be no longer childlike and innocent and help-less. And her voice, her incomparable voice, had an edge to it ; it was the voice of maturity, of experience, of the wisdom of the world.

" You can take it from me," said this voice, " that it doesn't do a man a bit of good to go on hanging about a girl, and worrying her when she doesn't want him."

" You mean—she doesn't like me ? "

" Like you ? As far as I know she likes you well enough."

" Then—for the life of me I can't see why——"

" Liking a man isn't wanting him. And you're not going the way to make Winny want you."

" Oh——"

He had drawn up in the middle of the pavement just to consider whether, after all, there wasn't something in it.

" You're—you're not offended ? " Her voice implored now and pleaded.

" That's all right."

" Well—if you're sure you're not—would you mind seeing me home ? "

" Certainly. With pleasure."

She was all helpless again and childlike, and he liked her that way best.

" I don't like the streets," she explained. " I'm afraid of them. I mean I'm afraid of the people in them. They stare at me something awful. So horribly rude, isn't it, to stare ? "

" Rude ? " said Ransome. " It's disgustin'."

" As if there was something peculiar about me. Do *you* see anything peculiar about me ? Anything, I mean, to make them stare ? "

He was silent.

" *Do* you ? " she insisted poignantly.

They were advancing headlong towards intimacy and its embarrassments.

" Well, no," he said, " if you ask me—no, I don't. Except that, don't you know, you're——"

" I'm what ? "

" Well——"

" Oh ! " (She became more poignant than ever.) " You *do* then——"

" No, I don't—on my honour I—I only meant that— well, you *are* a bit out of the way, you know."

Her large gaze interrogated him.

" Out of the way all round, I should fancy. Something rather wonderful."

" Something—rather—wonderful——" she repeated drowsily.

" Strikes me so—that's all."

" Strange ? "

" Sort of——"

"It *is* strange that we should be talking this way—when you think—Why, you don't even know my name."

"No more I do," said Ransome.

"My name is Violet. Violet Usher. Do you like it?"

"Very much," said Ransome.

He did not know if this was cock-a-tree; but if it was he found himself enjoying it.

"And yours is Randall. Mr. Randall Ransome, aren't you?"

"I say, you know, how did you get hold of that?"

"Why—Winny told me."

In the strangeness of it all he had forgotten Winny.

"Then she told you wrong. Now I think of it, Winny doesn't know my real name. My real name would take your breath away."

"Tell it me."

"Well—if you will have it—stand well back and hold your hat on. Don't let it catch you full in the face. John —Randall—Fulleymore—Ransome. Now you know me."

She smiled enchantingly. "Not quite. But I know something about you Winny doesn't know. That's strange, isn't it?"

It was, if you came to think of it.

They had crossed the Euston Road now, and Miss Usher turned presently up another side street going north. She stopped at a door in a long row of dingy houses.

"This is me," she said, "I've got a room here. It was awfully good of you to bring me."

"Not at all," he murmured.

"And you're sure you didn't mind my speaking to you like that? I wouldn't have done it if I hadn't been Winny's friend."

"Of course not."

She was not sure whether he were answering her question or assenting to her statement.

"And now," she said, "you're going home."

F

" I suppose so." But he remained rooted to the door-step, digging into a crevice in it with his stick.

From the upper step she watched him intently.

" And we shan't see each other again."

He was not sure whether it was a statement or a question.

" Shan't we ? " He said it submissively, as if she really knew.

She was opening the door now and letting herself in. Miss Usher had a latchkey.

" Where ? " said Miss Usher softly, but with incision. She had turned now and was standing on her threshold.

" Oh—anywhere——"

" Anywhere's nowhere." Miss Usher was smiling at him, but as she smiled she stepped back and shut the door in his excited face.

He turned away, more stupefied than ever.

For the first time in his life he had encountered mystery. And he had no name for it.

But he had made a note of her street, and of the number of her door.

VIII

THAT night Ransome was more than ever the prey of thought, if you could call it thought, that mad racing and careering of his brain which followed his encounter with Miss Usher. The stupefaction which had been her first effect had given way to a peculiar excitement and activity of mind. When he said to himself that Miss Usher had behaved queerly, he meant that she had acted with a fine defiance of convention. And she had carried it off. She had compelled him to accept her with her mystery as a thing long known. She had pushed the barriers aside, and in a moment she had established intimacy.

For only intimacy could have excused her interference with his innermost affairs. She had given him an amount of warning and advice that he would not have tolerated from his own mother. And she had used some charm that made it impossible for him to resent it. What could well be queerer than that he should be told by a girl he did not know that his case was hopeless, that he must give up running after Winny Dymond, that he was only persecuting a girl who didn't care for him? Ransome had no doubt that she had spoken out of some secret and mystic knowledge of her friend.

He supposed that women understood each other.

And after all what had she done that was so extraordinary? She had only put into words—sensible words—his own misgivings, his own profound distrust of the event.

What *was* extraordinary, if he could have analysed it, was the calmness that mingled with his disturbance.

Calmness with regard to Winny and to the issue taken out of his hands and decided for him ; calmness, and yet a pain, a distinct pain that he was not subtle enough to recognise as remorse for a disloyalty. And, under it all, that nameless, inexplicable excitement, as if for the first time in the affairs of sex he had a sense of mystery and of adventure.

He did not ask himself how it was that Winny had not stirred that sense in him. He did not refer it definitely to Violet Usher. It had moved in the air about her ; but it remained when she was gone.

So far was he from referring it to Miss Usher that when it died down he made no attempt to revive it by following the adventure. He was restrained by some obscure instinct of self-preservation, also by the absurd persist-ence with which in thought he returned again and again to Winny Dymond. That recurrent tenderness for Winny, a girl who had no sort of tenderness for him, was a thing he did not mean to encourage more than he could help. Still, it kept him from running after any other girl. He was not in love with Violet Usher, and so, gradually, her magic lost its hold upon his memory.

Autumn came, and with it another Grand Display at the Polytechnic Gymnasium, the grandest he had yet known. As if it had been some great civic function, it was attended by the Mayor of Marylebone in his robes. To be sure the Mayor, who was " going on " that night, left some time before the performance of Mr. J. R. F. Ransome on the Horizontal Bar.

But Ranny was not aware of the disappearance of the Mayor. He was not perfectly aware of his own amazing evolutions on the horizontal bar. He was not perfectly aware of anything but the face and eyes of Violet Usher fixed on him from the side gallery above. The gallery was crowded with other faces and with other eyes, all fixed on him ; but he was not aware of them. The gallery was for him a solitude pervaded by the presence of Violet Usher.

She was seated in the front row directly opposite him ; her arms were laid along the balustrade, and she leaned out over them, bending her dark brows towards him, immovable and intent. He did not know whether she was alone there. To all appearance she was alone, for her face remained fixed above her arms, and it was as if her eyes never once looked away from him.

And under their gaze an exultation seized him and a fierce desire, not only to exceed and to excel all other performers on the horizontal bar, but to go beyond himself ; beyond his ordinary punctual precision ; beyond the mere easy swing and temperate rhythm. Instead of the old good-natured rivalry, it was as if he struggled and did battle in some supreme and terrible fight. Each movement that he made fired his blood ; from the first flinging of his lithe body upwards, and the sliding of its taut muscles on the bar, to the frenzy of his revolving, triumphal, glorious to behold. Each muscle and each nerve had its own peculiar ecstasy.

And when he dropped from the high bar to the floor he stood tingling and trembling and breathless from the queer violence with which his heart threw itself about. So utterly had he gone beyond himself. And he knew that his demonstration had not been quite so triumphal, so glorious as he had thought it. There had been far too much hurry and excitement about it. And Booty told him he was all right, but perhaps not quite up to his usual form.

It was with the air of a conqueror that Ranny pushed his way through the packed line of spectators in the gallery. It was with a crushed and nervous air, as of some great artist, conscious of his aim and of his failure, that he presented himself to Violet Usher, sliding slant-wise into the place she made for him.

It was as if she had known that he would come to her. They shook hands awkwardly. And with the stirring of her body there came from her that faint warm odour of violets.

" I didn't expect to see you here," he said at last.

" Winny brought me ; else I shouldn't have come."

She was very precise in making Winny responsible for her appearance. He gathered that that was her idea of propriety.

" Well—anyhow—it's a bit of all right," he said. Then they sat silent for a while.

And the girl's face turned to Ranny with a flying look ; and it was as if she had touched him with her eyes, lightly and shyly, and was gone. Then her eyes began slowly to look him up and down, up and down, from his bare neck and arms, white against the thin crimson binding of his " zephyr," from his shoulders and from his chest where the lines and bosses of the muscles showed under the light gauze, and from his crimson belt, down the firm long slopes to his knees ; and it was as if her eyes brushed him, palpably, with soft feather-strokes. They rested on his face ; and it was as if they held him between two ardent hands. And over her own face as she looked at him there went a little wave of change. Her rich colour stirred and deepened ; her lips parted for the quick passage of her breath ; and her blue eyes looked grey as if veiled in a light vapour.

Ranny was seized with an overpowering, a terrible consciousness of himself and of his evolutions on the horizontal bar.

" Well," he said, as if in apology, " you've seen me figuring queerly."

" Oh, it's all right for men," she said. " Besides, I've seen *you* before."

" Why, you weren't here last time ? "

" No. Not here."

" Where, then ? Where on earth can you have seen me ? "

She bent her brows at him in that way she had, under the brim of her wide hat. " I saw you at Wandsworth—at the Sports—running in that race. When you won the cup."

" Oh, Lord," said Ranny, expressing his innermost confusion.

" Well, I'm sure you ran beautifully."

" Oh, yes, I *ran* all right."

" And you jumped ! "

" Anybody can jump," said Ranny.

" Can they ? "

" Oh, Lord, yes. You should see Fred Booty."

" I did see him. You won the cup off him."

She drew herself up, in that other way she had, as if challenged.

" And he'll win it off me next year. You bet. Look—here they are."

Some instinct, risen he knew not whence, compelled him to divert her gaze.

From below in the great hall came the sound of the rhythmic padding and tramping of feet. The Young Ladies of the Polytechnic were marching in. Right and left they wheeled, and right and left ranged themselves in two long lines under the galleries. Now they were marking time with the stiff rise and fall of black stockings under the short tunics. Facing them, at the head of her rank, was Winny Dymond, very upright and earnest. And with each movement of her hips the crimson sash of leadership swung in rhythm at her side.

Miss Usher turned to him. " Is Winny with them ? "

" Rather. There she is. Right opposite. Jolly she looks, doesn't she ? "

Miss Usher looked at Winny. The bent black brows

bent lower and a large blue eye slued round into her profile, darting a sudden light at him.

"Don't ask *me*," she said, "I'm sure *I* don't know." And she turned her shoulder on him and sat thus averted, gazing at her own hands folded in her lap.

Ransome leaned out over the balustrade and watched Winny. And for a moment, as he watched her, he felt again the old sense of tenderness and absurdity, mingled, this time, with that mysterious pain.

A bar-bell struck on the floor. A feminine voice gave the sharp word of command, and the Young Ladies formed up for their performance on the parallel bars.

Miss Usher still sat averted.

"Look," he said at last, "it's Winny's turn."

She turned slowly, reluctantly almost, and looked.

Winny Dymond, shy, but grave and earnest, was going through her little preliminary by-play at the bars. Then, with her startling suddenness, she rushed at them, and swung herself, it seemed to Ransome, with an increased abandonment, a wilder rhythm and motion ; and when she raised her body like an arch, far-stretching and wide-planted, it seemed to him that it rose higher and stretched farther and wider than before, that there was, in fact, something preposterous in her attitude. For as Miss Usher looked at Winny she drew herself up and her red mouth stiffened.

Ranny's tension relaxed when Winny flung herself from side to side again and over, and lighted on her feet in the little curtseying posture, perfunctory and pathetic.

He clapped his hands. "'Jove. That's good!" He was smiling tenderly.

He turned to Miss Usher, eager and delighted. "Well —what d'you think of it ? "

The eyes he gazed into were remote and cold. Miss Usher did not answer him. And he gathered from her silence that she disapproved profoundly of the performance. He wondered why.

"Oh, come," he said. "She's the best we've got. There's not one of those girls that can touch her on the bars. Look at them."

"I don't want to look at them. I didn't think it would be like that. I'm not used to it. I've never been to a gymnasium in my life before."

"You ought to come. You should join us, Miss Usher. Why don't you?"

"Thank you, Mr. Ransome, I'd rather not. I don't see myself!"

He didn't see her either. Some of his innocence had gone. She had taken it away from him. He was beginning to understand how Winny's performance had struck her. It was magnificent, but it was not a thing that could be done by a nice woman, by a woman who respected herself and her own womanhood and her own beauty; not a thing that could be done by Violet Usher. He was not sure that in her view it was consistent with propriety, with reticence, with a perfect purity. And he began to wonder whether his own view of it had not been a little shameless.

He rushed, for sheer decency, into a stuttering defence.

"Well, but—well, but—but it's all right, don't you know?"

"It's all right for men. They're different. But——"

"Not right for women?"

"If you reelly want to know—No. I don't think it is. It isn't pretty, for one thing."

"Oh, I say—how about Winny?"

"Winny's different. It doesn't seem to matter so much for her."

"Why not—for her?"

"Well—she's a queer creature anyhow."

"How d'you mean—queer?"

"Well—More like a boy, somehow, than a girl. She doesn't care. She'll do anything. And she's plucky. If she's taken a thing into her head she'll go through with it whatever you say."

" Yes, she's got pluck," he assented. " *And* cheek."

" Mind you, she's as good as gold, with all her queerness. But it *is* queer, Mr. Ransome, if you're a woman, not to care what you do, or what you look like doing it. And she's so innocent, she doesn't reelly know. She couldn't do it if she did. All the same I wish she wouldn't."

She seemed to brood over it in beautiful distress.

" It's a pity that the boys encourage them. Boys don't mind, of course. But *men* don't like it."

And with every word of her strange magical voice there went from him some shred of innocence and illusion. It was, of course, his innocence, his ignorance that had made him tolerant of a Grand Display ; that had filled him with admiration for the Young Ladies of the Polytechnic Gymnasium, and that had attracted him to Winny Dymond. Everything he had thought and felt about Winny was illusion. It was illusion, that sense she gave him of tenderness and of absurdity. Gymnastics were all very well in their way. But nice women, the women that men cared about, women like Violet Usher, did not make of their bodies a spectacle in Grand Displays. Little Winny, whatever she did, was all right, of course ; but now he came to think of it, he began to wish, like Violet Usher, that she wouldn't do it. It was as a boy and her comrade, that he had admired her. It was as a man that he criticised her now, looking at her through Violet Usher's eyes. And it was as a boy that he had cared and as a man that he had ceased to care.

In one night Ranny had suddenly grown up.

Of course, it might have been different if she had cared for *him*.

" What does it mean, the Combined Maze ? What is it ? "

Miss Usher was studying her programme.

The Combined Maze ? That wasn't so easy to explain.

But Ranny explained it. It was, he said, a maze, because you ran it winding in and out like, and combined, because men and women ran in it all mixed up together. They made patterns accordin' as they ran, and the patterns were the plan of the maze. You didn't see the plan. You didn't know it, unless you were leader. You just followed.

" I see. Men and women together."

" Men and women together."

" Are you running in it ? "

" Yes."

" Does Winny run in it ? "

" Rather. We run together. You'll see how it's done."

Miss Usher thought she saw.

And they ran in it together, Ransome with Winny before him, turning from him, parting from him, flying from him, and returning to him again. Always with the same soft pad of her feet, the same swaying of her sturdy, slender body, the same rising and falling on her shoulders of her childish door-knocker plat.

Winny was a child ; that was all that could be said of her ; and he, he was a man ; grown up suddenly in a single night.

He ran, perfunctorily, through all the foolish turnings and windings of the maze. He put his hands on Winny's waist to guide her when, in her excitement, she went wrong. He linked his arm with hers when they ran locked, shoulder to shoulder, in the Great Wheel ; but it was as if he held and caught, and was locked together with a child. Winny's charm was gone ; and with it gone the sense of tenderness and absurdity ; gone the magic and the madness of the running. For in Ranny's heart there was another magic and another madness. And it was as if Life itself had caught him and locked him with a woman in the whirling of its Great Wheel.

IX

HE haunted that door in the shutter more than ever in the hope of seeing Violet Usher. Not that he wanted to haunt it. It was as if, set his feet southwards as he would, they were turned back irresistibly and drawn eastwards in the direction of the door.

There was nothing furtive and secret in his haunting. He had a right to hang about Starker's, for he knew Miss Usher now. He had been formally introduced to her by Winny as they left the Polytechnic together, on the night of the Grand Display. Winny, preoccupied with her own performance on the parallel bars, had remained unaware of their communion in the gallery, and Violet Usher had evidently judged it best to say nothing about their previous interviews.

The introducing, of course, made all the difference in the world; for Ransome, reckless as he was, respected the conventions where women were concerned. He had seen too much of the secret and the furtive ways of other fellows, and he knew what their hanging about meant. It meant, in nine cases out of ten, that they wanted kicking badly. And Ranny would have told you gravely that, in his experience, it was the " swells " who wanted kicking most of all. The " fellows," the shop-assistants, and the young clerks, like himself, were fairly decent, but sometimes they wanted kicking too, and in any case the " flabby " way they fooled about with girls and their " silly goats' talk " outraged Ranny. It made a girl cheap, and kept other fellows off her. It didn't give her her chance. It wasn't cricket.

He was prepared to kick, personally, any fellow

he found making Winny Dymond or Violet Usher cheap.

Not that Winny lent herself to cheapness, but about Violet he was not quite sure. And if you had asked, Why not? he would have told you it was because she was so different. By which he meant so dangerously, so disastrously feminine and innocent and pretty. He knew now (she had " jolly well shown him ") that Winny could take care of herself; but Violet, no; she was too impulsive, too helpless, too confiding. To think of her waiting for him like that—for a fellow she'd never met before—in Oxford Street at closing time! How did she know that he wasn't a blackguard? Supposing it had been some other fellow? Ranny's muscles quivered as he thought of Violet's innocence and Violet's danger.

All this was luminously clear to Ranny.

But when he asked himself why, and to what end he himself desired to cultivate her acquaintance, it was there that obscurity set in. One thing he was sure about. He did not intend to marry her. If he couldn't afford to marry Winny he most certainly could not afford to marry Violet, not for years and years, so many years that you might just as well say never, and have done with it. Violet was not the sort of girl you could ask to wait for you years and years. His youth was not too sanguine to divine in her the makings of a more expensive woman than even a petty cashier could afford.

To be sure Ranny did not enter into any sordid calculations, neither did he think the thing out in so many words; for in this matter of Violet Usher he was incapable of any sustained and connected thought. It came to him —the utter hopelessness of it—in glimpses and by flashes, as he sat at his high desk in the counting-house.

But no flashes came to him with the question, Why then did he keep on running after Violet Usher? He ran because he couldn't help it; because of the sheer excitement of the running; because he was venturesome,

and because of the very mystery and danger of the
adventure.

But, though he hung round Starker's evening after
evening, from the middle to the very end of October, he
never once caught sight of Violet Usher. Winny he
caught, as often as not, now that he had given up trying
to catch her ; sometimes he caught her at Starker's, sometimes at their old corner by the Gymnasium ; and whenever he caught her he walked home with her. If Winny
did not positively seek capture she no longer positively
evaded it. She was no longer afraid of him, recognising,
no doubt, that he wanted nothing of her, that he would
never worry her again. It was as if she had given him
his lesson, and was content now that he had learned it.

One night, early in November, as they were going over
Wandsworth Bridge, the question that had been burning
in him suddenly flared up.

" What has become of your friend Miss Usher ? "

" Nothing," said Winny, " has become of her. She's
gone home. Her father sent for her."

" Whatever for ? "

" To look after her. She never should have left home."

Then she told him what she knew of Violet, bit by bit,
as he drew it out of her. She was very fond of Violet.
Violet had pretty ways that made you fond of her. Everybody was fond of Violet. Only her people—they'd been
a bit too harsh and strict with her, Winny fancied. Not
that she knew anything but what Violet had told her.

Where was her home ?

In the country. Down in Hertfordshire. Her father
was a farmer, a small farmer. The trouble was that
Violet couldn't bear the country. She wouldn't stay a
day in it if she could help it. She was all for life. She'd
been about a year in town. No, Winny hadn't known
her for a year. Only for a few months really, since she
came to Starker's. She'd been in several situations before
that. She was assistant at the ribbon counter at Starker's.

The clerks didn't have anything to do with the shop-girls as a rule ; but Winny thought the custom silly and stuck up. Anyhow she'd taken a fancy to Violet, seeing her go in and out. And Violet needed a deal of looking after. She was like a child. A spoilt child with little ways. Winny had tried her best to take care of her, but she couldn't be taking care of her all the time. She was glad she had gone home though she was so fond of her. But she was afraid she wouldn't stay long.

" You think," said Ransome, " she'll come back ? "

" I shouldn't be surprised if she turned up any day."

" And you'll take care of her ? "

" Yes, I shall take care of her."

He looked at her and for a moment it revived, it stirred in his heart, that odd mingled sense of absurdity and tenderness.

She would come back, he told himself ; she would come back. Meanwhile he could call his soul his own, to say nothing of his body. Under all the shock of it Ransome felt a certain relief in realising that Violet Usher had gone. It was as if some danger, half discerned, had been hanging over him and had gone with her.

But winter and spring passed, and she did not come back. They passed monotonously, like all the springs and winters he had known. He had got his rise at Michaelmas, but he was free from the obsession of the matrimonial idea, and all that he now looked forward to was an indefinite extension of the Athletic Life.

In June of nineteen-four he entered for the Wandsworth Athletic Sports. He hoped to win the silver cup for the Hurdle Race, against Fred Booty, as he had done last year.

Wandsworth was sure of its J. R. F. Ransome. Putney and Wimbledon, competing, were not sending any better men than they had sent last year. And this year, as Booty owned, Ransome was "a fair masterpiece," a young miracle of fitness. His admirable form, hitherto equal to young Booty's, was improved by strenuous training, and at his worst he had what Booty hadn't, a fire and a spirit, a power, utterly incalculable, of sudden uprush and outburst, like the loosening of a secret energy. When he flagged it would rise in him and sting him to the spurt. But, while it made him the darling of the crowd, it was apt to upset the betting of experts at the last minute.

There is a level field not far from Wandsworth which is let for football matches and athletic sports. Railings and broken hedges and a few elm-trees belt the field. All round the space marked out for the contest a ring of ropes held back the straining crowd; and all round, within the ring, went the course for the mile flat race. Down one side of the field, facing the Grand Stand, was the course for the jumping, for the hundred yards' flat race, and for the hurdle race, which was the last event. On this side, where the crowd was thickest, the rope was supplemented by a wooden barrier.

The starting-post was on the right near the entrance to the field; the winning-post on the left directly opposite the Grand Stand. Those who could not buy tickets for the Grand Stand had to secure front places at the barrier if they wished to see anything.

Here, then, there was a tight-packed line of men and women, youths and girls, with an excited child here and there squeezed in among them, or squatting at their feet under the barrier. Here were young Tyser and Buist and Wauchope of the Polytechnic, who had come to cheer. And here, by the winning-post, well in the front, having been there since the gates were open, were Maudie Hollis and Winny Dymond, in flower-wreathed hats and clean white frocks. Behind, conspicuous in their seats on the Grand Stand as became them, were Mr. and Mrs. Randall, and with them was Ranny's mother.

For all these persons there was but one event—the Hurdle Race. For all of them, expectant, concentrated on the imminence of the Final Heat, there was but one distraction, and that was the remarkable behaviour of a young woman who had arrived too late for a satisfactory place among the crowd.

She had wriggled and struggled through the rear, with such success that her way to the front row was obstructed only by the bodies of two small children. They were firmly wedged, yet not so firmly but that a determined young woman could detach them by exerting adequate pressure. This she did; and having loosened the little creatures from their foothold, she partly lifted, partly shoved them behind her and slipped into their places at the barrier. This high-handed act roused the resentment of a young man, the parent or guardian of the children. He wanted to know what she thought she was doing, shoving there, and told her that the kids had as much right to see the blooming show as she had, and he'd trouble her to give 'em back the place she'd taken. And it was then that the young woman revealed herself as remarkable. For she turned and bent upon that young man a pair of black brows with blue eyes smiling under them, and said to him in a vivid voice that penetrated to the Grand Stand, " Excuse me, but I *do* so want to see." And the young man, instead of making the obvious retort, took off his hat and begged her pardon and gave her more room than she had taken.

" Well," said Mr. Randall (for he had been observing her for some time with sidelong appreciation), " some people have a way with them."

" Some people have impudence," said Mrs. Randall.

" And if it was you or me, Bessie," Mrs. Ransome said, " it wouldn't have been made so easy for us."

" I see you wanting to shove anybody, Emmy," said her brother.

G

" If I did, I shouldn't begin with little innocent children.
I should shove someone of my own size."

Then they were silent and paid no more attention to
the young woman and her ways.

For far down at the end of the course the racers, the
winners of the first four heats, were being ranged for the
start, four abreast ; the two young men from Putney and
Wimbledon on the inside of the course, Fred Booty in the
middle, and Ransome outside. Booty knew that, starting
even with his rival, he hadn't much of a chance. As for
the young men from Putney and Wimbledon, they would
be nowhere.

Of those four young bodies, Ransome's was by far the
finest. Even Booty with his wild slenderness and faun-
like grace could not be compared with Ransome, so well-
knit, so perfect in every limb was he. Beside him the two
young men from Putney and Wimbledon were distinctly
weedy. He stood poised, with head uplifted, his keen
mouth tight shut, his nostrils dilated, his eyes gazing
forward, intent on the signal for the start. His brown
hair, soaked in the sweat of the first heat and then sun-
dried, was crisped and curled about his head. Under his
white gauze "zephyr" and black running drawers the
charged muscles quivered. His whole body was a quivering
vehicle for the leashed soul of speed.

The pistol shot was fired. They let themselves go.
From far up the course by the winning-post, where Winny
leaned out over the barrier, it was as if at the first row of
hurdles four bodies leaped into the air like one and wriggled
there. At the sixth row, well in sight, two bodies, Booty
and Ransome, soared clean and dropped together. Putney
and Wimbledon rose wriggling close behind their drop.
At the seventh row Ransome was in front, divided from
Booty by an almost imperceptible interval (Putney and
Wimbledon were several yards behind). At the eighth
and the ninth hurdles he rose gloriously and alone ;
Booty dropped with a dull thud a yard behind him.

Putney and Wimbledon were nowhere. Nobody looked at them as they went lolloping, unevenly, dejectedly, over their seventh hurdle.

And now Booty was catching up, but the race was Ransome's. He knew it. Booty knew it. The field knew it.

Ranny's mother knew it. Little shivers went up and down her back; there was a painful constriction in her throat, and tears of excitement in her eyes; her hand was clenched convulsively over her pocket-handkerchief which had rolled itself into a ball. She had been holding herself in; for she knew that these symptoms would increase when she saw Ranny, her boy, come running.

Below, at the barrier, there were hoarse cries, shrill cries, deep shouting. "Go it, Ransome! Go it, old Wandsworth! Wandsworth wins!" Tyser and Buist and Wauchope were yelling "Stick it, Ranny! Stick it!" "Stick it!" "Stick—it!" The last voice, which was Wauchope's, died away in a groan.

Somebody was leaning over the barrier, on a line with the last hurdles. Somebody stretched out an arm and shook a little white handkerchief at him as he came on. Somebody caught his eyes and struck him with a blue flash under black brows. She struck and fixed him as he ran to his last leap.

He looked at her and started and stood staggering with checked speed. And as he staggered, Booty rose slenderly and dropped and rushed on to the tape-line at the winning-posts. The white tape fluttered across him as he breasted it. Booty had won the race.

They cheered him; they were bound to cheer the winner. But at the barrier and from the Grand Stand there burst forth a more frantic uproar of applause as Ransome recovered himself and took his last hurdle at a stand.

It was all very well to cheer him; but he was beaten; beaten in the race that was his.

He staggered out of the course. Hanging his head, and heedless of his friends, and of Booty's hand on his bent shoulder, he went and hid himself in the dressing-tent.

And there in the dressing-tent, his faun-like face more sanguine than ever in his passion, Booty burst out like a young lunatic. He swore most horribly. He swore at the umpire. He swore at Ransome. He swore at everybody all round. The more Ranny congratulated him, the more he swore at him. He called Ranny a blanky young fool, and asked him what the blank he did it for. He said it was a blanky shame, and that if anybody tried to give *him* a blanky cup, he'd throw it at 'em. Even when they'd calmed him down a bit, he still swore that he'd give Ranny the cup; for Ranny'd given him the race. He explained to them in his hoarsest tones that it stood to reason he could never have got in with the pace Ranny'd got on him. It wasn't fair, he said. It was a fluke, a blanky fluke.

And round him Tyser and Buist and Wauchope clamoured in the tent and agreed with him, declaring that it wasn't fair. Of course it was a fluke, a blanky fluke.

And Ranny, though he told Booty to dry up and stow it; though he put it to Tyser and Buist and Wauchope that it wasn't any blanky fluke, that it couldn't well be fairer, seeing how he'd funked it at the finish, Ranny knew in his heart that somewhere there was something queer about it. He couldn't think why on earth he'd funked it.

That night, in her little room in St. Ann's Terrace, Winny lay awake and cried.

Violet Usher had come back.

X

IT was from the next day, Sunday, that he dated it—
what happened. It followed as a sequel to the events
of Sunday.

For Ransome was convinced that it never could have
happened if he had not gone with Wauchope on Sunday
evening to that Service for Men. He used to say that if
you traced it back far enough, poor old Wauchope was at
the bottom of it. It was poor old Wauchope who had
" rushed " him for the Service (in calling him poor old
Wauchope, he recognised him as the unknowing and
unwilling thing of Destiny). Thus it had its root and rise
in the extraordinary state of Wauchope's soul.

Wauchope had realised that he *had* a soul, and was
beginning to take an interest in it. That, of course, was
not the way he put it when he approached Ransome on
Saturday night after the Sports Dinner at the "Golden
Eagle." All he said was that he was "in for it." Been let
in by a curate johnnie who'd rushed him for a Service for
Men to-morrow night at Clapham. Wauchope wasn't
going because he wanted to, but because the curate was
such a decent chap he didn't like to disappoint him. He
ran a Young Men's Club in St. Matthias's, Clapham, and
Wauchope helped him by looking in now and then for a
knock-up with the gloves. The curate was handy with
the gloves himself. A bit cumbrous, but fancied himself
as a featherweight, in a skipping, dodging, dance-all-
round-you, land-you-one-presently sort of style. Well,
the curate johnnie had been handing round printed
invitations for this service. " All Welcome," don't you
know ? " Come, and bring a Friend." Wauchope had

promised, Honour Bright, he'd come and bring a friend. And Ransome, in a weak moment, had consented to be brought.

The service would be at eight, and would last, say, till nine. Half-past nine was the very earliest hour he could fix for his appointment with Miss Usher.

For he had seen her. She had risen up before him, to his amazement, on that Sunday evening, as he turned out of his own door on his way to supper with Wauchope at Clapham. He had walked with her for five minutes, wheeling his bicycle in the gutter, while they settled how and where they were to meet.

She was living in Wandsworth, lodging in St. Ann's Terrace, near to Winny Dymond, so that Winny could take care of her. She had got another situation at Starker's, in the millinery department.

He proposed that he should meet her at closing time to-morrow, and she smiled at him and said she didn't mind; but Winny would be there (he had forgotten Winny). Then he suggested next Saturday afternoon or Sunday about three; and she said she really couldn't say. Saturday and Sunday were such a long way off, and things might be different now that she was in the millinery. And she smiled again, and in such a manner that he had a vision, a horrible vision, of other fellows crowding round her on Saturdays and Sundays. He more than suspected that this was " cock-a-tree "; but it made him desperate, so that he said " Well—how about to-night ? "

Well—*to-night* she'd promised Winny she'd be good and go to church.

If he had been madder ; if he'd been more set on it, he would have gone off with her that minute ; he would have persuaded her to give up church ; he himself would have broken his promise to old Wauchope. But he did none of these things, and his abstention was the sign and measure of his coolness, of his sanity. He only said, as any cool and sane young man might say: How about after church ? And if he called when he got back from Clapham ? He wouldn't be a minute later than half-past nine.

And Violet had said : Oh, well—she didn't know about calling. You see she only had one room. And he had reckoned with that difficulty ; for Winny Dymond only had one room which she shared with Maudie. By calling, he'd meant, of course, on the doorstep, to take her for a walk.

But Violet, for some reason, didn't care about the doorstep. She'd rather, if he didn't mind, that he met her somewhere out of doors.

And so they had been drawn into an assignation at the old elm-tree by the Causeway on Wandsworth Plain.

Thus, if it had done nothing else to him, the Service for Men could be held responsible for throwing that meeting with Violet much too late.

Still, he had no misgivings. It was June ; and in June nine o'clock was still day-time. And when he went to the Service he hadn't any idea what it would do to him.

No more, of course, had poor old Wauchope. Wauchope was grateful and apologetic ; before they got there he said he didn't know what he might be letting Ransome in for. The curate johnnie was bossing the Service, but he understood they'd engaged another joker for the Address. What he, Wauchope, funked, personally, more than anything was the Address. And Ransome, generously, declared that whatever it was like, he'd stick it. He'd stand by Wauchope to the finish, like a man.

They left their bicycles in Wauchope's rooms, and walked the few hundred yards to St. Matthias's Mission Church.

St. Matthias's Mission Church was a brand-new yellow-brick building in the latest Gothic, with a red-tiled roof, where a shrill little bell swung tinkling under the arch in the high west gable.

Inside, cream distempered walls with brown stencillings ; in the roof, bare beams of pitch pine, stained and varnished ; north and south, clear glass windows shedding a greenish light ; one brilliant stained glass window above the altar at the east end.

Up and down the aisles between the open pews of pitch pine went the workers of the Mission, marshalling the men into their seats. By the west door, Wauchope's friend, the cumbrous curate, who fancied himself as a featherweight, stood smiling and shaking hands with each man as he came, and thanking him for coming, thus carrying out the idea that it was an entertainment. He had his largest smile, his closest grip for Wauchope and for Ransome, for they were men after his own heart. Ransome observed the curate critically, and without committing himself irretrievably to an opinion, he owned that he looked fit enough. There was not about him any sign that you could see of flabbiness or weediness. He was evidently a decent johnnie, and for all that happened afterwards Ransome forbore to hold him personally responsible.

The service, conducted by the curate, was extremely brief. Everything was left out that could be left, to make room for hymns wherever it was possible to place a hymn. The Psalms were chanted and the curate intoned the Prayers in a voice that was not his natural voice, but something far more poignant and impressive.

There were no boys in the choir, and the singing, that lacked their purifying and clarifying treble, had a strange effect, sombre yet disturbing. It acted on Ranny like an incantation.

Of course, if he had known what it was going to do to him, he would have kept away.

For though there was nothing in his flesh and blood and muscle that suggested an inebriate father, yet in his profounder and obscurer being he was Fulleymore Ran-

some's son. The secret instability that made Fulleymore
Ransome drink had had its effect on Ranny's nervous
system. His nerves, though he was not aware of it, were
finely woven and highly strung. He had a tendency to be
carried away and to be excited, exalted, and upset. Since
Saturday afternoon Ranny had remained more or less in
a state of tension induced by the hurdle race, by the
shock of seeing Violet Usher, and by the dinner at the
"Golden Eagle." And, coming straight from Violet, he had
entered St. Matthias's Mission Church keyed up to his
highest pitch. So that the Service for Men which subdued Wauchope and made him humble and ashamed and
sent him away trying to be a better man, that very same
Service worked Ranny up to a point when anything
became possible to him.

First of all, then, the intoning and the chanting acted on
him exactly like an incantation. Ranny's will, the spiritual
part of him, was lulled to sleep by the rhythmic voices,
and as his sense of decency had no reason whatever to
expect an outrage, it was also off its guard, quiescent,
passive to the charm. The rest of Ranny was exposed,
piteously, to the rhythm that swelled, that accentuated,
accelerated the vibration of his inner tumult.

Then, the obvious safety-valve was closed to him. A
sense of strangeness and of sudden shyness prevented
him from joining as he should have joined in the Service.
Ranny could not take it out all at once in singing. That
silence and passivity of his left him open at every pore
to the invasion of the powers of sound. Those young,
intensely vibrant bass and tenor voices sang all round
him, they sang at him and into him and through him.
There was a young man close behind him with a tenor
voice that pierced him like a pain. There was Wauchope
at his right ear thundering in a tremendous baritone.

First of all it was a trumpet-call that shook him.

> " ' Sold-ier-ers o-of Christ ! a-arise,
>   And pùt your armour on,' "

sang Wauchope. The sound of that singing made Ransome
feel noble ; and there is nothing more insidiously destructive than feeling noble.

And then, later on, it was a strange and a more poignant
cry that melted him, so that his very soul dissolved in
tenderness and yearning.

> " ' Jesu, Lover o-of my soul,' "

sang the young man with the tenor,

> " ' Let me to Thy bosom fly,
>   While the gathering wa-ters roll,
>   While the tempest sti-ill is high.' "

(Ranny felt them about him, the waters and the tempest.)

> " ' Other refuge ha-ave I none,
>   Hangs my helpless soul on Thee ;
>   Leave—ah ! leave me no-ot alone,
>   Still support and co-omfort me.' "

And as the infinite pathos and pleading of the tenor
voice played on him, Ranny sank, lost and shelterless and
alone, till at the word " Life " he rose again and exulted,
he rose above himself, even to the point of singing.

> " ' Thou of Life the fountain art,
>   Freely let me take of Thee ;
>   Spring Thou up with-in my heart ; ' "

(sang Ranny)

> " ' Rise to all eternity.' "

There was something about that hymn, and his own
sudden crying out in it, that made him peculiarly sus-
ceptible to the influences of the Address. When the
preacher rose in the pulpit, when he looked about him
with ardent and earnest eyes in a face ravaged by emotion,
when his wide and somewhat loose and mobile lips gave
out the text, Ranny had an obscure foreknowledge of
what would happen to him.

For he was not altogether virgin to the experience he
was undergoing. It belonged to certain moods of his

childhood and his adolescence when more than once, in Wandsworth Parish Church, he had been stirred mysteriously by the tender music of the Evening Service, and by the singing of certain hymns. There were layers upon layers of emotion sunk beyond memory in Ranny's soul. So that what happened to him now had the profound and vehement, though secret, force of a revival. The submerged feelings rose in him ; they were swollen, intensified, dominated beyond recognition by the virile and unspiritual passion that leaped up and ran together with them and made them one. It gave them an obscure but superb sanction and significance.

For that incantation not only called up the past ; with a still greater magic and mystery it evoked the future. It was a prophecy, a premonition of the things to be. It cried upon the secret, unseen powers of life. It brought down destiny.

"'Know ye not that your bodies,'" said the preacher —and he leaned out and looked to the young men on the right—"'your bodies'"—and he looked to the young men on the left—"'are the temples of the Holy Ghost?'" —and he looked straightforward and paused as if he saw invisible things.

He may have drawn a bow at a venture, but he seemed to have singled out Ranny from among all those young men. He leaned over his pulpit, and fixed his kindled and penetrating eyes on Ranny. He adjured Ranny to remember that Sin which he had never committed ; he implored him to recall the shame which he had never felt, and at the same time to purge himself of that unholy memory, and put away from him the sensual thoughts that had never occurred to him, and the abominable intentions that he had never had.

Then with a subtle and plastic inflection of his voice, like the poise of wings descending, he dropped from that almost inspired height of emotion, and became shrewd and practical, thoroughly informed and competent, a

physician with a flair for the secret of disease, a surgeon
of the Soul, relentless in his handling of the knife, a man
of the world who spoke to them of what he knew, in all
sincerity, as man to man. And then he soared again,
flapping his great wings that fanned emotion to a flame.

And through it all the young curate who had brought
them there sat folded more and more within his surplice,
and became more and more red as to his face, more and
more dubious as to his eyes. He was like some young
captain, wise though intrepid, who sees his brave battalions
routed through the false move of his general.

The magic worked. A man behind Ransome was heard
breathing heavily. The gentle drowsiness habitually
expressed by Wauchope's broad and somewhat flattened
features was intensified to stupefaction. His head had
sunk slightly forward, but he looked up, lowering at the
preacher with his little innocent eyes, half sullen, half
afraid.

Wauchope was merely uncomfortable. He suffered on
the surface. But Ranny was disturbed profoundly,
shaken, excited, and most curiously uplifted.

He and Wauchope compared notes afterwards on the
preacher whom they called "that imported josser."
They thought he rather fancied himself at that particular
job, and supposed that he was some sort of a " pro " who
had spoiled his " form " by overdoing it, and had lost the
confidence of his backers. They agreed that if Wauchope's
friend the curate had given them a straight talk it would
have been much straighter. As it was, nothing could
have been more devious, more mysterious and serpentine
than the discourse that turned and wound and wormed
its way into the last obscurities and secrecies of Ranny's
being.

In the Mission Church of St. Matthias's Ranny underwent
illumination. It was as if all that was dark and passionate
in him had been interpreted for him by the preacher.
Interpreted, it became in some perverse way justified.

Over and above that innermost sanction and recognition it had the seal outside it of men's acknowledgment, it took its place among the existent, the normal, the expected. Ranny was not alone in his passion and confusion. He was companioned, here and now, in the great enlightenment.

But even Ranny could not have foretold the full extent of his reaction to that sinuous and evocative Address.

Meanwhile, so carried away was Ranny that he joined Wauchope in a furious singing of the final hymn, " Onward, Christian so-o-oldier-ers ! "

He had felt noble ; he had felt tender ; now he was triumphant.

XI

W AUCHOPE, who hadn't a nerve in his composition, recovered soon after he got into the open air. But in Ransome, without intermission, the magic of that incantation worked.

The symptoms of its working were a frightful haste, anxiety, and fear. He left Wauchope without any explanation, and rode off to his appointment at a dangerous speed and with a furious ringing of his bell. He was afraid that if he were late by five seconds Violet Usher would be gone. It was incredible to him that she should be there. It was incredible that it should have come to this, that he should be flying in haste and anxiety and fear unspeakable to meet her at the elm-tree by the Causeway on Wandsworth Plain. The whole adventure was incredible.

Yet there could not be a better place for it than Wandsworth Plain, a three-cornered patch of bare ground, bounded on one side by the river Wandle, and on the other by a row of brown cottages and two little old inns, with steep tiled roofs and naked walls, " The Bell " and " The Crane." They were pure eighteenth century, and they give to Wandsworth Plain its lonely and deserted air as of a little river-side hamlet overlooked by time and the Borough Council. On a Sunday evening in summer they stand as if in perpetual peace, without rivalry, without regret, very bright and clean and simple, one washed yellow and the other chalk-white. The river runs under brown walls, shaded on one side by espalier limes, on the other overhung with elder bushes in flower. Lower down, on the banks, are willows and alders, and the wild hemlock

grows there, lifting up its great white whorls. Beyond
the farther wall and the limes there is a vast yard, stacked
with timber ; beyond the banks a dock ; and beyond all,
on the great River, unseen, a distance of crowded ware-
houses and grey wharves.

The elm-tree, muffled in green, leans out over the
stream as the lightning bowed it long ago, propped by
wooden stays, mutilated to the merest torso of a tree.
A sacred thing, the elm-tree is enclosed and guarded by
a wooden railing as in a shrine.

Ransome was ten minutes too early, and it was impossible that she should be there. Yet there she was, in
her white dress, leaning up against the wooden railing, as
if swept and then left there in her detachment, so in-
accessible, so isolated was she, so unaware or so disdainful
of the couples, the young devotees of passion, who had
made the elm-tree their meeting-place. She was there
too soon, yet about her there was no air of haste, but rather
of brooding and delay. You would have said of her in
her stillness that she could afford to wait, she was so
certain of her end.

She scarcely stirred from her place to greet Ransome as
he came. He leaned up against the railing close beside
her.

" I'm sorry," he said. " I tore like mad. Did you
think I was never coming ? "

She smiled with a curious smile.

" No," she said. " I knew that you would come."

And they stayed there. (Some instinct had impelled
him to call at the shop, and leave his bicycle with Mercier.
A bicycle was an encumbrance, a thing inappropriate to
the adventure.) They stayed while the couples, the young
devotees of passion, stood locked in each other's arms, or
moved away, slowly, like creatures in an enchantment,
linked together, and passed into the dusk. And in the
end his hand sought and found hers, secretly, behind the
shelter of her gown, and they too passed, hand-in-hand

and slowly, like creatures in an enchantment; they were drawn into the dusk, beyond the barrier at the Causeway, to the footpath by the river.

When they returned to the elm-tree it was all dark and secret there. They stood as those others had stood, creatures of the enchantment, locked, with hands on shoulders and faces looking close and seeing each other's eyes large and strange in the darkness.

Over Wandsworth Plain came the sound of the Parish Church clock striking ten.

When they reached St. Ann's Terrace the little brown house where Violet lodged was shut up, asleep behind drawn blinds.

Violet could let herself in. She had a key. At least she thought she had. She could have been almost sure she had brought it. But no, it was not in her purse, nor yet in her pocket. She turned the pocket inside out and shook it and there was no key. Oh, dear, she was afraid she had lost it, or else—perhaps—she hadn't brought it after all. She was that careless. She thought she must have left it in her room on the dressing-table.

They knocked three times and nobody answered. Nobody was there. They had all gone out early in the evening and evidently they had not come back. Sometimes, Violet said, they weren't back till eleven or past it.

Well, she didn't want to stand out there much longer. She wondered how she was ever going to get in.

They looked at each other and laughed at their helplessness. There is always something funny about being locked out. Ranny said, " What a lark ! "

Then he thought of the window.

It was low. He stepped on to the ledge, and stood there. He slipped the latch with the blade of his pocket-knife. He raised the sash and dropped into the room. He groped about in it till he found his way into the passage and opened the door and let Violet in.

She said she was all right now. Her candle would be

left there for her, on the shelf. But it wasn't, and Violet didn't like the dark. She was afraid of it. So Ranny lit a match. He lit several matches and lighted her all the way up the narrow staircase to the door of her little bed-room at the back. She took the matches from him and went in to look for the candle, leaving the door ajar and Ranny standing outside it on the mat.

He heard her soft feet moving about the room; he heard the spurt of the matches, and her little smothered cry of impatience as they went out one by one. It seemed ages to Ranny as he waited.

At last she found the candle and lit it and set it down somewhere where it was hidden behind the door.

And then she came to him with her eyes all shining in the dusk.

She filled the half-opened doorway; and round and about her and in the room beyond there hung, indescribable but perceptible, palpable almost as a touch, the thick scent of her hair. And they stood together on the thres-hold as they had stood by the elm-tree in the dark.

She closed her eyes and his hold tightened. She called his name thickly, "Ranny!" and suddenly it was as if his very nerves and the strength of his knees dissolved and flowed like water, and drawing he was drawn over the threshold.

"Don't worry about it, Ranny. It had got to be."

She said it, clinging to him with soft hands as he parted from her. For a moment she was moved beyond herself by his compunction, his passion of tenderness for the helpless thing she seemed.

What would have surprised him if he could have thought about it was that, above it all, above the tenderness and the compunction, he still felt that triumphant sense of

H

sanction and completion, of acquiescence in an end fore-appointed and foreseen.

But before he could think about it he was overtaken by an astounding, an incredible drowsiness.

He dragged himself home to his attic and his bed, where, astoundingly, incredibly, he slept.

XII

IT was about nine o'clock of another Sunday evening a
week later.

Winny Dymond was sitting on the edge of Violet's bed in
the little back room in St. Ann's Terrace. Violet in a
white petticoat and camisole, overcome by the heat, lay
stretched at length, like a drowsy animal, in the hollow of
the bed where she had flung herself. Her head, tilted back,
lay in the clasp of her hands. Her breasts, drawn upwards
by the raised arms, left her all slender to the waist. The
soft-folded, finely indented crook of her elbows made a
white frame for her flushed face. She was looking at
Winny with eyes narrowed to the slits of the sleepy, half-
shut lids.

In a thick, sweet voice, a voice too drowsy for anything
beyond the bare statement of the fact, she had been
telling Winny that she was engaged to be married to
Mr. Ransome.

Now she was looking at Winny (all her intelligence
narrowed to that thread-fine glint of half-shut eyes), looking to see how Winny would take it.

Winny took it with that blankness that leaves the brain
naked to all irrelevant impressions, and with a silence that
made all her pulses loud. She heard the rattle and roar of a
distant tram and the clock striking the hour in the room
below. She saw the soiled lining and the ugly warp of
Violet's shoes kicked off and overturned beside the bed.
Beyond the shoes, a stain that had faded rose and became
vivid on the carpet. Then a film came over Winny's eyes,
and on the far border of the field of vision, somewhere
towards the top of her head, a yellow chest of drawers with

99

white handles grew dim and quivered and danced like the
yellow and white spectre of a chest of drawers.

" I suppose you're surprised," said Violet.

" No, I'm not. Not at all."

And she wasn't. But she was amazed at her own calmness.

" I knew it," she said.

" Knew it ? "

" Yes."

Of course she had known it. If she hadn't how could
she have endured it now ?

" When did you know ?

" Last week. When you came back."

That was not true. She had known it before last week.
She had known it as long as she had known Violet. And
she had known that because of it Violet would come back.

She hadn't blamed Violet for coming back. Even now,
as she sat on Violet's bed and was tortured by those
lights under Violet's eyelids, even now she didn't blame
her. And if she turned her shoulder it was not because
she minded Violet looking at her (she was past minding
that), but because she was afraid to look at Violet. She
didn't want to see her lying there. It was almost as if she
were afraid of hating her.

Behind her Violet was stirring. She had drawn up her
outstretched limbs and raised herself on the pillows. Winny
felt her behind her, restless and alert.

Then she spoke again.

" You needn't mind, Winny. It's got to be."

" Mind ? What makes you think I'm minding ? "

" The way you sit there with your mouth shut, saying
nothing."

" There's nothing to say. I'm not surprised. You've not
told me anything I didn't know."

" Well, anyone would think you didn't approve of it.
Why can't you get up and say you hope we'll be happy or
something ? "

" Of course I hope you'll be happy. I want you to be happy."

(Of course she did.)

" Look here "—Violet was sitting up now—" *was* there anything between you and him ? "

Winny rose straight and turned and looked at her.

" You've no business to ask that," she said.

" Yes I have." She rose slowly, twisted herself, slid her foot to the floor, and stood up facing Winny. " If I'm going to marry him I've a right to know. Not that it'll make a scrap of difference."

" Who told you there was anything between us ? "

" Nobody told me. I mean—*was* there—before I came ? "

" There was never anything—never. Anyone who tells you anything different's telling you a lie. I'm not saying we weren't friends——"

Violet smiled.

" I'm not saying you were anything else. You can go on being friends. *I* shan't care. Only don't you go saying I came between you—that's all."

At that Winny fired.

" As if I'd do any such a thing ! I don't know what can have put it into your head."

Violet laughed.

" You should see *your face*," she said. " Why—anyone could tell you were gone on him. They've only got to look at you."

There are some insults, some insolences that cannot be answered.

" You can believe that," said Winny, " if you like—if it makes you any happier. But your believing it won't make it true."

She walked slowly, in her small dignity, to the chair where she had thrown down her hat. She took up the hat and put it on, deliberately, with a high bravery, before the glass.

Then she turned to her friend and smiled at her.

" It's all right," she said, " though you mightn't think it. Good-bye."

Whereupon Violet rushed at her and kissed her.

" It isn't your fault, and it isn't mine, Winky," she whispered. " It's got to be, I tell you."

She drew herself from the embrace, erect and rosy, in a sudden passion that had in it both triumph and despair.

" Wild horses couldn't have torn him and me apart."

And Winny didn't blame her ; even in the pain of the night that followed, when she lay awake in the bed she shared with Maudie Hollis, stifling her sobs lest she should waken Maudie, clutching the edge of the mattress where she had writhed out of Maudie's reach. For at the first sound of crying the proud beauty had turned to her friend and put her arms about her, and held her in a desolate and desolating embrace.

" Don't cry, Winny ; don't cry, dear. It isn't worth it," had been Maudie's consolation. For, though Winny hadn't said a word to her, she knew. And she had followed it up by declaring that she hated that Violet Usher ; and she hated Ransome ; she hated everybody who made little Winky, little darling Winky, cry.

But Winky didn't hate them. It had to be. Nothing could be more beautiful in its simplicity than her acceptance of the event.

And she didn't blame them. She didn't blame anybody. She had brought it on herself. The thing was as good as done last summer, when she had stopped Ranny making love to her. She had stopped it on purpose. She knew he couldn't afford to marry her, not for years and years ; she knew he had been trying to tell her so ; and it didn't seem fair, somehow, to let him get worked up all for nothing. That was how girls drove men mad. She considered that she was there to take care of Ranny, and she had seen, in her wisdom, that to keep Ranny well in hand would be less hard on him than to let him lose his head.

Violet hadn't seen it, that was all.

Besides, Violet was different. She had ways with her which made it no wonder if Ranny lost his head. In Winny's opinion the man didn't live who could resist Violet and her ways. She got round you somehow. She had got round Winny last year when she had come imploring her to take her to the Grand Display at the Polytechnic Gymnasium, teasing her and threatening that if she didn't take her she'd go off to the Empire by herself. She had spoken as if going to the Empire was a preposterous and unheard-of thing. Winny didn't know that Violet had gone there more than once, not by herself, but with the foreman of her department.

And she had had to take her, and that, of course, had done it. Though she had been afraid of this thing and had foreknown it from the beginning, she had taken her; though she had been afraid ever since she had seen Violet's face and watched her ways. So afraid was she that she had tried to keep Ranny from ever seeing Violet. Time and again she had hurried her away when she had seen Ranny coming, while the fear in her heart told her that those two were bound to meet. She had lived from hand to mouth on her precarious happiness, contented if she could stave off the evil day.

And it was all worse than useless. Violet had been aware that she was being hurried away when Ranny came in sight, and it had made her the more set. As for Winny's hope that Violet would forget all about Ranny when some other man appeared, it was futile as long as she took care of Violet. Taking care of Violet meant keeping her as far as possible out of the way of other men—so that there again! It seemed as if she had arranged it so that Ranny should be the only one. For Winny had divined her friend's disastrous temperament even while she maintained hotly

that there was no harm in her. And she had almost
quarrelled with Maudie because the proud beauty had said,
" Well—you'll see."

Winny knew nothing about Violet and the foreman.

And with the same innocence she never doubted that
when Violet and Ransome met that night at the Polytechnic it was for the first time.

And so she stitched with a good will at a white muslin
blouse for Violet's wedding present, and folded it herself and
put it away in the yellow chest of drawers with the rest of
Violet's wedding things. It lay there, all snowy white, with
a violet-scented sachet on the top of it, a sachet (Winny had
found it in the drawer) with a pattern of violets on a white
satin ground and the name " Violet " sprawling all across it
in embroidery.

XIII

RANSOME had barely risen from that sleep of exhaustion when he realised the disastrous character of the night's adventure. He was no longer uplifted by any sense of sanction and of satisfaction. Of the pride of life there remained in him only sufficient to prevent him from regarding his behaviour as in any sense a shame and a disaster to his own youth. Otherwise his mood was entirely penitential. He could not look at the thing as it affected himself. However it might be for him, he had wronged Violet, and that was calamity enough for any man to face. According to all his instincts and traditions, he had wronged her.

Of course, he was going to marry her. He was going to marry her at once; as soon as ever they could get their banns put up. It never occurred to him that delay could, in such a case, be possible.

For, from the very moment of that morning after, in Ranny's heart there was an awful and a sacred fear, a fear of fatherhood. It was the first thing he thought of as soon as he could think at all.

He wanted to put Violet right at once, before a suspicion of that possibility should have crossed her mind. It would have seemed to him abominable to risk it, to wait on, as fellows did, on the off-chance of a reprieve, till she came to him, poor child, with her whispered tale. That, to Ranny's mind, was where the shame came in; not in the fact, but in the compulsion of the fact. It was intolerable that any man should have the right to say of his own wife that he had been forced to marry her. Hence his desperate haste.

Violet couldn't understand it. She didn't want to be

married all at once. She said there was no hurry ; that he couldn't afford it ; that there was no rhyme nor reason in it ; let them go on as they were a bit ; let them wait and see.

In all this Ranny saw only a tenderness and a desire to spare him. But he stood firm. He was not concerned with reasons and with rhymes ; he wouldn't wait, he wouldn't see ; and (this astonished Violet and secretly enraged her) he absolutely refused to go on as they were.

For his fear was always before him.

It was no doubt to that refusal of his that he owed Violet's consent.

His family were appalled at the news of Ranny's engagement. It was so unexpected, so unlike him ; and how it had happened Ranny's mother couldn't think. She knew all his comings and goings for the last year. His temperance and discretion had given her a sense of imperishable security. She had made up her mind that Ranny wasn't one to be in a hurry ; and now she had been right only in her prophecy that when his time came there would be no holding him.

And there *was* no holding him.

They had all tried it. They had all been at him ; his Uncle Randall and his Aunt Randall and his mother and his father. For the first time in his life Mr. Ransome was roused to take an interest in his son, to acknowledge him as an adult, capable of formidably adult things. And though they all told him that he was too young to know his own mind, that he was doing foolish, and behaving silly, under the show of disapproval and disparagement it was clear that they respected him, that they realised his manhood, and that he was somehow important to them as he had never been important in his life before.

What was more, rage as they would at it, they were impressed by Ranny's firmness, his unalterable and imperturbable determination to marry, and to marry the unknown Violet Usher.

And on the main issue they gave way. They owned that

it was natural that the boy should want to marry; they saw that he would have to marry some day; and his mother went so far as to say she wanted him to marry and to settle down. What they did not understand, and most certainly did not approve of, what they did their best to talk him out of, was the awful hurry he was in. There wasn't any hurry, they said, there couldn't be, when he was so young. He couldn't afford to marry now, but he could afford it very well in two years' time. Why, he was only twenty-three, and in two years' time he'd have got his next rise, and he'd have saved more money.

"If you'd wait, Ranny," said his mother, "but the two years." And his father and his uncle said he *must* wait.

But Ranny wouldn't. He wouldn't wait six months. No, and he wouldn't wait three months and look about him. He wouldn't have waited three weeks if it hadn't been for the banns. It was no use their talking.

They knew it. It had been no use their talking seven years ago, when Ranny had refused to become a Pharmaceutical Chemist, and had given no reasons, because the only reason he could give was that life would be intolerable if spent in the perpetual presence of his father. And he didn't give them any reasons now.

Before the Ransomes and the Randalls knew where they were the banns had been put up in Wandsworth Parish Church and in the Parish Church of Elstree, in Hertfordshire, and Violet had been twice to tea.

He had looked for opposition down at Elstree, in Hertfordshire, fierce and insurmountable opposition from Mr. Usher, that father who had been so harsh to Violet. It was incredible that Violet's father would allow him to marry her, it was incredible that her mother would allow it. He would just have to marry her in spite of them.

But, as it happened, the attitude of Mr. and Mrs. Usher surpassed probability. Not only were they willing that he should marry Violet, they desired that he should marry her at once. The sooner the better, Mr. Usher said. If young

Ransome could marry her to-morrow he'd be best pleased. It was almost as if Mr. Usher knew. But, of course, he didn't, he couldn't possibly know. He would have scouted the proposition altogether if he hadn't had three other younger girls at home. It wasn't, Ranny reflected, as if Violet was the only one. So far from putting obstacles in Ranny's way, Mr. Usher positively smoothed it. Understanding that the young man was not, as you might call it, rolling, he said there wasn't much that they could do, but if at any time a hamper of butter and eggs and fruit and vegetables should come in handy, they'd send it along and welcome; he shouldn't even wonder if, in case of necessity, they could rise to a flitch of bacon or a joint of pork. Ranny was exquisitely grateful; though, as for the necessity, he didn't see himself depending on his father-in-law for his food supplies. He had no foreboding of the importance that hamper from Hertfordshire was to assume in the drama of his after-life. For the actual hour it stood simply as the measure of Mr. Usher's approval and goodwill.

He was much moved when at parting Mrs. Usher pressed him by the hand and asked him to be gentle with her girl. There was no harm, Mrs. Usher said, in poor Vi. She was a bit wilful and wild-like; all for life was Violet—but there, she'd be as good as gold when she had a home and a kind husband and children of her own. "Mark my words," said Mrs. Usher, "once the babies come she'll settle down."

And Ranny marked her words.

This unqualified backing that he got from Violet's parents went far to sustain Ransome in the conflict with his own. He could indeed have embraced Mr. and Mrs. Usher when, in consequence of one Sunday afternoon's communion with these excellent people, his mother declared herself more reconciled than she had been to the idea of Ranny's marrying. Between Ranny's mother and Mrs. Usher there was established in one Sunday afternoon the peculiar sympathy and intimacy of parents who live supremely in their children. With her rosy, full-blown, robust benevolence, Mrs. Usher was a powerful pleader. She put it to Mrs. Ransome that nothing mattered so long as the young people were happy. If in the pursuit of happiness the young people failed in the first year or two to make ends meet, surely among them all they could be given a helping hand. She was sure that Mr. Usher would do anything he could, in reason. The comfortable woman declared that she had taken a fancy such as never was to Ranny, so had Mr. Usher, and he wasn't, she could assure you, one to take a fancy every day. She had never had a boy (and it wasn't for not wanting), but if she *had* had one she'd have wished him to be just such another as Ranny. Ranny, she was certain, was that clever he'd be sure to get along. To which argument Mrs. Ransome had to yield. For she was confronted with a dilemma, having either to agree with Mrs. Usher or to maintain that her Ranny was not clever enough to get along. So that before Sunday evening she found herself partaking in the large-hearted tolerance and optimism of Violet's parents, and forcing her view upon Uncle and Aunt Randall.

Only Mr. Ransome held out. He refused to be worked upon by argument. To Ranny's amazement, the old Humming-bird bore himself in those days of stress, not with that peculiar savage obduracy that distinguished his more insignificant hostilities, but with a certain sad and fine insistence. It was as if for the first time in his life he was aware that he cared for his son Randall and was afraid of losing him. The Humming-bird could hardly have suffered more if the issue had been Randall's death and not his marriage. But when the thing was settled all he said was, " I don't like it, Mother, I don't like it."

How profoundly it had disturbed him was shown in this, that for the three weeks before Ranny's wedding-day he remained completely sober.

So precipitate, so venturesome was Ranny, that in a

month from that memorable Sunday he found himself married and established in a house. A house that in twenty years' time would become his own.

That was incredible, if you like. Cowardly caution and niggardly prudence had suggested rooms ; two low-rented, unfurnished rooms such as could be found almost anywhere in Wandsworth ; whereas a house in Wandsworth was impossible even if you sank as low as Jew's Row or Warple Way. For the first two days of his engagement Ranny had devoted every moment of his leisure to the drawing up and balancing of imaginary household accounts ; with the result that he wondered how he ever could have regarded marriage as a formidable affair. Why, in the seven years since he had begun to earn money, he had been steadily putting money by. Five pounds a year in the first three years, then ten, then twenty, and a whole fifty in the year and a half since he had got his rise. With the interest on his savings and his salary, his present income was not less than a hundred and twenty-five pounds a year.

In the night watches he grappled like a man with the financial problem. Scheme after scheme did Ranny throw on the paper from his seething brain. In the fifth—no, the thoroughly revised and definitive seventh, he made out that, by a trifling reduction in his personal expenditure, housekeeping on the two-room system would leave him with a considerable margin. (In the first rough draft—even in the second—he had allowed absurdly too much for food and clothing.) But, mind you, that margin existed solely and strictly on the two-rooms system.

And here Ranny's difficulties began ; for neither Violet nor her parents would hear of their living in two rooms. Violet, who had lived in one room, said that living in two rooms was horrible, and Mrs. Usher said that Violet was right. It was better for all parties to begin as you meant to go on. Begin in hugger-mugger and you may end in it. But if he gave Violet a home of her own that *was* a home

at the very start, she'd soon settle down in it. He needn't
worry about the hard work it meant. The only thing that
would keep Violet steady-like was downright hard work.
No ; she didn't mean anything cruel. They could have a
char once a fortnight for a scrub-down and the heavy
washing.

And Ranny began all over again and made out another
set of accounts on the house basis and allowing for the
char.

Impossible ; even in Jew's Row or Warple Way. Skimp
as he would in personal expenditure, on the house basis the
two ends of Ranny's income simply *wouldn't* meet.

All the same, he began looking for the house. The idea
of the house, the desire for the house worked in his brain
like a passion; the more impossible it was, the more ungovernable, the more irresistible he found it.

And, as he wandered forth on that adventure, seeking for
a house, one Saturday afternoon, accompanied by Violet,
Ranny fell into the hands of the Speculative Builder.

Not very far from Wandsworth, in the green pasture-
lands of Southfields, that great magician was already
casting into bricks and mortar his tremendous dream—the
city of dreams, the Paradise of Little Clerks.

As yet he had called into being only a few streets of his
city, stretching eastwards and southwards into the green
plain. About it, southwards and eastwards, there lay acres
of naked earth upturned, torn and tamed to his hand. Beyond were the fields with their tall elms, unbroken, virgin,
mournful in their last beauty, as they waited for the axe
and pick.

He had done terrible things to the green earth, that
speculative builder, but you could not say of him that he
had shut out the sky. The city ran very low upon the
ground in street after street of diminutive, two-storied
houses. Each house was joined on to the next, porch to
porch and bow-window to bow-window, alternating in an
endless series, a machine-made pattern that repeated ; a

pattern monotonous and yet fantastic in its mingling of purple, white, and red. Each had the same little mat of grass laid before each bow-window, the same little red-tiled path from gate to front door, the same front door decorated with elaborate panelling and panes of coloured glass, the same little machine-made iron gate, the same low red wall and iron railing and privet hedge ; so indistinguishably, so maddeningly alike were all these diminutive houses. Each roof had the same purple slates, each roof-tree the same red earth-work edging it like a lace ; the same red tiles roofed each porch, and faced each gable and the space between the stories. Only when your eyes became accustomed to the endless running pattern could you trace it clearly, grasp the detail, note that every two bow-windows were separated by one rain-pipe, every two porches sustained by one pillar, one diminutive magnificent purple pillar, simulating porphyry and crowned with a rich Corinthian capital in freestone, the outline of each porch being picked out and made clear and decisive with wood-work painted white. Then and not till then did you see that the all-important detail was the porphyry pillar, for it was as if every two houses sprang from it as two flowers from one stem.

Inside, each little house had the same narrow passage and steep stairs ; each had the same small room at the front and one still smaller at the back ; the same little scullery behind the same back door at the end of the passage that led off into the garden ; and upstairs the same bath-room over the scullery, the same bedrooms back and front, and the same tiny dressing-room with its little window looking out over the porch.

" Quite enough, if we can run to it," Violet said.

Violet, hitherto somewhat indifferent to the adventure, was caught by the redness and whiteness, the brand-newness and compactness of the little houses ; she was seduced beyond prudence by the sham porphyry pillar.

"Quite enough. More than we want, really," said Ranny.

But that was before they had seen the Agent and the Prospectus.

They went to the Agent, not because they could afford to take a house, but just for curiosity, just to say they'd been, just to supply Ranny with that information that he craved for, now that the passion of the house-hunt was upon him.

"No good going," said Violet. "The rent will be something awful—why, that pillar alone——"

And Ranny too said he was afraid the rent wouldn't be any joke.

But that was precisely what the rent was—a joke. A joke so good that Ranny took for granted it couldn't possibly be true. Ranny chaffed the Agent; he told him he was trying to get at him; he said you didn't find houses with bathrooms and gardens back and front, going for thirteen shillings a week, not in this country.

And the Agent, who was very busy and preoccupied with making notes in a large note-book at his table, mumbled all among his notes that that was right. Of course you didn't find 'em unless you knew where to look for 'em. And that was not because a good 'ouse couldn't be made to pay for thirteen shillings a week, if there was capital and enterprise at the back of the Company that built 'em. This here Estate was the only estate in England —or anywhere—where you could pick up a house, a house built in an up-to-date style with all the modern improvements, for thirteen shillings a week.

And Ranny with a fine shrewdness posed him. "Yes, but what about rates and taxes?"

They were included.

And as the Agent said it calmly, casually almost, making notes in his note-book all the time, Ranny conceived a ridiculous suspicion. He fixed him with a stare that brought him up out of his note-book.

"Included? *What's* included?"

I

"District rate," said the Agent, "poor rate, water rate, the whole bag of tricks for thirteen shillings."

That took Ranny's breath away. As for Violet, she said instantly that they must have the house.

"Of course you must 'ave it," said the Agent. He might have been an indulgent father. "Why not? Only thirteen shillings. And I can make you better terms than that."

It was then that he produced the Prospectus.

By this time, as if stirred by Violet's beauty, he had thrown off the mask of indifference; he was eager and alert.

They spent twenty minutes over that Prospectus from which it appeared that the profit of the Estate Company, otherwise obscure, came from what the Agent called the "ramifications" of the scheme, from the miles and miles of houses they could afford to build. Whereas Ranny's profit was patent, it came in on the spot, and it would come in sooner, of course, if he could afford to purchase outright.

"For how much?"

"Two hundred and fifty."

But there Ranny put his foot down. He said with decision that it couldn't be done, an answer for which the Agent seemed prepared.

Well, then—he could give him better terms again. Could he rise to twenty-five?

Ranny deliberated and thought he could.

Well, then—only twenty-five down, and the balance weekly.

The balance? It sounded formidable, but it worked out at exactly tenpence a week less than the rent asked for (twelve and twopence instead of thirteen shillings), and in twenty years' time—and he'd be a young man still then—the house would be his, Ranny's, as surely as if he had purchased it outright for two hundred and fifty pounds.

It was astounding. Such a scheme could only have been dreamed of in the Paradise of Little Clerks.

And yet—and yet—it was impossible.

Ranny said he didn't want to be saddled with a house. How did he know whether he'd want that particular house in twenty years' time?

Then he could let or sell, the Agent said. It was an investment for his money. It was property. Property that was going up and up. Even supposing—what was laughable—that he failed to sell—he would be paying for his property—paying for house and land—less weekly than if he rented it. Ordinarily you paid your rent out of income or investments. He would be investing every time he paid his rent. People made these difficulties because they hadn't grasped our system—or for other reasons. Maybe (the Agent fired at him a glance of divination) he was calculating the expense of furnishing?

He was.

Nothing simpler. Why—you furnished on the hire-purchase system.

"Not much," said Ranny. He knew all about the hire-purchase system.

So he backed out of it. He backed out of his Paradise, out of his dream. But to save his face he said he would think it over and let the Agent know on Monday.

And the Agent smiled. He said he could take his time. There was no hurry. The house wouldn't run away. And he gave Ranny a copy of the Prospectus with a beautiful picture of the house on it.

All the way home Violet reproached him. It was a shame, she said, that he couldn't afford the furniture. There was nothing in the world she wanted so much as that beautiful little house. She hung on his arm and pleaded. Would he ever be able to afford the furniture? And Ranny said he thought he could afford it in two years. Meanwhile the house wouldn't run away. It would wait two years.

And as if it had been waiting for him, motionless, from all eternity, the house, with its allurements and solicitations, caught him before six o'clock on the evening of that very day.

Ranny's mother, as if she had known what the house was after, played into its hands. Attracted by the Prospectus and the picture, she walked over to Southfields directly after tea. She looked at the house and fell in love with it at first sight. It had taken her no time to grasp the system. You couldn't get a house like that in Wandsworth, not for fifty or fifty-five, not counting rates and taxes. It was a sin, she said, to throw away the chance. As for furnishing, she had seen to that. In fact Ranny without knowing it had seen to it himself. For the last five years he had kept his father's books, conceiving that herein he was fulfilling an essentially unproductive filial duty. And all the time his mother, with a fine sense of justice, had been putting by for him the remuneration that he should have had. Out of his seven years' weekly payments for board and lodging, she had saved no less than a hundred pounds. Thus she had removed the one insurmountable obstacle from Ranny's path.

It might have been better for Ranny if she hadn't. Because, on any scheme, on the lowest scale of expenditure, with the most dexterous manipulation of accounts, the house left him without a margin. But who would think of margins when he knew that he would grow steadily year by year into a landlord, the owner of house property, and *that*, if you would believe it, for less rent than if he didn't own it ? So miraculous was the power of twenty-five pounds down.

As if he thought the house could, after all, run away from him, he bicycled to Southfields with a letter for the Agent, closing with his offer that very night.

And by a special appointment with the Agent, made as a concession to his peculiar circumstances, he and Violet went over before ten o'clock on Sunday morning to choose the house.

For after all they hadn't chosen it yet.

It was difficult to choose among the houses where all were exactly alike; but you could choose among the streets, for some were planted with young limes and some with plane trees, and one, Acacia Avenue, with acacias. Ransome liked the strange tufted acacias. "Puts me in mind of palm trees," he said. And finally his fancy and Violet's was taken by one house, Number Forty-Seven, Acacia Avenue, for it stood just opposite a young tree with a particularly luxuriant tuft. It was really as if the tree belonged to Number Forty-Seven.

Then they discovered that, outwardly uniform, these little houses had a subtle variety within. All, or nearly all, had different wall-papers. In Number Forty-Seven there were pink roses in the front sitting-room and blue roses in the back, and, upstairs, quiet, graceful patterns of love-knots or trellis-work. The love-knots, blue with little pink rose-buds, in the front room (*their* room) caught them. They were agreed in favour of Number Forty-Seven.

Then—it was on the following Saturday—they quarrelled. The Agent had written enquiring whether Mr. Ransome wished to give his residence a distinctive name. He didn't wish it. But Violet did. She wished to give his residence the distinctive and distinguished name of Granville. She said she couldn't abide a number, while Ranny said he couldn't stand a name. Especially a silly name like Granville. He said that if he lived in a house called Granville it would make him feel a silly ass. And Violet said he was a silly ass already to feel like that about it.

Then Violet cried. It was the first time he had seen her cry, and it distressed him horribly. He held out against his pity all Saturday evening. But on Sunday morning, when he thought of Violet, he relented. He said he'd changed his mind about that old family seat. Violet could call it what she liked.

She called it Granville.

The name, in large white letters, appeared presently in the fan-light above the door.

At Woolridge's, on Monday morning in his dinner-hour, Mr. Ransome of the counting-house strolled with great dignity and honour through seven distinct departments as a customer. He ear-marked, for a beginning, and subject always to the approval of a Lady, three distinct suites of furniture which he proposed, most certainly, to purchase outright. None of your hire-purchase systems for Mr. Ransome.

On Tuesday, accompanied by two ladies, he again appeared. Between two violent blushes, and with an air which would have been light and off-hand if it could, Mr. Ransome presented to his friend, the foreman, his mother—and Miss Usher. And as if the foreman had not sufficiently divined her, Miss Usher's averted shoulders, burning cheeks, and lowered eyelids made it impossible for him to forget that she was the Lady whose approval was the ultimate condition of the deal.

After an immensity of time, in which Mr. Ransome's dinner-hour was swallowed up and lost, Miss Usher decided finally on the suite in stained walnut, upholstered handsomely in plush, with a pattern which Ransome imagined to be Oriental, a pattern of indefinite design in yellowish drab and heavy blue upon a ground of crimson. A splendid suite. The overmantle alone was worth the nineteen pounds nineteen shillings he paid for it.

The furnishing of the chamber of the love-knots was arranged for, decorously, between Mrs. Ransome and the foreman. Over every item, from the wardrobe in honey-coloured maple picked out with black, to the china " set "

with crimson reeds and warblers on it, Ranny's friend,
the foreman, communed with Ranny's mother in an
intimate aside ; and Ranny's mother, in another aside
of even more accentuated propriety, appealed to flaming
cheeks and lowered eyelids and a mouth that gave an
almost inarticulate assent. The eyelids refused to open
on Ranny where he stood, turning his back on the women,
while he shook dubiously the foot-rail of the iron double
bedstead to test the joints ; and the mouth refused to
speak when Ranny was heard complaining that the bedstead was about three sizes too large for the room. Eyes
and mouth recovered only downstairs among the carpets,
where they again asserted themselves by insisting on a
Kidderminster with a slender pattern of blue on a drab
ground ; though Ranny's mother had advised the black
and crimson. Ranny's mother contended almost with
passion that drab showed every stain. But Violet would
have that carpet and no other.

And when by struggles and by prodigies of strength on
Ranny's part and on the part of Woolridge's men, by
every kind of physical persuasion, and by coaxing, by
strategy and guile, all that furniture from seven distinct
departments was at last squeezed into Granville—well,
there was hardly room to turn round. Granville, that
would have held its own under any treatment less severe,
was overpowered by Woolridge's.

"What's wrong with it ? " said poor Ranny as they
stood together one Saturday evening, and surveyed their
front sitting-room. He couldn't see anything wrong with
it himself.

They had been married that morning. Ranny had had
to bring his bride straight from her father's house to Granville. There could be no going away for the honeymoon.
Woolridge's wouldn't let Ranny go till the sales were over.

It was only a minute ago that he had had his arm round Violet's waist, and that her face had pressed his. It seemed ages. And suddenly Violet had shown sulkiness and irritation. He couldn't understand it. He couldn't understand how she could have chosen their first hour of solitude for finding fault with the arrangement of the room. He himself had been distinctly pleased ; proud too of having furnished throughout from Woolridge's, in a style that would last, and at a double discount which he owed to his payment in ready money, and to his connection with the firm.

Now he faced a young woman who had no understanding of his pride and no pity.

" It's *all* wrong," said she. " And I'll tell you for why. It's too heavy. You should have furnished in bamboo."

" Bamboo ? Sham-poo ! It wouldn't last," said Ranny.

" Who wants the silly things to last ? " said Violet. " Come to that, you never let on it was bamboo you wanted."

" How could *I* know what I wanted ? You rushed me so, you never gave me time to think."

" Oh, I say," said Ranny, " what a tiresome kiddy ! "

With that he kissed her and between the kisses he asked her with delirious rapidity : " Who gave you a drawing-room suite ? Who gave you a nice house ? Who let you call it Granville ? " But he knew. Nobody indeed knew better than Ranny how tight a squeeze it was ; and what a horrible misfit for Granville.

Then suddenly something in the idea of Granville tickled him.

" Whether is it," he enquired, " that the drawing-room suite is too large for Granville ? Or that Granville is too small for the drawing-room suite ? "

" It's too small for anything. And I think you might have waited."

" Waited ? "

"Yes. Why shouldn't we have gone on as we were?"

He couldn't criticise her in a moment that was still so blessed; otherwise it might have struck him that Granville was certainly too small for Violet's voice.

But it struck Ranny's mother as she heard it from the bedroom overhead where she laboured, spreading with her own hands the sheets for her son's marriage-bed.

"Why shouldn't we?" Violet's voice insisted.

"Because we couldn't."

He drew her to him. Her eyes closed and their faces met, flame to flame.

"Poor little thing," he said. "Is its head hot? And is it tired?"

"Ranny," she said, "is your mother still upstairs?"

"She'll be gone in a minute," he whispered thickly.

XIV

VIOLET'S connection with Starker's ceased on the day of her marriage. Violet herself would have continued it ; she had meant to continue it ; she had fought the point passionately with Ranny ; but Ranny had put his foot down with a firmness that subdued her. She had said, " Oh, well—just as you like. If you think you can get along without my pound a week." And Ranny with considerable warmth had answered back that he hoped to Heaven he could. And then, again and again, with infinite patience and gentleness, he explained that the privilege of acquiring Granville entailed duties and responsibilities incompatible with her attendance in Starker's Millinery Saloons. He pointed out that if they were dependent upon Granville, Granville was also dependent upon them. Granville, she could see for herself, was helpless—pathetic he was.

And Violet would laugh. In those first days he could always make her laugh by playing with the personality they had created. She would come out into the roadway on an August morning, as Ranny was going off to Woolridge's, and they would look at the absurd little house where it stood winking and blinking in the sun ; and morning after morning Ranny kept it up.

" Look at him," he would say, " sittin' there behind his little railin's, sayin' nothing, just waitin' for you to look after him."

And Violet would own that Granville was pathetic. But she triumphed. " You wouldn't feel about him that way," she said, " if he was only Number Forty-Seven."

Just at first there was no doubt that Violet was fond of

Granville. Just at first it was as if she couldn't do too
much for him, to keep him spick-and-span, clean from
top to toe and always with a happy polish. Just at first
he was, as Ranny said, "such a pretty little chap with
his funny purple pillar, and his little peepers winkin' at
you kind of playful, half the time." For the sun shone on
him all that August honeymoon. It streamed down the
Avenue between the rows of young acacias whose green
tufts with that light on them put Ranny more and more
in mind of palm trees. He was more and more in love
with the brand-new Paradise. He expressed all the charm
of Southfields, of Acacia Avenue, when he said it was
"so open, and so up-to-date." It made Wandsworth
High Street look old and tortuous and grimy by comparison.

But Ranny was more and more in love with Violet ; so
much in love that he could never have expressed her
charm. And yet he couldn't hide the effect it had on him.
The neighbours knew it was their honeymoon. They
smiled when they saw Ranny and Violet come out of
Granville every morning wheeling the bicycle between
them ; they smiled when Violet ran beside him as he
mounted ; most of all they smiled when Ranny, riding
slowly, turned right round in his saddle and the two
young lunatics waved and signalled to each other as if
they would never have done.

No doubt that in those first days Violet was in love
with Ranny. No doubt that she looked after him as much
as Violet could look after anything ; every bit as much as
she looked after Granville.

But the hard fact was that Granville and all his furniture
required a great deal of looking after.

Ranny too. To begin with, he had what Violet called
an awful appetite. Which meant that a joint and a loaf
went twice as fast as Violet had calculated ; so that she
found herself driven to pan bread and tinned meat in
self-defence. She had found that for some reason Ranny

didn't eat so much of these. What with his walking and his "biking," and his sitting, Ranny's activities wore through his ordinary everyday clothes at a frightful rate. And then his zephyrs and his flannels! Ranny's mother had always seen to them herself. She had washed them with her own hands. Ranny's wife sent them to the laundress, not too often. So that Ranny, the splendid, immaculate Ranny she had fallen in love with, appeared after his marriage a shade less immaculate, less splendid than he had been before.

It was not, of course, that Violet couldn't wash things. For, as Ranny's mother said to Mrs. Randall, You should see her own white blouses. There was washing for you! Mrs. Ransome owned quite handsomely that the girl "paid for it." By which she meant that Violet's appearance justified the extravagant amount of time she spent on it. And it was not that Granville demanded from her the downright hard work Mrs. Usher had considered salutary in her case. Ransome had seen to that. He had not agreed with Mrs. Usher. If he couldn't keep a servant, he could, and did, engage a charwoman for all the heavy work. It was not that the light work Violet did was unbecoming to her. On the contrary Violet bloomed in Granville. She had had to own that the unaccustomed exercise was a good thing, giving a fineness and a firmness to outlines that had been a shade too lax. It was that you can have too much of a good thing when you have it every day ; too much of light washing and light cooking, of the lightest of light sweeping, of dusting and the making of even one double bed.

Ransome did his best to spare her. He thought that she was tired of looking after Granville when in reality she was only bored. As for her fits of sullenness and irritation he had been initiated into their mystery on his wedding-day. The sullenness, the irritation had ceased so unmysteriously that Ranny in his matrimonial wisdom was left in no doubt as to its cause. There was even sweetness in it, for it proved that, however tired Violet might be of things in general, she was by no means tired of him.

Ransome himself was never tired in those days, and never, never bored. Granville as Number Forty-Seven might have palled upon him ; Granville as a personality assumed for him an everlasting charm. It was astonishing how right Violet had been there. Granville, after all, hadn't made him feel a silly ass. It kept him in a state of being tickled. It tickled Wauchope and Fred Booty. They met him with "What price Granville ? " They called him by turns Baron Granville of Granville, and the Marquis or the Duke of Granville. They "ragged" while Ranny lunged at them and said "Cheese it " ; until one day Booty, suddenly serious, asked, Why on earth, old chappie, he had called it Granville ? When Ranny replied significantly, " I didn't." Then they stopped.

But Granville tickled him only as it were on one side. The other side of Ransome was insensitive. His undeveloped taste was not aware of the architectural absurdity of Granville, with its perky gable, and its sham porphyry pillar. He could look at it, and yet think of it quite gravely and with a secret tenderness as his home, and more than all as the home he had given Violet, the blessed roof and walls that sheltered her.

And all the time, in secret, it was taking hold of him, the delicious thought of property, of possession, of Granville as a thing that in twenty years' time would be his own. Brooding over Granville, Ranny's brain became fertile in ideas. He was always calling out to Violet : " Vikes ! I've got *another* idea ! When he gets all dirty next year I'll paint him green. That'll give him a distinctive character, if you like." Or, " How would it be if I was to cover him up all over with creepers, back and front ? " Or, " Some day I'll whip off those tiles and clap him on a balcony. He'd look O.K. if he only had a balcony over his porch."

His porch was the one thing wrong with Granville ; because it wasn't absolutely and entirely his. The porphyry pillar, for instance ; he had only half a share in it ; the other half belonged to Number Forty-Five ; and you couldn't rightly tell where Number Forty-Five's share ended and his began. Still it wasn't as if anybody ever wanted to swarm up the pillar. But there was a party-wall and that was a serious thing. It was so low that a child could clear it at a stride. And when the postman and errand boys and tradespeople went their rounds, instead of going down Forty-Five's front walk and up Granville's, they all straddled insolently over the party-wall. Ransome said it was "like their bally cheek," by which he meant that it was an insult to the privacy and dignity of Granville. And he stopped it by setting a high box, planted with a perfect little hedge of euonymus, on Granville's half of the top of the party-wall. And he and Violet hid behind the window curtains all one Saturday afternoon, and watched "the poor johnnies being sold."

There was no end to the fun he was getting out of Granville. Every evening he hurried home from Wool-ridge's that he might put in an hour's work in his garden before supper. He was never tired of digging and plant-ing and watering the long strip at the back, or of clipping the privet hedge that screened his green mat at the front. Only Violet got tired of seeing him doing it. More than once when Ranny's innocent back was turned she watched it, scowling. She was so far "gone on him" that she couldn't bear to see him taken up with Granville. She hated the very flowers as his hands caressed them. She hated the little tree he had planted at the bottom of the back garden. For the little tree had kept him out one night till nearly ten o'clock, after Violet had expressly told him that she was going to bed at nine.

.

Violet was not tired ; but she was tired of Granville.

After six weeks of it she began to long secretly for Starker's Millinery Saloons. In the Saloons you walked looking beautiful through a flowery and a feathery grove of hats. You had nothing to do but to try hats on and to sell them, and each sale was a personal triumph for the seller. Violet knew she could sell more hats than any other of the girls at Starker's ; she knew she had a pretty way of putting on a hat, of turning slowly round and round in it to show the side and crown, of standing motionless before a customer while her blue eyes made play that advertised the irresistible fascinations of the brim. At Starker's she went from one triumph to another.

For gentlemen came to the Millinery Saloons, gentlemen whose looks said plainly that they found her prettier than the ladies that they brought ; gentlemen who sometimes came again alone, who for two words would buy a hat and give it you. At Starker's there was always a chance of something happening.

At Granville nothing happened, nothing ever could happen. Granville, when it didn't keep you doing things, gave you nothing to look at, nothing to think about, nothing to take an interest in, and nobody to take an interest in you. It left you sitting in a lonely window looking out into a lonely Avenue, an Avenue where nobody (nobody to speak of) ever came. And not only did Violet long for Starker's Millinery Saloons, she longed for Oxford Street ; she longed for the adventurous setting forth in bus or tram, with the feeling that anything might happen before the day was over ; she longed for the still more adventurous stepping out of the little door in Starker's shutter into the amorously hovering crowd, for the furtive looking round with eyes all bright for the encounter ; above all she longed for somebody, no matter who, to come, somebody to meet her somewhere and take her to the Empire.

And nobody but Ranny ever came.

Sometimes, of course, he took her to Earl's Court or the Coliseum ; but going there with Ranny wasn't any fun. Ranny's idea of fun was not Earl's Court or the Coliseum ; it was to mount a bicycle and ride from that lonely place, Acacia Avenue, into places that were more lonely still. Sometimes they would have tea at a confectioner's, but what Ranny loved best was to put bits of cake or chocolate in his pocket, and to eat them in utter loneliness sitting in a field. In short, Ranny loved to take her into places where there was nothing for them to do, nothing for them to look at, and nobody to look at them. If Violet hadn't been gone on Ranny she couldn't have endured it for a day.

Then in the late autumn the bicycle rides ceased. Violet was overtaken, first with a dreadful lassitude, then with a helplessness as great as Granville's. And with it a sullenness that had no sweetness in it, for Violet defied her fate. And now when she raised her old cry again, " I can't see *why* I shouldn't have gone on at Starker's like I did," instead of saying, " Somebody's got to look after Granville," Ranny answered, " *This* is why."

All through the winter the charwoman came every day. And one midnight, in the first week of March, nineteen-five, Violet's child was born. It was a daughter.

XV

IN that night Ransome acquired a dreadful knowledge. Granville was not a place where you could be born with any decency. It seemed to participate horribly in Violet's agony, to throb with her tortures and recoils, to fill itself shuddering with her cries, such cries as Ransome had never heard or conceived, that he would have believed impossible. They were savage, inhuman; the cries and groans of some outraged animal; there was menace in them and rebellion, terror and an implacable resentment.

And as Ransome heard them his heart was torn with pity and with remorse too, as though Violet's agony accused him. He could not get rid of the idea that he had wronged her; an idea that he somehow felt he would never have had if the baby had been born a month later. He swore that she should never be put to this torture a second time; that if God would only spare her he would never, never quarrel with her, never say an unkind word to her again. He couldn't exactly recall any unkind words; so he nourished his anguish on the thought of the words he had very nearly said, also of the words he hadn't said, and of the things he hadn't done for her. Casting about for these he found that he hadn't taken her to Earl's Court or the Coliseum half as often as he might. He had been wrapped up in himself, that's what he had been; a selfish, low brute. He felt that there was nothing he wouldn't do for Vi, if only God would spare her.

But God wouldn't. He wasn't sparing her now. God had proved that he was capable of anything. It was incredible to Ransome that Violet should live through that night. He wouldn't believe his mother and the

K 129

doctor and the nurse when they told him that everything was as it should be. He knew that they were lying ; they must be ; it wasn't possible that any woman would go through that and live.

All this Ransome thought as he sat in the front parlour under the little creaking room. He *would* sit there where he could hear every sound, where it was almost as if he was by her bed and looking on.

And he wouldn't believe it was all over when at midnight they came and told him, and when he saw Violet lying in her mortal apathy, and when he kissed her poor drawn face. He couldn't believe that Violet's face wouldn't look like that for ever, that it wouldn't keep for ever its dreadful memory, the resentment that smouldered still under its white apathy.

For there could be no doubt that that was Violet's attitude—resentment, as of some wrong that had been done her. He didn't wonder at it. He resented the whole business himself.

It was a pity, though, that she didn't take more kindly to the baby, seeing that, after all, the poor little thing was innocent, it didn't know what it had done.

Ranny would not have permitted himself this reflection but that a whole fortnight had passed and Violet had not died. Ranny's fatherhood was perturbed by Violet's indifference to the baby. He spoke of it to the doctor, and suggested weakness as a possible explanation.

" Weakness ? " The doctor stared at him and smiled faintly. " What weakness ? "

" I mean," said Ranny, " after all she's gone through."

The doctor put his hand on Ranny's shoulder. " My dear boy, if half the women went through as little and came out of it as well——"

Ranny flared up.

" I like that—your trying to make out she didn't suffer. Tortures weren't *in* it. How'd you like——"

But the doctor shook his head.

" We can't alter Nature, my dear boy. But I'll tell you for your comfort—in all my experience I've never known a woman have an easier time."

" D'you mean—d'you mean—she'll get over it ? "

" Get over it ? She's got over it already. She's as strong as a horse."

He turned from Ranny with a swing of his coat-tails that but feebly expressed his decision and his impatience. He paused before the closed doorway for a final word.

" There's no earthly reason why she shouldn't nurse that baby."

" What's that, sir ? " said Ranny, arrested.

" She *must* nurse it. It's better for her. It's better for the child. If I were her husband I'd insist on it—*insist*. If she tells you she can't do it, don't believe her."

" I say, I didn't know there'd been any trouble of that sort."

" That's all the trouble there's been," the doctor said. And he entered on a brief and popular exposition of the subject, from which Ranny gathered that Violet was flying in the face of that Providence that Nature was. Superbly and exceptionally endowed and fitted for her end, Violet had refused the task of nursing-mother.

" Why ? "

The doctor shrugged his shoulders, implying that anything so abstruse as young Mrs. Ransome's reasons was beyond him.

He left Ranny struggling with the question : If it isn't weakness—*What* is it ?

For Violet persisted in her strange refusal, in spite of Ranny's remonstrances, his entreaties, his appeals.

" It's been trouble enough," she said, " without that."

She was sitting up in her chair before the bedroom fire. They were alone. The nurse was downstairs at her supper. The Baby lay between them in its cradle, wrapped in a white shawl. Ranny was watching it.

" I should have thought," he said at last, " you couldn't have borne to let the little thing——"

But she cut that short. " Littie thing ! It's all very well for *you*. You haven't been through what I have ; if you had, p'r'aps you'd feel as I do."

The Baby stirred in its shawl. Its eyes were still shut, but its lips began to curl open with a queer waving, writhing movement.

" What does it mean," said Ranny, " when it makes that funny face ? "

" How should *I* know ? " said Violet.

Little sounds, utterly helpless and inarticulate, came now from the cradle.

" What nice noises it makes," said Ranny. He was stooping by the cradle, touching the Baby's soft cheek with his finger.

" Look at it," he said.

But Violet would not look.

The Baby's face puckered and grew red. Its body writhed and stiffened. It broke into a cry that frightened him.

" Oh, Lord ! " said Ranny, " do you think I've hurt it ? Hadn't you better take it up or something ? "

But Violet did not take it up. He looked at her in astonishment. She looked at him and her face was sullen.

The Baby screamed high.

Ranny put his arm under the small warm thing and lifted it up out of its cradle. He had some idea of laying it on its mother's lap.

The Baby stopped screaming.

Ranny held it, with the nape of its absurdly loose and heavy head supported on his left wrist, and its little soft hips pressed into the hollow of his right hand. And as he held it he was troubled with a compassion and a tenderness unlike anything he had ever known before. For the Baby's helplessness was unlike anything he had ever known.

And its innocence! Why, its hand, its incredibly tiny hand, had found his breast and was moving there for all the world as if he had been its mother. And to Ranny's amazement, with the touch, a queer little pricking pang went through his breast, as if a thin blood vessel had suddenly burst there.

"D'you see that, Vi? Its little hand? What a rum thing a baby is!"

But even that didn't move Violet, or turn her from her purpose, though she smiled.

From that moment Ranny's paternal instinct raised its head again. It had been crushed for the time being in his revolt against Violet's sufferings. But now it was indescribable, the feeling he had for his little daughter Dorothy. (Violet, since they *had* to call the Baby something, had called it Dorothy.) Meanwhile, he hid his feeling. He maintained a perverse, a dubious, a critical silence while his mother and his mother-in-law and his Aunt Randall and the nurse overflowed in praise which, if the Baby had understood them, must have turned its head.

Ranny was reassured when the other women were about him ; because then Violet did show signs of caring for the Baby, if only to keep them in their places and remind them that it was her property and not theirs. She would take it out of their arms, and smooth its hair and its clothes, and kiss it significantly, scowling sullen-sweet, as if their embraces had rumpled it and done it harm. For as long as the nurse was there to look after it, the Baby's adorable person was kept in a daintiness and sweetness so exquisite that it was no wonder if Ranny's mother, in her transports, called it " Little Rose," and " Honeypot," and " Fairy Flower " ; when all that Ranny said was, " It's a mercy it's got hair."

XVI

JUST at first the miracle of the Baby drew a crowd of
pilgrims from Wandsworth to Acacia Avenue. Granville had become a shrine.

People Ransome hardly knew and didn't care for, friends
of his mother and of his Aunt Randall, came over of a
Sunday afternoon to see the Baby. And Wauchope and
Buist and Tyser of the Polytechnic came; and old
Wauchope got excited and clapped Ranny on the back
and said, " Go it, Granville! Steady does it. Here's to
you and many more of them." And Booty brought
Maudie Hollis, who was not too proud and too beautiful
to go down on her knees before the Baby, while young
Fred stood aloof in awe, and grew sanguine to the roots
of the hair that rose, tipping his forehead like a monumental
flame.

As for the Humming-bird, he was amazing. He insisted
on the Baby being christened in Wandsworth Parish
Church (marvellous, he was, throughout the ceremony);
and he actually appeared at Granville afterwards with the
christening party.

That Sunday afternoon Ransome saw Winny Dymond
for the first time since his marriage. He saw her, he could
swear that he saw her, standing with Maudie Hollis in a
seat near the door. He was certainly aware of a little
figure in a long dark coat, and of a face startlingly like
Winny's, and of eyes that could only have been hers,
profound and serious eyes, fixed upon the Baby. But

135

when he looked for her afterwards as the christening party passed out of the church, led by Mrs. Randall carrying the Baby, Winny was nowhere to be seen. No doubt the christening party scared her.

He thought of Winny several times that week. He wondered what she had been doing with herself all those months, and why it was she hadn't come to see them.

And the very next Saturday, as Ransome, on his return from Woolridge's, was wheeling his bicycle with difficulty through the little gate, the door of Granville opened, and Winny came out.

Ransome was so surprised that he let the bicycle go, and it went down with a horrid clatter, hitting him a malicious blow on the ankle as it fell. He was so surprised that, instead of saying what a man naturally would say in the circumstances, he said, " Winky ! "

It would have been like her either to have laughed at his clumsiness, or to have flown to help him, but Winky wasn't like herself. She stood in an improbable silence and gravity and stared at him, while her lips moved as if she drew back her breath, and her feet as if she would have drawn herself back, but for the door she had closed behind her ; so inspired was she with the instinct of retreat.

Her scare (for plainly she was scared) lasted only for a second ; only till he spoke again and came forward.

" So it's little Winky, is it ?   Well, I never ! "   He laughed for pure pleasure.

She smiled faintly and came off her doorstep to take the hand he held out to her.

" I came," she said, " to see Violet and the Baby."

At that he smiled also, half furtively.   " And have you seen them ? "

" Oh, yes.   I've been sitting with Violet for the last hour.   I must be going now."

" Going ?   Why, what's the hurry ? "

" Well——"

"Well——" He tried to sound the little word as she did. He remembered it, the funny little word that summed up her evasiveness, her reluctance, her absurdity.

She was still standing by the doorstep, stroking the sham porphyry pillar with her childish hand, as if she wanted to see what it was made of.

"It isn't *reelly* marble," Ransome said.

She gazed at him, wondering. "*What* isn't?"

"That pillar."

"Oh—I wasn't thinking——" She took her hand away suddenly as if the pillar had been a snake and stung her. Then she looked at it.

"How beautiful they make them." She paused, absolutely grave. Then, "Oh, Ranny, you *have* got a nice house," she said.

"Have you seen it?"

"No. Not *all* of it." She spoke as if it had been a palace.

"Come in and have a look round," said Ranny.

"Well——"

There was distinct yielding in her voice this time. Winny was half caught.

"I *do* love looking at houses."

He lured her in. She came over the threshold as if on some delicious yet perilous adventure, with eyes that shone and with two little teeth that bit down her lower lip ; a way she had when she attempted anything difficult and at the same time exciting. He showed her everything except the room she had seen already, the room with the love-knots and the rosebuds where Violet and the Baby were. Winny admired everything with joy and yet with reverence, from the splendid overmantle in the front sitting-room to the hot-water tap in the bathroom.

"My word ! " Winny said, " what I'd give to have a bath like that ! "

"I say," said Ransome, suddenly moved, "you take a lot more interest in it all than Virelet does."

" She's used to it," said Winny. " Besides, I always take an interest in other peoples' houses."

She pondered. They were both leaning out of the back bedroom window now, looking down into the garden.

" Think of all those little empty houses, Ranny, and the people that'll come and live in them. It seems somehow so beautiful their coming and finding them and getting things for them ; and at the same time it seems somehow sad." She paused.

" I don't mean that *you're* sad, Ranny. You know what I mean."

He did. He had felt it too, the beauty and the sadness, but he couldn't have put it into words. It was the sadness and the beauty of life.

It was queer, he thought, how Winny felt as he did about most things in life.

But Winny's joy over the house was nothing to her joy over the garden, the garden that Ranny had made, and over the little tree that he had planted. It was the most beautiful and wonderful tree in the whole world. For in her eyes everything that Ranny did and that he made was beautiful and wonderful. It could not be otherwise ; because she loved him.

And oh ! she had the most intense appreciation of Granville, of the name and of the personality. She took it all in. Trust Winny.

And as they stood in the gateway at parting, he told her of the system by which in twenty, no, in not much more than nineteen years' time Granville would be his own.

" Why, Ranny, it sounds almost too good to be true ! "

" I know it does. That's why sometimes I think I'll be had over it yet. I say to myself, Granville looks jolly innocent, but he'll score off me, you bet, before he's done."

" He *does* look innocent," said Winny.

He did. (And how Winny took it in !)

" *That's* what tickles me," said Ranny. " Sometimes,

when I come home of a evening and find him still sittin'
there, cockin' his little eyes as if he was goin' to have a
game with me, it comes over me that he's up to something,
and—what do you think I do ? "

" I don't know, Ranny." She almost whispered it.

" I burst out laughin' in his face."

" How *can* you ? " She was treating Granville as he
did, exactly as if it was alive.

" Well—you see how comical he is."

" Yes. I see it." (Of course she saw it.) " Still—
there's something about him all the same."

There was something about everything that was
Ranny's, something that touched her, something that
made her love it, because she loved him. Winny couldn't
have burst out laughing in its face.

" I'm glad I came," she said. " Because now I can see
you."

He misunderstood. " I hope you will, Winky—very
often."

" I mean—see you when you're not there."

He looked away. Something in her voice moved him
unspeakably. For one moment he saw into the heart of
her—placid, profound, and pure.

He was going down the Avenue with her now. For in
that moment he had felt the beauty of her and the sadness. He couldn't bear to think of her " seeing herself
home," going back alone to that little room in St. Ann's
Terrace, where some day, when Maudie married, she would
be left alone. The least he could do was to walk with her
a little way.

" I say, Win," he said presently, " why ever haven't
you come before ? " He really wondered.

There was a long silence. Then, " I don't know, Ranny,"
she said simply.

They had come to the end of Acacia Avenue before
either of them spoke again. Then Ranny conceived
something brilliant.

" What did you think of the Baby ? " he said.

She fairly shone at him, and at the same time she was earnest and very grave.

" Oh, Ranny," she said. " It's the most beautiful baby that ever was. Isn't it ? "

Ranny smiled superbly.

" They tell me so ; but I dunno. *Is* it ? "

" Of course it is."

She had turned, parting from him at last, and she flung that at him as she walked backwards, smiling in his face.

" Well—I must be going back to Vi," he said.

And he went back.

XVII

IN April Ransome looked confidently for Violet to
" settle down." Mrs. Usher had assured him again and
again that the next month would bring the blessed change.

" She'll be all right," said Mrs. Usher, " when the nurse
goes and she has you and Baby to herself."

And at first it seemed as though Violet's mother knew
what she was talking about.

April put an end to their separation. April, like a second
honeymoon, made them again bride and bridegroom to
each other. Nature, whom Ranny had blasphemed and
upbraided, triumphed and was justified in Violet's beauty
that bloomed again and yet was changed to something
almost fine, almost clear ; as if its coarse strain had been
purged from it by maternity. Something fine and clear
in Ranny responded to the change.

And, as in their first honeymoon, Violet's irritation
ceased. She was sullen-sweet, with a kind of brooding
magic in her ways. She drew him with eyes whose glamour
was tenderness under lowering brows ; she bound him
with arms that, for all their incredible softness, had a
vehemence that held him as if it would never let him go ;
and in the cleaving of her mouth to his there was a savage
will that pressed as if it would have crushed between
them all memory and premonition. This was somewhat
disastrous to fineness and clearness, and Ransome's no
doubt would have perished but for the persistence with
which he held Violet sacred as the mother of his child.

Her attitude to the child was still incomprehensible to
him, but he was beginning to accept it, perceiving that it
had some obscure foundation in her temperament. There

were moments when he fell back on his old superstition
(exploded by the doctor) and told himself that Violet was
one of those who suffer profoundly from the shock of
childbirth. And in that case she would get over it in
time.

But time went on and Violet showed no signs of getting
over it, no signs, at any rate, of settling down. On the
contrary, before very long she slipped into her old slack
ways. With all her fierce vitality it was as if she had no
strength to turn her hand to anything. The charwoman
came every week. (That was no more than Ransome was
prepared for.)

The charwoman worked heavily against odds, doing all
she knew. And yet, in the searching light of summer, it
was plain, as Ransome pointed out, that Granville was
undergoing a slow deterioration.

First of all the woodwork cracked and the paint came off
in blisters, and the dirt that got into the seams and holes
and places stayed there. Granville was visited with a
plague of fine dust. It settled on everything ; it penetrated ; it worked its way in everywhere. Violet, going
round languidly with a silly feather-brush, made no head-
way against the pest.

" For Heaven's sake get it out," said Ransome, " or we
shall all be swallowed up in it and die."

" Get it out yourself, if you can," said Violet. " You'll
soon see how you like my job."

She was developing more and more a power of acrimonious
and unanswerable retort.

" Can't you let it be, Ranny ? " (He had found the
feather brush.)

" No. It's spoiling all my O.K. cuffs and collars."

" I can't help your cuffs and collars. What do you
suppose it's doing to mine ? "

Ransome went on flourishing the feather brush. Presently he began to cough and sneeze.

" If you wouldn't rouse it," said Violet, " it would do less harm."

He admitted that the dust was terrible when roused.

So the dust got the better of them. Ransome was not the sort of man who could go about poking his nose into cupboards and places, or flourish a feather brush with a serious intention. He was even more incapable of badgering a beautiful girl whom he had already wronged sufficiently, who declared herself to be sufficiently handicapped by Baby.

Since the Baby came he had abstained from comment on his wife's shortcomings ; though in the matter of meals, for instance, she had begun to add unpunctuality to incompetence. Ransome would have considered himself " pretty flabby," if he couldn't rough it. But he found himself looking forward more and more to the days they spent at Wandsworth, those rare but extensive Sundays that covered the hours of two square meals, not counting tea-time. Then there was the hamper from Hertfordshire. To be sure, in common decency, it could only be regarded as a lucky windfall, but providentially the windfall was beginning to occur at frequent intervals. The Ushers must have had an inkling. Everybody who came to the house could perceive the awful deterioration in the food.

The next thing Ransome noticed was a faint, a very faint, but still perceptible deterioration in himself. And by " himself " Ranny meant in general his physique and in particular his muscles. They were not flabby—Heaven forbid !—but they were not the superb muscles that they had been. All last year he had attended the Gymnasium religiously once a week, just to keep in form. This year his wife was having a bad time and it wasn't fair to leave her too much by herself. Instead of going to the Polytechnic he practised with his dumb-bells in the back bedroom. And now and then after Violet had gone to bed he sprinted. There was no need to worry about himself.

What Ranny worried about was the steady, slow deterioration in the Baby.

It began in the third month of its existence. Up till then the Baby hadn't suffered. It was naturally healthy, and even Violet owned that it was good. By which she meant that it slept a great deal. And for a whole month after she had it to herself she had made tremendous efforts to keep it as the nurse had kept it. She saw (for she was not unintelligent) that trouble taken now would save endless trouble in the long run, in dealing with its inconceivably tender person. As for its food, Violet had been firm about the main point, but it was no strain to order once for all from the dairy an expensive kind of milk which Ranny paid for.

Only, whereas Nurse had made a Grand Toilette for Baby every other day, insisting that the little frocks and vests and flannels should be put on all clean together, Violet observed a longer and longer interval. On Sundays, when Ranny's mother saw her, Baby was still a Little Rose, a Honeypot, and a Fairy Flower. On other days, when tiresome people dropped in unexpectedly, Violet hid everything under a clean overall when she could lay her hands on one.

But from Ranny she hid nothing; and presently it came upon him with a shock that to caress and handle Baby was not the same perfect ecstasy that it had been. It puzzled him at first; then it enraged him; and at last he spoke to Violet.

"Look here," he said, "if you want that child to be a Little Rose and a Honeypot and a Fairy Flower, you'll have to keep it cleaner. That's got to be done, d'you see, whatever's left."

Violet sulked for twenty-four hours after that outburst, but for a whole week afterwards he noticed that Baby was distinctly cleaner.

But whether it was clean or whether it was dirty, Ranny loved it and became more and more absorbed in it.

And with Ranny's absorption Violet's irritability re
turned and increased, and sullenness set in for days at a
time without intermission.

" *This*," said Ranny, " is the *joie de veeve*."

Three more months passed.

For Ransome every day brought a going forth and a
returning, a mixing with the world, with men and with
affairs, the affairs of Woolridge's. His married life had done
one good thing for him. It taught him to appreciate his
life at Woolridge's, and to discern variety where variety
had not been too apparent. There was the change from
Granville to Woolridge's and from Woolridge's to Granville. There was the dinner-hour when he rose from his
desk and went out to an A B C shop with Booty or some
other man. Sometimes the other man had ideas, views of
life and so forth, that interested Ransome ; if he hadn't,
at any rate he was a man. That is to say he didn't sulk or
nag or snap at you ; or nip the words out of your mouth
and twist them ; he wasn't perverse ; he didn't do things
that passed your comprehension, and he let you be. For
Ransome the world of men brought respite. Even at home,
in that world of women, of one woman, when things (he
meant the one woman) were too much for him, menacing
his as yet invincible hilarity, he could turn his back on
them, and work in the garden or play with the Baby. Or
he could leave them for a while and mount his bicycle and
ride out into the open country. For Ransome life still
had interests and surprises.

For the Baby surprise and interest lurked in the feeblest
of its sensations ; every day brought, for the Baby, excitement, discovery and adventure. And then, it had
attached itself to Ransome. It behaved as if it had some
secret understanding with its father. Its sense of comedy,
like Ranny's, seemed imperishable. It would respond
explosively to devices so old, so stale, so worn by repetition,

L

that the wonder was they didn't alienate it, or disgust. The rapid approach and withdrawal of Ranny's hand, his face suddenly hidden behind its pinafore and exposed, still more suddenly, with a cry of " Peep-bo ! " its own inspired seizing of Ranny's hair, would move it to delirious laughter or silent strangling frenzy. And when Ranny wasn't there and nobody took any notice of it, it had its own solitary and mysterious ecstasies of mirth.

It was all very well for Ranny and the Baby.

But for Violet it was one interminable, intolerable monotony. Always the same tiresome things to be done for Granville and for the Baby and for Ranny, when she did them ; and when she didn't there was nothing to do but to sit still, with no outlook, no interest, no surprise, no possibility of variety and adventure.

Now and then they would leave the Baby at Wandsworth with its grandmother, and Ranny would take her to Earl's Court or the Coliseum. But these bright hours were rare, and when they passed the gloom they had made visible was gloomier. And brooding over it she suffered a sense of irremediable wrong.

Nothing to look forward to but bed-time ; the slow, soft-footed ascent to the room with the walls of love-knots and rosebuds, Ranny carrying the Baby. Nothing to look forward to but the dark when the Baby slept and Ranny (who *would* hang over it till the last minute) couldn't see the Baby any more, the dark when he would turn to her with the old passion and the old caresses.

And even into the darkness and into their passion there had come a difference, subtle, estranging and profound. Between them there remained that sense of irremediable wrong. In Violet it roused resentment and in Ransome a tender yet austere responsibility. For he blamed himself for it.

Violet blamed the Baby.

And in those three months Winny Dymond came and

went. By some fatality she contrived to call either on a Sunday when they had all gone to Wandsworth or on a Saturday when Ransome was not there. Once or twice in summer when he was kept at the counting-house during stocktaking or the sales (for Woolridge's season of high pressure came months earlier than Starker's), Winny had dropped in towards supper-time when Violet had asked her to keep her company. But she always left before Ranny could get back, because Violet told her (as if she didn't know it) that Ranny would be too tired to see her home.

One Saturday evening in August he had come in about nine o'clock after a turn on Wimbledon Common. Granville with its gate, its windows and all its doors flung open, had a scared, abandoned look. A strange sound came from Granville, the sound of a low singing from upstairs, from—yes, it was from the front bedroom.

He went through the lower rooms and out into the garden. Nobody was there. The Baby's cradle and pram were empty. And still from upstairs the voice came singing. In all his knowledge of her he had never known Violet sing.

He went upstairs. The door of the front bedroom was closed as if on a mystery. He knocked and opened it tentatively, like a man who respected mysteries. The voice had left off singing and was saying something. It was a voice he knew, but not Violet's voice.

It was saying, with a lilt that was almost a song, " Upsy daisy, upsy daisy, den ! "

There was a pause and then—" Diddums ! " and a sound of kissing.

He found Winny Dymond sitting there, alone, with the Baby on her knee. He caught her in the act of slipping a night-gown over its little naked body that was all rosy from its bath. The place was full of the fragrance of soap and violet powder and clean linen.

" Hello, Winky ! " he said. " What a lark ! " He stood fascinated.

But Winky with a baby in her lap was not capable of levity. It struck him that the Baby was serious, too.

" Violet's just this minute gone out for a breath of air," she said. " I'm putting Baby to bed for her. She's been very fretful all day."

" Who ? Virelet ? "

" No, Baby. (Did it then !)."

" How's that ? " (He sat perched on the foot-rail of the bedstead ; for there was not much room to spare, what with the wardrobe and Winny and the bath.)

" I don't know. But I fancy she isn't very well."

The Baby confirmed her judgment by a cry of anguish.

" I say, what's wrong ? "

" I think," said Winny, " it's the hot weather and the bottles."

" The what ? "

" The bottles. They're nasty things and you can't be too careful with them."

His face was inscrutable.

" Do you think," she said, " you could find me a nice clean one somewhere ? I've got *two* in soak."

He smiled in spite of himself at the gravity, the importance of her air.

He went off to look all over the house for the nice clean one that Winny was certain must be somewhere. In a basin by the open window of the bedroom he found the two horrors that she had put there to soak.

" What's wrong with these ? " said he.

For one moment it was as if Winny were indignant.

" You put your nose to them and you'll soon see what's wrong."

He did and saw. It was not for nothing that he had been born over a chemist's shop in Wandsworth High Street. He had heard his father and his mother (and Mercier even) comment on the sluts whose sluttishness sent up the death-rate of the infant population.

He kept his back to Winny as he stood there by the window.

"The bi——!" A bad word, a word that he would not for worlds have uttered in a woman's presence, half formed itself on Ranny's lips. He turned. "Well," he said aloud, "I *am*—— Let's throw the filthy things away. They're poisonous."

"No, I'll see to it. Just bring me another."

"There isn't another."

She gazed at him with eyes where incredulity struggled with terror that responded to his fierceness. She didn't believe, and she didn't want Ranny to believe that Violet could be so awful.

"There *must* be, Ranny, somewhere."

"There isn't, I tell you."

"Then run round to the chemist's and get *three*."

"All right, but it's no good. The kid's been poisoned. Goodness knows how long it's been going on."

She looked at him, reproachfully, this time.

"No, no; it's only the hot weather come on sudden."

The Baby set up a sorrowful wail as if it knew better and protested against Winny's softening of the facts.

"Poor lamb, she's hungry. Jest you run, there's a dear."

He ran. The chemist, a new-comer, had set up his shop very conveniently at the corner of Acacia Avenue.

As Ransome approached, a familiar figure emerged from the shop doorway; it stood there for a moment as if undecided, then turned and disappeared round the corner.

It was Leonard Mercier.

"What on earth," thought Ranny, "is old Jujubes doing here?"

The flying wonder of it had barely flicked his brain

when it was gone. Ranny's thoughts were where his heart was, where he was back again in an instant, in the bedroom with Winny and the Baby.

He prepared the child's food under Winny's directions (it was wonderful how Winny seemed to know) ; and before nightfall, what with rocking and singing, she had soothed the Baby to a sleep.

Nightfall, and Violet hadn't come back.

" I'm glad she's got out at last," Winny said. " She's had such an awful day."

" You think she doesn't get out enough, then ? "

She hesitated.

" I do. Not really out ; because of Baby."

They sat near, they spoke low, so as not to wake the child that slept on Winny's knee.

" The kid doesn't give her many awful days. It's such a jolly kid. Anyone would think she'd be happy with it."

" She's so young, Ranny. You should think of that. She's only like a child herself. She's got to be looked after. She doesn't know much about babies. She hasn't had one very long, you see."

" *You* know, Winny. How's that ? You haven't had one at all."

" No. I haven't had one. I can't say how it is."

He smiled. " To look at you anyone would say you'd nursed a baby all your life."

So she had—in fancy and in dreams.

" It comes more natural to some," she said. " All Violet wants is telling. You should tell her, Ranny."

" Tell her what ? "

" Well—tell her to take Baby out more. Tell her to give her a bath night *and* morning. Tell her little babies get ill and die if you don't keep everything about them as clean as clean. Tell her anything you like. But don't tell her to-night."

" Why not ? "

" Because she's upset."

" What's upset her ? "

" I don't know. *You'll* upset her if you go flying out at her about those old bottles like you did ; and if you go calling her bad names. *I* heard you."

Was it possible ? (Why, he hadn't let it out, or, if he had, it had gone, quite innocently, through the open window.)

" If you're not as gentle as gentle with her you'll upset her something awful. You've got to be as gentle with her as you are with Baby."

So she thought he wasn't gentle, did she ? She thought he bullied Violet and upset her ? Whatever could Violet have been saying about him ? Well—well—he couldn't tell her that he *had* been as gentle with her as he was with Baby, and that the gentler he was the more Violet was upset.

He didn't know that Winky was punishing him in order to punish herself for having given Violet away.

" All right, Winky," he said. " If you think I'm such a brute."

" I don't think anything of the sort, Ranny. You know I don't."

She rose with the sleeping child in her arms and carried it to its cot. He followed her and turned back the blanket for her as she laid Baby down. But it was Winny and not Baby that he looked at.

And he thought " Little Winky's grown up."

To be sure her hair was done differently. He missed the door-knocker plat.

But that was not what he meant. He had only thought of it after she had left him.

It was past ten before Violet came back. He found her in the sitting-room, standing in the light of the gas flame

she had just lit. Her eyes shone ; her face was flushed.
She panted a little as if (so he thought) she had hurried,
being late.

" Well," he said to her, " have you had your little run ? "

She stared and flung three words at him.

" I wanted it ! "

And still she stared.

" Vi——" he began.

" Well—what's the matter with you ? "

" Nothing's the matter with *me*. But I'm afraid Baby's
going to be ill."

She stood before him, her breast heaving. She drew
her breath in and let it out again in a snort of exasperation.

" What makes you think so ? "

" Something Winny said."

" What does she know about it ? "

He wanted to say " A jolly sight more than you do,"
but he stopped himself in time.

He began to talk gently to her.

And Violet was horribly upset.

Wrap it up as tenderly as he might there was no mistaking the awfulness of the charge he brought against her.
He had as good as taxed her with neglecting Baby. She
had recourse to subterfuge ; she sheltered herself behind
lies, laid on one on the top of the other, little silly trans-
parent lies, but such a thundering lot of them that Ranny
could say of each that it was jolly thin and of the whole
that it was a bit too thick.

That brought her round, and he wondered whether
gentleness was the best method for Violet after all. He was
disgusted, for he hated subterfuge.

And she might just as well have owned up at once ; for
-in a day or two she was defenceless. The Baby was ill ;
and the illness was accusation and evidence and proof
positive and punishment all rolled into one ; Baby's sufferings being due to the cause that Ransome had assigned.
It had been poisoned, suddenly, from milk gone sour in

the abominable bottles, and slowly, subtly poisoned from the still more abominable state of its Baby's Comforter. Ransome and his wife sat up three nights running and the doctor came twice a day. And every time, except on the last night, when the Baby nearly died, the doctor spoke brutally to Violet. *He* knew that gentleness was not a bit of good.

XVIII

STILL, that was in August and they could put a good half of it down to the hot weather.

Besides, the Baby got over it. With all its accusing and witnessing, it was, as Ranny said, a forgiving little thing ; it had never in its life done anybody any harm. It did not hurt Violet now.

And the hot days passed ; weeks passed ; months passed, and winter and spring. The Baby had one little attack after another. It marked the passage of the months by its calamities ; and still these might be put down to the cold weather or the stress of teething. Then, in a temperate week of May, nineteen-six, it did something decisive. It nearly died again of enteritis ; and again it was forgiving and got over it.

There could be no doubt that things would have been simpler if it had been cruel enough to die. For the question was : What were they to do now ?

Things, Ransome said, had got to be different. They couldn't go on as they were. The anxiety and the discomfort were intolerable. Still, that he had conceived an end to them, showed that he did not yet utterly despair of Violet. She had been terrified by the behaviour of the Baby and by the things, the brutal things, the doctor had said to her, and she had made another effort. Ransome's trouble was simply that he couldn't trust her. He said to himself that she had good instincts and good impulses if you could depend on them. But you couldn't. With all her obstinacy she had no staying power. He recognised in her a lamentable and inveterate flabbiness.

If he had known all about her he might have formed a

larger estimate of her staying power. But he did not yet know what she was. That bad word that he had once let out through the window had been in Ranny's simple mind a mere figure of speech, a flowering expletive, flung to the dark, devoid of meaning and of fitness. He did not know what Violet's impulses and her instincts really were. He did not know that what he called her flabbiness was the inertia in which they stored their strength, nor that in them there remained a vigilant and indestructible soul, biding its time, holding its own against maternity, making more and more for self-protection, for assertion, for supremacy. He felt her mystery, but he had never known the ultimate secret of this woman who ate at his board and slept in his bed and had borne his child. It was with his eternal innocence that he put it to her, What were they to do now?

And that implacable and inscrutable soul in her was ready for him. It prompted her to say, that she couldn't do more than she did, and that if things were to be different he must get someone else to see to them. He must keep a servant. He should have kept one for her long ago.

Poor Ranny protested that he'd keep twenty servants for her if he could afford it. As it was, a charwoman every week was more than he could manage, and she knew it. And she said, looking at him very straight, that there was one way they could do it. They could do as other people did. In half the houses in the Avenue they let apartments. They must take a lodger.

Violet had thrown out this suggestion more than once lately. And he had put his foot down. Neither he, nor Granville, he said, could stand a lodger. A lodger would make Granville too hot by far to hold him.

Now in their stress he owned that there was something in it. He would think it over.

Thinking it over, he saw more than ever how impossible it was. The charwoman, advancing more and more, had been a fearful strain on his resources, and the expenses of

the Baby's birth had brought them to the breaking point.
And then there had been Baby's illnesses. Before that
there was the perambulator.

But that was worth it. He remembered how last year
he had seen an ernomous poster in High Street, with the
words in scarlet letters : " Are you With or Without a
Pram for Baby ? " He had realised then for the first
time that he was without one. And the scarlet letters
had burnt themselves into his brain, until, for the very
anguish of it, he had gone and bought a pram and wheeled
it home under cover of the darkness, disguised in its
brown paper wrappings to heighten the surprise of it.
Violet had not been half so pleased nor yet so surprised as
he had expected ; but he had got his money back again
and again on that pram with the fun he'd had out of it.

But before that again, in their first year, things had had
to be done for the house and garden. Ranny shuddered
now when he thought of what the lawn-mower alone had
cost him. And that tree ! And then the little pleasures
and the outings—when he totted them all up he found
that he had taken Violet to Earl's Court and the Coliseum
far, far oftener than he could have believed possible.
Looking back on that first year he seemed to have been
always taking her somewhere. She wasn't happy when
he didn't.

No, and she hadn't been very happy when he did. He
would never forgot that week they had spent at Southend
last Whitsuntide, when he got his holiday. And it had
all eaten into money. Not that he grudged it ; but
the fact remained. His margin was gone ; half his savings
were gone ; his income had suffered a permanent shrinkage
of two pounds a year.

Impossible to keep a servant without the aid of the
lodger he abhorred. But with it not only possible but
easy, easy as saying how d'you do. Except for the presencè
of the loathsome lodger nothing would be changed. The
back bedroom was there all ready, eating its head off ;

and for all they used the front sitting-room, they might just as well not have had one.

They could get somebody who would be out all day.

He thought about it for three weeks, but before he made up his mind he talked it over with his mother. She had come to see them late one evening in June, and he had walked back with her. She was tired, she said, and they had found a seat in a little three-cornered grove where the public footpath goes to Wandsworth High Street.

In this favourable retreat Ranny disclosed to his mother as much as he could of his affairs. Mrs. Ransome didn't like the idea of the lodger any more than he did, but she admitted that it was a way out of it. " Only," she said, " if I was you I should have a lady. Someone you know about. Someone who might look after Vi'let."

" That's right. But Virelet would have to look after her, you see."

" Vi'let's no more idea of looking after anybody than the cat."

" It isn't her fault, mother."

" I'm not saying it's her fault. But it's a pity all the same you should have to put up with it."

" It's larks for me to what Vi puts up with. I shouldn't mind, if——"

He drew back, shy before the trouble of his soul.

" If what, Ranny ? " she said gently.

" If she seemed to care a bit more for the kid. Sometimes I think she actually——"

Though he could not say it Mrs. Ransome knew.

" Don't you think that, Ranny. Don't you think it, my dear."

She was playing at the old game of hiding things, and she expected him to keep it up. She had never admitted for one moment that his father drank ; and she wasn't going to admit, or to let him admit, for a moment that his wife was a bad mother.

So she changed the subject.

" That's a nice little girl I see sometimes down at your place. That Winny Dymond. Is she a friend of Vi'let's ? "

Ranny said she was.

" Has Vi'let known her long ? "

" I think so. I can't say exactly how long."

" Before she was married ? "

" Yes."

Something in his manner made her pause, pondering.

" Did *you* know her before you married, Ran ? "

" Ages before."

His mother sighed.

" I suppose," said Ranny, harking back, " some women *are* like that."

" Like what now ? " She didn't want to go back to it. She was afraid of what she might be driven to say.

" Not caring much about their own kids."

" Oh, Ranny, why do you 'arp on it ? "

" Because I don't understand it. It's just the one thing I can't understand. What does it *mean*, mother ? "

" Well, my dear, sometimes it means that they can't care for anything but their 'usbands. It's 'usband, 'usband with them all the time. There's some," she elaborated, " that care most for their husbands and there's some that care most for their children."

(He wondered which would Winny Dymond care for most ?)

" And there's some," said Mrs. Ransome, " that care most for both, and care different, and that's best."

(Winny, he somehow fancied, would have been that sort.)

" Which did *you* care for most, Mother ? "

" You mustn't ask me that question, Ranny. I can't answer it."

But he knew. He felt her yearning towards him even then. There was something very artful, and at the same time very comforting about his mother. She had made him feel that Violet was all right, that he was all right, that everything in fact was all right; that he was indeed twice-blest since he had a wife who loved him better than her child, and a mother who loved him better than her husband.

" Talking of husbands," he said, " how's the Torpichen Badger ? "

She shook her head at him in the old way; keeping it up.

" Oh, Ranny, you mustn't call your father that."

" Why not ? "

" It's a whisky, my dear."

(He could have sworn there was the ghost of a smile about her soft mouth.)

" So it is. I forgot. Well, how's the Hedgehog ? "

For all her smile Mrs. Ransome seemed to be breaking down all of a sudden, as if in another moment the truth would have come out of her; but she recovered and she kept it up.

" He's had the Headache come on more than ever. I've never known a time when His Headache has been so bad. Most constant it is."

Ranny preserved a respectful silence.

" He's worrying. That's what it is. Your father's got too much on His mind. The business isn't doing quite so well as it did now He can't see to things. And here's that Mercier saying that he's going to leave."

" What ? Old Eno ? What's he want to leave for ? "

" To better himself, I suppose. You can't blame him."

They rose and went on their way that plunged presently into Wandsworth High Street.

By the time he got home again Ransome had braced himself to the prospect of the thing he hated. They might let the rooms, perhaps, for a little while, say, till Michaelmas when he would have got his rise. ´Yes, perhaps ; if they could find a lady.

But Violet wouldn't hear of a lady. Ladies gave too much trouble ; they nagged at you and they beat you down.

Well, then, if she liked, a gentleman. A gentleman who would be out all day, and whose hours of occupation would coincide strictly with his own. But he impressed it on her that no rooms were to be let in his absence to any applicant whom he had not first inspected.

So they settled it.

Then, as if they had scented trouble, Mr. and Mrs. Usher came up from Hertfordshire the very next Saturday. They looked strangely at each other when the idea of the lodger was put before them, and Mr. Usher took Ranny out into the garden.

" I wouldn't do it," Mr. Usher said. " Let her work, let her work with her 'ands. A big strapping girl like her, it won't hurt her. Why, my Missis there could turn out your little doll-'ouse in a hour. Don't you take no gentlemen lodgers. Don't you let her do it, Randall, my boy. Or there'll be trouble."

The advice came too late. That very evening Violet informed her husband that she had let the rooms.

And while Ranny raged she assured him that it was all right. She had done exactly what he had told her. She had let them to a friend of his—Leonard Mercier.

XIX

SHE gathered from his silence that it was all right. Not a muscle of Ranny's face betrayed to her that it was all wrong.

Ever since his marriage he had kept Leonard Mercier at a distance. He had had to meet him, of course, and Violet had had to meet him, now and again, at dinner or supper in his father's house ; but Ranny was not going to let him hang round his own house if he could help it. When Jujubes suggested dropping in on a Sunday, Ranny assured him that on Sundays they were always out. And Mercier had met the statement with his atrocious smile. He understood that Randall meant to keep himself to himself. Or was it, Mercier wondered, his young wife that he meant to keep ?

And wondering he smiled more atrociously than ever. It pleased him, it excited him to think that young Randall regarded him as dangerous.

But Randall did not regard him as dangerous in the least. To Ranny, Jujubes, in his increasing flabbiness, was too disgusting to be dangerous. And his conversation, his silly goat's talk, was disgusting too. Ranny had thought that Violet would find Jujubes and his conversation every bit as disagreeable as he did.

Even now, while some instinct warned him of impending crisis, he still regarded Leonard Mercier as decidedly less dangerous than disgusting. He wasn't going to have the flabby fellow living in his house. That was all ; and it was enough.

And in this moment that his instinct recognised as critical, he acquired a wisdom and a guile that ages of

experience might have failed to teach him. With no
perceptible pause, and in a voice utterly devoid of any
treacherous emotion he enquired what Mercier was doing
there, and learned that Mercier was leaving Wandsworth
next week, on the thirteenth, and would be established as
chief assistant in the new chemist's shop in Acacia Avenue.

He remembered. He remembered how last year he had
seen Jujubes coming out of the chemist's shop and looking
about him. So *that* was what he was after ! There had
been no chance for him last year ; but Southfields was a
rising suburb, and this summer the new chemist was able
to increase his staff.

It was not surprising that Mercier should want to leave
Wandsworth, nor that the new chemist should desire to
increase his staff, nor that these two desires should coincide
in time. Nothing indeed could be more natural. But still
Ranny's instinct told him that there had been a curious
persistency about old Eno.

Well, he would have to interview old Eno, that was all.

He waited a whole hour, to show that he was not
excited ; and then, without saying a word to Violet, he
whirled himself furiously down to Wandsworth.

The interview took place very quietly over his father's
counter. He found his quarry alone there in the shop.

Leonard Mercier greeted him with immense urbanity.
He could afford to be urbane. He was dressed, and knew
that he was dressed, with absolute correctness in the
prevailing style, a style that disguised and restrained his
increasing flabbiness, whereas, though Ranny's figure was
firm and slender, his suit was shabby. Leonard Mercier
had the prosperous appearance of a man unencumbered
with a wife and family. And unless you insisted on hard
tissues he was good-looking in his own coarse way. His
face, with all its flabbiness, had its dark accent and distinction ; and these were rendered even more emphatic by
the growth of a black moustache which he had trained
with care. The ends of it were waxed and drawn finely to

a point. His finger-nails and his skin, his hair and his moustache showed that the young chemist did not disdain the use of the cosmetics that lay so ready to his hand.

The duologue was brief.

" Hello, old chappy. So you're going to be my new landlord ? "

" Not *much*."

" What's that ? "

" Some error of my wife's, I fancy."

" As *I* understand it Mrs. Ransome's let me two rooms and I've taken them."

" That's right. But you can't have 'em."

" But I've engaged them."

" Sorry, Jujubes. You were a trifle previous. I'm not letting any rooms just yet."

" Mrs. Ransome told me the contrary."

" Then Mrs. Ransome didn't know what she was talking about."

" Rats ! When *you* told *her*——"

" It's immaterial," said Ranny with great dignity, " what I told her. For I've changed my mind. See ? "

" You can't change it. You can't play fast and loose like that. I've engaged those rooms from a week to-day. Where am I to go to ? "

" You can go to hell if you like," said Ranny with marked amiability.

Up to that point Mercier had been amiable too. But when Ranny told him where he might go to he began to look unpleasant.

Unpleasant, not dangerous ; oh, no, not dangerous at all. Ranny looked at him and thought how he would go in like a pillow if you prodded him, and of the jelly, the jelly on the floor, he would make if you pounded.

" You've got to account to me for this," said Mercier. " Those rooms are let to me from the thirteenth, and on the thirteenth I come into them, or you pay me fifteen bob for the week's rent."

" Have you got that down in black and white ? "
He had not.

" Well—if you come into those rooms on the thirteenth
I shouldn't wonder if you get it down in black and
blue."

Whereupon Mercier pretended that he was only joking.
He was glad that the counter was between him and young
Randall, the silly ass. And Ranny said it was all right
and offered him (magnanimously) the fifteen shillings,
which Mercier (magnanimously) refused on the grounds
that he had been joking. Then Ranny beholding Jujubes
for the lamentably flabby thing he was, and considering
that after all he had not dealt quite fairly with him,
undertook to find him quarters equal if not superior to
Granville—where, he assured him, he would not be
comfortable. And having shaken hands with Jujubes
across the barrier of the counter, he strode out of the shop
with a formidable tightening and rippling of muscles under
his thin suit.

Mercier leaned back against the shelves of white jars
and pondered. Recovering presently, he made a minute
inspection of his finger-nails. He then stroked his moustache into a tighter curl that revealed the rich red curve
of his upper lip. And as he caught the pleasing reflection
of himself in the looking-glass panel opposite he smiled
with a peculiar atrocity.

Up till then his mood had been the petty fury of a
shopman baulked of his bargain and insulted. Now, in
that moment, the moment of his recovery, another thought
had occurred to Mercier.

It accounted for his smile.

Ransome went back to Granville with his mind unalterably made up. He was not going to let any rooms to
anybody, ever. The letting of rooms, was, if you came to

think of it, a desecration of the sanctity of the home and an outrage to the dignity of Granville. When he thought of Jujubes sprawling flabbily in the front sitting-room, strolling flabbily (as he would stroll) in the garden, sleeping (and oh, with what frightful flabbiness he would sleep !) in the back bedroom next his own, filling the place (as he would) with the loathsome presence and the vision and the memory of Flabbiness, he realised what it was to let your rooms. And realising it, he had no doubt that he could make Violet see the horror and the nuisance of it. Come to that, she shrank from trouble, and Jujubes would have been ten times more trouble than he was worth.

In fact Ranny, having settled the affair so entirely to his own satisfaction, could no longer perceive any necessity for caution and rushed on it recklessly at supper ; though experience had taught him to avoid all unpleasant subjects at the table. The unpleasantness soaked through into the food, as it were, and made it more unappetising and more deleterious than ever. Besides, Violet was apt to be irritable at meal-times.

" It's off, Vikes, that letting."

He saw nothing at all unpleasant in the statement as it stood, and he was not prepared for the manner in which she received it.

" Off ?   What d'you mean ? "

" I've been down and I've seen Mercier."

" He told you what ? "

She had raised her head.   Her red mouth slackened as if with the passage of some cry inaudible.   Her eyes stared, not at her husband, but beyond and a little above him ; there was a look in them of terror and enraged desire, as if the object of their vision were retreating, vanishing.

But it was all vague, meaningless, incomprehensible to Ranny.   He only remembered afterwards, long afterwards, that on that night when he had spoken of Mercier she had " looked queer."

And the queerest thing was that she did not know
Mercier then, or hardly ; hardly to speak to.

He answered her question.

" He told me he'd taken the rooms, of course."

" And so he *did* take them ! "

" Yes, he took them all right. But I had to tell him
that he couldn't have them."

" But you can't act like that. You can't turn him out
if he wants to come."

" Oh, *can't* I ? *He* knows that. Jolly well he knows it.
He won't want to come. Anyhow, he isn't coming."

" You stopped him ? "

" Should think I did. Rather," said Ranny cheerfully.

She shot at him from those covering brows of hers a
look that was malignant and vindictive. It missed him
clean.

" Y—y—you—— ! " Whatever word she would have
uttered she drew it back with her vehement breath.
" *What* did you do that for ? "

" Why, because I don't want the fellow in the house."

" Why—don't—you want him ? " Her shaking voice
crept now as if under cover.

" Because I don't approve of him. That's why."

" What have you got against him ? "

" Never you mind. I don't approve of him. No more
would you if you knew anything about him. Don't you
worry. You couldn't stand him, Vi, if you had him
here."

She pushed her plate violently away from her with its
untasted food, and planted her elbows on the table. She
leaned forward, her chin sunk in her hands, the raised
arms supporting this bodily collapse. Foreshortened,
flattened by its backward tilt, its full jowl strained back,
its chin thrust towards him and sharpened to a V by the
pressure of her hands, its eyes darkened and narrowed
under their slant lids, her face was hardly recognisable as
the face he knew.

But its sinister, defiant, menacing quality was lost on Ranny. He said to himself, "She's rattled, poor girl; and she's worried. That's why she looks so queer."

"You haven't told me yet," she persisted, "what you've got against him."

And Ranny replied in a voice devoid of rancour, "He's a low swine. If we took him in I should have to build a pigsty at the bottom of the garden for him, and I can't afford it. Granville isn't big enough for him and me. And it wouldn't be big enough for him and you, neither. You'd be the first to come and ask me to chuck him out." He spoke low, for he heard the neighbours talking in the next garden.

"Fat lot you think of *me* !" she cried.

"It's you I *am* thinking of."

She rose from the table, dragging the cloth askew in her trailing, hysterical stagger. She lurched to the French window that, thrown back against the wall, opened on to the little garden. And she stood there, leaning against the long window and pressing her handkerchief to her mouth till the storm of her sobbing burst through.

The people in the next garden stopped talking.

"For God's sake," said Ranny, "shut that window."

He got up and shut it himself, moving her inert bulk aside gently for the purpose. And she stood against the wall and laid her face on it and cried.

And Ranny called upon the Lord in his helplessness.

He went and put his arm round her and she thrust him from her; and then whimpered weakly.

"Wh—wh—wh—why are you so unkind to me?"

"Unkind! Oh, my Aunt Eliza!"

"You don't care. You don't care," she moaned. "You don't care what happens to me. I might die to-morrow and you wouldn't care."

"Oh, come——" he ventured.

But Violet wouldn't come. She was off, borne from him on the rising tide of hysteria.

" It's true ! It's true ! " she cried. " Else you wouldn't use me like you do."

" But look here. Whatter you goin' on about ? Just because I don't want you to have anything to do with Mercier."

She raised her flaming face at that.

" It's a lie ! It's a beastly lie ! I never had anything to do with Mercier."

" Who said you'd had anything to do with him ? "

" You did. And I hardly know him. I've hardly seen him. I've hardly spoken to him be — be — before."

" I never said you had."

" You thought it."

" You know I didn't. How *could* I think it ? "

" You *did*. That's why you wouldn't let him come. You won't trust me with him."

" Trust you with him ? I should think I *would* trust you. Him ! The flabby swine ! "

Violet's sobs sank lower. They shook her inwardly, which was terrible to see.

And as he looked at her he remembered yet again how in the beginning he had wronged her. *That* was what made her think he wouldn't trust her. There would always be that wrong between them.

He drew her (unresisting now) to the other side of the room and lowered her to the couch that stood there. He looked into the teapot where the drained leaves were still warm. He filled it up again with boiling water from the kettle on the gas-ring, and poured out a cup and gave it her to drink, supporting her stooping head tenderly with his hand. Her forehead burned to his touch.

" Poor little Vi," he said. " Poor little Vi."

She glanced at him ; slantwise, yet the look made his heart ache.

" Then you *do* trust me ? " she muttered.

" You *know* I do."

They sat there leaning against each other till the room grew dim. Then they rose, uncertainly ; and hand-in-hand, as it were under the old enchantment, they went upstairs into the dark room where the Baby slept.

To-night he did not look at it.

XX

THAT was on the eighth of June.
    He remembered, because it was a Saturday,
Saturdays and Sundays being the landmarks of his existence by which alone he measured the distances and marked
the order of events. The habit of so regarding them was
contracted in his early days at Woolridge's, when only in
and by those hours snatched from Woolridge's did he live.
All other days of the week were coloured and had value
according to their nearness to Saturday and Sunday.
Monday was black, Tuesday brown, Wednesday a browny
grey, Thursday a rather clearer grey (by Thursday you
had broken the back of the week), Friday distinctly rosy,
and Saturday and Sunday, even when it rained, a golden
white.

He hadn't been married a year before all the seven were
shady ; the colours ran into each other till even Sundays
became a kind of greyish drab. And still he continued
to date things by Saturdays and Sundays ; as he did now
in his mind, exultantly, thus : " Saturday, the eighth :
Jujubes knocked out in the first round."

Not that the dates went for very much with Ranny,
to whom interesting things so seldom happened. He remembered this one more because of his scoring off Jujubes
than because of the scene with Violet and its sequel. He
was used to scenes and sequels and was no longer concerned
to note their correspondence and significance. So that he
never noted now that it was on and after Thursday the
thirteenth that what he called the Great Improvement had
begun.

He meant the improvement in Violet's appearance. He

had accepted the fact that, in all household matters, his wife was a slut and a slattern ; yet it staggered him when it first dawned on him that, in the awful deterioration of Granville and the Baby, the standard of her own toilette had gradually lowered. Then gradually he got inured to it. The tousled, tumbling hair, the slipshod feet, the soiled blouse gaping at the back, were, he reflected bitterly, in perfect harmony with Granville, and of a piece with everything. He had ceased to censure them ; they belonged so inalienably to the drab monotone ; they were so indissolubly a part of all his life. And somehow she bloomed in spite of them. Ranny's unconquerable soul still cried " Stick it ! " as he grappled with her shameless blouses.

And now, suddenly, she had changed all that. She had become once more the creature of mysterious elegance, of beauty charged with magical reminiscence, in the trim skirt and stainless blouse, clipped by the close belt ; and with the bit of narrow black velvet ribbon round her throat. Even in the morning she appeared once more with a clear parting in her brushed and burnished hair. Even in the morning her soft skin was once more sweet in its sheer cleanness. And in the evening there soaked through and fell and hung about her that old fragrance of violets that invariably turned his head.

And she had bought new stockings and new shoes ; openwork stockings that showed her white feet through, and little, little shoes with immense steel buckles. And her new mushroom with the big red roses round it assaulted, battered, and beat into cocked hats all the other mushrooms in the Avenue.

But it was the stockings and the shoes that made him kiss her feet when, on Sunday the sixteenth, he first saw them coming down the stairs.

" Do you like my shoes ? " she said. And she stuck them out one after the other. As she was standing four steps above him they were on a level with his mouth ; so he kissed them one after another, on the instep, just above the buckles.

" Do you like my dress ? "

" It's ripping."

" Do you like my hat ? "

" It's an A1 hat ; but it's those feet that fetch me."

He had not been so fetched for a whole year. It was a most peculiar fetching.

They went to church together (they had hired a little girl for the last week to mind the toddling Baby in the mornings). It might have been for church that she had put on that hat. It could only be for him that she wore the shoes. All through the service Ranny's heart was singing a hymn to the blessed little feet that had so fetched him, the blessed little tootsy-woots in the blessed little shoes. He knelt, adoring, to the hem of the new white dress. He bowed his head under the benediction of the hat.

The fact that Mercier was established in the chemist's pew opposite and was staring at the hat, and under it, did not interfere with his devotions in the least. He could even afford to let old Jujubes walk home with them, though he managed to shake him off adroitly at his shop door. Nothing could really interfere with his devotions. For he felt that those things, especially the shoes, were the outward and visible signs of an inward and spiritual grace. Some grace that had descended out of Heaven upon Violet.

The signs would be, no doubt, expensive ; they should not have been so much as dreamed of before Michaelmas when he would get his rise ; that splendiferous get-up would in all probability just about clean him out, rise and all ; but he tried not to look on the dark side of it. He was not one to quench the spirit or the smoking flax.

But, as the hours and the days went by, it was borne in upon him that there was absolutely no connection between Violet's inward state and that regenerated outside. This perturbed him ; and it would have perturbed him more

but that he had other things to think of, and that in any
case he believed that a woman's clothes do not necessarily
point to an end beyond themselves.

Now, if he had been less preoccupied and had paid more
heed to dates, he would have noted three things : that it
was on and after the evening of Thursday the twentieth
that her mood of gay excitement and of satisfaction died
and gave place to restlessness, irritation and expectancy
(a strained and racking, a dismayed and baulked expectancy) ; that Thursday, the twentieth, was early closing
day in Southfields ; and that consquently Leonard Mercier
was at large. And having gone thus far in observation he
must have seen that it was on and after Thursday the
twenty-seventh (early closing day again) that she became
intolerable.

Intolerable. There was no other word for it. The
" *joie de veeve* " was so intense that it was not to be
borne. She had days of stupor now that followed fits of
fury. He didn't know which was the worse, the fury or
the stupor.

But it was the stupor that made him burst out one night
(at supper ; it was always at supper that these things
happened).

She had brought it on herself by asking what he wanted
now when he had broken the frightful silence by addressing
her affectionately as " Vikey."

" What I want," said Ranny then, " is a change. I want
bracing ; and bright surroundings, and entertaining
society. I shall go and live at Brookwood."

At last it was too much for anybody (the fury, this time).
It was too much for the charwoman, even once a fortnight,
and she refused to come again. It was too much for the
little girl who minded Baby in the mornings, and she left.
Her mother said she wouldn't " have her put upon," and
complained that Mrs. Ransome had served her something
shameful. Ransome hardly liked to think how Violet
could have served the little girl.

Before long he had an inkling. For presently a new and incredible quality revealed itself in Violet.

Up till now she had never been unkind to the Baby. She had neglected it ; she had been indifferent to it ; but it had seemed impossible, not only to Ransome but to Violet herself, that she could be positively unkind. He had charged the neglect to her ignorance and the indifference to the perversity of her passion for her husband. It was thus that his mother had explained the mystery, and at moments it looked as if she might be right.

But now that the little thing was on its feet, padding about with a pathetic and ridiculous uncertainty, stumbling and upsetting itself, sitting down suddenly and clutching at things as it overbalanced, and dragging them with it in its fall, Violet could only think of it as a perfect and omnipresent nuisance, a thing inspired to torment her with its malignant and deliberate activity. And from this she went on to think of it as grown-up at fifteen months, a mature person, infinitely responsible. Its misfortunes, its infirmities, its innocences were counted to it as sins. When jam spread itself over Baby's face and buried itself in Baby's neck, and leaped forth and ran down to the skirts of its clothing, Baby was " a nasty little thing ! " and " a naughty, naughty girl ! "

Then once, in a fit of exasperation, Violet slapped Baby's hands and found such blessed relief in that exercise that the slapping habit grew on her. Cries of anguish went up from Granville, till the neighbours two doors on either side complained.

But tiny hands, slapped till (as she said) she was tired of slapping them, gave no scope, offered no continuous outlet to the imprisoned spirit within. Violet, under a supreme provocation, advanced to arm-dragging and shaking.

She found that shaking on the whole did her most good.

And then, one Sunday morning, Ransome caught her at it.

He caught her, coming up softly behind her and pinning her, so that her fingers relaxed their hold and he swung her from him.

" I'm not going to have that, my girl," he said.

He was deadly quiet about it ; and the deadliness and quietness subdued her. But he kept the child away from her all day till it dropped off to sleep at bed-time.

After that he never knew another peaceful moment. All his life was narrowed suddenly into the circle of one terror and one care. It was like a nightmare while it lasted. And it tethered him tight. He couldn't get off by himself now on Saturdays and Sundays, for he was afraid to leave the child with Violet and Violet with the child. He came pounding home from Woolridge's at a frantic pace, for he never knew now what might be happening, what might have happened in his absence.

And so on to the last days of July.

In that month, Granville, so long deteriorating, was at its worst. The paper on the walls was blistering here and there like the paint ; the red and blue roses and the rose-buds wilted, with an effect of putrefaction, and the love-knots faded.

The front sitting-room, furnished so proudly and expensively, had been long abandoned because of the attendance it exacted. In there you could positively smell the dust. The pile of the plush held it and pierced through it, as grass holds and pierces through the earth. Ranny had a landed estate in his chairs and sofa. And the bright surfaces of polished wood and looking-glass were blurred as if the breath of dissolution had passed over them. Ranny's silver prize cups, standing in a row on the little sideboard, were tarnished every one. Violet had no pride in them. That sitting-room was not supposed to be sat in ; yet Ranny sat in it sometimes with Baby, as a refuge from the other.

For the other was awful. It had the look, not only of
being lived in, but of having lived ; of having lived hard,
brutally, squalidly, and of being worn out. A room of
which Ranny said that, go into it when you would, it looked
as if it had been up all night. A stained, bleared-eyed,
knocked-kneed sinner of a room.

And oh ! the scullery, where the shining sink had grown
a grey rough skin, a sort of fungoid coat, from the grease
that clung to it, and the gas-stove, furred with rust, skulked
like some obscene monster in its corner. He was afraid,
morally and physically afraid, to look at that thing of
infamy behind the back door. He tried to pretend the
scullery wasn't there.

And in the middle of it, and through the fury and the
stupor, Violet bloomed.

That was what he could not understand ; how between
her own cruelty and that squalor she had the heart to
bloom.

He dreaded every interruption and delay that detained
him at Woolridge's, every chance encounter that kept him
from that lamentable place where he feared and yet
desired to be.

Yet it was in those last days of July that Granville, as
if it had passed through its mortal crisis, took, suddenly,
a turn for the better.

He came into his house late one evening and found
peace and order there, and the strange, pungent smell of a
thorough cleaning. There was a clean white cloth spread
in the sitting-room for supper, spoons and forks and the
china on the dresser and the table glistened ; everything
that could be made to shine was shining. From the gas-
stove in the scullery there came the alluring smell of a
beefsteak pie baking. It was wonderful. And it all
seemed to have been done by some divine, invisible agency.
There was nobody about ; not at any rate at the back ;
and overhead there was no sound of footsteps.

He was gripped by a sense of mystery, almost of disaster ;

as if a wonder so extreme had something ominous in it. Then he went into the front sitting-room.

On the plush sofa, which had been moved from its place against the wall and drawn right across the bow of the window, Violet lay, veiled from the street by white Nottingham lace curtains. Pure white they were; such whiteness as was not to be seen in the newest houses in the Avenue. The furniture had been polished till it looked like new. All in a row Ranny's silver prize cups shone again as on the day when he bore them from the field. The smell of dust was gone. Instead of it there came towards him a sweet smell of violets and of woman's hair.

On the sofa in the window Violet lay like a suburban odalisk, voluptuous, heavy-scented. The flesh of her neck and arms showed rosy under the thin white muslin of her gown that clung to her in slender folds and fell away, revealing the prone beauty of her body. The dim light came on her through the Nottingham lace curtains as light might come through some Oriental lattice of fretted ivory. She bloomed, like a heavy flower, languid, sullen-sweet, heavy-scented.

It was Thursday, the twenty-fifth.

Ransome looked about him and smiled.

" I say, this is a bit of all right. Did you do it yourself, Vi ? "

Her large eyes opened on him in the pale light; dark they were with a sensuous mockery in them.

" Do I look as if I'd done it myself ? " she said.

She certainly didn't.

" Did you get a woman in then, or what ? "

She hesitated a moment.

" Yes. I got a woman in."

And the miracle continued; so that Ranny said that Granville was not such a bad little fellow, after all, if you took him the right way and humoured him.

Then he began to make discoveries.

The first was on the Sunday morning when he went to

N

his drawer for a pair of clean socks. He had no hope of finding so much as one whole one. And yet, there were all his socks sorted, and folded, and laid in a row ; and every single one of them had been made whole with exquisite darning. The same with his shirts and vests and things ; and they had been in rags when he had last looked at them. And something had been done to his cuffs and collars, too.

Then there was the Baby. Her hair, that used to cling to her little head in flat rings as her sleep had crushed it, was all brushed up and fluffed into feathery ducks'-tails that shone gold in gold. She came to him lifting up her little clean pinafore and frock to show him. She knew that she was fascinating.

" It must be Mother, bless her," he said to himself.

But it wasn't Mother ; or if it was she lied about it.

Then Violet let it out.

It was on the night of Tuesday, the first of August, at bed-time Ransome was leaning over the cot where the Baby lay, tossed half-naked between sleep and waking, drowsy with dreams. She was adorable with her Little Rose face half unfolded, and the Honeypot smell of her silken skin.

Violet stood beside him, looking at the two, sullenly but with a certain unwonted tolerance. She was strange and still, as if the unquiet spirit that had torn her was appeased.

" I say, it's worth while keeping this kid clean, Vi. It repays you."

" It pays Winny, I suppose. Else she wouldn't do it."

" Winny ? "

" Yes. What are you staring at ? She's a pretty kid," she added, as if the admission had been wrung from her.

" She's not been here ? " said Ransome.

" Hasn't she ! She was here all morning and all day yesterday and pretty nearly every day last week."

" But—how did she get off ? Why—it's sale-time ! "

" She's chucked them."

" What's she done that for ? "

" You'd better ask her."

His instinct told him that he would do well to let it pass. He said no more that night.

But in the morning, over his hurried breakfast, he returned to it.

" I don't like this about Winny," he said. " Has she got another job or what ? "

" She's got what she wanted."

" What's that ? "

" A job at Johnson's."

Johnson's was the new drapers at the other corner of Acacia Avenue, opposite the chemist's.

" Johnson's ? " Ranny could not conceal his innocent dismay. Johnson's operations and his premises were so diminutive that for Winny—after Starker's—the descent seemed awful.

" Are you sure she wanted it ? "

" She must have wanted it pretty badly when she's willing to take seven bob a week less screw. And if she'd waited till Michaelmas she'd have got her rise."

Ranny bent his head low over his cup. He felt his face burning with a shame that he could not comprehend. He knew that Violet was looking at him and that made it worse.

" You needn't worry," she was saying. " It isn't your fault if she makes a fool of herself."

" Makes a fool of herself ? What do you mean ? "

The heat in his face mounted and flamed in his ears ; and he knew that he was angry.

" *You* ought to know," she sneered.

He was hotter. He was intolerably hot.

" I don't, then," he retorted.

" You silly cuckoo, d'you mean to say you don't know she's gone on you ? Lot of pains she takes to hide it You've only got to look at her to know."

At that the fire in him blazed out. He rose, bringing his fist down on the table.

"You ought to be ashamed of yourself," he said. "A low animal wouldn't say a thing like that. When she's been so good to you! Where would you be, I should like to know, if it hadn't been for Winny?"

She looked at him under her lowered brows; and in her look there was that strange tolerance, and mockery and a feigned surprise. And with it all a sort of triumph, as if she were rich in some secret and insolent satisfaction and could afford her tolerance.

"Me?" she mocked. "Do you suppose it's me she comes for?"

"I don't know and I don't care. But as long as she does come you've got to be decent to her? See?"

"I *am* decent to her. *I* don't mind her coming. What difference does it make to *me?*"

"I should say it makes a thundering lot of difference, if you ask me. Considering the work you've managed to get out of her for nothing."

"It isn't my business. I can't help it, if she likes to come here and work for nothing."

. "You make me sick," said Ranny.

His eyelids stung him as if they had been cut by little, little knives close under the eyeballs. He turned from her, shamed, as if he had witnessed some indecency, some outrage on a beautiful innocent thing.

Outside in the sunlight his tears dazzled him an instant and sank back into their stinging ducts.

Yes, it had stung him. And he had got to end it, somehow, for Winny's sake. He had no idea how to set about it. He could not let the little thing come and do his wife's work for her, like that, on the sly, for nothing. And yet he could not tell her not to come.

And he asked himself again and again, "Why, why does she do it ? Why ? Like that—for nothing ? "

His heart began to beat uncomfortably, trying to tell him why. But he did not listen to it. He was angry with his heart for trying to tell him things he did not know and did not want to know.

No. He ought not to let her keep on coming. But what was he to do ? How could he tell her not to come ?

He went home through Wandsworth that evening and called at St. Ann's Terrace. Winny was there. She came down to him where he waited on the doorstep. As they stood there he could see over the low palings of the gardens the window of the little house where he had climbed in that night, that Sunday night, more than two years ago.

He said he had come to ask her to spend Bank Holiday with them. They might go for a sort of picnic to Richmond Park, and she must come back to supper.

That was his idea, his solution, his inspiration ; that she must come ; that she must be asked, must be implored to come ; but as a guest, in high honour, and in festival.

They settled it. And still he lingered awkwardly.

" I say—is it true that you've left Starker's ? "

" Yes."

" What did you do that for, Winky ? "

He did not know that he was going to ask her that ; but somehow he had to.

She paused, but with no sign of embarrassment ; looking at him with her profound and placid eyes. It was as if she had to search for the truth before she answered him.

" I thought it best," she said at last. " I didn't want to stay."

" Were you wise ? "

She smiled.

" Yes, Ranny. I think so."

No. There was not a trace of embarrassment about her, such embarrassment as she would have been bound to feel if Violet had been right. She had spoken in measured

tones, as if from some very serious, secret and sincere conviction.

She went on. "You see, Maudie won't want me any -
more. They're going to be married when Fred gets his
holiday." \
"Yes. But it isn't such a good thing for *you*, is it ? "

Her deed thus exposed, presented to her in all the high
folly of it, she seemed to flinch, as if she herself were struck
with the frightful indiscretion of her descent from Starker's.

"It's quieter. That's more what I want."

He smiled. Pressed home, she was evasive as she had
ever been.

"Look here," he said as if he were changing the subject. "*You've* been found out."

"Found out, Ranny ? "

"Yes. What have you been about this last week ?
I can't have you going and doing Vi's work for her, you
know."

"Oh *that!* That was nothing. I just put things straight
a bit, and now she's got to keep them straight."

He sighed, and reverted. "I don't like your throwing
up that good job. I don't reelly."

He meant to go, leaving it there, all that she had done,
unacknowledged, unexplained between them, as she would
have it left. And instead of going he stood rooted to that
doorstep, and to his amazement he heard himself saying,
"I wish I could do something for you, Winny."

And then (he took his own breath away with the abrupt-
ness of it). "Look here—why not come and make your
home with us, when Maudie's married ? "

She smiled dimly, as if she hardly saw him, as if, instead
of standing beside him on the doorstep, she were saying
good-bye to him from somewhere a long way off.

"Oh, no, Ranny, that would never do."

"Why not ? There's that back room there doing nothing. We don't want it. You'd be welcome to it if it was
any good."

She shook her head slowly. "It's very kind of you, but it wouldn't do. It really wouldn't. I don't mean the room, Ranny—it's a dear little room—I mean—I mean, you know——"

Now at last she was embarrassed, helpless, shaken from her defences by the suddenness of his proposal.

"All right, Winky," he said gently.

Then she broke down, but without self-pity, tearless, in her own fashion.

"Oh, Ranny, *please* don't think I'm horrid and ungrateful."

"That's all right," he said feebly.

He turned as if to go ; but she recalled him.

"There's one thing you could do," she said.

"What's that ? I'll do anything."

"Well—You can let me come over Saturdays and Sundays sometimes and look after Baby while you take Violet somewhere."

He said nothing and she went on.

"If I were you, Ranny, I'd take her somewhere every week. I'd get her out all I could."

And he said again for the third time, very humbly :

"All right."

And as he went he called over his shoulder, "Don't forget Monday."

As if she was likely to forget it !

XXI

AND after all Monday, that is to say the day at Richmond, never came.

On Monday morning when Violet got up she was seized with a slight dizziness and sickness. It passed off. She declared that earthquakes shouldn't stop her going to Richmond, and dressed herself in defiance of all possible disturbance. Ransome took the Baby over to Wandsworth, to his mother, to be looked after. At ten o'clock he joined Winny and Maudie and Fred Booty at St. Ann's Terrace where they had arranged that Violet was to meet them. Following on her bicycle she would be there at ten sharp, when the five would go on to Richmond by the tram that passed Winny's door.

Ransome had no sooner left Granville than Violet slipped out to the chemist's at the corner.

Ten o'clock struck, and the quarter and the half-hour, and Violet had not appeared at St. Ann's Terrace.

Ransome proposed that the others should go on without him ; he said he thought there must be something wrong, and that he had better go and see what had happened. They argued about it for a while and finally Maudie and Fred Booty started. Winny refused flatly to go with them. She was convinced that they would meet Violet on the road to Southfields. She must have had a puncture, Winny said.

But they did not meet her.

And there was no sign of her downstairs at Granville.

"Hark ! What's that ? " said Winny, listening at the foot of the stair. " Oh, Ranny ! "

From the room above there came a low, half-stifled sound of sobbing and groaning.

He dashed upstairs.

In a few minutes he returned to Winny in the front sitting-room.

" What's the matter ? Is she ill ? " she said.

" No, I don't think so. She won't tell me. She's horribly upset about something."

" Shall I go to her ? "

" No ; better not, Winny. Look here, she won't come to Richmond. She says we're to go without her."

" We can't, Ranny."

" I don't know. Upon my word I think we may as well. She'll be more upset if we don't go. She says she wants to be left to herself for *one* day."

A sort of tremor passed over her eyes. They did not look at him ; they looked beyond him, as if somewhere they saw something that frightened her.

" You mustn't leave her, Ranny," she said.

He laughed. " She doesn't want me. She's just told me so."

" Whether she wants you or not you've got to stay with her."

She said it sternly.

" I say, you needn't talk like that. To hear you anyone would think I fair neglected her."

She bit her lip. Her eyes wandered in their troubled way. She looked like a thing held there under his eyes against its will and seeking some way of escape.

" I don't think you neglect her, Ranny," she said at last.

" Well, then, what *do* you think ? "

She turned. " I think I'm going for a little spin somewhere by myself. I shall come back in time for dinner. Then I shall go down to Wandsworth and fetch Baby."

" I'll do that."

" No, you won't. You'll stay with Violet," she said.

" And what about your holiday ? "

" My holiday's all right. Don't you worry."

She was out of the house and in the garden. Mechanically he wheeled her bicycle out into the road. He was utterly submissive to her will.

She mounted and he ran by her side ; she pressed on her pedals, compelling him to run fast and faster ; she set her mouth hard, grinning, and forced the pace, and he ran at the top of his speed and laughed. At the end of the Avenue she turned, waved to him gaily and was gone.

Upstairs on her bed, in the room of the love-knots, Violet lay and writhed. She lay on her face. She had wetted her pillow with her tears ; she had flung it aside and was digging her hands into Ransome's pillow with a tearing, disembowelling motion. Every now and then, with the regularity of a machine, she gave out a sob and a groan that shook her.

He found her so.

She turned on her side as he entered, and showed him her face scarlet and swollen with crying.

" What have you come for ? " she said. " I *told* you to go."

" I haven't gone. I'm not going."

" But you've got to go. You shall go. D'you hear ? I won't have you hanging about, watching and tormenting me. What are you afraid of ? What d'you think I'm going to do ? "

She turned and raised herself on her elbow and stared about her as if at a host of enemies surrounding her, then she sank back helpless.

" Won't you tell me what it is, Vi ? " he said tenderly.

He sat beside her, leaning over into her hot lair, and made as though he would have put his hand on her shoulder. She writhed from him.

" Why can't you let me be," she cried, " when I don't want you ? I don't want you, I tell you, and I wish you'd go away. You've done enough harm as it is."

He rose and went to the foot of the bed and stood there, regarding her sombrely.

"What did you mean by that? What harm have I done you?"

She had flung herself down again.

"You *know*—you *know*," she moaned into the pillow.

"My God, I wish I did!"

Then he remembered.

"Unless—you mean——"

"You ought to know what I mean without my telling you."

"Well, if I do you needn't cast it up to me. I married you right enough, Vi."

"Yes, that's what you did. And that's why I hate you."

"It seems to me a queer reason. But, come to that, what else could we do?"

She sat up, pulling herself together like a woman who had things to say and meant to say them now.

"We could have done as I wanted. We could have gone on as we were."

"That's what you wanted, was it?"

"You know it was. I never asked you to marry me. I asked you not to. And you *would*—you *would*. I didn't *want* to marry you."

"And why didn't you want? That's what I'd like to get at."

"Because I knew what it would be."

"Has it been so very bad then?"

She sat up straighter, wringing her hands as if she wrung her words out. "It's been awful—something awful. All the things I don't like—all the time. And it's made me hate the sight of you. It's made me wish I'd died before I'd seen you. And I want to get away. I want to get out of this horrid, hateful little house. I knew I would. I knew—I knew——"

"My God—if *I'd* known——"

" *You?* If *you'd* known ! I wish to God you had. I wish you had just ! If that would have stopped you marrying me. Oh, you *knew* all right ; only you didn't care. You never have cared. I suppose you think it's what I'm made for."

" I don't follow. It may be all wrong. I'll allow it *is* all wrong, all the time. What I want to know is what's up now ? "

" Can't you see what's up ? Can't you think ? "

He thought. And presently he saw.

" You don't mean to say it's—it's another ? "

" Of course it is. What else have I been talking about ? "

" Are you sure, Vi ? "

He was very grave, very gentle.

" Sure ? D'you think I wouldn't make sure, when it's what I'm afraid of all the time ? "

" Don't you want it ? Have you never wanted it ? "

" Want it ? Want it ? I'll hate it if it comes. But it won't come. It shan't come. I won't have it. I won't live and have it. I shall die anyway."

" Oh, no, you won't," he said.

But she flung herself back and writhed and sobbed again. He sat down and watched with her. In silence and utter hopelessness he watched. Presently she lay motionless, worn out.

At one o'clock Winny knocked at the door and said dinner was ready.

Violet stirred. " What's the good of sitting staring there like a stuck ox ? " She raised herself. " Since you *are* there you can get me that eau-de-Cologne."

He brought it. He bathed her hands and forehead and wiped them with his handkerchief.

She dragged herself downstairs and sat red-eyed through

dinner, the materials for the picnic which Winny had
unpacked and spread.

The day wore on. Violet dragged herself to her bed
again, and lay there all afternoon while Ransome hung
about the house and garden, unable to think, unable to
work, or take an interest in anything. He was oppressed
by a sense of irremediable calamity.

At four o'clock he made tea and took it to Violet in her
room.

She sat up, weak and submissive, and drank, crying
softly.

She turned her face to him as she sank back on her
pillow. " I'm sorry, Ranny," she said ; " but you
shouldn't have married me. I'm not that sort. I told
you ; and you see."

He could not remember when she had ever told him.
But it was clear that he saw. For he said to himself,
" They say a lot of things they don't mean when they're
like this."

XXII

THAT was the first and by far the most impressive of their really great scenes. There was no doubt about it, Violet could make scenes, and there was no end to the scenes she made. But those that followed, like those that had gone before, were beyond all comparison inferior. They lacked vehemence, vividness, intensity. After that first passion of resentment and revolt, Violet declined upon sullenness and flat, monotonous reproach.

Ransome put it all down to her condition. He set his mouth with a hard grin and stuck it. He told himself that he had no illusions left, that he saw the whole enormous folly of his marriage, and that he saw it sanely, as Violet could not see it, without passion, without revolt, without going back for one moment on anything that he or she had done. He saw it simply as it was, as a thing that had to be. She, being the more deeply injured of the two, must be forgiven her inability to see it that way. He had done her a wrong in the beginning and he had made reparation, and it was not the reparation she had wanted. She had never reproached him for that wrong as many women would have ; on the contrary, he remembered how, on the night when it was done, she had turned to comfort him with her, " It had got to be." She had been generous. She had never hinted at reparation. No ; she certainly had not asked him to marry her.

But that also had had to be. They couldn't help themselves. They had been caught up and flung together and carried away in a maze ; like the Combined Maze at the Poly., it was, when they had to run—to run, locked together.

What weighed on him most for the moment was the financial problem. He lived in daily fear of not being able to pay his way without breaking into the rest of his small savings. His schemes, that had looked so fine on paper, had left, even on paper, no margin for anything much beyond rent and clothing and their weekly bills. There had been no margin at all for Baby; Baby who, above all, ought to have been foreseen and provided for. Baby had been paid for out of capital. So that from the sordid financial point of view Violet's discovery was a calamity.

It was a mercy he had got his rise at Michaelmas. But even so they were behindhand with their bills. That, of course, would not have happened if he hadn't had to buy a new suit that winter. Ranny had found out that his bicycle, though it diminished his travelling expenses and kept him fit, was simply "ruination" to his clothes.

It was awful to be behindhand with the bills. But if they got behind with the rent they would be done for. He would lose Granville. His rent was not as any ordinary rent that might be allowed to run on for a week or two in times of stress. Granville was relentless in exaction of the weekly tribute. If payments lapsed, he lost Granville and he lost the twenty-five pounds down he paid for it.

And Granville that scourged him was itself scourged of Heaven. That winter the frosts bound the walls too tight and the thaws loosened them. The rain, beating through from the south-west, mildewed the back sitting-room and the room above it. The wind made of Granville a pipe, a whistle, a Jew's harp to play its tunes on; such tunes as set your teeth on edge.

Ransome said to himself bitterly that his marriage had not been his only folly. He should have had the sense to do as Booty had done. Fred had married soon after Michaelmas, when he too had got his rise. He and Maudie had not looked upon houses to their destruction; they had simply taken another room in St. Ann's Terrace where she had lived with Winny. And she had kept her job at Starker's, and meant to keep it for another year or so. Fred wasn't going to have any kids he couldn't provide for. Ranny's case had been a warning to him.

And Ranny's case was lamentable that winter, after he had paid for his suit. They lived almost entirely now on hampers sent from Hertfordshire. The hampers were no longer treated as mysterious windfalls; they came regularly once a week and were shamefully and openly allowed for in the accounts. And regularly once a week the young Ransomes had their Sunday dinner at Wandsworth; they reckoned it as one square meal.

All this squeezing and pinching was to pay for a little girl to look after Baby in the mornings. They had found another and had contrived to keep her. For Violet, though she went on making scenes with Ranny, was quiet enough now when Ranny wasn't there, if only Baby was kept well out of her way. In the autumn months and in the early winter she even had her good days, days of passivity, days of exaltation and of rapt brooding, days when she went as if sustained by some mysterious and secret satisfaction, some agreeable reminiscence or anticipation. And if Ransome never noticed that these days were generally Thursdays, it was because Thursday (early closing day in Southfields) had no interest or significance for Ranny. And of all Violet's moods he found the one simple explanation in her state.

On the whole he observed a change for the better in his household. Things were kept straighter. There was less dust about, and Ranny's prize cups had never ceased to shine. His socks and vests were punctually mended, and Baby at his home-coming was always neat and clean. He knew that Winny had a hand in it. For Winny, established at Johnson's at the corner, was free a good half-hour before he could get back from Oxford Street ; and as often as not he found her putting Baby to bed when Violet was out or lying down. But he did not know, he was nowhere near knowing, half the things that Winny did for them. He didn't want to know. All that he did know made him miserable or pleased him according to his mood. Of course, it couldn't really please him to think that Winny worked for him for nothing ; but to know that she was there, moving about his house, loving and caring for his child as he loved and cared for it, whether it was sick or well, clean or dirty, gave him pleasure that when he thought about it too much became as poignant as pain. For there was nothing, absolutely nothing, that he could do for Winny to repay her. He did not know that Winny paid herself in a thousand inimitable sensations every time she touched the things that he had touched, or that belonged to him ; that with every stitch she put into his poor clothes her fingers satisfied their longing, as it were in an attenuated, reiterated caress ; that to feel the silken flesh of his child against her flesh was for Winny to know motherhood.

Her life had in it the wonder and beauty and mystery of religion. All the religion that she knew was in each service that she did for Ranny in his house. Acacia Avenue, with its tufted trees, with its rows of absurd and pathetic and diminutive villas, was for Winny a shining walk between heavenly mansions. She handled each one of Ranny's prize cups as if it had been the Holy Grail.

And religion went hand-in-hand with an exquisite iniquity. In all that she did there was something unsanctioned, something that gave her the secret and essential thrill of sin. When Winny made that beefsteak pie for Ranny she had her first taste of fearful, delicious, illegitimate joy. For it was not right that she should be there making beefsteak pies for Ranny. It was Violet who should have been making beefsteak pies. But once plunged in Winny couldn't stop. She went on till she had

o

mended all Ranny's clothes and sewed new Poly. ribbon on all the vests he ran in. She loved those vests more than anything he wore. They belonged to the old splendid Ranny who had once been hers.

And under it all (if she had cared to justify herself) under the mystery and the beauty and the wonder, there was the sound practical common sense of it all. As long as Violet was comfortable with Ranny she would stay with him. But she would not be comfortable if she had too many things to do ; and if she became uncomfortable she would leave him ; and if she left him Ranny would be unhappy. So that the more you did for her the more likely she was to keep straight. Keeping Violet straight had always been Winny's job ; it always would be ; and she was more than ever bound to stick to it now that it meant keeping Ranny's home together. In Winny's eyes the breaking up of a home was the most awful thing that could happen on this earth. In Leonard Mercier (established so dangerously near) she recognised a possible leader of the forces of disruption. When she left Starker's for Johnson's (where, as she put it to herself, she could look after Violet), she had hurled her small body into the first breach. Johnson's was invaluable as a position whence she could reconnoitre all the movements of the enemy.

But it was a strain upon the heart and upon the nerves ; and the effect on Winny's physique was so evident that Ranny noticed it. He noticed that Winny was more slender and less sturdy than she used to be ; her figure, to his expert eye, suggested the hateful possibility of flabbiness. He thought he had traced the deterioration to its source when he asked her if she had chucked the Poly.

She had.

What did she do that for ? Well—she didn't think she cared much for the Poly. now. It was different somehow. At least that was the way she felt about it. (" Same here," said Ranny.) And she couldn't keep up like she did. The running played her out.

He saw her, then, a tired, indifferent little figure, padding through the circles and the patterns of the Combined Maze; padding listlessly, wearily, with all the magic and the joy gone out of her.

"We had grand times there together," he said then. "Do you remember the Combined Maze?"

She remembered.

"Sometimes I think that life's like that—a maze, Winny. A sort of Combined Maze—men and women—mixed up together."

She thought so too.

Violet had got used to Winny's being there. She took it for granted, as if it also were one of those things that had to be. She depended on it, and owned herself dependent. When Winny was there, she said, things went right, and when she wasn't there they went wrong. She didn't know how they had ever got along without her.

Ransome was surprised to see in Violet so large a heart and a mind so open. For not only did she tolerate Winny, she clung, he could see that she clung, to her like a child. She even tolerated what he wouldn't have thought a woman would have stood for a single instant, the fact, the palpable fact, that Ranny couldn't get along without her any more than she could.

And if they could the Baby couldn't. Baby (she was Dorothy now and Dossie) cried for Winny when Winny wasn't there. She would run from her mother's voice to hide her face in Winny's skirts. Baby wasn't ever really happy without Winny.

That was how she had them, and she knew it, and the Baby knew it; and the two of them simply rode roughshod over Ranny and his remonstrances.

"What are you doing there, Winky?" he would say

when he caught her on a Sunday morning in the bath-
room, with Baby happy on a blanket at her feet.

" Washing·Dossie's pinafores," she would sing out.

" I wish to Goodness I could stop you."

" But you can't. Can he, Lamby Lamb? Laugh at
him, then. Laugh at Daddy."

And the Lamby Lamb would laugh.

He knew, and they knew, that he couldn't stop her
except by doing the work for her ; and the more things he
did the more things she found to do that he couldn't do,
such as washing pinafores. So he gave it up ; and gradually
he too began to take it for granted that Winny should be
there.

And she was more than ever there after April of nineteen
seven, when the little son was born. The little son that
they called Stanley Fulleymore.

When *he* came more and more of Ranny's savings had to
go. He didn't care. For he had gone again through deep
anguish, again believing that Violet would die, that she
couldn't possibly get over it. And she *had* got over it ;
beautifully, the doctor said. He assured him that she hadn't
turned a hair. And after it she bloomed as she had never
bloomed before ; she bloomed to excess ; she coarsened
in sheer exuberance and rioting of health. She was built
magnificently, built as they don't seem able to build women
now, built for maternity.

" You don't think," said Ranny to the doctor, " that
it really does her any harm ? "

For she had tried to frighten him with the harm she said
it did her.

" My dear Ransome, if she had a dozen children it
wouldn't do her any harm."

It was the same tale as before, and he couldn't understand it. For of the flame of maternity, the flame that
burned in Winny, it was evident that Violet hadn't got a
spark. If she had been indifferent to her daughter Dorothy,
she positively hated her son, Stanley Fulleymore. She

intimated that he was a calamity, and an ugly one at that. One kid, she said, was bad enough ; what did he expect that she should do with two ?

She did nothing ; which was what he had expected. She trailed about the house, glooming ; she sank supine under her burden and lay for ever on the sofa. When he tried to rouse her she burst into fury and collapsed in stupor. The furies and the stupors were worse than he had ever known. They would have been unendurable if it had not been for Winny.

And in the long days when Winny was not there he was always afraid of what might happen to the children. He had safeguarded them as far as possible. He had engaged an older and more expensive girl, who came from nine to six, five days a week and Saturday morning. Soon after six, Winny would be free to run in and wash the Baby and put Dossie to bed.

Shamelessly he accepted this service from her ; for he was at his wits' end. As often as not he took Violet out somewhere (to appease the restlessness that consumed her), leaving Winny in charge of the babies. Winny had advised it, and he had grown dependent on her judgment. He considered that if anybody understood Violet it was Winny.

And slowly, month by month, the breach that Winny had hurled herself into widened. It was as if she stood in it with arms stretched wide, holding out a desperate hand to each of them.

Everything conspired to tear the two asunder. In summer the heat of the small rooms became intolerable. Ransome proposed that he should sleep in the back bedroom and leave more air for Violet and the children.

Violet was sullen but indifferent. " If you do," she said, " you'll take Dossie. I won't have her."

He took Dossie. The Baby was safe enough for all her dislike of it, and for all it looked so sickly. For it slept

It slept astoundingly. It slept all night and most of the day. There never was such a sleeper.

He thought it was a good sign. But when he said so to Winny she looked grave, so grave that she frightened him.

Then suddenly the Baby left off sleeping. Instead of sleeping he cried. He cried piteously, inveterately; he cried all night and most of the day. He never gave them any peace at all. His crying woke little Dossie and she cried; it kept Ransome awake; it kept Violet awake, and she cried too, hopelessly, helplessly; she was crushed by the everlasting, irremediable wrong.

And it was then, in those miserable days, that she turned on Winny, until Ransome turned on her.

" It's shameful the way you treat that girl, after all she's done for you."

" What's she been telling you ? " There was fright in Violet's eyes.

"-She's not told me anything. I've got eyes. I can see for myself."

" Oh, you've got eyes, have you ? Jolly lot you see ! "

But she was penitent that night and asked Winny to forgive her. She implored her not to leave off coming.

And Winny came and went now in pain instead of joy. Everything in Ranny's house pained her. Violet's voice that filled it pained her, and the crying of the little children. Ranny's face pained her. Most of all it pained her to see Dossie's little cot drawn up beside Ranny's bed in the back room ; they looked so forlorn, the two of them ; so outcast and so abandoned.

She went unhindered and unheeded into Ranny's room, tidying it and putting the little girl to bed. But into Violet's room she would not go more than she could help. She hated Violet's room ; she loathed it ; and she dared not think why.

One Saturday evening in the last week of September

Ransome had come home late after a long solitary ride in the country. Violet, who was busy making a silk blouse for herself, had refused to go with him. Winny had laid it down as a law for Ranny that Violet was never to be left for very long to herself, if he wanted her to be happy. And, of course, he wanted her to be happy. But if ever there was a moment when he could leave her with a clear conscience it was when she was dressmaking. She gave herself to it with passion, with absorption. He had known her to sit for hours over a new blouse in apparently perfect happiness.

And to-day he could have sworn that she was happy. She had risen of her own accord and kissed him good-bye and told him to enjoy himself and not hurry home. She would be all right, and Winny had said she would drop in for tea. He left her sewing white lace on to blue silk in a matchless tranquillity.

And he *had* enjoyed his ride, and he had not hurried home, for he knew that the children would be all right (even if Violet's happy mood had changed) as long as Winny was there to look after them.

He rode far out into the open country, into the deep-dipping lanes, between fields, and through lands scented with autumn. And as he rode he was a boy again. Never since his marriage had he known such joy in freedom and such ecstasy in speed. There was a wind that drove him on, and the great clouds challenged him and raced with him as he went.

He came home against the wind, but that was nothing. The wind was a challenge and a defiance of his strength ; it set the blood racing in his veins, and cooled it in his face when it burned. It was good to be challenged by the wind and to defy it. It was good to struggle. It was all good that happened to him on that day.

Night had fallen when he returned. Granville was lit up behind its yellow blinds. Winny stood at the open door with the lighted passage way behind her. Granville

in the autumnal dark, with the gas turned full on inside
it, looked all light, all quiet flame, as if the walls
that were the substance of it had been cut clean
away, leaving a mere shell, a mere framework for its
golden incandescence.

So small, so fragile, so insubstantial was the shell, that
Winny's slight figure in the doorway showed in proportion
solid and solitary and immense, as if it sustained the
perishable fabric.

She was leaning forward now, bearing up the shell on
her shoulders. She was looking out, up and down the
Avenue.

" That you, Winny ? " he said.

" Yes. I'm looking for Vi."

" She gone out ? "

" Gone into Wandsworth."

" What did she go for ? "

" To have a dress tried on."

" I say, she *is* going it ! "

" There's a girl in St. Ann's," said Winny, " what makes
for her very cheap."

He sighed and checked his sigh. " You bin slavin',
Win ? "

" No. Why ? "

" You looked fagged out."

Winny's face was white under the gas-light.

She said nothing. She stood there looking out while he
propped his bicycle up against the window-sill.

He followed as she turned slowly and went through the
passage to the back room.

" Kids asleep ? "

" Yes. Fast."

She went to the dresser, and he helped her to take down
the cups and plates and set the table for their supper. In
all her movements there was a curious slowness and constraint, as if she were spinning time out, thread by thread.
It was five-and-twenty past eight.

" Who's that for ? " she asked as he laid a third place at the side.

" Well, I should think it was for you."

She started ever so slightly and stared at the three plates, as if their number put her out in some intricate calculation.

" I must be going," she said.

" Not you. Not much ! "

She submitted, moving uneasily about the place, but busy, folding things and putting them away. He ran upstairs to wash. She could hear him overhead, splashing, rubbing, and brushing.

When he came down again she was sitting on the sofa with her hands clasped in front of her, her head bent, her eyes fixed, gazing at the floor.

" I suppose we've got to wait for Vi," he said.

" Oh, yes."

They waited.

" I say, it's a quarter to nine, you know," he said presently.

" Hungry, Ran ? "

" My word ! I should think I was just. D'you think she's gone to Mother and had supper there ? "

" She—might have."

" Well, then, let's begin. Come along."

She shook her head. There was a slight spasm in her throat as if the idea of food sickened her.

" What's the matter ? "

" Nothing—nothing. I'm all right. I don't want to eat anything, that's all. I must be going soon."

" You're tired out, Win. You've got past it. Tell you what, I'll make you a cup of tea."

" No, Ranny, don't. I'd rather not."

She rose, and yet she did not go. He had never known Winny so undecided.

Then suddenly she stooped. On the floor of the hearth-rug she had caught sight of some bits of blue silk left from

Violet's sewing. With an almost feverish concentration of purpose she picked up each one of the scraps and snippets ; she threw them on the hearth. Slowly, deliberately, spinning out her thread of time, she gathered what she had strewed ; she gathered into a handful the little scraps and snippets of blue silk, powdered with the grey ashes from the hearth, and dropped them in the fire, watching till the last shred was utterly destroyed.

There was a faint cry overhead and Ransome started up. The cry or his movement clinched her resolution.

" *I'll* go, Ranny," she said.

And as she went she drew a letter in a sealed envelope from the bosom of her gown and laid it on the table.

" Vi said I was to give you that if she wasn't back by eight. It's nine now."

He stared and let her go. He waited. He was aware of her footsteps in the front room upstairs, of the baby crying, and of the sudden stilling of his cry. Then he opened the letter.

He read in Violet's tottering, formless handwriting :

" DEAR RANDALL,
        " This is to let you know I've gone and that I'm not coming back again. I stuck to you as long as I could but it was misery. You and me aren't suited to live together, and it's no use us going on any more pretending. If you'd take me back to-morrow I wouldn't come. I can't live without Leonard Mercier, nor he without me. I daresay you know it's him I've gone with.

        " We're awfully sorry for all the trouble we're bringing on you. But we couldn't help ourselves. We were driven to it. I've been off my head all this year thinking how I must do it, and all the time being afraid to take the step. And ever since I made up my mind to it I've been quiet inside and happy, which looks as if it was meant and had got to be.

        " You needn't blame Leonard. He held off till he couldn't

hold off any more, because he was a friend of yours and
didn't want to hurt you.   It was really me made him.
It's a tragedy but it would be a bigger tragedy if we didn't,
for we belong to one another.   And he's taking me to Paris
to live so as nobody need know anything about it.   He's
got a post in a shop there.   And we're starting on a Saturday so as you can have Sunday to turn round in.

   " You'll forgive me, Ranny dear.   It's what I've always
told you—you shouldn't have married me.   You should
have married a girl like Winny.   She was always fond of
you.   It was a lie what I told you once about her not
being.   I said it because I was mad on you, and I knew
you'd marry her if I let you alone.   So you can say it's
all my fault, if you like.

                                        " Yours truly,
(she had hesitated, with some erasures, over the form
of valediction)   " Vi."

   There was a postscript :
   " You can do anything you like to me as long as you
don't touch Leonard.   It's not his fault my caring for him
more than you."
   And in a small hand squeezed into the margin he made
out with difficulty two more lines.   " You needn't be
afraid of being fond of Baby.   There was never anything
between me and Leonard before July of last year."
   He did not read it straight through all at once.   He
stuck at the opening sentence.   It stupefied him.   Even
when he took it in, it did not tell him plainly what it was
that she had done besides going away and not coming back
again.   It was as if his mind were unable to deal with more
than one image at a time, as if it refused to admit the hidden
significance of language.
   Realisation came with the shock of the name that
struck at him suddenly out of the page in a flash that
annihilated the context.   The name and his intelligence
leaped at each other and struck fire across the darkness.

His gorge rose at it as it would have risen at a foul blow under the belt.

Leonard Mercier; he saw nothing else; he needed nothing else but that; it showed him her deed as the abomination that it was. If it had been any other man he thought he could have borne it, for he might still have held her clean.

As it was, the uncleanness was such that his mind turned from it instinctively as from a thing unspeakable. He closed his eyes, he hid his face in his hands, as if the two had been there with him in the room. And still he saw things. There rose before him a sort of welter of grey slime and darkness in which were things visible, things white and vivid, yet vague, broken and unfinished, because his mind refused to join or finish them ; things that were faceless and deformed, like white bodies that tumble and toss in the twilight of evil dreams. These white things came tumbling and tossing towards him from the grey confines of the slime ; urged by a persistent and abominable life, they were borne perpetually on the darkness and were perpetually thrust back into it by his terror.

He turned the letter and read it to the end, to the last scribble on the margin : " You should have married a girl like Winny Dymond." " It was a lie what I told you once about her." " You needn't be afraid of being fond of Baby." There was nothing evocative, nothing significant for him in these phrases, not even in the names. His mind had no longer any grip on words. The ideas they stood for were blurred; they were without form or meaning; they rose and shifted like waves, and like waves they disappeared on the surface of the darkness and the slime.

He was roused from his sickening contemplation by a child's cry overhead. It came again ; it pierced him ; it broke up the horror and destroyed it. He woke with it to a sense of sheer blank calamity, of overpowering bereavement.

His wife had left him. That was what had happened

to him. His wife had left him. She had left her little children.

It was as if Violet had died and her death had cleansed her.

When the child cried a third time he remembered Winny. He would have to tell her.

XXIII

HE rose and went to the fire-place mechanically. His impulse was to tear up and burn Violet's letter and thus utterly destroy all proof and the record of her shame. He was restrained by that strong subconscious sanity which before now had cared for him when he was at his worst. It suggested that he would do well to keep the letter. It was—it was a document. It might have value. Proofs and records were precisely what he might most want later on. He folded it and replaced it in its envelope and thrust it into the breast-pocket of his coat.

And it occurred to him again that he had got to tell Winny.

He could hear her feet going up and down, up and down, in the front room overhead where she walked, hushing the crying baby. Presently the crying ceased and the footsteps, and he heard the low humming of her cradle-song ; then silence ; and then the sound of her feet coming down the stairs.

He would have to tell her now.

He drew himself up, there where he was, standing by his hearth, and waited for her.

She came in softly and shut the door behind her and stood there as if she were afraid to come too near. Her face was all eyes ; all eyes of terror, as before a grief too great, a bereavement too awful for any help or consolation. She spoke first.

" What is it, Ranny ? " Her low voice went light like a tender hand that was afraid to touch his wound.

" She's left me ; that's all."

Her lips parted, but no words came ; they parted to

ease the heart that fluttered with anguish in her breast. She moved a little nearer into the room, not looking at him, but with her head bowed slightly as if her shoulders bore Violet's shame. She stood a moment by the table, looking at her own hand as it closed on the edge, the fingers working up and down on the cloth. It might have been the hand of another person, for all she was aware of its half-convulsive motion.

"Oh, Ranny, *dear*——" At last she breathed it out, the soul of her compassion, and all her hushed sense of his bereavement.

"Did you know?"

She shook her head, slowly, closing in an extremity of negation the eyes that would not look at him.

"No—No——" It was as if she had said, "Who *could* have known it?" Yet her voice had an uncertain sound.

"But you had an idea?"

"No," she said, taking courage from his incredible calmness. "I was afraid; that was all."

And then, as one utterly beaten by him and defenceless, she broke down. "I tried so hard—so hard, so as it shouldn't happen."

It was as if she had said, "I tried so hard—so hard to save her for you; but she had to die."

"I know you did."

But it was only then, in the long pause of that moment, that he knew; that he saw the whole full, rich meaning and intention of the things that she had done for him.

And now, as if she were afraid lest he should see too much, as if somehow his seeing it would sharpen the perilous edge she stood on, would wind up to the pitch of agony her tense feeling of it all, Winny suddenly became evasive. She found her subterfuge in stark matter-of-fact.

"You haven't had any supper," she said.

"No more have you."

"I don't want anything."

" I'm sure *I* don't. But you must. You'll be ill, Winny, if you don't."

White-faced and famished they kept it up, both struck by the indecency of eating in the house of sorrow. Then for his sake she gave in, and he for hers.

" If you will, I will," she said.

" That's right," said he.

And together helping each other, they filled the kettle and set it on the fire to boil, moving in silence and with soft footsteps, as in the house where death was. And together they sat down to the table and forced themselves to eat a little, each for the sake of the other, encouraging each other with such difficult, broken speech as mourners use. They behaved in all ways as if the ghost of a dead Violet sat in her old place, facing Ranny. The feeling, embraced by each of them with the most profound sincerity, was that Ranny's bereavement was irreparable, supreme. Each was convinced with an inassailable and immutable conviction that the thing that had happened was, for each of them, the worst that could happen.

Half through the meal he got up suddenly and left her. He was seized with violent sickness, such sickness as he had never yet known and would have believed impossible. The sounds of his bodily anguish reached her from the room above. They stirred her emotion to a passion of helpless, agonising pity. If she could only go up to him and put her hand on his forehead and do things for him ! But she couldn't ; and she felt poignantly that if she did Ranny somehow wouldn't like it. So, as there was nothing she could do for him, she laid her head down on her arms and wept.

She raised it suddenly, like a guilty thing, and dashed the tears from her eyes, as if she were angry with them for betraying her.

Ranny had recovered and was coming downstairs again. As he came in he saw at once what she had been doing.

" You've been crying, Winny ? "

She said nothing.

"I wouldn't if I were you," he said. "There's no need."

She rose and faced him bravely, for there were things that must be thought of.

"What are you going to do, Ranny?" she said.

"Nothing. What is there to be done?"

"Well——" She paused, breathing painfully.

"Look here, Winny, you're dead-beat and you must go home to bed. Do you know it's past ten?"

She drew herself up. "I'm not going."

"You must, dear, I'm afraid."

He smiled, and the smile and his white face made her heart ache. Also they made her more determined.

"You must have somebody. You can't be left like this all by yourself. Do you think I can go and leave you, when you're ill and all?"

"I'm all right now. I wish I could see you home, but I can't leave the house with the kids, you see, all alone."

"Ranny," she said, "I'm not going." She was very grave, very earnest, absolutely determined, and, child that she still was, absolutely unaware of the impossibility of the thing that she proposed. She was blind to herself, blind to all appearances, blind to all aspects of the case but one, his desolation and his necessity.

"I can't leave you. I wouldn't be happy if I didn't stay. You might be taken bad or something, in the night."

"You can't stay, Winny. It wouldn't do." They were the words she had used to him, in her wisdom, when he had asked her to make her home with him and Violet.

But the vision of propriety, which he raised and presented thus for her consideration, it was nothing to her. She swept it all aside.

"But I *must*," she said. "There's Baby."

He remembered then that little one, above in Violet's deserted room. Almost she had persuaded him, but for that secret sanity which had him in its care.

P

"I'll take him. You must go now," he said firmly. "Now this minute."

He looked for her hat and coat, found them and put her into them, handling her with an extreme inflexibility of manner and tenderness of touch, as if she had been a child.

"Well, then," she compromised. "Let me help you move him."

He let her; and they went upstairs and into Violet's room. Winny had removed every sign of disorder left by Violet in the precipitancy of her flight. Between them, very gently, they carried the cot with the sleeping baby in it, out of the room of the love-knots and the rosebuds into Ranny's room. They set the cot close up against the side of his bed with the rail down so that Ranny's arms might reach out to Baby where he lay. Dossie's little bed was drawn up at the foot. They stood together for a moment, looking at the two children, at Dossie, all curled up and burrowing into her pillow, and at Baby, lying by Ranny's bed as a nursling lies by its mother.

They were silent as the same thought tore at them.

Night after night, for years, as long as Dossie and Baby were little, Ranny would lie like that, on that narrow bed of his, shut in by the two cots, one at his side and the other at his feet. And to Winny it had come, for Ranny had rubbed it in to her (tenderly enough; but he had rubbed it in) that this was the last night when she could stand beside him there. She had tried so hard to hold him and Violet together; and all the time it had been Violet who had held her and him. It was Violet's presence that had made it possible for her to go in and out with Ranny in his house.

She stooped for a final, reassuring look at Baby.

"Can you manage with him?" she whispered.

He nodded.

"I've made him his food in that saucepan. You'll have to heat it on the gas-ring—in there."

" In there " was Violet's room.

They went downstairs together.

" I wish I could see you home," he said again.

" I'm all right." But she paused on the doorstep. " You ought to have somebody. You can't be left all alone like this. Mayn't I run down and fetch your mother ? "

" No," he said, " you mayn't. I'll go down myself to-morrow morning, if you wouldn't mind coming in and looking after the kids for a bit."

" Of course I'll come. Good night, Ranny."

" Good night, Winky. And thanks——" His throat closed with a sharp contraction on the words. She slipped into the darkness and was gone.

He was thankful that he had had the sense to see the impossibility of it, of her spending the night in his house with nobody in it but the two of them and the two children.

But it was only when, in the act of undressing, he was reminded of Violet's letter by its bulging in his breast-pocket that he glimpsed the danger they had escaped. Up till then he had only thought of Winny, of her reputation, of her post at Johnson's (imperilled if she were not in by eleven), of all that she would not and could not think of in her thought for him. Now, that inner sanity, that secret wisdom which had made him preserve Violet's letter as a possibly valuable document, suggested that if Winny had stayed all night in the house with him that document would have lost its value. Not that he had meant to do anything with it, that he had any plan, or any certain knowledge. Those two ideas, or rather, those two instinctive appreciations, of the value of the document and of the awfulness of the risk they ran, were connected in his mind obscurely as the stuff of some tale that he had been told, or as something he had seen some time in the papers. He put them from him as things that he himself had no immediate use for ; while all the time subconscious sanity guarded them and did not let them go.

But that was all it did for him. It did not lift from him his oppression, or fill with intelligible detail his blank sense of calamity, of inconsolable bereavement. This oppression, this morbid sense, amounted almost to hallucination ; it prevented him from thinking as clearly as he might about all that, the value of the document and the rest of it, and about what he ought to do. It was with him as he lay awake on his bed, shut in by the two cots ; it, and the fear of forgetting to feed Baby, got into his dreams and troubled them ; they watched by him in his sleep ; they woke him early and were with him when he woke.

Dossie woke too. He took her into his bed and played with her, and in playing he forgot his grief. A little before seven he got up and dressed. He washed Dossie and dressed her as well as he could, with tender, clumsy fingers that fumbled over all her little strings and buttons. Pain, and pleasure poignant as pain, thrilled him with every soft contact with her darling body. He tried to brush her hair as Winny brushed it, all in ducks'-tails and in feathers.

He went down and busied himself, hours earlier than he need, making the fire, getting ready Dossie's breakfast and Baby's and his own. Foraging in the larder, he came upon a beefsteak pie that, evidently, Winny had made for him, as if in foreknowledge of his need. When he had washed up the breakfast things and the things that were left over from last night, he went upstairs and made his bed, clumsily. Then he went down again and tidied the sitting-room. In all this he was driven by his determination to leave nothing for Winny to do for him when she came. He went to and fro, with Dossie toddling after him and laughing.

Upstairs, Baby laughed in his cot.

And all the time, Ranny, with his obsession of bereavement and calamity, was unaware of the peace, the exquisite, the unimaginable peace that had settled upon Granville.

At half-past eight Winny looked in (entering by the open door of Granville) to see what she could do.

She found him in the bath-room, trying to wash Baby. He had put the little zinc bath with Baby in it inside the big one.

"Whatever did you do that for, Ranny?" Winny asked while her heart yearned to him.

He said he had to. The little beggar splashed so. Good idea, wasn't it?

Almost he had forgotten his bereavement.

Winny shook her head.

"Anyhow I've washed him all right."

"Yes," said she. "But you'll never dry him."

"Why not?"

"You can't. Not in here. There isn't room for you to set. Where's your chair and your flannel apron?"

"Flannel apron?"

"Yes. If you don't wear one you'll not get any hold on him. He'll slip between your knees before you know he's gone."

"Not if I keep 'em together."

"*Then* there's no lap for him. What he wants is petticoats."

(Petticoats? That was the secret, was it? He had tried to soap Baby, bit by bit, as he had seen Winny do, holding him, wrapped in a towel, on his knees—a disastrous failure. It was incredible how slippery he was.)

"There's his blanket. I thought I'd dry him on the floor."

"He'll catch his death of cold, Ranny, if you do.

There, give him to me. We'll take him downstairs to the fire."

He gave her the little naked, dripping body, and she wrapped it in the warm blanket and carried it downstairs.

" You bring the towels and the powder-puff, and all his vests and flannels and things," said Winny.

He brought them. She established herself in the low chair by the fire downstairs. He played with Dossie as he watched her. And all the time, through all the play, his obscure instinct told him that she ought not to be there. It suggested that if he desired to preserve the integrity of the document, Winny and he must not be known to be alone in the house together.

But it was a question of petticoats. He realised it when he saw Baby sprawling in the safe hollow of her lap. He had meant to tell Winny that she mustn't stay ; but she had him by those absurd petticoats of hers, and behind her petticoats he shielded himself from the upbraidings of his sanity.

But Winny knew. She was not going to stay, to be there with him more than was strictly necessary. When, with exquisite gentleness, she had inserted Baby into all his little vests and things, she put on him his knitted Baby's coat and hat, and gave him to Ranny to hold while she arrayed Dossie in her Sunday best. Then she packed them both into the wonderful pram, and wheeled them out into the Avenue, far from Ranny.

For she knew that Ranny didn't want her. He wanted to be left alone to think.

XXIV

HE had been incapable of thinking until now, the first moment (since it had happened) that he had been left alone. Last night the thing had stupefied him so that he could not think. If he had tried to describe what had been before him last night, he would have said there was a lot of cotton-wool about. It had been all like wool, cotton-wool, nothing that the mind could bite on, nothing that it could grasp. Last night Winny had been there and that had stopped his thinking. It was absurd to say that what had happened had disturbed his night's rest. What had disturbed his night's rest had been his fear lest he should forget to feed Baby. And in the morning there had been too many things to do, there had been Dossie and Baby. And then Winny again.

And now they were all gone. There was silence and a clear space to think in. His brain too was clear and clean. The clouds of cotton-wool had been dispersed in his movements to and fro.

As an aid to thinking he brought out of his breast-pocket Violet's letter. He spread it on the table in the back sitting-room and sat down to it, seriously, as to a document that he would have to master, a thing that would yield its secret only under the closest examination. He was aware that he had not by any means taken it all in last night.

That she had gone off with Leonard Mercier, *that* he had indeed grasped, *that* he knew. But beyond that the letter gave him no solid practical information. It did not and it was not meant to give him any clue. In going off Violet had disappeared and had meant to disappear. He gathered from it that she had been possessed by one thought and by one fear, that he would go after her and bring her back.

"What on earth," he said to himself, "should I go after her for?"

She made that clear to him as he read on. Her idea was that he would go after her, not so much to bring her back as to do something to Mercier, to inflict punishment on him, to hurt Mercier and hurt him badly. That was what Violet was afraid of; that was why she tried to shield Mercier, to excuse him, to take the whole blame on herself. And, evidently, that was what Mercier was afraid of too. That was why he had bolted with her to Paris. They must have had that in their minds, they must have planned it months before. He must have been trying for the post he'd got there. Ransome could see further, with a fierce shrewdness, that it was Mercier's "funk" and not his loyalty that accounted for his "holding off." "He held off because I was his friend, did he? He held off to save his own skin, the swine!"

And now she drew him up. What was all this about Winny Dymond? He must have missed it last night. "She was always fond of you. It was a lie what I told you about her not being. I said it because I was mad on you. I knew you'd have married her if I'd let you alone."

She was cool, the way she showed herself up. That's what she'd done, had she? Lied, so that he might think Winny didn't care for him? Lied, so that he mightn't marry her? Lied, so that she might get him for herself? For her fancy, for no more than a low animal would feel. He could see it now. He could see what she was. A woman who could fancy Mercier must have been a low animal all through and all the time.

How he had ever cared for her he couldn't think. There must have been some beastliness in him. Men *were* beasts sometimes. But he was worse. He was a fool to have

believed her lie. Even her beastliness sank out of sight
beside that treachery.

Well—she'd been frank enough about it now. She must
have had a face, to own that she'd lied to him and trapped
him! After that, what did it matter if she *had* left him?
" I daresay you know who I've gone with." What did it
matter who she'd gone with? Good God! What did it
matter what she'd done?

He could smile at her fear and at the cause of it. Mercier must have terrified her with his funk. The postscript
said as much. " You can do anything you like to me, so
long as you don't hurt Leonard." He smiled again at
that. What did she imagine he'd like to do to her? As
for Mercier, what should he want to hurt the beast for?
He wouldn't touch him—now—with the end of a barge-
pole.

Oh, well, yes, he supposed he'd have to leather him if he
came across him. But he wouldn't have any pleasure in
it—now. Last year he would have leathered him with
joy; his feet had fairly ached to get at him, to kick the
swine out of the house before he did any harm in it. Now
it was as if he loathed him too much in his flabbiness to
care for the contact that personal violence involved.

Yet, through all the miserable workings of his mind
the thought of Mercier's flabbiness was sweet to him. It
gave him a curious consolation and support. True, it
had been the chief agent in the process of deception;
it had blinded him to Mercier's dangerous quality; it had
given him a sense of false security; he could see, now,
the fool he'd been to imagine that it would act as any
deterrent to a woman so foredoomed as Violet. Thus it
had in a measure brought about the whole catastrophe.
At the same time it had saved him from the peculiar
personal mortification such catastrophes entail. In comparison with Mercier he sustained no injury to his pride
and vanity of sex. And Mercier's flabbiness did more for
him than that. It took the sharpest sting from Violet's

infidelity. It removed it to the region of insane per-
versities. It removed Violet herself from her place in
memory, that place of magic and of charm where if she
had remained she would have had power to hurt him.

When he considered her letter yet again in the calmness
of that thought, it struck him that Violet herself was
offering him support and consolation. " You shouldn't
have married me. You should have married a girl like
Winny Dymond "—" I knew you'd marry her if I let
you alone." Why, after all these years, had she confessed
her treachery ? Why had she confessed it now at the precise
moment when she had left him ? There was no need. It
couldn't help her. No, but it was just possible (for she
was quite intelligent) that she had seen how it might help
him. It was possible that some sort of contrition had
visited her in that last hour, and that she had meant to
remind him that he was not utterly abandoned, that there
was something left.

That brought him to the lines, almost indecipherable,
squeezed in her last hurried moment into the margin of
the letter. " You mustn't be afraid of being fond of
Baby. There was nothing between me and Leonard before
July of last year."

She had foreseen the supreme issue ; she had provided
for the worst sting, the unspeakable suspicion, the intolerable terror. It was as if she had calculated the precise
point where her infidelity would touch him.

Faced with that issue, Ranny's mind, like a young thing
forced to sudden tragic maturity by a mortal crisis, worked
with an incredible clearness and capacity. It developed
an almost superhuman subtlety of comprehension. He
looked at the thing all round ; he controlled his passion
so that he might look at it. It was of course open to him
to take it that she had lied. Passion indeed clamoured
at him, insisting that she did lie, that lying came easier
to her than the truth. But, looking at it all round without
passion, he was inclined to think that Violet had not

lied. She had not given herself time or space to lie for
lying's sake. If she had lied, then, she had lied for a
purpose. A purpose that he could very well conceive.
But if she lied for *that* purpose she would have given importance and prominence to her lie. She wouldn't have
hidden it away in an almost invisible scrawl on an inade-
quate margin.

Of course, she might have lied to deceive him for another
purpose, for his own good. But there again conscious
deception would have made for legibility at the least.

Besides, she had put it in a way that left no room for
doubt. "You needn't be afraid of being fond of Baby."
Even passion had to own that the words had the ring of
remorse, of insight, of certainty, and, above all, of haste.
Such haste as precluded all deliberation. Evidently it
was an afterthought. It had come to her, inopportunely,
in the last moment before flight, and she had given it
the place and the importance she would naturally give
to a subject in which she herself was not in any way
concerned.

There remained the possibility that she might be mis-
taken. But the dates upheld her. In the beginning he
and she had, of necessity, gone very carefully into the
question of dates. He remembered that there had been a
whole body of evidence establishing the all-important point
beyond a doubt. All of his honour that he most cared for
she had spared. She had not profaned the ultimate
sanctity, nor poisoned for him the very sweetness of his
life.

There were sounds in the front garden. Winny was
bringing in the children. He went out to meet them as
they came up the flagged walk. Dossie toddled, clinging
to the skirts of Winny, who in all her tenderness and
absurdity, with her most earnest air of gravity and ab-

sorption in the adventure, pushed the pram. In the pram, tilted backwards, with his little pink legs upturned, Baby fondled, deliciously, his own toes. He was jerking himself up and down and making for the benefit of all whom it might concern his very nicest noises.

Ranny stood in the doorway, silent, almost austere, like a man escaped by a hair's-breadth from great peril.

When he caught sight of the silent and austere young man in the doorway, Baby let go his fascinating toes. He chuckled with delight. He jerked himself more than ever up and down. He struggled to be free, to be lifted up and embraced by the young man. Silence and austerity were no deterrent to Baby, so assured was he of his position, of his welcome, of the safe, warm, tingling place that would presently be his in the hollow of the young man's arm. The desire of it made Baby's arms and his body writhe, with a heartrending agitation, in his little knitted coat.

All this innocent ecstasy of Baby the young man met with silence and austerity and sombre eyes.

With Winny's eyes on him he indeed lifted Baby up, disclosing, first, his pathetically bunched and bundled back, and then his face, exquisitely contorted.

And Winny, who had *forgotten* for a minute, laughed. " He is funny, isn't he ? He smiles just like you do, all up in the corners like."

At that the young man's arms tightened and he gripped Baby with passion to his breast. He kissed him, looking down at him, passionately, sombrely.

Winny saw, and the impulse seized her to efface herself, to vanish.

" I must be going," she said, " or I shall be late for dinner. Can you manage, Ranny ? There's a beefsteak pie. I made it yesterday."

As she turned Dossie trotted after her ; and as she vanished Dossie cried, inconsolably.

He managed, beautifully, with the beefsteak pie.

His sense of bereavement which still weighed on him was no longer attached in any way to Violet. He could not say precisely what it *was* attached to. There it was. Only, when he thought of Violet, it seemed to him incomprehensible, not to say absurd, that he should feel it.

XXV

IN the afternoon Winny came again for the children, so that he could go to Wandsworth unencumbered. The weather was favourable to her idea, which was not to be in Ranny's house more than she could help, but to be seen, if seen she must be, out of doors with the children, in a public innocence, affording the presumption that Violet was still there.

Above all, she was not going to be seen with Ranny, or to be seen by him too much, if she could help it. With her sense of the sadness of his errand, the sense (that came to her more acutely with the afternoon) of things imminent, of things, she knew not what, that would have to be done, she avoided him as she would have avoided a bereaved person preoccupied with some lamentable business relating to the departed.

He was aware of her attitude; he was aware, further, that it would be their attitude at Wandsworth. They would all treat him like that, as if he were bereaved. They would not lose, nor allow him to lose for an instant, their awestruck sense of it. That was why he dreaded going there, why he had put it off till the last possible moment, which was about three o'clock in the afternoon. His uncle Randall would be there. He would have to be told. He might as well tell him while he was about it. His wife's action had been patent and public; it was not a thing that could be hushed up, or minimised, or explained away.

As he thought of all this, of what he would have to say, to go into, to handle, every moment wound him up to a higher and higher pitch of nervous tension.

His mother opened the door to him. She greeted him

with a certain timidity, an ominous hesitation ; and from
the expression of her face you might have gathered, in
spite of her kiss, that she was not entirely glad to see him ;
that she had something up her sleeve, something that she
desired to conceal from him. It was as if by way of con-
cealing it that she let him in stealthily with no more opening
of the door than was absolutely necessary for his entrance.

" You haven't brought Vi'let ? " she whispered.

" No." >

They went softly together through the shop, darkened
by the blinds that were drawn for Sunday. In the little
passage beyond he paused at the door of the back parlour.

" Where's Father ? "

She winced at the word " Father," so out of keeping
with his habitual levity. It was the first intimation that
there was something wrong with him.

" He's upstairs, my dear, in His bed."

" What's the matter with him ? "

" It's the Headache." She went on to explain, taking
him as it were surreptitiously into the little room, that the
Headache had been frequent lately, not to say continuous ;
not even Sundays were exempt.

" He's a sad sufferer," she said.

Instead of replying with something suitable, Ranny set
his teeth..

She had sat down helplessly, and as she spoke she gazed
up at him where he remained standing by the chimney-
piece ; her look pleaded, deprecated, yet obstinately en-
deavoured to deceive. But for once Ranny was blind to
the pathos of her deception. Vaguely her foolish secrecy
irritated him.

" Look here, Mother," he said, " I want to talk to you.
I've got to tell you something."

" It's not anything about your Father, Ranny ? "

" No, it is not."

(She turned to him from her trouble with visible relief.)

" It's about my wife."

" Vi'let ? "

" She's left me."

" Left you ? What d'you mean, Ranny ? "

" She's gone off—Bolted."

" When ? "

" Last night, I suppose—to Paris."

She stared at him strangely, without sympathy, without comprehension. It was almost as if in her mind she accused him of harbouring some monstrous hallucination. With her eternal instinct for suppression she fought against it, she refused to take it in. He felt himself unequal to pressing it on her more than that.

" Would she go there—all that way—by herself, Ranny?" she brought out at last.

" By herself ? Not much ! "

" Well—how——"

And still she would not face the thing straight enough to say, " How did she go, then ? "

He flung it at her brutally, exasperated by her obstinacy.

" She went with Mercier."

" With *'im? She*——"

Her face seemed suddenly to give way under his eyes, to become discoloured in a frightful pallor, to fall piteously into the lines of age.

This face that his words had so crushed and broken looked up at him with all its motherhood, mute yet vibrant, brimming in its eyes.

"Sit down, dear," she said. " You'll be tired standing."

He sat down, mechanically, in the nearest chair, bending forward, contemplating his clenched hands. His posture put him at her mercy. She came over to him and laid one hand on his shoulder ; the other touched his hair, stroking it. He shrank as if she had hurt him and leaned back. She moved away, and took up a position in a seat that faced him. There she sat and gazed at him, helpless and passive, panting a little with emotion ; until a thought occurred to her.

" Who's looking after the little children ? "

" Winny—Winny Dymond."

" Why didn't you send for *me*, Ranny ? "

" It was too late—last night."

" I'd have come, my dear. I'd have got out of me bed."

" It wouldn't have done any good."

There was a long pause.

" Were you alone in the house, dear ? "

He looked up, angry. " Of course I was alone in the house."

She sat silent and continued to gaze at him with her tender, wounded eyes.

Outside in the passage the front door bell rang. She rose in perturbation.

" That's them. Do you want to see them ? "

" I don't care whether I see them or not."

She stood deliberating.

" You'd better—p'r'aps—see your uncle. I'll tell him, Ranny. Your Father's not fit for it to-day."

" All right."

He rose uneasily and prepared himself to take it standing.

He heard them come into the shop, his Uncle and his Aunt Randall. He heard his uncle's salutation checked in mid-career. He heard his mother's penetrating whisper, then mutterings, commiserations. Their communion lasted long enough for him to gather that his mother would have about told them everything.

They came in, marking their shocked sense of it by soft shufflings at the door of the parlour, his sanctuary. He felt obscurely that he had become important to them, the chief figure of a little infamous tragedy. He had a moment's intense and painful prescience of the way they would take it ; they would treat him with an excruciating respect, an awful deference, as a person visited by God and afflicted with unspeakable calamity.

And they did. It was an affair of downcast eyes and

Q

silent, embarrassed and embarrassing hand-shakings.
Ransome met it with his head in the air, clear-eyed,
defiant of their sympathy.

"I think," his mother said, "we'd better come upstairs
if we don't want to be interrupted." For on Sundays the
back parlour was assigned to the young chemist, Mercier's
successor, who assisted Mr. Ransome.

Upstairs, the ordered room, polished to perfection,
steadfast in its shining Sunday state, appeared as the
irremovable seat of middle-class tradition, of family virtue,
of fidelity and cleanliness, of sacred immutable propriety.
And into the bosom of these safe and comfortable sanctities Ranny had brought horror and defilement and
destruction.

His Uncle Randall, try as he would, could not disguise
from him that this was what he had done. Because of
Ranny's wife, Respectability, the enduring soul of the
Randalls and the Ransomes, could never lift up its head
superbly any more. All infamies and all abominations
that could defile a family were summed up for John Randall in the one word, Adultery. It was worse than robbery
or forgery or bankruptcy; it struck more home; it did
more deadly havoc among the generations. It excited
more interest; it caused more talk; and therefore it
marked you more and was not so easily forgotten. It
reverberated. The more respectable you were the worse
it was for you. If, among the Randalls and the Ransomes,
such a plunge as Violet's was unheard of, it made the
more terrific splash, a splash that covered the whole
family. The Ransomes, to be sure, stood more in the
centre, they were more deplorably bespattered, and more,
much more intimately tainted. But, by the very close-
ness of their family attachment, the mud of Violet's
plungings would adhere largely to the Randalls, too.
The taint would hang for years around him, John Randall,
in his shop. He had hardly entered his sister's room
before he had calculated about how long it would be

before the scandal spread through Wandsworth High
Street. It wasn't as if he hadn't been well known. As a
member of the Borough Council he stuck in the public
eye where other men would have slipped through into
obscurity. It was really worse for him than any of them.

All this was present in the back of John Randall's mind
as he prepared to deal efficiently with the catastrophe.
Having unbuttoned his coat and taken off his gloves with
exasperating, slow, and measured movements, he fairly
sat down to it at the table, preserving his very finest
military air. The situation required before all things a
policy. And the policy which most appealed to Mr.
Randall, in which he showed himself most efficient, was
the policy of a kindly hushing-up. It was thus that for
years he had dealt with his brother-in-law's inebriety.
Ranny's case, to be sure, was not quite so simple ; still, on
the essential point Mr. Randall had made up his mind—
that, in the discussion that must follow, the idea of
adultery should not once appear. If they were all of
them as a family splashed more or less from head to foot
with mud of a kind that was going to stick to them, why,
there was nothing to be done but to cover it up as soon as
possible.

It was in the spirit of this policy that he approached his
nephew. It involved dealing with young Mrs. Ransome
throughout as a good woman who had become, somehow,
mysteriously unfortunate.

" I'm sorry to hear this about your wife, Randall. It's
a sad business, a sad business for you, my boy."

From her seat on the sofa beside Ranny's mother,
Aunt Randall murmured inarticulate corroboration of
that view.

Ranny had remained standing. It gave him an advantage in defiance.

" I've never heard anything," his uncle continued
heavily, " that's shocked and grieved me more."

" I wouldn't worry about it if I were you, Uncle."

At that Mr. Randall fumed a little feebly, thereby losing some of the fineness of his military air. It was as if his nephew had disparaged his importance, ignored his stake in the family's reputation, and as good as told him it was no business of his.

" But I *must* worry about it. *I* can't take it like you do, as cool as if nothing had happened. Such a thing's never been known, never so much as been named in your mother's family, or your father's, either. It's—it's so unexpected."

" I didn't expect it any more than you did."

" You needn't take that tone, Randall, my boy. I'm sorry for you, but you're not the only one concerned. Still, I'm putting all that aside, and I'm here to help you."

" You can't help me. How can you ? "

" I can help you to consider what's to be done."

" There isn't anything to be done that I can see."

" There are several things," said Mr. Randall, " that can be done." He said it as if he were counsel giving an opinion. " You can take her back ; you can leave her alone ; or you can divorce her. First of all I want to know one thing. Did you give her any provocation ? "

" What do you mean by provocation ? "

" Well—did you give her any cause for jealousy ? "

Ranny's mother struck in. " He wouldn't, John." And his Aunt Randall murmured half-audible and shocked negation.

Ranny stared at his uncle as if he wondered where he was coming out next.

" Of course I didn't."

" Are—you—quite—sure about that ? "

" You needn't ask him such a thing," said Ranny's mother, and Ranny fairly squared himself.

" Look here, Uncle, what d'you want to get at ? "

" The facts, my boy."

" You've got all there are."

" How about that young woman up at your place ? "

"What young woman ? "

"That Miss——"

Ranny's mother supplied his loss. "Miss Dymond."

"What's she got to do with it ? " said Ranny.

"I'm asking you. What *has* she ? "

"Nothing. You can keep her out of it."

"That's what I should advise *you* to do, my boy."

Ranny dropped his defiance and sank his flushed forehead. "I *have* kept her out of it." His voice was grave and very low.

"Not if she's there. Taking everything upon her and looking after your children."

"What harm's she doing looking after them ? "

"You'll soon know if you take it into a court of law."

"Who told you I was going to take it ? "

"That's what I'm trying to get at. *Are* you ? "

"Am I going to divorce her, you mean ? "

That was what he had meant. It was also what he was afraid of, what he hoped to dissuade his nephew from. Above all things he dreaded the public scandal of divorce.

"Yes," he said. "Is it bad enough for that ? "

"It's bad enough for anything. But I don't know what I'm going to do."

"Well, it won't do to have that young woman's name brought forward in the evidence."

"Who'd bring it ? "

"Why, *she* might." (Randall's face was blank.) "Your wife, if she defends the suit. That would be her game, you may be sure."

It would, Randall reflected. That was the very point suggested last night by his inner sanity, the use that might be made of Winny. Winny's innocent presence in his house might ruin his case if it were known. What was worse, far worse, it would ruin Winny. Whatever he did he must keep Winny out of it. ,

"I haven't said I was going to bring an action."

" Well—and I don't advise you to.   Why have the
scandal and the publicity when you can avoid it ? "

" Why, Ranny," his mother cried, " it would kill your
Father."

Ranny scowled.   Her cry failed to touch him.

Mr. Randall went on.   He felt that he was bringing his
nephew round, that he was getting the case into his own
hands, the hands that were most competent to deal with
it.   It was only to be expected that with his experience he
could see farther than the young man, his nephew.   What
Mr. Randall saw beyond the scandal of the Divorce Court
was a vision of young Mrs. Ransome, wanton with liberty
and plunging deeper, splashing as she had not yet splashed,
bespattering them all to the furthest limits of her range.
The question for Mr. Randall was how to stop her, how
to get her out of it, how to bring her to her sober senses
before she had done more damage than she had.

He wondered, had it occurred to Randall that he might
take her back ?

" Have you any idea," he said, " what made her do
it ? "

" Good God, what a question ! "

Mr. Randall made a measured, balancing movement of
his body while he drummed with his fingers on the table.

" Well——" It was as if he took his question back,
conceding its enormity.   He leaned forward now in his
balancing, and lowered his voice to the extreme of confidence.

" Have you any idea how far she's gone ? " (It was as
near as he could get to it.)

" She's gone as far as Paris," said Ranny, with a grin.
" Is that far enough for you ? "

Mr. Randall leaned back as with relief, and stopped
balancing.   " It might be worse," he said, " far worse."

" How d'you mean—worse ?   Seems to me about as
bad as it can be."

" It's unfortunate—but not so serious as if——" He

paused profoundly. He was visibly considering it from some private and personal point of view. "She might have stayed in London. She might have carried on at your own door or here in Wandsworth."

His nephew, Randall, was now regarding him with an attention the nature of which he entirely misconceived. It gave him courage to speak out—his whole mind and no mincing matters.

"If I were you, Randall, the first thing I should do is to get rid of that young woman—that Dymond girl——" He put up his hand to ward off the imminent explosion. "Yes, yes, I know *all* you've got to say, my boy, but it won't do. She's a young girl——"

"She's as good as they make them," said Ranny, glaring at him, "as good as my mother there."

"Yes, yes, yes. I know all about it. But you mustn't have her there."

"Have her where?"

"Where I know she's been—where your mother says she's been—in your house. Now, don't turn on your mother; she hasn't said a word against her. I'm not saying a word. But you mustn't—have—her—about, Randall. You mustn't have her about. There'd be talk and all, before you know where you are. It isn't right and it isn't proper."

"No, Ranny, it isn't proper," said his mother, and his aunt said, No, it wasn't, too.

Ranny laughed unpleasantly.

"You think it's as improper as the other thing, do you?"

He addressed his uncle.

"What other thing?" said Mr. Randall. It had made him wince even while he pretended not to see it. It had brought him so near.

"What my wife's done."

"Well, Randall, since you ask me, to all appearances—appearances, mind you—it is."

" Appearances ? "

" Well, you must save appearances, and you must save 'em while you can."

" How am I to save them I should like to know ? "

" By actin' at once. By stoppin' it all before it gets about. You can't have your wife over there in Paris carryin' on. You must just start—soon as you can—to-morrow—and bring her back."

" Not much ! "

" It's what you got to do, Randall. She's been unfortu-nate, I know ; but she's young, and you don't know how she may have been led on. 'S likely's not you haven't looked after her enough. You don't know but what you may have been responsible. You got to take her back."

" What should I take her back for ? " said Ranny, with false suavity.

" To save scandal. To save trouble and misery and disgrace all round. You got to think of your family."

" What do you mean by my family ? Me and my children ? "

" I mean the family name, my boy."

A frightful lucidity had come upon Ranny, born of the calamity itself. It was not for nothing that he had attained that sudden violent maturity of his. He saw things as they were.

" You mean yourself," he said. " Jolly lot you think of me and my children if you ask me to take her back. Not me ! I'll be damned first."

" You married her, Randall, against the wishes of your family ; and you're responsible to your family for the way she conducts herself."

" I should rather think I *was* responsible ! If I wasn't— if I was a bletherin' idiot—I might take her back——"

" I don't say if she leaves you again you'll take her back a second time. But you got to give her a chance. After all, she's the mother of your children. You married her."

" Yes. That's where I went wrong. That's what made

her do it, if you want to know. *That's* the provocation I gave her. It's what she always had against me—the children, and my marrying her. And she was right. She never ought to have had children. I never ought to have married her—against her will."

"Well, I can't think what you did it for—in such haste."

"I did it," said Ranny in his maturity, his lucidity, "because it was the way I was brought up. I suppose, come to that, I did it for all you."

He saw everything now as it was.

"How d'you make that out? Did it for us!"

Then Ranny delivered his soul, and the escape, the outburst was tremendous, cataclysmic.

"For you and your rotten respectability! What you brought me up on. What you've rammed down my throat all along. What you're thinking of now. You're not thinking of me; you're thinking of yourself, and how respectable you are, and how I've dished you. You don't want me to take my wife back because you care a rap about me and my children. It's because you're afraid. That's what it is, you're afraid. You're afraid of the rotten scandal; you're afraid of what people'll say; you're afraid of not looking respectable any more. You know what my wife's done—you know what she *is*——"

"She's a woman, Randall, she's a woman."

"She's a—Well, she *is*, and you know it. You know what she is, and you want me to take her back so as you can lie about it and hush it all up and pretend it isn't there. Same as you've done with my father. He's a drunkard——"

"For shame, Randall," said his uncle.

"He is, and you know it, and he knows it, and my mother knows it. And yet you go on lying about him and pretending. I'm sick of it. I'm sick of hearing about how good he is, and his Headaches—Headaches!"

"Oh! Ranny, dear," his mother wailed piteously.

"I'm not blaming him, Mother. Poor old Humming-bird, he can't help it. It's the way he's made. I'm not blaming Virelet. She can't help it, either. It's my fault. If I'd wanted her to stick to me I oughtn't to have married her."

"What ought you to have done then?" his uncle enquired sternly.

"Anything but that. That's what started her. She couldn't stand it. She'll stick to Mercier all right, you'll see, because she isn't married to the swine; whereas if I took her back to-night she'd chuck me to-morrow. Can't you see that she's like that? She's done the best day's work she ever did for herself and me too."

"Well, how you can speak about it so, Ranny," said his mother.

"There you're at it again, you know—pretendin'. You go on as if it was the most horrible thing that could happen to anyone, her boltin', when you know the most horrible thing would be her comin' back again. To look at you and Uncle and Aunt there, anyone would think that Virelet was the best wife and mother that ever lived, and that she'd only left me to go to heaven."

"Well, there's no good my saying any more, I can see," said Mr. Randall. And he rose, buttoning his coat with dignity that struggled in vain against his deep depression. He was profoundly troubled by his nephew's outburst. It was as if peace and honesty and honour, the solid, steadfast tradition by which he lived, had been first outraged, then destroyed in sheer brutality. He didn't know himself. He had been charged with untruthfulness and dishonesty; he, who had been held the soul of honesty and truth, who had always held himself at least sincere.

And he didn't know his nephew Randall. He had always supposed that Randall was refined and that he had a good heart. And to think that he could break out like this, and be coarse and cruel, and say things before ladies that were downright immoral——

"Well," he said as he shook hands with him, "I can't understand you, my boy."

"Sorry, Uncle."

"There—leave it alone. I don't ask you to apologise to me. But there's your mother. You've done your best to hurt her. Good-bye."

"He's upset, John," said Ranny's mother, "and no wonder. You should have let him be."

"I'm not upset," said Ranny wearily. "What beats me is the rotten humbug of it all."

And no sooner did Mr. Randall find himself in the High Street with his wife than he took her by the arm in confidence.

"He was quite right about that wife of his. Only I thought—if he could have patched it up——"

"Ah, I daresay he knows more than we do. What I can't get over is the way he spoke about his poor father."

"Well—I wouldn't say it to Emma, but Fulleymore *does* drink. Like a fish he does."

(It was his sacrifice to honesty.)

"But Randall was wild. He didn't quite know what he was saying. Poor chap! It's hit him harder than he thinks."

Ranny, alone with his mother, put his arm round her neck and kissed her. (She had gone into her room and returned dressed, ready to go back with him to South-fields.)

"I'm sorry, Mother, if I hurt you."

"Never mind, Ranny, I know how hurt you must have been before you could do it. It was what you said about your Father, dear. But there—you've always been good to him no matter what he's been."

"Is he *very* bad, Mother?"

"He is. I don't know, I'm sure, how I'm going to leave

him ; unless he can manage with Mabel and Mr. Ponting. She's a good girl, Mabel. And he's got a kind heart, Ranny, that young man."

" D'you think I haven't ? "

" I wasn't meaning you, my dear. Come, I'm ready now."

They went downstairs. Mrs. Ransome paused at the kitchen door to give some final directions to Mabel, the maid, and a message for Mr. Ponting, the assistant ; and they went out.

As they were going down the High Street, her thoughts reverted to Ranny's awful outburst.

" Ranny, I wish you hadn't spoken to your uncle like you did."

" I *know*, Mother—but he set my back up. He was talkin' through his Sunday hat all the time, pretendin' to stick up for Virelet, knowin' perfectly well what she is, and cussin' and swearin' at her for it in his heart, and naggin' at me because there wasn't anybody else to go for."

" He was trying to help you, Ranny."

" If God can't help me, strikes me it's pretty fair cheek of Uncle to presume "—He meditated.

" But he wasn't tryin' to help me. He was thinkin' how he could help his own damned respectability all the blessed time. He knows what a bloomin' hell it's been for Virelet and me this last year—and he'd have forced us back into it—into all that misery—just to save his own silly skin."

" No, dear, it isn't that. He doesn't think Vi'let should be let go on living like she is if you can stop her. He thinks it isn't proper."

" Well, that's what I say. It's his old blinkin', bletherin' morality he's takin' care of, not me. Everybody's got to live like he thinks they ought to, no matter how they hate it. If two Kilkenny cats he knew was to get married and one of them was to bolt he'd fetch her back and tie 'em both up, heads together, so as she shouldn't do it again. And if they clawed each other's guts out he wouldn't care. He'd say they were livin' a nice, virtuous, respectable and moral life.

"What rot it all is !

"Stop her ? As if anyone could stop her ! God knows she can't stop herself, poor girl. She's made like that. I'm not blamin' her."

For, with whatever wildness Ranny started, he always came back to that—He didn't blame her. He knew whereof she was made. It was proof of his sudden, forced maturity, that unfaltering acceptance of the fact.

" Talk of helpin' ! Strikes me poor Vi's helpin' more than anybody, by clearin' out like she's done."

That was how, with a final incomparable serenity, he made it out.

But his mother took it all as so much wildness, the delirium, the madness, born of his calamity.

" He'd have been all right if I'd been ass enough to play into his hands and gone blowin' me nose and grizzlin' and whinin' about my misfortune, and let *him* go gassin' about the sadness of it and all that. But because I kept my end up he went for me.

"Sadness ! He doesn't know what sadness is *or* misfortune.

" My God ! If every poor beggar had the luck I've had—to be let off without having to pay for it ! "

Up till then his mother had kept silence. She had let him rave. " Poor boy," she had said to herself, " he doesn't mean it. It'll do him good."

But when he talked about not having to pay for it, that reminded her that paying for it was just what he would have to do.

" How'll you manage," she said now, " about the children ? I can take them for a week or two or more while you get settled."

" Would you ? "

It *was* a way out for the present.

"I'd take them altogether—I'd love to, Ranny—if it wasn't for your Father bein' ill."

In spite of the cataclysm, she still by sheer force of habit kept it up.

"I don't want you to take them altogether," he said.

"I could do it—if you was to come with them——"

That indeed was what she wanted, the heavenly possibility she had sighted from the first. But she had hardly dared to suggest it. Even now, putting out her tremorous feeler, she shrank back from his refusal.

"If you could let Granville—and come and live with us."

His silence and his embarrassment pierced her to the heart.

"Won't you?" she ventured.

"Well—I've got to think of them. For them, in some ways, the poor old Humming-bird might, you see, be almost as bad as Virelet."

She knew. She had known it all the time. She had even got so far in knowledge as to see that Ranny's father was in a measure responsible for Ranny's marriage. If Ranny had had more life, more freedom, and more happiness around him in his home, he would not have been driven, as he was, to Violet.

"Well, dear, you just think it over. If you don't come you must get somebody."

Yes. He must get somebody. He had thought of that.

"It can't be Winny Dymond, dear."

"No," he assented. "It can't be Winny Dymond."

"And you'll have to come to me until I can find you someone."

They left it so. After all, it made things easier, the method that his mother had brought to such perfection, her way of skating rapidly over brittle surfaces, of circumnavigating all profound unpleasantness, and of plunging, when she did plunge, only into the vague, the void.

And through it all he was aware of the brittleness, the

unpleasantness, the profundity of what was immediately
before him, how to deal with poor Winny and her innocent
enormity ; the impropriety, as it had been presented to
him, of her devotion.

But even this problem, so torturing to his nerves, was
presently lost sight of in the simple, practical difficulty
of detaching Winny from the children ; or rather, of
detaching the children from Winny, of tearing, as they
had to tear, them from her, piecemeal, first Baby, then
Dossie, with every circumstance of barbarous cruelty.

It was a spectacle, an operation of such naked agony
that before it the most persistent, the most incorruptible
sense of propriety broke down. It was too much altogether
for Mrs. Ransome.

Dossie was the worst. She had strength in her little
fingers and she clung.

And the crying, the crying of the two, terrible to Ranny,
terrible to Winny, the passionate screams, the strangled
sobs, the long, irremediable wailing, the terrifying con-
vulsive silences, the awful intermissions and shattering
recoveries of anguish—it was as if their innocence had
insight, had premonition of the monstrous, imminent
separation, of the wrong that he and she were about to do
to each other in the name of such sanctities as innocence
knows nothing of. For outrage and wrong it was to the
holy primal instincts, drawing them, as it had drawn
them long ago, seeking to bind them again, body and
soul, breaking all other bonds ; insult and violence to honest
love, to fatherhood and motherhood, to the one (one and
threefold) perfection that they could stand for, he and
she.

It ended by its sheer terror in Winny's staying just for
that evening, to put the little things to sleep. For nobody
else, not Ranny, and not his mother, was able to do that.
The dark design of their torturers was to take these innocent
ones by night, drugged with their sleep, and pack them in
the pram, snugly blanketed, and thus convey them in

secrecy to Wandsworth, where it was hoped they would wake up, poor lambs, to a morning without memory.

"Well—Winky," he said. But it was not yet well. He had to stand by and see Winky stoop over Baby's cot (it was her right) for the last look.

She knew it was her last look, in that room—in that way that had been the way of innocence.

"Well, I never!" said Ranny's mother as he returned from seeing Winky home. (So much was permitted him. It was even imperative.)

"Did they ever cry like that for their Mammy?"

He smiled grimly. His illumination was more than he could bear.

XXVI

IT was in the cruelty of it, in that sudden barbarous
tearing of the children from Winny, of Winny from
Ransome, and of Ransome from his home, in that hurried
surreptitious flight through the darkness, that he most
felt the pressure and the malignant pinch of poverty.
Owing to his straitened circumstances, with all his
mother's forethought and goodwill, with all the combined
resources of their ingenuity, they could do no better to
meet his lamentable case than this. "This," indeed, was
imperative, inevitable. He reflected bitterly that, if he
had been a rich man, like the manager or the secretary
of Woolridge's, instead of a ledger clerk (that was all that
his last rise had made him) at a hundred and fifty a year,
he would have been spared "this." It would have been
neither inevitable nor imperative. It simply wouldn't
have happened. He would have had a house with a staff
of competent servants, a nurse for the children, a cook and
maybe a housemaid to manage for him, and so forth.
Winny wouldn't have come into it. It would never have
occurred to her to run the risks she had run for him.
There would have been no need. She would have remained, serene, beautiful in sympathy, outside his calamity,
untouched by its sordidness, its taint. All the machinery
of his household would have gone on in spite of it, without
any hitch or dislocation, working all the more smoothly in
the absence of its mistress.

That was how rich people came out of this sort of thing,
right side up, smiling, knowing as they did that there was
nothing to spoil the peace of it for them, or make them
apt to mistake it for anything but the blessing that it was.

Thus they got, as you may say, the whole good out of it without any waste. At the worst, if they didn't like it, rich people, driven to flight, depart from the scene of their disaster with dignity, in cabs.

But Ranny's departure, with all its ignominy, was not by any means the worst. The worst, incomparably, was the going back on Monday evening to settle up. There was a man coming from Wandsworth with a handcart for the cots, the high chair and all the babies' furniture, and the kids' toys and the little clothes, their whole diminutive outfit, and for what he needed of his own. And when all the packing was done he would still have to go into things.

By the things he had to go into he meant the drawers and the cupboards in his wife's room.

And such things! It was as if the whole tale of her adultery, with all its secret infamy, its squalor, its utter callousness, was there in that room of the love-knots and the rosebuds.

In the locked wardrobe—the key was on the chimney-piece where he could find it—he came on her old skirts, draggled and torn and stained as he had known them, on the muslin gown of last year, loathsome and limp, bent like a hanged corpse ; and on her very night-gown of the other night, dreadfully familiar, shrinking, poor ghost of an abomination, in its corner. And under them, in a row, the shoes that her feet had gone in, misshapen, trodden-down at heel, gaping to deliver up her shame.

These things Winny had collected and put away in order, and hidden out of his sight as best she could. Seeing, she too, the tale they told, she had hung a sheet in front of them and locked the door on them and laid the key aside, to break in some degree the shock of them. For they were things that had been good enough for him, but not good enough for Violet's lover. She had gone to him in all her bravery, leaving them behind, not caring who found them.

And there was more to be gone through before he had

finished with it. There were the drawers, crammed with little things, the collars, the ribbons and the laces, and one or two trinkets that he had given her, cast off with the rest, all folded and tidied by Winny, smoothed and coaxed out of the memories they held, the creases that betrayed the slattern; and with them, tucked away by Winny, defiled beyond redemption, almost beyond recognition, the sachet, smelling of violets and with the word " Violet " sprawling all across it in embroidery.

All these things, the dresses, the shoes, and the rest of them, he gathered up in handfuls and flung into an old trunk which he locked and pushed under the bed.

Then he set his teeth and went on with his task. In the soiled linen basket, among his own handkerchiefs as he counted them, he found one queerly scented and of a strange, arresting pattern. It had the monogram "L. M." stitched into the corner. She must have borrowed it from the beast. Or else—the beast had been in the house and had left it there.

That finished him.

Finished as he was in every sense, thoroughly instructed, furnished with details that fitted out and rounded off all that was vague and incomplete in his vision of the thing, he was still unprepared for the question with which his mother met him.

" Have you told Mr. and Mrs. Usher ? "

He hadn't.

He had forgotten Mr. and Mrs. Usher, forgotten that this prolongation of his ordeal would be necessary.

" Well, you'll have to."

" Of course I'll have to."

" Will you go and see him ? "

" No. I—can't. I'll write."

He wrote in the afternoon of the next day at Woolridge's, in the luncheon hour when he had the ledger clerks' pen to himself. He was very brief.

He received his father-in-law's reply by return. Mr. Usher made no comment beyond an almost perfunctory expression of regret. But he said that he must see Randall. And, as the journey between Elstree and Wandsworth was somewhat long to be undertaken after office hours, he proposed the "Bald-Faced Stag," Edgware, as a convenient half-way house for them to meet at, and Wednesday, at seven or thereabouts, as the day and hour. Thus he allowed time for Randall to receive his letter and, if necessary, to answer it. No telegraphing for Mr. Usher, except in case of death, actual or imminent.

Ransome supposed that he would have to see him and get it over. Soon after seven on Wednesday, then, Mr. Usher having ridden over on his mare Polly and Ransome on his bicycle, they met in the parlour of the "Bald-Faced Stag," Edgware. Mr. Usher's friend the landlord had undertaken that they should not be disturbed.

It was impossible for Ransome not to notice something queer about his father-in-law, something utterly unlike the bluff and genial presence he had known. Mr. Usher seemed to have shrunk somehow and withered, so that you might have said the catastrophe had hit him hard, if that, his mere bodily shrinkage, had been all. What struck Ransome as specially queer about Mr. Usher was his manner and the expression of his face. You could almost have called it crafty. Guilty it was, too, consciously guilty, the furtive face of a man on the defensive, armed with all his little cunning against a possible attack, having entrenched himself in the parlour of the "Bald-Faced Stag" as on neutral territory.

"What say to a bit of supper, my boy, before we begin business?"

It was a false and feeble imitation of his old heartiness.

Over a supper of cold ham and cheese and beer they discussed Ransome's father's health and his mother's health, and Mrs. Usher's health, which was poor, and Mr. Usher's prospects, which were poorer, not to say bad. He leaned on this point and returned to it, as if it might have a possible bearing on the matter actually in hand, and with a certain disagreeable effect of craftiness and intention. It was as if he wished to rub it in that whatever else Randall forgot he wasn't to forget *that*, that he had nothing to look to, nothing to hope for in his father-in-law's prospects ; as if he, Mr. Usher, had arranged this meeting at the "Bald-Faced Stag" for the express purpose of making that clear, of forestalling all possible misunderstanding. He kept it before him, with the cheese and beer, on the brown oil-cloth of the table from which poor Randall found it increasingly difficult to lift his eyes.

It was almost a relief to him when Mr. Usher pushed his plate away with a groan of satiety, and began.

"Well, what's all this I hear about Virelet ? "

Randall intimated that he had heard all there was.

"Yes, but what's the meaning of it ? That's what I want to know."

Randall put it that its meaning was that it had simply happened, and suggested that his father-in-law was in every bit as good a position for understanding it as he.

"I daresay. But what I'm trying to get at is—did you do anything to make it happen ? "

"What on earth do you suppose I did ? "

"There might be faults on both sides, though I don't say as there were. But did you do anything to prevent it ? Tell me that."

"What could I do ? I didn't know it was going to happen."

"You should have known. You was warned fair enough."

"Was I ? Who warned me, I should like to know ? "

"Why, I did, and her mother did. Told you straight. Don't you go for to say that I let you marry the girl under false pretences, or her mother either. I told you what sort Virelet was, straight as I·could, without vilifying my own flesh and blood. Did you want me to tell you straighter ? Did you want me to put a name to it ? "

His little eyes shot sidelong at Randall, out of his fallen, shrunken fatness, more than ever crafty and intent.

He was pitiful. Randall could have been sorry for him but that he showed himself so mean. His little eyes gave him so villainously away. They disclosed the fulness of his knowledge ; they said he had known things about Violet ; he had known them all the time, things that he, Randall, never knew. And he hadn't let on, not he. Why should he ? He had been too eager, poor man, to get Violet married. His eagerness, that had appeared as the hardy flower of his geniality, betrayed itself now as the sinister thing it was—when you thought of the name that he could have given her !

Randall did not blame him. He was past blaming anybody. He only said to himself that this explained what had seemed so inexplicable—the attitude, the incredible attitude of Mr. and Mrs. Usher ; how they had leaped at him in all his glaring impossibility, an utter stranger, with no adequate income and no prospects ; how they had hurried on the marriage past all prudence ; how they had driven him on and fooled him and helped him to his folly.

But he was not going to let them fool him any more.

" Look here, Mr. Usher, I don't know what your game is and I don't care. I daresay you *think* you told me what you say you did. But you didn't. You didn't tell me anything—not one blessed thing. And if you had it wouldn't have done any good. I wouldn't have believed you. You needn't reproach yourself. I was mad on Virelet. I meant to marry her and I did marry her. That's all."

" Well," said Mr. Usher, partially abandoning his position, " so long as you don't hold me responsible——"

" Of course, I don't hold you responsible."

" I'm sure me and the Missis we've done what we could to make it easier for you."

He gazed before him, conjuring up between them a quiet vision of the long procession of hampers, a reminder to Randall of how deeply, as it was, he stood indebted.

"And we can't do no more. That's how it is. No more we can't do."

"I'm not asking you to do anything. What do you *want?*"

"I want to know what you're going to do, my boy."

"Do?"

"Yes, do."

"About what?"

"About Virelet. Talk of responsibility, you took it on yourself contrary to the warnings what you had, when you married her. And having taken it you ought to have looked after her. Knowing what she is you ought to have looked after her better than you've done."

"How *could* I have looked after her?"

"How? Why, as any other man would. You should have made her work, work with her 'ands, as I told you, 'stead of giving her her head, like you did, and lettin' her sit bone-idle in that gimcrack doll-house of yours from morning till night. Why, you should have taken a stick to her. There's many a man as would, before he'd a let it come to that. Damn me if I know why you didn't."

"Well, really, Mr. Usher, I suppose I couldn't forget she was a woman."

"Woman? Woman? I'd a womaned 'er! Look 'ere, my boy, it's a sad business, and there's no one sorrier for you than I am, but there's no good you and me broodin' mournful over what she's done. Course she'd do it, 's long's you let her. You hadn't ought to 'ave let 'er. And seein' as how you have, seems to me what you've got to do now is to take her back again."

"I can't take her back again."

"And why not?"

"Because of the children—for one thing."

That argument had its crushing effect on Mr. Usher.

It made him pause a perceptible moment before he answered.

" Well—you needn't look to me and her mother to 'ave her——"

Randall rose, as much as to say that this was enough ; it was too much ; it was the end.

" We've done with her. You took her out of our 'ands what 'ad a hold on her, and you owe it to her mother and me to take her back."

" If that's all you've got to say, Mr. Usher——"

" It isn't all I've got to say. What I got to say is this. Before you was married, Randall, I don't mind telling you now, my girl was a bit too close about you for my fancy. I've never rightly understood how you two came together."

There, as they fixed him, his little eyes took on their craftiness again and his mouth a smile, a smile of sensual tolerance and understanding, as between one man of the world and another.   /

" I don't know, and I don't want to know. But however it was—I'm not askin', mind you—however it was "— He was all solemn now—" you made yourself responsible for that girl. And responsible you will be held."

It may have been that Mr. Usher drew a bow at a venture ; it may have been that he really knew, that he had always known. Anyhow, that last stroke of his was, in its way, consummate. It made it impossible for Randall to hit back effectively ; impossible for him to say now, if he had wished to say it, that he had not been warned (for it seemed to imply that if Mr. Usher's suspicions were correct, Randall had had an all-sufficient warning) ; impossible for him to maintain, as against a father whom he, upon the supposition, had profoundly injured, an attitude of superior injury. If Mr. Usher had deceived Randall, hadn't Randall, in the first instance, deceived Mr. Usher ? In short, it left them quits. It closed Randall's mouth, and with it the discussion, and so that the balance as between them leaned if anything to Mr. Usher's side.

" Well, I'm sorry for you, Randall."

As if he could afford it now Mr. Usher permitted himself a return to geniality. He paused in the doorway.

" If at any time you should want a hamper, you've only got to say so."

And Randall did not blame him. He said to himself, " Poor old thing. It's funk—pure funk. He's afraid he may have to take her back himself. And who could blame him ? "

Funny that his father-in-law should have taken the same line as his Uncle Randall. Only, whereas his Uncle Randall had reckoned with the alternative of divorce, his father-in-law had not so much as hinted at the possibility.

It was almost as if Mr. Usher had had a glimpse of what was to come when he had been in such haste, haste that had seemed in the circumstances hardly decent, to saddle Ransome with the responsibility.

For, if Ransome had really thought that Violet was going to let him off without his paying for it, the weeks that followed brought him proof more than sufficient of his error. He had sown to the winds in the recklessness of his marriage and of his housekeeping, and he reaped the whirlwind in Violet's bills that autumn shot into the letter-box at Granville.

He called there every other day for letters ; for he was not yet prepared, definitely, to abandon Granville.

The bills, when he had gathered them all in, amounted in their awful total to twenty pounds odd, a sum that exceeded his worst dreams of Violet's possible expenditure. He had realised, in the late summer and autumn of last year, before the period of compulsory retirement had set in, that his wife was beginning to cost him more than she had ever done, more than any woman of his class, so far as he knew, would have dreamed of costing ; and this summer, no sooner had she emerged triumphant than—with two children now to provide for—she had launched out upon a scale that fairly terrified him. But all her past extravagance did nothing to prepare him for the extent to which, as he expressed it, she could " go it," when she had, as you might say, an incentive.

The most astounding of the bills his whirlwind swept him was the bill from Starker's—from Oxford Street, if you please—and the bill (sent in with a cynical promptitude) from the chemist in Acacia Avenue at the corner. That, the chemist's, was in a way the worst. It was for scent, for toilette articles, strange yet familiar to him from their presence in his father's shop, for all manner of cosmetics, for things so outrageous, so unnecessary, that they witnessed chiefly to the shifts she had been put to, to her anxieties and hastes, to the feverish multiplication of pretexts and occasions. Still, they amounted but to a few pounds and an odd shilling or two. Starker's bill did the rest.

That, the high resplendent " cheek " of it, showed what she was capable of ; it gave him the measure of her father's " funk," for, of not one of the items, from the three-guinea costumes (there were several of them) down to the dozen of open-work Lisle thread hose at two and eleven the pair, had Ransome so much as suspected the existence. The three-guinea costumes he could understand. It was the three night-gowns, trimmed lace, at thirteen, fifteen and sixteen shillings apiece, that took his breath away, as with a vision of her purposes. Still, to him, her husband, Starker's statement of account represented directly, with the perfection of business precision, the cost of getting rid of her ; it was so simply and openly the cost of her outfit, of all that she had trailed with her in her flight.

Yet, as he grasped it, he saw with that mature comprehension which was now his, that, awful as it was, that total of twenty pounds odd represented, perfectly, the price of peace. It was open to him to repudiate his wife's debts, in which case she would appear in the County Court, which, with its effect of publicity, with the things that would be certain to come out there, was almost as bad as the Divorce Court. Then the unfortunate tradespeople would not be paid, a result of her conduct which was intolerable to Ranny's decency. Besides, he wanted to be rather more than decent, to be handsome, in his squaring of accounts with the woman whom, after all, in the beginning he had wronged. He could even reflect with a humour surviving all calamity, that though twenty odd pounds was a devil of a lot to pay, his deliverance was cheap, dirt cheap, at the money.

But that was not all. There was Granville.

He hated Granville. He could not believe how he ever could have loved it. The fact that he was gradually becoming his own landlord only made things worse. It gave Granville a malignant power over him, that power which he had once or twice suspected, the power to round on him and injure him and pay him back. He knew he was partly responsible for Granville's degradation. He had done nothing for this property of his. He had not given it a distinctive character ; he had not covered it with creepers or painted it green or built a balcony. He had left it to itself.

He asked himself what it would look like in seventeen years' time when it would be his. In seventeen years' time he would be forty-two. What good would he be then ? And what good would Granville be to him ? What good was it now ? In its malignancy it demanded large sums to keep it going and if it didn't get them it knew how to avenge itself. Slowly perishing, it would fall to dust in seventeen years' time when it came into his hands.

But he had not dreamed of the extent to which Granville could put on the screw.

He was enlightened by the agent of the Estate Company to which Granville owed its being. The agent, after a thorough inspection of the premises, broke it to Ransome that if he did not wish to lose Granville, he would have to undertake certain necessary repairs, the estimate for which soared to the gay tune of ten pounds eight shillings and eightpence. It was the state of the roof, of the south-west wall, and of the scullery drain that most shocked the agent. Of the scullery drain he could hardly bring himself to speak, remarking only that a little washing down from time to time with soda would have saved it all. The state of that drain was a fair disgrace ; and it was not a thing of days ; it dated from months back—years, he shouldn't be surprised. It was fit to breed a fever.

Of course, it wasn't quite as bad as the agent had made out. But Ranny, knowing Violet, believed him. It gave him a feeling of immense responsibility towards Granville, and the Estate Company, and the agent.

Finally, owing to Violet's reckless management, his debts to the grocer, the butcher, and the milkman had reached the considerable total of nine pounds eighteen shillings and eleven pence. It would take-about forty pounds odd to clear his obligations.

The question was how on earth was he to raise the money? Out of a salary of twelve pounds a month ?

He would have to borrow it. But from whom ? Not from his father. To whatever height his mother kept it up, she could not conceal from him that his father was in difficulties. Wandsworth was going ahead, caught by the tide of progress. The new Drug Stores over the way were drawing all the business from Fulleymore Ransome's little shop. Even with the assistance of the young man, Mr. Ponting, Fulleymore Ransome was not in a state to hold his own. But John Randall, the draper, if you like, was prosperous. He might be willing, Ransome thought, to lend him the money, or a part of it, at a fair rate of interest.

And John Randall indeed lent him thirty pounds ; but not willingly. His reluctance, however, was sufficiently explained by the fact that he had recently advanced more than that sum to Fulleymore. He was careful to point out to Randall that he was helping him to meet only those catastrophes which might be regarded as the act of God— Violet's bills and the deterioration of Granville. He was as anxious as Randall himself to prevent Violet's appearance in the County Court, and he certainly thought it was a pity that good house property should go out of his nephew's hands. But he refused flatly to advance the ten pounds for the weekly arrears, in order to teach Randall a lesson, to make him feel that he had some responsibility, and to show that there was a limit to what he, John Randall, was prepared to do.

For days Ransome went distracted. The ten pounds still owing was like a millstone round his neck. If he didn't look sharp and pay up *he* would be County-Courted too. He couldn't come down on his father-in-law. His father-in-law would tell him that he had already received the equivalent of ten pounds in hampers. There was nobody he *could* come down on. So he called at a place he had heard of in Shaftesbury Avenue, where there was a " josser " who arranged it for him quite simply by means of a bill of sale upon his furniture. After all, he did get some good out of that furniture.

And he got some good, too, out of Granville when he let it to Fred Booty for fifteen shillings a week.

He was now established definitely in his father's house. The young man Mr. Ponting had shown how kind his heart was by turning out of his nice room on the second floor into Ranny's old attic. The little back room, used for storage, served also as a day nursery for Ranny's children. Six days in the week a little girl came in to mind them. At night Ranny minded them where they lay in their cots by his bed.

It was all that could be done ; and with the little girl's

board and the children's and his own breakfast and supper and his Sunday dinner, it cost him thirty shillings a week. There was no way in which it could be done for less, since it was not in him to take advantage of his mother's offer to let him have the rooms rent free.

And underneath Ranny's rooms, between the bedroom at the back and the back parlour, between the parlour and the shop, between the shop and the dispensing room, Fulleymore Ransome dragged himself to and fro, more than ever weedy, more than ever morose, more than ever sublime in his appearance of integrity ; and with it all so irritable that Ranny's children had to be kept out of his way. He would snarl when he heard them overhead ; he would scowl horribly when he came across the " pram," pushed by the little girl, in its necessary progress through the shop into the street and back again.

But at Ranny he neither snarled nor scowled, nor had he spoken any word to him on the subject of the great calamity. No reproach, no reminder of warnings given, none of that reiterated " I told you so," in which, Ranny reflected, he might have taken it out of him. He also seemed to regard his son Randall as one smitten by God and afflicted, to whose high and sacred suffering silence was the appropriate tribute. His very moroseness provided the sanctuary of silence.

And all the time he drank ; he drank worse than ever ; furtively, continuously he drank. Nobody could stop him, for nobody ever saw him doing it. He did it, they could only suppose, behind Mr. Ponting's back in the dispensing-room.

They were free to suppose anything now ; for, since Ranny's great delivering outburst, they could discuss it ; and in discussion they found relief. Ranny's mother owned as much. She had suffered (that also she owned) from the strain of keeping it up. Ranny's outburst had saved her, vicariously. It was as if she had burst out herself.

There were, of course, lengths to which she would never go, admissions which she could not bring herself to make. There had to be some subterfuge, some poor last shelter for her pride. And so, of the depression in Fulleymore's business she would say before Mr. Ponting, "It's those Drug Stores that are ruining him." And Mr. Ponting would reply gravely, "They'd ruin anybody."

Mr. Ponting was a fresh-coloured young man and good-looking, with his blue eyes and his yellow hair sleeked backwards like folded wings, so different from Mercier. Mr. Ponting had conceived an affection for Ranny and the children. He would find excuses to go up to the storeroom, where he would pretend to be looking for things while he was really playing with Dossie. He would sit on Ranny's bed while Ranny was undressing, and together they would consider, piously, the grave case of the Humming-bird, and how, between them, they could best "keep him off it."

"It's the dispensary spirits that he gets at," Mr. Ponting said. "That's the trouble."

(And it always had been.)

"The queer thing is," said Ranny, "that you never fairly see him tight. Not to speak of."

"That's the worst of it," said Mr. Ponting. "I wish I *could* see your father tight—tumbling about a bit, I mean, and being funny. The beastly stuff's going for him inside, all the time—undermining him. There isn't an organ," said Mr. Ponting solemnly, "in your father's body that it hasn't gone for."

"How d'you know?"

"Why, by the medicines he takes. He's giving himself strophanthus now, for his heart."

"I say—d'you think my mother knows that?"

"It's impossible to say what your mother knows. More than she lets on, I shouldn't be surprised."

Mr. Ponting pondered.

" It's wonderful how he keeps it up. His dignity, I mean."

" It's rum, isn't it ? " said Ranny. He was apparently absorbed in tying the strings of his sleeping suit into loops of absolutely even length. " But he always *was* that mysterious kind of bird."

He began to step slowly backwards as he buttoned up his jacket. Then, by way of throwing off the care that oppressed him, and lightening somewhat Mr. Ponting's burden, he ran forwards and took a flying leap over the Baby's cot into his own bed.

Mr. Ponting looked, if anything, a little graver. " I wouldn't do that, if I were you," he said.

" Why not ? " said Ranny over his blankets, snuggling comfortably.

" Oh, I don't know," said Mr. Ponting vaguely.

In a day or two Ranny himself knew.

His arrangements had carried him well on into October. In the last week of that month, on a Tuesday evening, he appeared at the Regent Street Polytechnic, where he had not been seen since far back in the last year. It was not at the Gymnasium that he now presented himself but at the door of that room where every Tuesday evening, from seven-thirty to eight-thirty, a qualified practitioner was in attendance.

It was the first time that Ransome had availed himself of this privilege conferred on him by the Poly.

He said he wouldn't keep the medical man a minute.

But the medical man kept Ranny many minutes, thumping, sounding, intimately and extensively overhauling him. For more minutes than Ranny at all liked, he played about him with a stethoscope. Then he fired off what Ranny supposed to be the usual questions.

" Had any shock, worry, or excitement lately ?

" Been overdoing it in any way ?

" Gone in much for athletics ? "

Ranny replied with regret that it was more than three years since he had last run in the Wandsworth Hurdle Race.

He was then told that he must avoid all shock, worry, or excitement. He mustn't overdo it. He must drop his hurdle-racing. He mustn't bicycle uphill, or against the wind ; he mustn't jump ; he mustn't run——

" Not even to catch a train ? "

" Not to catch anything."

And the doctor gave him a prescription that ran :

> " Sodæ Bicarb., one dram.
> Tinct. Strophanthi, two drams—"

He remembered. That was the stuff he'd measured for old Mr. Beesley's heart-mixture. It was the stuff that Ponting said his father was taking now.

If anyone had told him three years ago that his heart was rocky he'd have told them where to go to. It had been as sound as a bell when he entered for the Poly. Gym.

Well, he supposed that was about the finishing touch— if they wanted to do the thing in style.

He went slowly over Wandsworth Bridge and up the High Street, dejected, under the autumn moon that had once watched his glad sprinting.

S

XXVII

AND in all this time he had not heard again from Violet, nor had he written to her.

Then—it was in the first week of November—Violet wrote.

She wrote imploring him to set her free. It was rooted in her, the fear that he would compel her to come back, that he had the power to make her. She wanted (he seemed to see it) to feel safe from him for ever. Leonard had promised to marry her if she were free. She intimated that Leonard was everything that was generous and honourable. She wanted (she who had abused him so for having married her), she wanted to marry Mercier, to have a hold on him and be safe. Marriage was her idea of safety now.

She went on to say that if he would consent to divorce her, it would be made easy for him, she would not defend the suit.

That meant—he puzzled it out—that meant that it would lie between the two of them. Nobody else would be dragged into it. Winny's name would not by any possibility be dragged in. Violet would have no use for Winny, since she was not going to defend the suit. She might—at the worst—have to appear as witness, if the evidence of Violet's letters (her own admission) was not sufficient. It looked as if it would be simple enough. Why should he not release her? He had no business not to give her the chance to marry Mercier, to regulate the relation, if that was what she wanted.

It was his own chance too, his one chance. He would be a fool not to take it.

And as it came over him in its fulness, all that it meant

and would yet mean, Ranny felt his heart thumping and bounding, dangerously, in its weakened state.

On a Wednesday evening in November, he presented himself once more at the Regent Street Polytechnic and at the door of an office where, on Wednesday evenings, an experienced legal adviser held himself in readiness to give advice, that legal adviser who had been the jest of his adolescence, whose services he had not conceived it possible that he should require.

He had a curiously uplifting sense of the gravity and impressiveness of the business upon which at last, inconceivably, he came. But this odd elation was controlled and finally overpowered by disgust and shame, as one by one, under the kind but acute examination of the legal man, he brought out for his inspection the atrocious details. And he had to show Violet's letter of September, the document, supremely valuable, supremely infamous, supported by the further communication of November. The keen man asked him, as his uncle and his father-in-law had asked, if he had given any provocation, any cause for jealousy, misunderstanding, or the like? Had his own conduct been irreproachable? When all this part of it was over, settled to the keen man's satisfaction, Ranny was told that there was little doubt that he could get his divorce if—that was the question—he could afford to pay. Divorce was, yes, it was a costly matter, almost, you might say, the luxury of the rich. A matter, for him, probably of forty or fifty pounds—well, say, thirty, when you'd cut expenses down to the very lowest limit. Could he, the keen but kindly man enquired, afford thirty?

No, he couldn't. He couldn't afford twenty even. With all his existing debts upon him he couldn't now raise ten.

He asked whether he could get his divorce if he put it off a bit until he could afford it?

The legal man looked grave.

"Well—yes. If you can show poverty——"

Ranny thought he could undertake to show *that* all right.

At the legal man's suggestion he wrote a letter to his wife assuring her that it was impossible for her to desire a divorce more than he did; that he meant to bring an action at the very moment when he could afford it, pointing out to her that her debts which he had paid had not made this any easier for him; that in the meanwhile she need not be anxious; that he would not follow her or molest her in any way; and that in no circumstances would he take her back.

And now Ranny's soul and all his energy were set upon the one aim of raising money for his divorce. It was impossible to lay his hands upon that money all at once. He could not do it this year, nor yet the next, for his expenses and his debts together exceeded the amount of his income; but gradually, by pinching and scraping, it might be done perhaps in two or three years' time.

His chief trouble was that in all these weeks he had seen nothing of Winny. He had called twice at the side door of Johnson's, but they had told him that she was not in; and, hampered as he was with the children, he had not had time to call again. Besides, he knew he had to be careful, and Winny knew it too. That, of course, would always help him, her perception of the necessity for care. There were ways of managing these things, but they required his mother's or his friends' co-operation; and so far Mrs. Ransome had shown no disposition to co-operate. Winny was not likely to present herself at Wandsworth without encouragement, and she had apparently declined to lend herself to any scheme of Maudie's or of Fred Booty's. With Winny lying low there was nothing left for him but the way he shrank from, of persistent and unsolicited pursuit.

November passed and they were in December, and he had not seen her. After having recovered somewhat under the influence of the drug strophanthus, he now became depressed, listless, easily fatigued.

Up till now there had been something not altogether

disagreeable to Mrs. Ransome in the misfortunes of her son. They had brought him back to her. But he had not wanted to come back; and now she wondered whether she had done well to make him come, whether (after all he had gone through) it was not too much for him, realising as he did his father's awful state. It had gone so far, Mr. Ransome's state, that there was no way in which it could be taken lightly.

And she was depressed herself, perceiving it. Mr. Ransome's state made him unfit for business now, unfit to appear in the shop, above all unfit for the dispensary. Fit only to crawl from room to room and trouble them with the sad stare of his peaked and peevish face. He required watching. He himself recognised that in his handling of tricky drugs there was a danger. The business was getting out of hand. It was small and growing smaller every month, yet it was too much for Mr. Ponting to cope with unassisted. They were living, all three of them, in a state of tension most fretting to the nerves.

The whole house fairly vibrated with it. It was as if the fearful instability of Mr. Ransome's nervous system communicated itself to everybody around him. At the cry or the sudden patter of Ranny's children overhead, Mr. Ransome would be set quivering and shaking, and this disturbance of his reverberated. Ranny set his teeth and sat tight and "stuck it"; but he felt the shattering effect of it all the same.

And the children felt it too, subtly, insidiously. Dossie became peevish, easily frightened; she was neither so good nor so happy with her Granny and the little girl as she had been with Winny. Baby cried oftener. Ranny sometimes would be up half the night with him.

All this Mrs. Ransome saw and grieved over and was powerless to help.

In Christmas week the state of Mr. Ransome became terrible, not to be borne. Ranny was working hard at the counting-house; he was worn out and he looked it.

The sight of him, so changed, broke Mrs. Ransome down.

" Ranny," she said, " I wish you'd get away somewhere for Christmas. Me and Mabel'll look after the children. You go."

He said there wasn't anywhere he cared to go to.

" Well—is there anything you'd like to do? "

" To do? "

" For Christmas, dear. To make it not so sad like. Is there anybody," she said, " you'd like to ask? "

No, there wasn't. At any rate, if there was he wouldn't ask them. It wouldn't be exactly what you'd call fun for them, with the poor old Humming-bird making faces at them all the time.

His mother looked at him shrewdly and said nothing. But she sat down and wrote a letter to Winny Dymond, asking her to come and spend Christmas Day with them, if, said Mrs. Ransome, she hadn't anywhere better to go to and didn't mind a sad house.

And Winny came. She hadn't anywhere better to go to, and she didn't mind a sad house in the least.

They wondered, Ranny and his mother, how they were ever going to break it to the Humming-bird.

" Your Father won't like it, Ranny. He's not fit for it. He'll think us heartless, having strangers in the house when He's suffering so."

But Mr. Ransome, when asked if he was fit for it, replied astoundingly that he was fit enough if it would make Randall any happier.

It did. It made him so happy that his recovery dated from that moment. He had only one fear, that Dossie would have forgotten Winky.

But Dossie hadn't, though after two months of Wandsworth she had forgotten many things, and had cultivated reserve. When Ranny said, " Who's this, Dossie? " she tucked her head into her shoulder and smiled shyly and said, " Winty." But they had to pretend that Baby remembered, too. He hadn't really got what you would call a memory.

And, after all, it was Ranny (Winny said to herself) who remembered most. For he gave her for a Christmas present, not only a beautiful white satin " sashy," scented with lavender (lavender, not violets, this time), but a wonderful hot-water bag with a shaggy red coat that made you warm to look at it.

" Ranny ! Fancy you remembering that I had cold feet ! "

That night he went home with her to Johnson's side-door, carrying the sachet and the hot-water bag and the things his mother had given her.

Upstairs, in the attic she shared with three other young ladies, the first thing Winny did was to turn to the Cookery Book she had bought a year ago and read the directions: " How to Preserve Hot-Water Bags "—to preserve them for ever.

XXVIII

THUS nineteen-seven, that dreadful year, rolled over into nineteen-eight. By nineteen-ten, at the very latest, Ransome looked to get his divorce. He had no doubt that he could do it, for he found it far less expensive to live with his mother at Wandsworth than with Violet at Granville. He knew exactly where he was, he had not to allow so considerably for the unforeseen. His income had a margin out of which he saved. To make this margin wider he pinched, he scraped, he went as shabby as he dared, he left off smoking, he renounced his afternoon cup of tea and reduced the necessary dinner at his A B C shop to its very simplest terms.

The two years passed.

By January, nineteen-ten, he had only paid off what he already owed. He had not raised the thirty pounds required for his divorce. Indomitable, but somewhat desperate, he applied to his Uncle Randall for a second loan at the same interest. He did not conceal from him that divorce was his object. He put it to him that his mind was made up unalterably, and that since the thing had got to be, sooner or later, it was better for everybody's sake that it should be sooner.

But Mr. Randall was inexorable. He refused, flatly, to lend his money for a purpose that he persisted in regarding as iniquitous. Even if he had not advanced a further sum to young Randall's father, he was not going to help young Randall through the Divorce Court, stirring all that mud again. Not he.

"You should wash your dirty linen at home," he said.

"You mean keep it there and never wash it. That's what it comes to," said young Randall furiously.

"It's been kept. And everybody's forgotten that it's there by this time. Why rake it up again?" said his Uncle Randall.

And there was no making him see why. There was no making any of them see. Mrs. Ransome wouldn't hear of the divorce. "It'll kill your Father, Ranny," she said, and stuck to it.

And Ranny set his mouth hard and said nothing. He calculated that if he put by twelve shillings a week for twenty-five weeks that would be fifteen pounds. He could borrow the other fifteen in Shaftesbury Avenue as he had done before, and in six months he would be filing his petition.

As soon as he was ready to file it he would tell Winny he cared for her. He would ask her to be his wife.

He had not told any of them about Winny. But they knew. They knew and yet they had no pity on him, nor yet on her. When he thought of it Ranny set his face harder.

Yet Winny came and went, untroubled and apparently unconscious. She was not only allowed to come and go at Wandsworth as she had come and gone at Granville, by right of her enduring competence; she was desired and implored to come. For if she had (and Mrs. Ransome owned it) a "way" with the children; she had also a way with Mrs. Ransome, and with Mr. Ransome. The Humming-bird, growing weedier and weaker, revived in her presence; he relaxed a little of his moroseness and austerity. "I don't know how it is," said Ranny's mother, "but your Father takes to her. He likes to see her about."

Saturday afternoons, and Sundays, and late evenings in summer were her times, so that of necessity she and Ranny met.

Not that they pleaded necessity for meeting. Since his awful enlightenment and maturity, Ransome had never thought of pleading anything ; for he did not hold himself accountable to anybody or require anybody to tell him what was decent and what wasn't. And Winny was like him. He couldn't imagine Winny driven to plead. She had gone her own way without troubling her head about what people thought of her, without thinking very much about herself. As long as she was sure he wanted her, she would be there, where he was. He felt rather than knew that she waited for him, and would wait for him through interminable years, untroubled as to her peace, profoundly pure. He was not even certain that she was aware that she was waiting and that he waited too.

In the spring of nineteen-ten it looked as if they would not have very long to wait. He had measured his resources with such accuracy that by June, if all went well, he could set about filing his petition.

And now, seeing the thing so near and yet not accomplished, Ranny's nerve went. He began to be afraid, childishly and ridiculously afraid, of something happening to prevent it. He had a clear and precise idea of that something. He would die before he could file his petition, before he could get his divorce and marry Winny. His heart to be sure was better ; but at any moment it might get worse. It might get like his father's. It might stop altogether. He thought of it as he had never thought of it before. He humoured it. He never ran. He never jumped. He never rode uphill on his bicycle. He thought twice before hurrying for anything. Against these things he could protect himself.

But who could protect him against excitement and worry and anxiety ? Why, this fear that he had was itself the worst thing for him imaginable. And then worry. He *had*

to worry. You couldn't look on and see the poor old
Humming-bird going from bad to worse, you couldn't
see everybody else worrying about him, and not worry
too. He would go away and forget about it for a time,
and when he came back again the terrible and intolerable
thing was there.

And at the heart of the trouble there was a still more
terrible and intolerable peace. It was as if Mr. Ransome
had made strange terms with the youth and joy and innocent life that had once roused him to such profound resentment and disgust. His vindictive ubiquity had ceased.
When the spring came he could no longer drag himself up
and downstairs. His feet and legs were swollen ; they were
like enormous weights attached to his pitifully weedy
body. His skin had the sallow smoothness, the waxen
substance that marked the deadly, unmistakable progress
of his disease. He could not always lie down in his bed.
Sometimes he lived, day and night, motionless in his
invalid's chair, with his legs propped before him on a foot-
rest. He would sit for hours staring at them in lamentable
contemplation. He could measure his span of life from
day to day as the swelling rose or sank. On his good days
they wheeled him from his bedroom at the back to the
front sitting-room.

And through it all, as by some miracle, he preserved
his air of suffering integrity.

It was quite plain to Ranny that his father could not
live long. And if he died ? Even in his pity and his grief
Ranny could not help wondering whether, if his father
died any time that year, it would not make a difference,
whether it would not, perhaps, at the last moment prevent
his marrying ?

Partly in defiance of this fear, partly by way of committing himself irretrievably, he resolved to speak to Winny.
He desired to be irretrievably committed, so that, whatever
happened, decency alone would prevent him from drawing
back. Though he could not in as many words ask Winny

to marry him before he was actually free, there were things that could be said, and he saw no earthly reason why he should not say them.

For this purpose he chose, in sheer decency, one of his father's good days which happened to be a fine warm one in May and a Saturday. He had arranged with Winny beforehand that she should come over as early as possible in the afternoon and stay for tea. He now suggested that, as this Saturday was such a Saturday as they might never see again, it would be a good plan if they were to go somewhere together.

" Where ? " said Winny.

Wherever she liked, he said, provided it was somewhere where they'd never been before. And Winny, trying to think of something not too expensive, said, " How about the tram to Putney Heath ? "

" Putney Heath," Ranny said, " be blowed ! "

" Well, then—how about Hampton Court or Kew ? "

But he was "on to" her. " Rot ! " he said. " You've been there."

" Well——" Obviously she was meditating something equally absurd.

" What d'you say to Windsor ? "

But Winny absolutely refused to go to Windsor. She said there was one place she'd never been to, and that was Golder's Hill. You could get tea there.

" Right—o ! " said Ranny. " We'll go to Golder's Hill."

" And take the children," Winny said.

Well, no, he rather thought he'd leave the kids behind for once.

" Oh, Ranny ! " Voice and eyes reproached him. " You couldn't ! You may never get a day like this again."

" I know. That's why," said Ranny.

The kids, Stanley, aged three, and Dossie, aged five, understanding perfectly well that they were being thrown over, began to cry.

" Daddy, take *me*—take *me*," sobbed Dossie.

" And me ! " Stanley positively screamed it.

" I say, you know, if they're going to howl," said Ranny.

" You *must*—— "

" That's it, I mustn't. They can't have everything they choose to howl for."

" There," said Winny. " See ! Daddy can't take you if you cry. He can't, really."

(She had gone—perfidious Winny !—to the drawer where she knew Stanley's clean suit was. Stanley knew it too.)

The children stopped crying as by magic. With eyes where pathos and resentment mingled they gazed at their incredible father. Tears, large crystal tears, hung on the flame-red crests of their hot cheeks.

Winny turned before she actually opened the drawer.

" Who wants," said she, " to go with Daddy ? "

" Me," said Dossie.

" Me," said Stanley.

" Well, then, give Daddy a kiss and ask him nicely. Then perhaps he'll take you."

And they did, and he had to take them. But it was mean, it was treacherous of Winny.

" What did you do that for, Winky ? " he said, going over to her where she rummaged in the drawer.

" Because," she said, " you promised."

" Promised what ? "

" Promised you'd take them. Promised Stanny he should wear his knickers. They told me you'd promised."

And he had.

" I forgot," he said.

" *They'd* never have forgotten."

She was holding them, the ridiculous knickers, to the nursery fire.

It took ten minutes to get Stanley into them, into the little blue linen knickers he had never worn before, and into his tight little white jersey ; and then there was

Dossie and her wonderful rig-out, the clean white frock and the serge jacket of turquoise-blue and the tiny mushroom hat with the white ribbon. It took five minutes more to find Stanley's hat, the little soft hat of white felt in which he was so adorable. They found it on Ranny's bed, and then they started.

It was a great, an immense adventure, right away to the other side of London.

" We'll take everything we can," said Ranny. And they did. They took the motor-bus to Earl's Court Tube Station, and the Tube (two Tubes they had to take) to Golder's Green. The adventure began in the first lift.

" Where we goin' ? " the children cried. " Where we goin', Daddy ? "

" We're going down—down—ever so far down, with London on the top of us—All the horses "—Winny worked the excitement up and up—" All the people—All the motor-buses on the top of us——"

" On top of me ? "

" And on me ? " cried Dossie. " And on Daddy and on Winky ? "

" Will it make us *dead ?* " said Stanley. He was thrilled at the prospect.

" No. More alive than ever. We shall come rushing out, like bunny rabbits, into the country on the other side."

Ever so far down into the earth they went, with London, and then Camden Town, and then Hampstead Heath—a great big high hill—right on the top of them ; and then, all of a sudden, just as Winny had said, they came rushing out, more alive than ever, into the country, into the green fields.

But there was something wrong with Ranny. He wasn't like himself. He wasn't excited or amused or interested in anything. He looked as if he were trying not to hear what Winny was saying to the children. He was abstracted. He went like a man in a dream. He behaved almost as

if he wanted to show that he didn't really belong to
them.

Of course, he did all the proper things. He carried his
little son. He lifted him and Dossie in and out of the
trains as if they had been parcels labelled "Fragile, with
Care." But he did it like a porter, a sulky porter who was
tired of lifting things ; and they might really have been
somebody else's glass and china for all he seemed to care.

Ranny was angry. He was angry with the little things
for being there. He was angry with himself for having
brought them and with Winny for having made him bring
them ; and he was angry with himself for being angry.
But he couldn't help it. Their voices exasperated him.
The children's voices, the high reiterated sing-song, "Where
we goin' ? " Winny's voice, poignantly soft, insufferably
patient, answering them with all that tender silliness, that
persistent, gentle, intolerably gentle tommy-rot.

For all the time he was saying to himself, "She doesn't
care. She doesn't care a hang. It's them she cares for.
It's them she wants. It's them she's wanted all the time.
She's that sort."

And as he brooded on it, hatred of Winky, who had so
fooled him, crept into his heart.

"Oh, Daddy!" Dossie shouted with excitement (they
had emerged into the beautiful open space in front of
Golder's Green Station). "Daddy, we're bunnies now!
We'll be dea' little baby bunnies. You'll be Father Bunny,
and Winky'll be Mrs. Mother Bun! *Be* a bunny, Daddy."

Perceiving his cruel abstraction, Dossie entreated and
implored. "*Be* it ! "

But Daddy refused to be a bunny or anything that was
required of him. So silent was he and so stern that even
Winny saw that there was something wrong. She knew
by the way he let Stanny down from his shoulder to the
ground, a way which implied that Stanny was not so
young nor yet so small and helpless as he seemed. He
could walk.

Stanny felt it ; he felt it in the jerk that landed him ; but he didn't care, he was far too happy.

"He's a young Turk," said Winny, and he was. By his whole manner, by the swing of his tiny arms, by his tilted, roguish smile, by his eyes, impudent and joyous (blue they were, like his mother's, but clear, tilted and curled like Ranny's), Stanny intimated that Daddy was sold if he imagined that to walk was not just what Stanny wanted. And in spite of it he was heart-rending, pathetic ; so small he was, with all his baby roundness accentuated absurdly by the knickers.

"He's just such another as you, Ranny," Winny said. (She was uncontrollable !) "Such a little man as he is, in those knickers."

"Damn his knickers," said Ranny to himself behind his set teeth. But he smiled all the same ; and by the time they had got into the wonderful walled garden of Golder's Hill he had recovered almost completely.

It was not decent to keep on sulking in a place which had so laid itself out to make you happy ; where the sunshine flowed round you and soaked into you and warmed you as if you were in a bath. The garden, enclosed in rose-red walls and green hedges, was like a great tank filled with sunshine ; sunshine that was visible, palpable, audible almost in its intensity ; sunshine caught and contained and brimming over, that quivered and flowed in and around the wall-flowers, tulips and narcissus, that drenched them through and through and covered them like water, and was thick with all their scents. You walked on golden paths through labyrinths of brilliant flowers, through arches, tunnels and bowers of green. You were netted in sunshine, drugged with sweet live smells, caged in with blossoms, pink and white, of the espaliers that clung, branch and bud, like carved lattice-work, flat to the garden wall.

Neither could he well have sulked in the great space outside, where the green lawns unrolled and flung them-

selves generously, joyously to the sun, or where, on the
light slope of the field beyond, the trees hung out their
drooping vans, lifted up green roof above green roof,
sheltering a happy crowd.

And even if these things, in their benignant, admonishing,
reminding beauty, had not restored his decency, he was
bound to soften and unbend, when, as they were going
over the rustic bridge, Stanny tried to turn himself upside
down among the water-lilies. And as he captured Stanny
by a miracle of dexterity, just in time, he realised, as if it
had been some new and remarkable discovery, that his
little son was dear to him.

By slow stages, after many adventures and delays, they
reached the menagerie on the south side.

" Oh, Daddy, Daddy, look at that funny bird ! "
Dossie tugged and shouted.

In a corner of his yard, round and round, with incon-
ceivable rapidity and an astounding innocence, as if he
imagined himself alone and unobserved, the Emu danced
like a bird demented. On tip-toe, absurdly elongated,
round and round, ecstatically, deliriously, he danced.
He danced till his legs and his neck were as one high
perpendicular pole and his body a mere whorl of feathers
spinning round it, driven by the flapping of his wings.

" He *is* making an almighty fool of himself," said
Ranny.

" What does he do it for, Daddy ? "
" Let's ask the keeper."
And they asked him.

" 'E's a Emu, that's what 'e is," said the keeper.
" That's what he does when he goes courtin'. Only there
won't be no courtin' for him this time. 'Is mate died
yesterday."

" And yet he dances," Winny said.
" And yet he dances. Heartless bird ! " said Ranny.
They looked at the Emu, who went on dancing as if
unobserved.

T

"Scandalous, I call it," Ranny said. "Unfeelin'."

"Perhaps," said Winny, "the poor thing doesn't know."

"Per'aps he does know, and that's why he's dancin'."

Winny gazed, fascinated, at the uplifted and ecstatic head.

"I know," she said. "It's his grief. It's affected his brain."

"It's Nacher," said the keeper, "that's what it is. Nacher's wound 'im up to go, and he goes, you see, whether or no. It's the instint in 'im and the time of year. 'E don't know no more than that."

"But that," said Winny, "makes it all the sadder."

She was sorry for the Emu, so bereaved and so deluded, dancing his fruitless, lamentable dance.

"He *is* funny, isn't he?" said Stanny.

And they went slowly, spinning out their pleasure, back to that part of the lawn where there were innumerable little tables covered with pink cloths, set out under the trees, and seated at the tables innumerable family parties, innumerable pairs of lovers, pairs of married people, pairs of working women and of working girls on holiday; all happy for their hour, all whispering, laughing, chattering, and drinking tea.

On the terrace in front of the big red house were other tables with white covers under awnings like huge sunshades, where people who could afford the terrace sat in splendour and in isolation and listened to the music, played on the verandah, of violins and 'cello and piano.

Ransome and Winny and the children chose a pink-covered table on the lawn under a holly tree in a place all by themselves. And they had tea there, such a tea as stands out for ever in memory, beautiful and solitary. What the children didn't have for tea, Ranny said, was not worth mentioning.

And after tea they sat in luxurious folding chairs under the terrace and listened to the violins, the 'cello and piano.

Other people were doing the same thing as if they had been invited to do it, as if they were all one party, with somewhere a friendly host and hostess imploring them to be seated, to be happy and to make themselves at home.

And down the slope of the lawn, Stanny and Dossie rolled over and over in the joy of life. And up the slope they toiled, laughing, to roll interminably down.

And the moments while they rolled were golden, priceless to Ranny. Winny, seated beside him on her chair, watched them rolling.

" It's Stanny's knickers," she said, " that I can't get over ! "

" I don't want to hear of them again " (the golden moments were so few). " You make me wish I hadn't brought those kids."

" Oh, Ranny ! " Her eyes were serious and reproachful.

" Well—I can't get you to myself one minute."

" But aren't we having quite a happy day ? " she said. " What with the beautiful flowers, and the music and the Emu——"

" You were sorry, Winky, for that disgraceful bird, and you're not a bit sorry for me."

" Why should I be ? "

" My case is similar."

Her eyes were serious still, but round the corners of her mouth a little smile was playing in secret by itself. She didn't know it was there, or she never would have let it play.

" Don't you know that I want to say things to you ? "

She looked at him and was frightened by the hunger in his eyes.

" Not now, Ranny," she said. " Not yet."

" Why not ? "

" I want "—she was desperate—" I want to listen to the music."

At that moment the violins and the 'cello were struggling together in a cry of anguish and of passion.

"You *don't*," he said savagely.

He was right. She didn't. The music, yearning and struggling, tore at her heart, set her nerves vibrating, her breast heaving. It was as if it drew her to Ranny, urgently, irresistibly, against her will.

"Not now, Ranny," she said, "not now." And it was as if she asked him to take pity on her.

"No," he said. "Not now. But presently, when I see you home."

"No. Not even then. Not at all. You mustn't, dear," she whispered.

"I shall."

They sat silent and let the music do with them as it would.

And the sun dropped to the fields and flooded them and sank far away, behind Harrow on the Hill. And they called the children, the tired children, to them and went home.

Stanny had to be carried all the way. He hung on his father's shoulder, utterly limp, utterly helpless, utterly pathetic.

"He's nothing but a baby after all," said Winny.

They were going over Wandsworth Bridge.

"Do you remember, Ranny, the first time you ever saw me home, going over this bridge? What a moon there was."

"I do. That *was* a moon," said Ranny.

There was no moon for them to-night.

It was in a clear twilight, an hour later, that he saw her home.

They went half the way without speaking, till they came to the little three-cornered grove beside the public footpath. It was deserted. He proposed that they should sit there for a while.

" It's the only chance I'll ever get," he said to himself. She consented. The plane trees sheltered them and made darkness for them where they sat.

" Winky," he said after an agonising pause, " you must have thought it queer that I've never thanked you for all you've done for me."

" Why should you ? It's so little. It's nothing."

" Do you suppose I don't know what it is and what you've done it for ? "

" Yes, Ranny, you know what I did it for, and you see it's been no good."

" How d'you mean, no good ? "

" It didn't do what I thought it would."

" What was that ? "

" It didn't keep poor Vi and you together.

" Reelly "—She went on as if she were delivering her soul at last of the burden that had been two heavy for it—" I can see it all now. It did more harm than good."

" How do you make that out ? "

" D'you mind talking about it ? "

" Not a bit."

" Well, don't you see—it made it easier for her. It gave her the time and everything she wanted. If I hadn't been there that night she couldn't have gone, Ranny. She wouldn't have left the children. She wouldn't, reelly. And I hadn't the sense to see it then."

" I'm glad you hadn't."

" Oh, why ? "

" Because then you wouldn't have been there. I knew you were trying to keep it all together. But it was bound to go. It couldn't have lasted. *She'd* have gone anyhow. You don't worry about that now, do you ? "

" Sometimes I can't help thinking of it."

" Don't think of it."

" I won't so long as you know what I did it for."

He meditated.

" I know what you did it for in the beginning. But—
Winks—You were there *afterwards*."

" Afterwards——? "

" After Virelet went you were doing things."

" Well—and didn't you want me ? "

" Of course I wanted you. Did you never wonder why
I let you do things? Why I can bear to take it from you?
Don't you know I couldn't let any other woman do what
you do for me ? "

" I'm glad if you feel like that about it."

" I don't believe you've any idea how I feel about it.
I don't believe you understand it yet." His voice
thickened.

" I couldn't have let you, Winny, if I hadn't cared for
you. I should have been a low animal, a mean swine to
let you if I hadn't cared. I'm not talking as if my caring
paid you back in any way. I couldn't pay you back, if I
worked for you for the rest of my life. But that's what
I'm going to do if I can get the chance."

She could feel him trembling beside her and she was
afraid.

" Would you let me ? " he said. " Would you have
me, Winny ? Do you care for me enough to have me ? "

" You know I've always cared for you."

" Would you marry me if I was free ? "

" Don't talk about it, dear. You mustn't."

" And why mustn't I ? "

" It's no good. You're not free. You married Vi,
dear, and whatever she's done you can't unmarry her."

" Can't I ? That's precisely what I can do ; and it's
what I'm going to do."

" You're not. You couldn't."

It seemed to him that she shrank from him in horror.

" You don't understand. You're talking as if she and I
cared for each other. That's at an end. It's done for.
She's asked me to divorce her."

" Asked you ? When ? "

" More than two years ago, and I promised. She wants to marry Mercier, and she'd better. I'd have been free two years ago if I'd had the money. But I've got it now. I've been saving for it. I've been doing nothing else, thinking of nothing else from morning till night for more than two years, because I meant to ask you to marry me."

" All that time ? "

" All that time."

" But, Ranny, you know you *needn't*. I'm quite happy."

" Are you ? "

" Yes. You mustn't think I'm not and that you've got to make anything up to me, because that would make me feel as if I'd—there's a word for it, I know, but I can't think of it. It's what horrid girls do to men when they're trying to get hold of them—as if I'd comp—comprised——"

" D'you mean compromised ? "

" Yes."

" I make you feel as if you'd compromised me ? "

" That's right.'"

" Well, I *am* jiggered ! If that doesn't about take the biscuit ! Winky, you're a blessing, you're a treasure, you're a treat, I could live for a fortnight on the things you find to say."

He would have drawn her to him but she held herself rigid.

" Well, but—I haven't—have I ? "

" If you mean, have you made me want to marry you, you *have*. Haven't I told you I've thought of nothing else for more than two years ? "

" D'you want it so badly, Ranny ? "

" I want *you* so badly. Didn't you know I did ? Of course you knew."

" No, Ranny, I didn't. I thought all the time perhaps some day poor Virelet would come back."

" She'll never come back."

" But, if she did ? If she changed her mind ? Perhaps she's changed it now and wants to come back and be good."

"If she did I wouldn't take her."

He felt her eyes turn on him through the dark in wonder.

"But you'd have to. You couldn't not."

"I could, and I would."

"No, Ranny, you wouldn't. You'd never be cruel to poor Vi."

"Don't talk about her. Don't think about her."

"But we must. There she is. There she's always been——"

"And here we are. And here we've always been. Have you ever thought for a minute of *yourself?* Have you ever thought of *me?* I'm sick of hearing you say ' poor Vi.' Poor Vi! D'you know why I won't take her back ? Why I can't forgive her ? It's not for what you know she's done. It's for something you never knew about. I've a good mind to tell you."

"No—don't. I'd rather not know. Whatever it was she couldn't help it."

"You ought to know. It was something she did to you."

"She never did anything to me, Ranny."

"Didn't she ? She did something to me that came to the same thing. I suppose you think I cared for her before I cared for you ? "

"Well—yes."

"I didn't then. It was the other way about. And she knew it. And she lied to me about you. She told me you didn't care for me."

"She told you——? "

"She told me."

"I didn't think that Virelet would have done that."

"Nor I."

She paused considering it.

"How did you find out it was a lie, Ranny ? Oh—oh—I suppose I showed you——"

"Not you. She owned up herself."

"When ? "

" That night she went off. She wrote it in that letter. She told me why she did it too. It was because she knew I cared for you and was afraid I'd marry you. She wasn't going to have that. Now you know what she is."

" Why did you believe her ? "

" Why, Winky, you, you little wretch, you took care of that all right."

" But Ranny, if you cared for me, why did you marry her ? "

" Because I was mad and she was mad and we neither of us knew what we were doing. It was something that got hold of us."

" Aren't you mad now, Ranny ? "

" Rather ! But I know what I'm doing all the same. I didn't know when I married Virelet."

" Don't talk as if you didn't care for her. You *did* care."

" Of course I cared for her. But even that was different somehow. *She* was different. Why do you bother about her ? "

" I'm only wondering how you'd feel if you was to see her again."

" I shouldn't feel anything—anything at all. Seeing her would have no more effect on me than if she was a piece of clockwork." He paused.

" I say—you're not afraid of her ? " he said.

" No. I've been through all that and got over it. I'm not afraid of anything."

" You mean you're not afraid to marry me ? "

" No. I'm not afraid."

He felt her smile flicker in the darkness.

It was then that in the darkness he drew her to him, and she let herself be drawn, her breast to his breast and her head against his shoulder. And as she rested there she trembled, she shivered with delight and fear.

XXIX

HE had seen her home. At her door in the quiet Avenue he had held her in his arms again and kissed her. Her eyes shone at his under the lamplight.

He went back slowly, reviving the sweet sense of her.

A great calm had followed his excitement. He was sustained by an absolute certainty of happiness. It was in his grasp, nothing could take it from him. He would raise the rest of the money on Monday. He would see that lawyer on Wednesday. Then he would take proceedings. Once he had set the machinery going it couldn't be stopped. The law simply took the thing over, took it out of his hands, and he ceased to be responsible.

So he argued ; for at the back of his mind he saw more clearly than ever (he could not help seeing) something that might stop it all, disaster so great, so overwhelming that when it came his affairs would be swallowed up in it. In the face of that disaster it would be indecent of him to have any affairs of his own, or at any rate to insist on them. But he refused to dwell on this possibility. He persuaded himself that his father was better, that he would even recover, and that the business would recover too. For the last six months Ponting had been running it with an assistant under him, and between them they had done wonders with it, considering.

And on the Sunday something occurred that confirmed him in his rosy optimism.

His father was having another good day and they had wheeled him into the front sitting-room. Upstairs in the small back room Ransome was getting the children ready for their Sunday walk, when his mother came to him.

" Ranny," she said, " take off their hats and coats, dear. Your Father wants them."

" What does he want them for ? "

" It's his fancy. He's gettin' better, I think. I don't know when I've seen him so bright and contented as' he's been these last two days. And so pleased with everything you do for him—There, take them down, dear, quick."

He took them down and led them into the room. But they refused to look at their grandfather ; they turned from him at once ; they hid their faces behind Ranny's legs.

" They're afraid of me, I suppose," said Mr. Ransome.

" No," said Ranny, " they're not." But he had to take Stanny in his arms and comfort him lest he should cry.

" You're not afraid of Gran, are you ? Show Gran your pretty pinny, Doss."

He gave her a gentle push, and the child stood there holding out her pinafore and gazing over it at her grandfather with large, frightened eyes. Mr. Ransome's eyes looked back at her. They were sunken, sombre, wistful, unutterably sad. He did not speak. He did not smile. It was impossible to say what he was thinking.

This mutual inspection lasted for a moment so intense that it seemed immeasurable. Then Mr. Ransome closed his eyes as if pained and exhausted.

And Ranny stooped and whispered, " Kiss him, Dossie, kiss poor Gran."

The child, perceiving pity somewhere and awed into submission, did her best, but her kiss barely brushed the sallow, waxen face. And as he felt her there, Mr. Ransome opened his eyes suddenly and looked at her again, and Dossie, terrified, turned away and burst out crying.

" She's shy. She's a silly little girl," said Ranny as he led her away. He knew that, in the moment when the child had turned from him, his father had felt outcast from life, and utterly alone.

Mr. Ransome stirred and looked after him. " You come back here," he said. " I've something to say to you."

Ranny took the children to his mother and went back. Mr. Ransome was sitting up in his chair. He had roused himself. He looked strangely intelligent and alert.

He signed to his son to sit near him.

" How old are those children ? " he said.

" Dossie was five in March and Stanny was three in April."

" And they've been—how long without their mother ? "

" It'll be three years next October."

" Why don't you get rid of that woman ? " said Mr. Ransome. It was as if with effort and with pain and out of the secret, ultimate sources of his being that he drew the energy to say it. They would never know what he was thinking, never know (as Ranny had once said) what was going on inside him. And of all impossible things, *this* was what he had come out with now !

" Do you mean that, Father ? "

" Of course I mean it."

" Well then—as it happens—it's what I'm going to do."

" You should have done it before."

" I couldn't."

" Why not ? "

" I hadn't the money."

Mr. Ransome closed his eyes again as if in pain.

" I'd have given it you, Randall," he said presently. He had opened his eyes, but they wandered uneasily, avoiding his son's gaze. " If I'd had it. But I hadn't. I've been doing badly."

And again his eyelids dropped and lifted.

" Things have gone wrong that hadn't ought to if I'd been what I should be."

There was anguish in Ranny's father's eyes now. They turned to him for reassurance. As if in some final act of humility and contrition, he unbared and abased himself, he laid down the pretension of integrity.

His shawl had slipped from his knees. His hands moved over it as if, having unbared, he now sought to cover himself. Ransome stooped over him and drew the shawl up higher and wrapped it closer with careful, tender touches.

"Don't worry about that," he said.

"Your Mother'll be all right, Randall. She's got a bit of her own. It's all there, except what she put into the business. You won't have to trouble about her." He paused. "Have you got the money now?" he said.

"I shall have. To-morrow, probably."

"Then don't you wait."

"It'll be beastly work you know, Father. Are you sure you don't mind?"

"What *I* mind is your being married to that woman. I never liked it, Randall."

He closed his eyes. His face became more than ever drawn and peaked. His mouth opened. With short, hard gasps he fought for the breath he had so spent.

Ransome's heart reproached him because he had not cared enough about his father. And he said to himself, "He must have cared a lot more than he ever let on."

The way to the Divorce Court had been made marvellously smooth for him. His mother couldn't say now that it would kill his father.

But on Monday morning things did not go with Ransome entirely as he had expected. Shaftesbury Avenue refused to lend him more than ten pounds on the security of his furniture. Still, that was a trifling hitch. Now that the proceedings had been consecrated by his father's sanction there could be no doubt that his mother would be glad to lend him the five pounds. He would ask her for it that evening as soon as he got home.

But he did not ask her that evening, nor yet the next. He did not ask her for it at all. For, as soon as he got home she came to him out of his father's room. She stood at the head of the stairs by the door of the room, leaning against the banisters. And she was crying.

" Is Father worse ? " he said.

" He's going, my dear. There's a trained nurse just come. She's in there with the doctor. But they can't do anything."

He drew her into the front room and she told him what had happened.

" He was sittin' in his chair there like he was yesterday —so bright—and I thought he was better, and I made him a drop of chicken broth and sat with him while he took it. Then I left him there for a bit and went upstairs to the children—Dossie was sick this morning——"

" Dossie——? "

" It's nothing—she's upset with something she's eaten— and I was there with her ten minutes per'aps, and when I came back I found your Father in a fit. A convulsion, the doctor says it was, he said all along he might have them, but I thought he was better. And he's had another this evening and he hasn't come round out of it right. He doesn't know me, Ranny."

He had nothing to say to her. It was as if he had known that it would happen, and that it would happen like this, that he would come home at this hour and find his mother standing at the head of the stairs and that she would tell him these things in these words. He even had the feeling that he ought to have told *her*, to have warned her that it would be so.

On Wednesday evening, at eight o'clock, when Ransome should have been in the lawyer's room at the Polytechnic, he was standing by his father's bed. Mr. Ransome had partially recovered consciousness and he lay supported by his son's arms in preference to his own bed. For his bed had become odious to him, sinking under him, falling from him treacherously as he sank and fell, whereas Ranny's muscles adjusted themselves to all his sinkings and fallings. They remained and could be felt in the disintegration that presently separated them from the rest of Ranny, Ranny's arms being there, close under him, and Ranny's face a long way off at the other end of the room.

The process of dissolution had nothing to do with Mr. Ransome. It went on, not in him but outside him, in the room. He was almost unaware of it, it was so inconceivably gradual, so immeasurably slow. First of all the room began to fill with grey fog, and for ages and ages Ranny's face and his wife's face hung over him, bodiless, like pale lumps in the fog. Then for ages and for ages they were blurred, and then withdrawn from him, then blotted out.

This dying, which was so eternally tedious to Mr. Ransome, lasted about twenty minutes, so that at half-past eight, when Ranny should have been listening to his legal adviser, he was trying to understand what the doctor was trying to tell him about the causes, the very complicated causes of his father's death.

And with Mr. Ransome's death there came again on Ranny and his mother and on all of them the innocence and the immense delusion in which they had lived, in which they had kept it up, in the days before Ranny's wife had run away from him and before Ranny's enlightenment and his awful outburst. Only the innocence was ten times more persistent, the delusion ten times more solemn and more unutterably sacred now. Mr. Ransome's death made it impossible for them to speak or think or feel about him otherwise than if he had been a good man. If Ranny could have doubted it he would have stood reproved. From the doctor's manner, from his Uncle Randall's manner and his Aunt Randall's, from Mr. Ponting's and the assistant's manner, and from the manner, the swollen grief, uncontrolled and uncontrollable, of the servant

Mabel, he would have gathered that his father was a good man.

But Ransome never doubted it. He spoke, he thought, he felt as if his father's death had left him inconsolable. It was the death of a man who had made them all ashamed and miserable ; who had tried to take the joy out of Ranny's life as he had already taken it out of Ranny's mother's face ; who had hardly ever spoken a kind word to him ; who, if it came to that, had never done anything for him beyond contributing, infinitesimally, to his existence. And even this Mr. Ransome had done by accident and inadvertence, thinking (if he could be said to have been thinking at all) of his own pleasure and not of his son's interests ; for Ranny, if he had been consulted, would probably have preferred to owe his existence to some other parent.

And even in his last act, his dying, in his choice of that hour, of all hours open to him to die in, Mr. Ransome had inflicted an incurable injury upon his son. He had timed it to a minute. And Ranny knew it. He had had the idea firmly fixed in his head that if he did not go to the Polytechnic and find out how to set about filing his petition that Wednesday night, he would never get his divorce. Things would happen, they were bound to happen if he gave them time.

And yet that death, so ill-timed, so disastrous for Ranny in its consequences, Ranny mourned as if it had been in itself an affliction, an irreparable loss. He felt with the most entire sincerity that now that the Humming-bird was dead he would never be happy again.

On the Sunday after the funeral, which was on the Saturday, he sat in the front parlour with his mother and Mr. and Mrs. Randall, listening with a dumb but poignant acquiescence to all that they were saying about his father. Their idea now was that Mr. Ransome was not only a good man, a man of indissoluble integrity, but a man of unimaginably profound emotions, of passionate affections concealed under the appearance of austerity.

"No one knows," Mrs. Ransome was saying, "what 'E was thinking and what 'E was feeling—what went on inside him no one ever knew. For all he said about it you'd have thought he didn't take much notice of what happened—Ranny's trouble—and yet I know he felt it something awful. It preyed on 'is mind, poor Ranny being left like that. Why, it was after that, if you remember, that he began to break up. I put all his illness down to that.

"And then the children—you might say he didn't take much notice of them, but 'E was thinking about them all the time, you may depend upon it. 'E sent for them the Sunday before he died. I'm glad he did, too. Aren't you, Ranny?"

"Yes, Mother," Ranny said and choked.

"It'll be something for them to remember him by when they grow up. But they'll never know what was in his heart. None of us ever knew nor ever will know, now."

"He was a good man, Emmy, and a kind man—and just. I never knew anyone more just than Fulleymore. We were saying so only last night, weren't we?"

"Yes, John," said Mrs. Randall. "We were saying you could always depend upon his word. And as *you* say there were things in him we never knew—and never shall know."

And so it went on, with tearful breaks and long, oppressive silences, until someone would think of some as yet unmentioned quality of Mr. Ransome's. Every now and then, in the silences, one of them would be visited by some involuntary memory of his unpleasantness and of the furtive vice that had destroyed him, and would thrust the thought back with horror, as outrageous, indecent and impossible. They all spoke in voices of profound emotion and with absolute, unfaltering conviction.

"We shall never know what was in him." Always they

U

came back to that, they dwelt on it, they clung to it.
Under all the innocence and the delusion, it was as if,
through their grief, they touched reality, they felt the
unaltered, unapparent splendour, and testified to the
mystery, to the ultimate and secret sanctity of man's
soul.

Of all that Ransome was aware obscurely, he shared
their sense of that hidden and incalculable and enduring
life. But his own grief was different from theirs. It was
something unique, peculiar to himself and incommunicable.

Even he had not realised what was at the bottom of his
grief until he found himself alone with it, walking with it
on the road to Southfields. He had left the Randalls
with his mother and had escaped, with an irritable longing
for the darkness and the open air. He knew that the reason
why he wanted to get away from them was that his grief
was so different from theirs.

For they were innocent ; they had nothing to reproach
themselves with. If they had not loved his father quite
so much as they thought they did, they had done the next
best thing ; they had never let him know it. They had
behaved to him, they had thought of him, in consequence,
more kindly, more tenderly than if they *had* loved him ;
in which case they would not have felt the same obligation
to be careful. They had never hurt him. Whereas he——

That was why he would give anything to have his father
back again. It was all right for them. He couldn't think
what they were making such a fuss about. They had
carried their behaviour to such a pitch of perfection that
they could perfectly well afford to let him go. There was
no reason why they should want him back again, to show
him——

All this Ranny felt obscurely. And the more he thought
about it the more it seemed to him horrible that anybody

should have lived as his father had lived and die as he had died, without anybody having really loved him. It was horrible that he, Ranny, should not have loved him. For that was what it came to ; that was what he knew about himself ; that and nothing else was at the bottom of his grief and it was what made it so different from theirs. It was as if he realised for the first time in his life what pity was. He had never known what a terrible, what an intolerable thing was this feeling that was so like love, that should have been love and yet was not. For he didn't deceive himself about it as his mother (mercifully for her) was deceiving herself at this moment. This intolerable and terrible feeling was not love. In love there would have been some happiness.

Walking slowly, thinking these things, or rather feeling them, vaguely and incoherently, he had come to the grove by the public footpath. It was there that he had sat with his mother more than six years ago, when she had as good as confessed to him that she had not loved her husband ; not, that was to say, as she had loved her child.

And it was there, only the other night, that he had sat with Winny. One time seemed as long ago as the other.

And it was there that Winny was sitting now, on their seat, alone, facing the way he came, as if positively she had known that he would come.

He realised then that it was Winny that he wanted, and that the grief he found so terrible and intolerable was driving him to her, though when he started he had not meant to go to her, he had not known that he would go.

She rose when she saw him and came forward.

" Ranny ! Were you coming to me ? "

" Yes." (He knew it now.) " Let's stay here a bit. I've left Uncle and Aunt with Mother."

" How is she ? "

" Oh—well, it's pretty awful for her."

" It must be."

He was sitting near her but a little apart, staring at the

lamp-lit road. She felt him utterly removed from her. Yet he was there. He had come to her.

"I don't think," he said presently, "Mother'll ever be happy again. *I* shan't, either."

She put her hand on his hand that lay palm downwards between them on the seat and that was stretched towards her, not as if it sought her consciously, but in utter helplessness. There was no response in it beyond a nervous quivering that struck through her fingers to her heart.

He went on. "It's not as if *he* had been happy. He wasn't. Couldn't have been."

She fell to stroking gently that hand under her own. Its nervous quivering ceased.

"You know that funny way he had—the way he used to go poppin' in and out as if he was lookin' for somebody? That's what I can't bear to think of. Like as if he'd wanted something badly and wouldn't let on to anybody about it. Nobody knew what was going on inside him all these years. That's the horrible thing. We ought to have known and we didn't. There he was, poppin' in and out, and he might have been a mile off for all we could get at him. We didn't know anything about him—not reelly."

He mused. "That's it. We don't know anything about anybody— ever. I didn't know anything about Virelet—don't know now. I never shall know. Come to that, I don't know anything about you. Nor you about me—reelly."

"Oh, Ranny," she whispered. It was her one protest against the agony he was making her share with him.

"What do we know about anything? What does it all mean? The whole bloomin' show? The Combined Maze? They shove us into it without our leave. They make us do things we don't want to do and never meant to do. I didn't want to care for Virelet. I wanted to care for you. I didn't want to marry her nor she me. I didn't mean to. I meant to marry you. But I did care for her and I did marry her. I don't suppose *he* wanted to do

like he did or ever meant to. And look how he was treated
—shoved in—livin' his horrible little life down there—
doin' the things he didn't mean—lookin' for things he never
got—and then shunted like this, all anyhow, God knows
where—before he could put a hand on anything. There's
no sense in it.

"I wouldn't mind so much if I'd only cared for him. But
I didn't. I wanted to—I meant to—but I didn't. There
you are again. It's all like that and there's no sense in it."

"But you *did* care, Ran, dear. You're caring now.
You couldn't talk like this about him if you didn't care."

"No. I'm talkin' like this—because I didn't care.
Not a rap. My God! If I thought Stanny would ever
feel to me as I felt to my father, I'd go and kill myself."

"But he won't, dear. You haven't behaved to him like
your father behaved to you," said Winny calmly.

"What do you mean?"

"You know what I mean. At any rate, you will know
presently when you can look at it as it reely is. Nobody
could have done more for your father than you did. If
he'd been the best father in the world you couldn't have
done more."

"Doin' things is nothing. Besides, I didn't. D'you
know, I wouldn't go into his business when he wanted me
to? I wouldn't do it, just because I couldn't bear bein'
with him all the time. And he knew it."

"I don't care if he did know it, Ranny. You'd a perfect
right to live your own life. You'd a right to choose what
you'd do and where you'd be. As it was, you never had
any life of your own where your father was about. I can
remember how it was, dear, if you don't. If you'd given
in because he wanted you to; if you'd been boxed up
with him down there from morning till night, you'd never
have had any life at all. Not as much as *that!* And then,
instead of caring for him as you did, you'd have got to
hate him, and then he'd have hated you; and your mother
would have been torn between you. That's how it would

have been, and you knew it. Else you'd never have left
him."

" I say—fancy your knowin' all that ! "

" Of course I know it. I knew it all the time."

" Who told you ? "

" You don't have to be told things like that, Ranny."
The hand she was stroking moved from under her hand
and caught it and grasped it tight.

" Didn't I always know you were a dear ? " she went
on. " You said I didn't know anything about you. But I
knew that much."

" Yes—but—how did you know I cared for him ? "

" Oh, why—because—you couldn't have called him the
Humming-bird and all those funny names you did if you
hadn't cared. And, of course, he knew that too. That's
what he wouldn't let on, dear—the lot he knew. It must
have made him feel so nice and comfortable inside him to
know that whatever he was to do you'd go on calling
him a Humming-bird."

" D'you think it did—reelly ? "

" Why—don't you remember how it used to make your
mother smile. Well, then."

Well, then, she seemed to say, it was all right.

That was how she brought him round, to sanity when
he thought his brain was going and to happiness when he
felt it so improbable, not to say impossible, that he should
ever be happy again.

A fortnight passed.

In the three days following the death he had not thought
once about his own concerns. He simply hadn't time to
think of them. Every minute he could spare was taken up
with the arrangements for his father's funeral. Sunday
had been given over to mourning and remorse. It was
Monday morning and the weeks following it that brought

back the thought of his divorce. They brought it back, first, in all its urgency, as a thing vehemently and terribly desired, then as a thing, urgent indeed, but private and personal and, therefore, of secondary importance, a thing that must perforce stand over until the settlement of his father's affairs, till finally (emerging from the inextricable tangle in which it had become involved) it presented itself as it was, a thing hopeless and unattainable.

His father's affairs were worse than anything he had believed. For, except for that terror born of his own private superstition, he had not really looked forward to disaster on an overwhelming scale. He had imagined his father's business as surviving him only for a little while, and his father's debts as entailing perhaps strict economy for years. But he was not prepared for the actual figures.

And how his father, limited as he was in his resources and destitute, you would have thought, of all opportunity for wild expenditure, how he could have contrived to owe the amount he owe, passed Ranny's understanding.

Into that pit of insolvency there went all that was fetched by the sale of the stock and the goodwill of the business, and all that Mrs. Ransome had put into the business, including what she had saved out of her tiny income. As for Ranny's savings and the sum he had borrowed—the whole thirty pounds—they went to pay for the funeral and the grave and the monumental stone.

There could be no divorce. Divorce was not to be thought of for more than two years when he would have got his rise.

He broke the news to Winny, sitting with her in their little half-way grove, the place consecrated to Ranny's confidences.

" I can't do different," he said, summing it all up.

" Of course you can't. Never mind, dear. Let's go on as we are."

It was what Violet had said to him, but with how different a meaning.

" But Winky—it means waiting years. It'll be more than two before I can get a divorce—and we can't marry till six months after. That's three years. I can't bear to ask you to wait so long."

" Don't worry about me. I'm quite happy."

" You don't know how much happier you would be. Me too."

She pressed her face against his shoulder.

" I don't think I could be any happier than I am."

" You don't know," he repeated. " You don't know anything at all."

" I know I love you and you me, and that's enough."

" Oh—is it ? "

" It's the great thing."

" Winny, d'you know, that if poor Father hadn't died when he did—We missed it by a day. To think it could happen like that ! "

He clinched it with, " This Combined Maze has been a bit too much for you and me."

XXX

MRS. RANSOME for the first time in her life was thinking. She called it thinking, although that was no word for it, for its richness, its amplitude, its peculiar secret certainty. You might say that for the first time in her life Mrs. Ransome was fully conscious ; that, with an extraordinary vividness and clarity she saw things, not as she believed and desired them to be, but as they were.

She saw, for the first time since Mr. Ransome's death, that she was happy ; or rather, that she had been happy for more than two years, that is to say, ever since Mr. Ransome's death. And this vision of her happiness, of her iniquitous and disgraceful satisfaction, was shocking to Mrs. Ransome. She would have preferred to think that ever since Mr. Ransome's death she had been heartbroken.

But it was not so. Never in all her life had she been so at peace ; never since her girlhood had she been so gay. This state of hers had lasted exactly two years and four months, thus clearly dating from her bereavement. For it was in May of nineteen-ten that he had died, and she was now in September nineteen-twelve.

She might not have been aware of it but that it, her happiness, had only six months more to run.

For two years and four months she had had her son Ranny to herself. She had been the mistress of his house, the little house that she loved, and the mother of his children whom (next to her son Ranny) she adored. For two years and four months she had made him comfortable with a comfort he had never dreamed of, which most certainly he had never known. With tenderness and care and vigilance unabridged and unremitted, she had brought Granville and Stanley and Dossie to perfection. It had not been so hard. Stanley and Dossie she had found almost perfect from the first, more perfect than Ranny she had found them, because they were not so near to her own flesh and not loved so passionately as he.

And Granville, once far from perfect, had responded to treatment like a living thing. Maudie and Fred Booty had cherished it, they handed it on to Mrs. Ransome spotless and intact. Spotless and intact she had kept it. Spotless and intact no doubt it would be kept when, in six months' time, she in her turn would hand it over to Winny Dymond, to Ranny's second wife.

He had only just told her.

That was what hurt her most, that she had only just been told, when for more than two years he had been thinking of it. It was no use saying that he couldn't have told her before because he wasn't free. He wasn't free now ; not properly, like a widower.

That he would, after all, get rid of poor Violet who hadn't, in all those years, troubled him or done him any harm, *that* had been a blow to her. She hadn't believed it possible. She had thought the question of divorce had been settled once for all, five years ago, by his Uncle Randall. And John Randall in the meanwhile had justified his claim to be heard, and his right to settle things. He had cancelled the debt that poor Fulleymore had owed him. To be sure, he could afford it. He was more prosperous and prominent than ever. He was, therefore, less than ever likely to approve of the divorce.

If the idea of divorce had been appalling five years ago, it was still more appalling now. Since, after all, poor Violet had removed herself so far and kept so quiet, the scandal of her original disappearance had somehow diminished with every year, while, proportionately, with every year, the scandal, the indecency, the horror of the

Divorce Court had increased, until now it seemed to be a monstrous thing.

And that Ranny should have chosen this time of all times! When they'd paid off all the creditors and got clear, and stood respected and respectable again. As if his poor father's insolvency, which, after all, he couldn't help (since it was the Drug Stores that had ruined him), as if that wasn't enough disgrace for one family, he must needs go and rake up all that awful shame and trouble, after all these years, when everybody had forgotten that there *had* been any trouble and any shame.

That was what Mrs. Ransome found so hard to bear. And that she had been deceived; that he should have let her go on thinking that it wasn't possible, up to the last minute (it was Saturday and he was going to the lawyer on Monday), she who had the first right to be told.

All these years he had deceived her. All these years he had meant to do it the very minute he had got his rise.

For Ransome had attained the summit of his ambition. He was now a petty cashier with a pen all to himself at the top of the counting-house, and an income of two hundred a year. Short of making him assistant secretary (which was ridiculous) Woolridge's could do no more for him.

And Winny Dymond (Mrs. Ransome reflected bitterly), though he hadn't been free to speak to her, though he was practically (it didn't occur to Mrs. Ransome that what she meant was theoretically) a married man, Winny had known it all the time.

It was extraordinary, but Mrs. Ransome, who was really fond of Winny, felt towards her more acute and concentrated bitterness than she had felt towards Violet whom she hated. She was able to think of Ranny's first wife as poor Violet, though Violet had made him miserable and destroyed his home and had left him and his children. And the thought of his marrying Winny Dymond was intolerable to Mrs. Ransome, though she had recog-

nised her as the one woman Ranny ought to have married,
the one woman worthy of him, and she would have continued to welcome her in that capacity as long as Ranny
had refrained from marrying her.

For Ranny's mother knew that in Violet her motherhood had had no rival. Violet's passion for Ranny, Ranny's
passion for Violet, had not robbed her of her son. Violet,
not having in her one atom of natural feeling, and caring
only for her husband's manhood and his physical perfection, had left to Mrs. Ransome all that was most dear
to her in Ranny. Married to Violet he was still dependent
on his mother. He clung to her, he deferred to her judgment, he came to her for comfort. If he had been ill it
was she and not Violet who would have nursed him.
Whereas Winny would take all that away from her. She
would take—she could not help taking—Ranny utterly
away ; not from malice, not from selfishness, not because
she wanted to take him, but because she could not help
it. She was so made as to be all in all to him, so made as
to draw him to her all in all. There would be absolutely
nothing of Ranny left over for his mother, except the
affection he had always felt for her, which, for a woman of
Mrs. Ransome's temperament, was the least thing that
she claimed. Her instinct had divined Winny infallibly,
not only as a wife to Ranny, but as a mother. A mother
Winny was and would be to him far more than if she had
used her womanhood to bear him children.

So that, without the smallest preparation, she saw herself required at six months' notice to give up her son. And
while she blamed him for not having told her, she overlooked the fact that if she had been told she could not
have borne the knowledge. It would have poisoned for
her every day of the eight hundred and forty-five days
for which in her ignorance she had been so happy.

She did not attempt to deny that she had been happy.
But what she had *said* to Ranny when he told her was,
" It's a mercy your poor father doesn't know."

And in that moment she thought of her happiness with a sharp pang as if it had been unfaithfulness to her dead husband.

It was at half-past seven on a Saturday evening in the last week of September, nineteen-twelve, that Mrs. Ransome sat all alone in the back sitting-room at Granville and meditated miserably on those things. Upstairs in his bedroom overhead she could hear Ranny moving very softly, for fear of waking Stanley. She knew what he was doing. He was changing, making himself smart enough to take Winny Dymond to the Earl's Court Exhibition.

Upstairs in his bedroom overhead, Ranny moved very softly for fear of waking Stanley. He was changing into a new grey suit, making himself more smart than he had been for years to take Winny to the Earl's Court Exhibition.

In that shirt, glistening, high-collared, in a grey-blue tie, in grey-blue socks and brown boots, Ranny looked very smart indeed. And the suit, the suit looked splendid, the fold down the legs of the trousers being as yet unimpaired.

And Ranny looked young, ever so young still, though he was thirty-two. The faint lines at the corner of his eyes and of his mouth accentuated agreeably their upward tilt. He had gained distinction by the increasing firmness of his face. Virile in its adolescence, it had kept its youth in its maturity. Ranny's face expressed him. It was fine and clean ; it had not one mean or faltering line in it. And his figure had not, after all, deteriorated. Flabbiness was as far from him as it had been in his youth.

With infinite precautions, Ranny opened a drawer where he found a small japanned tin box, very new. This he unlocked softly, and from a little canvas bag that lay in the compartment specially reserved for it he took a sovereign, one of four, that represented rather more than a week's proportion of his new salary.

He had made up his mind that when the day came he would spend no less a sum. So great a rise could not be celebrated on less. If a cashier of Woolridge's could have been capable of saving, say, one and ninepence out of that sovereign, the man who was engaged to Winny Dymond would have died rather.

Of course, it was a thundering lot to spend. But then Ranny desired, he was determined to spend a thundering lot. It was extravagant, but he wished to be extravagant. It was reckless, irresponsible, but reckless and irresponsible was what he felt. He meant to go it. He meant to have his fling just for once. And he meant that Winny who had never had hers, nor any share in anybody else's, should taste, just for once, the rapture of a fling. She should have it for three solid hours of that delicious night, in one mad, flaming, stupendous orgy at the Earl's Court Exhibition.

For it wasn't really his rise that called for it. That was only a means to his divorce and marriage. It was his engagement that he proposed to celebrate.

The engagement, though he could hardly believe it, was a fact. True, it could not be made public until a decent interval after the divorce ; but it had been acknowledged. and settled between him and Winny as soon as ever he knew that he had got his rise. They would never celebrate it at all if they didn't celebrate it now before all the beastliness began.

For he knew perfectly well that it would be beastly. Winny would feel it even more than he did. She would feel it for him. Things that they had both forgotten would be raked up again, all the misery and all the shame. Now that it was imminent he dreaded the Divorce Court. His Uncle Randall could not have shrunk more painfully from this public washing of his dirty linen. He would come out of the Great Washhouse feeling almost, but not quite as unclean as if his linen had been kept at home and never washed at all.

And the trail of all that nastiness would spread over the six months of their engagement ; it would poison everything.

He didn't mean to think about it or let Winny think. They were going to enjoy themselves to-night while they could, while they still felt innocent and clean and jolly.

He stooped for a moment over the crib where his little son lay curled and snuggling, his face hidden, his head, with its crop of dark hair, showing like the fur of some soft burrowing animal. He freed the little mouth muffled in bed-clothes, and tucked the blankets closer. He picked up Stanny's Teddy bear that had fallen lamentably to the floor, and laid it where Stanny would find it beside him when he woke.

Treading softly, he went into the next room where Dossie lay in her own little bed beside his mother's, her little seven-year-old girl body stretched out in all its dainty slenderness (so unlike Stanny's. He saw with a pang of sudden passion the sweet difference). Her face, laid sideways in her golden brown hair, showed already a fine edge, nose and mouth and chin turned subtly, and carved out of their baby softness to the likeness of his own. He stooped and kissed Dossie's hair, and took without touching the sweetness of her mouth. Then he ran softly down the stairs.

His mother heard him running and came to the door of the room. "You're not going out like that," she said, "without an overcoat ? It'll rain before you're back, I know, and that new suit'll be ruined."

"Rot ! It *can't* rain on a night like this. Good night, Mother. Don't go sittin' up. I don't know when I'll be in."

" I'll hot some cocoa for you last thing and leave it on the trivet."

" Shan't want cocoa."

" What shall you want then ? "

" Oh, Lord ! " His nerves were all on edge. He couldn't bear it. " *Nothing !* " he cried as he rushed out.

At the gate it struck him that he had been a brute to her. He turned. He rushed back to her. He put his arm round her and kissed her.

" You're all right now, aren't you ? "

" Yes, Ran, dear, I'm all right." She smiled. " Run away and don't keep Winny waiting."

(Heaven only knew what it cost her.)

And Ranny looked back, laughing, through the doorway. " You know, Mother, it reelly *is* all right. And you're an angel."

And she said. " There ! Go along with you."

He went.

" Ranny, how nice you look ! "

Winny herself was looking nice and knew it. She wore a green cotton gown trimmed with white pipings, and a thing she called a Peggy hat that was half a bell and half a bonnet and had diminutive roses sewn on it here and there like buttons.

They were going down the long entrance to the Exhibition, between painted walls, in brilliant illumination and in publicity that might have been trying if they had had eyes for anything except each other.

Winny's eyes were brimming with joy and tenderness as she looked at him. If she loved the new grey suit, the brown boots and the Trilby hat, she did not love them more than the shabby blue serge with the place she knew in the lining where she had mended it. All the same it was impossible to see him in such things without that little breathless thrill of wonder and excitement. There wasn't one man at Earl's Court that night who could compare with Ranny. He made them all look weedy, flabby; pitiful, uninteresting things.

And then, all of a sudden (they were at the pay-gate), as she looked, astonishment, grief and anxiety appeared on Winny's face. Something had dismayed her tenderness, dashed her joy. She had seen Ranny take out of his waistcoat pocket gold—not ten shillings, but a whole sovereign. And a dreadful fear awoke in her.

He was going to spend it all.

She knew it, something told her; she could see by the way he smacked it down, careless like. And Winny couldn't bear it; she couldn't bear to think that Ranny who had pinched and scraped and done without things for years, should go and throw away all that on her!

But anybody could see that he was going to do it, by the strange excitement and abstraction in his eyes, by the way he gathered up the change and took Winny by the arm and walked off with her. His eyes and the close crook of his arm drawing her along with him in his course, the slight leaning of his body towards hers as they went, his stride and the set of his head proclaimed that he had got her, that she couldn't escape, that he meant to go it, that he had the right to spend on her more than he could possibly afford.

She could see what he was thinking. In one tremendous burst he was going to make up to her now for all that she had missed. What was more, he was going to rub it into her that he had the right to. She couldn't realise their happiness as he did. They had been cheated out of it so long that she couldn't believe in it, couldn't believe that it was actually in their grasp, the shining, palpitating joy that for five years had been dangled before them only to be jerked out of their hands. He wanted to make her feel it; to make her taste and touch and handle the thing that seemed impossible and yet was certain.

x

Ranny was intoxicated, he was reckless with certainty. And Winny couldn't bear it. All the way up between the painted walls she was trying to think what she could do to prevent his spending a whole sovereign. She knew that it was no use fighting Ranny. The more she hung on to him to stop him, the more Ranny would struggle and break loose. Persuasion was no good. The more she reasoned, the more determined he would be to spend that sovereign and the more ways he would find to spend it.

It was to be one of those mortal combats between man's will and woman's wit. Winny meant to circumvent Ranny and to defeat him by guile.

And at first it looked as if it could be done easily. For at first the Exhibition seemed to be on Winny's side.

They had emerged from between the painted walls into Shakespeare's England, into the narrow crooked streets under the queer old overhanging houses with the swinging signs—hundreds of years old Ranny said they were. And in the streets there were strange crowds, young men and young women who went shouting and singing and were marvellously and fantastically dressed. And they had glimpses through lattice windows of marvellous and fantastic merchandise. Marvellous and fantastic it seemed to Winny at first sight. But when she saw that it was just what they were selling in the shops to-day the delicious confusion in her mind heightened the effect of fantasy and of enchantment.

" I didn't think it would be like this," she said.

But why it was like that and why it was called Shakespeare's England, what on earth Shakespeare had to do with it, Winny couldn't think.

" Shakespeare ? Why, he wrote books, didn't he ? "

" Plays, Winky, plays."

" Plays then."

And when Ranny told her that it meant that England was like this in Shakespeare's time, hundreds of years ago, and reminded her that they had a scene from one of his plays on at the Coliseum the other day, Winny thought that only made it more marvellous and more like a dream than ever.

And she thought Ranny was more marvellous than ever, with the things he knew.

And then, having lured him into this tangled side issue, she began, as cool and off-hand as you please. He gave her the opening when he asked her what she'd like to do next.

" This is good enough for me," she said.

For the most marvellous thing about Shakespeare's England was that you could walk about in it free of charge.

He looked at her almost as if he knew what she was up to.

" But you've seen it, Winky. You've seen all there is of it. You don't want to stay here all night, do you ? "

He had her there, with his reminder of the hours they had to put in.

" Well——" She was lingering in the most natural manner as if fascinated by the exterior of the Globe Theatre. For she wished to spin out the time.

She saw Ranny's hand sliding towards his pocket.

" Would you like to go inside it ? " he said.

" No, Ranny, dear, I wouldn't. At least, I'd rather not if you've no objection."

She spoke firmly, seriously, as if she knew something against the Globe Theatre, as if the Globe Theatre were disreputable or improper.

Then (it was wonderful how she contrived the little air of excited inspiration) : " Tell you what," she said, " let's go and sit down somewhere and listen to the band. There's nothing I love so much as listening to a band."

She knew that they charged nothing for listening to the band.

It was a prompting from the Exhibition itself, proving, here again, that it was on her side, an entirely friendly and benignant power.

"All right," said Ranny. "*That's* in the Western Garden."

He took her by the arm and drew her, not to the Western Garden but to a street (he seemed to know it by instinct) through which Shakespeare's England, iniquitously, treacherously, led them to their doom, the Water Chute.

For there the Exhibition threw off her mask and revealed herself as the dangerous Enchantress that she was. Hung with millions of electric bulbs, crowned and diademed and laced with jewels of white flame, she signalled to them out of the mystery and immensity of the night. For a moment they were dumb, they stood still, as if they paused on the brink and struggled, protesting against this ravishing of their souls by the Exhibition. Straight in front of them, monstrous, yet fragile, its substance withdrawn into the darkness, its form outlined delicately in beads of light, in brilliants, in crystals strung on invisible threads, the Water Chute reared itself like a stairway to the sky, arch above arch, peak above peak, diadem above diadem, tilted at a frightful pitch. Chains of light, slung like garlands from tall standards, ringed the long lake that stretched from their feet to the bottom of the stair. The water, dark as the sky, showed mystic and enchanted, bordered with trembling reeds of light.

From somewhere up in the sky, under the topmost diamonded arch, there came a rambling and a rushing——

It thrilled them, agitated them.

And their youth rose up in them. They looked at each other, and their eyes, the eyes of their youth, shone with the same excitement and the same desire.

She knew that he had deceived her, that this was not the Western Garden where the band played; she was aware that the Exhibition was not to be trusted either; that it was in league with him against her; that if she yielded to it they were lost. And yet she yielded. The deep and high enchantment was upon her. The Exhibition had her by the hair. She was borne on, breathless, unprotesting, to the white palings where the pay-gate was.

It was worth it. She had to own it. Never before had either of them tasted such ecstasy; from the precipitous climb in the truck that hauled them, up and up, to the head of the high diamonded stair; the brief, exciting passage along the gangway to the boat that waited for them, its prow positively overhanging the topmost edge, the sliding lip of danger, where the rails plunged shining to the blackness below; the race they had for the front seat where, Ranny said, they would get the best of it; and then—the down-rush!

It was as if they had been shot, exulting, from the sky to the water, sitting close, sitting tight, linked together, each with an arm round the other's waist, and the hand that was free grasping the rail, their bodies bowed to the hurricane of their speed, with the rapture in their throats mounting and mounting, a towering, toppling climax of delight and fear, as the boat shot from the rails into the water and rose like a winged thing and leaped, urging to the heights that had sent it forth, and dropped, perilously again, with a shudder and a smack, once, twice; so tremendous was the impetus.

They heard young girls behind them scream for joy; but they were dumb, they were motionless; they drank rapture through set teeth; it went throbbing through them and thrilling, prolonging its brief life in exquisite reverberations.

And as if that wasn't enough, they went and did it all over again.

And Winny struggled; she tried to hold him back; she put forth all her innocent guile; she pitted her fragile charm against the stupendous magic of the Exhibition. She loitered, spell-bound to all appearance, in the bazaar, before the streaming, shining booths that poured out their strange merchandise, Italian, French, Indian, Chinese and Japanese.

"I don't want to do anything but walk about and look at things," she said. "Why, we might have travelled for years and not seen as much."

Winny seemed to be scoring points in the bazaar.

Then, before she knew where she was, Ranny, with all the power of the Exhibition at his back, had bought her a present, a little heart-shaped brooch made of Florentine turquoises.

That came of looking at things. She might have known it would.

"I'm tired of these shops," said Winny. "We shall be too late to hear anything of the band."

Thus she drew him to the Western Garden, so that for the moment she seemed to have it all in her own hands. For here there were more lights, an even more extravagant and fantastic display of electric jewellery, more garlands of diamond and crystal, illuminating, decorating everything. And there were rubies hanging in strange trees, and at their feet the glamour of light dissolved, half of it perished, gone from the world, drunk up by the earth, half living on where grey walks wound like paths in a dream, between rings of spectral green, islands of dimmed, mysterious red, so transformed, so unclothed and clothed again by glamour, as to be hardly discernible as beds of geraniums in grass.

Here they wandered for what seemed an eternity of bliss.

"What more do you want?" said Winny. "Isn't this beautiful enough for anybody?" Neither of them had any idea that the beauty and the glamour of it was in their own souls as they drank each other's mystery.

"Let's just sit and listen to the band," she said. And they sat and listened to it for another eternity, till Ranny became restless. For thirteen and elevenpence halfpenny was burning in his pocket.

The thought of it made him take her to a restaurant where they sat for quite a long time and drank coffee and ate ices. Winny submitted to the ices. They were delicious, and she enjoyed them without a shadow of misgiving. She was in fact triumphant, for she looked on ices as the close and crown of everything, and she calculated that out of that sovereign there would be exactly eleven and two-pence halfpenny left.

"Well—it's been lovely. And now we must go home," she said.

"Go home? Not much. Why we've only just begun." He looked at her. "D'you suppose I don't know what *you're* up to? You're jolly clever, but you can't take *me* in, Winky. Not for a single minute."

"Well, then, Ranny, let me pay for *something*." And she took out her little purse.

After that it was sheer headlong, shameful defeat for Winky. He had found her out, he had seen through her manœuvres, and he and the Exhibition, the destructive and terrible Enchantress, had been laughing at her all the time. A delirious devil had entered into Ranny with the coffee and the ices, urging him to spend. And Winny ceased to struggle. He knew at what point she would yield, he knew what temptations would be irresistible. He got round her with the Alpine Ride; the Joy Wheel fairly undermined her moral being; and on the Crazy Bridge Ranny's delirious devil seized her and carried her away, reckless, into the Dragon's Gorge.

Emerging as it were from the very jaws of the Dragon, they careered arm-in-arm through the rest of the Exhibition, two rushing portents of youth and extravagance and laughter; till, as if the Enchantress had twisted her wand and whisked them there, they found themselves inside the palisades of the Igorrote Village.

A swarm of half-naked savages leaped at them.

It was Ranny who recovered first.

"It's all right, Winky. They're the Philippine Islanders."

"Well, I never——"

"Nor I. Talk of travellin'——"

But it was all very well to talk. The sight had sobered them. Gravely and silently they went through that village. At last, Ranny paused outside a hut no bigger than a dog-kennel. It bore the label : " Beda And His Fiancée Kodpat Undergoing Trial Marriage."

Ranny laughed. " By Jove that tickles *me*," he said.

" What does it mean, Ranny ? "

" Why, I suppose it means they try it first and if they don't like it they can chuck it."

" What an idea ! "

" It's a rippin' good idea, Winky. Shows what a thunderin' lot of sense these simple savages have got. You bet they're not quite so simple as they seem. They know a thing or two. Why, they must be hundreds of years ahead of us in civilisation, to have thought it all out like that. Think of it, that fellow Beda's had a better chance than me."

They turned away from Beda and Kodpat, and presently Winny stood entranced before the little house that contained Baby Francis (born in the Exhibition) and his mother. She looked so long at Baby Francis that Ranny couldn't bear it.

" Oh, look at him, Ranny ! Isn't he a little lamb ? "

Winny's eyes were tender and her face quivered with a little dreamy smile.

" D'you want to take him home and play with him ? Shall I ask if he's for sale ? "

" Oh, Ranny ! "

She turned away. And he drew her arm in his. " You won't be happy till you've got him, Winky."

She said nothing to that ; only her mouth, without her knowing it, kept for him its little dreamy smile.

" I believe," said Ranny, " you've never reelly got over Stanley's goin' into knickers."

" I *love* his knickers," she protested.

" Yes, but you'd love *him* better if he was that size, wouldn't you ? "

"I couldn't love him better than I do, Ranny. You know I couldn't. And I wouldn't like him to be any different to what he is."

She was very serious, very earnest, almost as if she thought he'd really meant it.

Silent in the grip of an emotion too thick and close for utterance, they wandered back again to the enchanted garden where the band had played for them. The garden was silent, too. The bandstand was empty, black, unearthly as if haunted by some thin ghost of passionate sound; and empty, row after row of seats in the great parterre, except for a few couples who sat leaning to each other, hand in hand, finding a happy solitude in that twilight desolation.

Like worshippers strayed into some church, they joined this enraptured, oblivious company of devotees, choosing seats as far as possible from any other pair.

"Hadn't we better be going?"

They had sat there in silence, holding each other's hands. The excitement, the delirious devil in them, had spent itself, and under it they felt the heaving, dragging ground-swell of their passion.

To Winny it had never come before like this. Up till now it had been enough simply to be with Ranny. Merely to look at him gave her profound and poignant pleasure. To touch him in those rare accidental contacts the adventure brought them, to feel the firm muscles of his arm under his coat sleeve, stopped her breath with a kind of awe and wonder, as if in Ranny's body thus discerned she came unaware upon some transcendent mystery.

Yet Winny knew now why, in what way, and with what terrible strength she loved him and he her. She loved him, primarily and supremely, for himself, for the simple fact that he was Ranny. She loved him also for his body, for his slenderness, and for his strong-clipping limbs, and she loved him for his face because it could not by any possibility be anybody else's.

And in her joy and tenderness, in their engagement and in the whole adventure, this going out with him and all the rare, shy contacts it occasioned, instalments of delight, windfalls of bliss that Heaven sent her to be going on with, in the very secrecy and mystery of it all, Winny felt that disturbing yet delicious sense of something iniquitous, something perilous, something, at any rate, unlawful. It was the same sense that she had known and enjoyed in the days when she went into the scullery at Granville to make beef-steak pies for Ranny ; the same sense, but far more exquisite, far more exciting.

She did not connect it in any way with Violet. Violet had ceased to exist for them. Violet had of her own act annihilated herself. But Winny knew that until Ranny was divorced from his wife the law continued to regard him as married to her. So that, while firm land held and would always hold her, she was aware that he and she were walking on the brink, and that by the rule of the road Ranny went, so to speak, upon the outer edge where it was far more dangerous. She knew that he had more than once looked over ; and she knew (though nothing would induce *her* to look) that the gulf was there, not far from her adventurous feet.

Still, it was wonderful how all these years they had kept their heads.

So she said, " Hadn't we better be going ? I think we ought to."

She had unlaced her hand from his and had turned in her seat to face him with her decision.

" Not yet."

" Well—soon. It's getting rather chilly, don't you think ? "

At that he jumped up. " Are you cold, Winky ? "

" My feet are, sitting."

" I forgot your little feet."

He raised her.

" It isn't late," he said. " We can walk about a bit."

They walked about, for he was very restless again.

" Wherever does that music come from ? " Winny said.

Sounds came to them of violins and 'cellos, of trombones and clarionets, playing a gay measure, a dance, insistent, luring, irresistible.

They followed it.

In a vast room fronted by a latticed screen, all green and white, roofed by a green and white awning and having a pattern of lattice work, green and white, upon its inner walls, on a vast polished floor was a crowd of couples dancing to the music they had heard. It came loud through the open lattices, the insistent, luring, irresistible measure, violent now in solicitation, in appeal ; and over it and under went the trailing, shuffling slur of the feet of the dancers and the delicate swish of women's gowns as they whirled.

Standing close outside they could see into the hall through the lattices of the screen. They saw forty or fifty couples whirling slowly round and round to the irresistible measure ; some were stiff and awkward, palpably shy ; some with invincible propriety whirled upright and rigid, like toys wound up to whirl ; some were abandoned to the measure with madness, with passion, with a corybantic joy. Here and there a girl leaned as if swooning in her lover's arms ; her head hung back ; her lower lip drooped ; her face showed the looseness and blankness of a sensuous stupor. Other faces, staring, upraised, wore a look of exaltation and of ecstasy. All were superbly unaware.

Winny's face pressed closer and closer to the lattice. One of her little feet went tap-tapping on the gravel, beating the measure of the waltz. For at the sound of the music, at the sight of the locked and whirling couples, her memory revived ; she heard again the beating of the measure old as time ; she felt in her limbs the start and strain of the wild energy ; and instinct, savage and shy, moved in the rhythm of her blood, and desire for the joy of the swift running, of the lacing arms and flying feet.

In her body she was standing outside the Dancing Saloon at the Earl's Court Exhibition, with her face pressed to the lattice; she was twenty-seven last birthday in her body; but in her soul she was seventeen, and she stood on the floor of the Polytechnic Gymnasium, beating time to the thud of the bar-bell. She was Winny of the short tunic and the knickers, and the long black stockings, and had her hair (tied by a great bow of ribbon) in a door-knocker plat.

"Oh, Ranny"—She looked at him with her shining eyes, half tender and half wild. "If we only *could*——"

Something gave way in him and dissolved, and he was weak as water when he looked at her.

The violins gave forth a penetrating, excruciating cry. And he felt in him the tumult evoked, long ago, one Sunday evening by the music in the Mission Church of St. Matthias's.

Only he knew now what it meant.

His voice went thick in his throat.

"I mustn't, Winky. I daren't. Some day—you and I——"

It was the supreme temptation of the great Enchantress; and they fled from it. The violins shrieked out and cried their yearning as they went.

A scud of rain lashed the carriage windows as their train shot out of the Underground at Walham Green. When they stepped out on to the platform at Southfields, the big drops leaped up at them.

"Well, I never," said Winny. "Who'd have thought it would have done that?"

They scuttled into shelter.

" It'll be a score for Mother. She said it would come
and I said it wouldn't."

" It'll ruin your new suit."

" And there won't be much left of your dress."

" My dress'll iron out again. It's me poor hat."
(The Peggy hat was not made for rain.)

" I'll take it off and pin it up in me skirt. It's you I'm
thinking of."

She felt his coat to see what resistance it would offer to
the rain. It offered none. It made no pretence about it.

" It'll be soaked and it'll never be the same again," she
wailed.

But Ranny remained god-like in his calm. There was
still one and sixpence of his sovereign left.

" You can keep your hat on. We're going to take a cab."

If he had said he was going to take an aeroplane she
couldn't have been more amazed. It was only seven
minutes' walk to Acacia Avenue. And it was not a common
cab, it was Parker's fly that he was taking.

She surrendered because of the new suit.

" I can count the times I've ridden in a cab," she said.
" This is the third. First time it was going to Father's
funeral. Second time it was poor Mother's funeral. I've
never been happy in a cab till now."

" Poor little girl! Next time it'll be coming from our
wedding. Will you be happy then ? "

" I'm so happy now, Ranny, that I can't believe it."

" It'll only be six months, or seven·at the outside."

" Are you sure ? "

" Certain."

The worst of the cab was that it cut short their moments.
It had been standing a whole minute before Johnson's
side door. He sent it away.

For fifteen seconds, measured by hammer-strokes of
their hearts, they were alone. On the streaming doorstep,
under the dripping eaves he held her. He kissed her sweet
face all wet with rain.

" Little Winky—little darling Winky." He pushed back her Peggy hat and his voice lost itself in her hair.

" They're coming," she whispered.

There was a sound of footsteps and of a bolt drawn back. Somebody behind the door opened it just wide enough to let Winny through, then shut it on him.

It was intolerable, unthinkable, that she should disappear like that. Through a foot of space, in a hair's-breadth of time, she had slipped from him.

XXXI

NOBODY had seen them, for at this hour Acacia Avenue was deserted. The long monotonous pattern of it stretched before him, splendidly blurred, rich with lamplight and rain, bordered with streaming stars, striped with watered light and darkness, glowing, from lamp to lamp, with dim reds and purples that the daylight never sees, and with the strange gas-lit green of its tree-tufts shivering under the rain.

Otherwise the Avenue was depressing in its desolation. The more so because it was not quite deserted. At the far end of it the lamplight showed a woman's figure, indistinct and diminished. This figure, visibly unsheltered, moved obliquely as if it were driven by the slanting rain and shrank from its whipping.

He could not tell whether it were approaching or going from him. It seemed somehow to recede, to have got almost to the end of the road, past all the turnings; in which case, he reflected, the poor thing could not be far from her own door.

There was no mistaking his. Among all those monotonous diminutive houses it was distinct because of its lamppost, and its luxuriantly tufted tree. The gas was still turned on in the passage, so that above the door the white letters of its name, Granville, could be seen. There was no other light in the windows. Entering, he closed the door noiselessly, locked it, slipped the chain, and turned the gas out in the passage. The lamp-light from outside came in a turbid dusk through the thick glass of the front door. A small bead of gas made twilight in the sitting-room at the back.

The house was very still.

His mother had evidently gone to bed ; but she had left a fire burning in the sitting-room, and she had set a kettle all ready for boiling on the gas-ring, and on the table a cup and saucer, a tin of cocoa and a plate of bread and cheese.

He turned up the gas, put the tin of cocoa back into its cupboard and carried the bread and cheese to the larder in the scullery. He tried the back door to make sure that it was locked, and paused for a moment on the mat. He was thinking whether he had better not undress in there by the fire and spread his damp things round the hearth to dry.

And as he stood there at the end of the passage he was aware of something odd about the window of the front door. Properly speaking, when the passage was dark, the window should have shown clear against the light of the lamp outside, with its broad framework marking upon this transparency the four arms of a cross. Now it showed a darkness, a queer shadowy patch on the pane under the left arm of the cross.

The patch moved sideways to and fro along the lower panes ; then suddenly it rose, it shot up and broadened out, darkening half the window, its form indiscernible under the covering cross.

And as it stood still there came a light tapping on the pane. He thought that it was Winny, that she had run after him with some message, or that perhaps somebody else had run to tell him that something was wrong.

He went to the door ; and as he went the tapping began again, louder, faster, a nervous, desperate appeal.

He opened the door and the lamplight showed them to each other.

" Good God." He muttered it. " What are you doing here ? "

It was his instinct not his eyes that knew her.

She had not come forward as the door opened ; she had

swerved and stepped back rather, gripping her skirts tighter round her as she cowered. Sleeked by the rain, supple, sinuous and shivering, she cowered like a beaten bitch.

Yet she faced him. Shrinking from him, cowering like a bitch, backing to the edge of the porch where the rain beat her, she faced him for a moment.

Then she crept to him cowering ; and as she cowered, her hands, as if in helplessness and fear, let fall the skirts they had gathered from the rain. Her eyes, as she came, gazed strangely at him ; eyes that cowered, bitch-like, imploring, agonised, desirous.

She crept to the very threshold.

" Let me in," she said. " You will, won't you ? "

" I can't," he whispered. " You know that as well as I do."

Her eyes looked up sideways from their cowering. They were surprised, bewildered, incredulous.

" But I'm soaked through. I'm wet to me skin."

She was on the threshold. She had her hand to the door.

He could see her leaning forward a little, ready to fling her body upon the door if he tried, brutally, to shut it in her face. It was as if she actually thought that he would try.

He knew then that he was not going to shut the door.

" Come in out of the rain. And for God's sake don't make a noise."

" I'm not making a noise. I didn't even ring the bell."

He drew back before her as she came in, creeping softly in a pitiful submission. Though the passage was lighted from the street through the wide-open door, she went as if feeling her way along it, with a hand on the wall.

Ransome turned. He had no desire to look at her.

He struck a match and lit the gas, raised it to the full flame, and then, though he had no desire to look at her, he looked. He stared rather.

Y

Outside in the half-darkness he had known her, as if she stirred in him some sense, subtler or grosser than mere sight. Now, in the full light of the hanging lamp, he did not know her. He might have passed her in the street a score of times without recognising this woman who had been his wife ; though he would have stared at her, as indeed he would have been bound to stare. It was not only that her body was different, that her figure was taller, slenderer and more sinuous than he had ever seen it, or that her face was different, fined down to the last expression of its beauty, changed, physically, with a difference that seemed to him absolute and supreme. It was that this strange dissimilarity, if he could have analysed it, would have struck him as amounting to a difference of soul. Or rather, it was as if Violet's face had never given up her soul's secret until now ; never until now had it so much as hinted that Violet had any soul at all. The comparative fineness and sharpness of outline might have reminded him of his wife as she had looked when she came out of her torture after the birth of her first child, but that no implacable resentment and no revolt was there. It was plainly to be seen (nor did Ransome altogether miss it) that here were a body and soul that had suffered to extremity, and were now utterly beaten, utterly submissive.

This suggestion of frightful things endured was more lamentable by contrast with the shining sleekness, the drenched splendour of her attire. Ransome saw that her clothes helped to build up the impression of her strangeness. Violet was dressed as his wife, at the most frenzied height of her extravagance, had never dressed, as even Mercier's wife could not have dressed, nor yet his mistress. The black satin coat and gown that clung to her body like a sheath showed flawless though they streamed with rain, the lace at her throat, the black velvet hat with the raking plume that had once been yellow, the design and quality of the flat bag slung on her arm were details that belonged (and

Ransome knew it) to a world that was not his nor Mercier's either. And as he took them in he conceived from them an abominable suspicion.

His eyes must have conveyed his repulsion, for she spoke as if answering them.

" You mustn't mind my clothes. They're done for."

She looked down, self-pitying, at her poor slippered feet standing in a pool of rain.

" I'm making such a mess of your nice hall."

A little laugh shook in her throat and turned into a fit of coughing. He saw how instantly one hand went to her mouth and pressed there while the other struggled blindly, frantically, with the opening of her bag.

" What is it ? "

" My hanky——" She coughed the words out. It, the childish word, moved him to a momentary compassion.

" Here you are."

She stepped back from him as she stretched out her arm ; then she turned and leaned against the wall, hiding her face and muffling her cough in Ransome's pocket-handkerchief.

Each gesture, each surreptitious and yet frantic effort at suppression, showed her a creature that some brute had beaten, had terrified and cowed. The old Violet would have come swinging up the path ; she would have pushed past him into the warm and lighted room ; this one had come creeping to his door. She took no step to which he did not himself invite her.

" Come in here a minute," he said.

He put his hand upon her arm to guide her. He led her into the warm room and drew up a chair for her before the fire.

" Sit down and get warm."

She shook her head ; and by that sign he conceived the hope that she would soon be gone. She looked after him as he went to the door of the room to close it. When she heard the click of the latch her cough burst out violently and ceased.

She crouched down by the hearth holding out her hands to the blaze. He stood against the chimney-piece, looking down at her, silent, not knowing what he might be required to say.

She peeled off the wet gloves that were plastered to her skin ; she drew out the long pins from her hat, took it off and gazed ruefully at the lean plume lashed to its raking stem. With the coquetry of pathos, she held it out to him.

" Look at me poor feather, Ranny," she said.

He shuddered as she spoke his name.

" You'd better take your shoes off, and that coat," he said.

She took them off. He set the shoes in the fender. He hung the coat over the back of the chair to dry. As she stood upright the damp streamed from her skirts and drifted towards the fire.

" How about that skirt ? "

" I could slip it off, and me stockings too, if you didn't mind."

" All right," he muttered, and turned from her. He could hear the delicate silken swish of her draperies as they slid from her to the floor.

She was slenderer than ever in the short satin petticoat that was her inner sheath. Her naked feet, spread to the floor, showed white but unshapely. She stood there like some beautiful flower rising superbly from two ugly, livid, and distorted roots.

But neither her beauty nor her ugliness could touch him now.

" Look here," he said, " I'll get you some dry things."

His mind was dulled by the shock of seeing her, so that it was unable to attach any real importance or significance to her return. He knew her to be both callous and capricious, therefore he told himself that there was no need to take her seriously now. The thing was to get rid of her as soon as possible. He smothered the instinct that had warned him of his danger, and persuaded himself that dry things would meet the triviality of her case.

He went upstairs very softly to his room. In a jar on the chimney-piece he found a small key. Still going softly, he let himself into the little unfurnished room over the porch where boxes were stored. Among them was the trunk which contained Violet's long-abandoned clothes. He unlocked it, rummaged, deliberated, selected finally a serge skirt, draggled but warm ; a pair of woollen stockings, and shoes, stout for all their shabbiness.

And as he knelt over the trunk his mind cleared suddenly, and he knew what he was going to do. He was going to fetch a cab, if he could get one, and take her away in it. If she was staying in London he would take her straight back to whatever place she had come from. If she had come from a distance he would see her started on her journey home. He was prepared, if necessary, to hang about for hours in any station, waiting for any train that would remove her. If the worst came to the worst he would take a room for her in some hotel and leave her there. But he would not have her sitting with him till past midnight in his house. It was too risky. He knew what he was about. He knew that there was danger in any course that could give rise to the suspicion of cohabitation. He knew, not only that cohabitation in itself was fatal, but that the injured husband who invoked the law must refrain from the very appearance of that evil.

Of course, he knew what Violet had come for. She was beginning to get uneasy about her divorce. And, personally, he couldn't see where the risk came in unless the suit was defended. And it wasn't going to be defended. It couldn't be. The suspicion of collusion would in his case be a far more dangerous thing. It was what he had been specially warned against.

These two ideas, collusion and cohabitation, struggled

for supremacy in Ranny's brain. They seemed to him mutually exclusive ; and all it came to was that, with his suit so imminent, he couldn't be too careful. He must not, even for the sake of decency, show Violet any consideration that would be prejudicial to his case. Whereupon it struck him that the most perilous, most embarrassing detail of the situation was the disgusting accident of the weather. In common decency he couldn't have turned her out of doors in that rain. And under all the confused working of his intelligence his instinct told him that what happened was not an accident at all. His inmost prescience hinted at foredoomed, irremediable suffering ; profound, irreparable disaster.

But with his mind set upon its purpose he gathered up the shabby skirt, the stockings and the shoes, he took his own thick overcoat from its peg in the passage ; he warmed them well before the sitting-room fire.

Violet watched him with an air of detachment, of innocent incomprehension, as if these preparations in no way concerned herself. She was sitting in the chair now, with her bare feet in the fender.

He then put the kettle on the fire, and her eyes kindled and looked up at him.

" What are you going to do ? " she asked.

" I'm going to make you a cup of hot tea before you go."

" I *can't* go," she whispered.

He was firm.

" I'm awfully sorry, Virelet. But you've got to."

"But Ranny—you couldn't turn a cat out on a night like this."

" Don't talk nonsense about turning out. You know you can't stay here. I can't think what on earth possessed you to come. You haven't told me yet."

She did not tell him now. She did not look at him.

She sat bowed forwards, her elbows on her knees, and her
chin propped on her hands, while she cried, quietly, with
slow tears that rolled down her bare, undefended face.

He made the tea and poured it out for her, and she took
the cup from him and drank, without looking at him,
without speaking. And still she cried quietly. Now and
then a soft sob came from her in the pauses of her
drinking.

Ransome sat on the table and delivered himself of what
he had to say.

"I don't know what's upsetting you," he said. "And
you don't seem inclined to tell me. But if you're worrying about that divorce, you needn't. You'll get it all right.
The—the thing'll be sent you in a week or a fortnight."

"Ranny," she said, "are you really doin' it?"

"Of course I'm doing it."

"I didn't know——"

"Well—you might have known."

He was deaf to the terror in her voice.

"I'd have done it years ago if I'd had the money. It
isn't my fault we've had to wait for it. It was hard luck
on both of us."

He stopped to look at her, still, like some sick animal,
meekly drinking, and still crying.

He waited till her cup was empty and took it from her.
"More?"

"No thank you."

He put down the cup, turned, and went towards the door.
There was a savage misery in his heart and in all his
movements an awful gentleness.

She started up.

"Don't go, Ranny. Don't leave me."

Her voice was dreadful to his instinct.

"I must."

"You're going to do something. What are you going
to do?"

"I'm going to leave you to change into those things.

I'm going to look for a cab, and I'm going to take you back to wherever you came from."

" You don't know where I came from. You don't know why I've come."

There was the throb of all disaster in her voice. His instinct heard it. But his intelligence refused to hear. It went on reasoning with her who was unreasonable.

" I don't know," it said, " why you want to stick here. It won't do either of us any good."

" Has it began ? " she said. " Can't anything stop it ? "

" Yes. You can stop it if you stay here all night. If you want it to go right you must keep away. It's madness your coming here at this time of night. I can't think why you—I should have thought you'd have known——"

" Oh, Ranny, don't be hard on me."

" I'm not hard on you. You're hard on yourself. You want a divorce and I want it. Don't you know we shan't get it—if——"

" But I *don't* want it—I don't indeed."

" What's that ? "

" I don't want it. I didn't know you were divorcing me. I never thought you'd go and do it after all these years."

" Rot ! You knew I was going to do it the minute I had the money."

" You don't understand. I've come to ask you if you'll forgive me—and take me back."

" I forgave you long ago. But I can't take you back. You know *that* well enough."

She made as if she had not heard him.

" I'll be good, Ranny. I *want* to be good."

He also made as if he had not heard.

" Why do you want me to take you back ? "

" That's why. So as I can be good. Father's turned me out, Ranny."

" Your father ? "

" I went to him first. I didn't think I'd any right to come to you—after I'd served you like I did."

" Oh, never mind how you served me. What's Mercier been doing ? "

" He's got married."

" Just like him. I thought he was going to marry *you* ? "

" He wouldn't wait for me. He couldn't. He thought you were never going to get your divorce. He *had* to settle down so as to get on in his business. He wanted a Frenchwoman who could help him, and he daren't so much as look at me—after, for fear she'd divorce him."

" I told you he was a swine."

" He wasn't. It wasn't *his* fault. He'd have married me two years ago if you could have divorced me then."

Her mouth was loose to the passage of her sigh, as if for a moment she felt a sensuous pleasure in her own self-pity. She did not see how his mouth tightened to the torture as she turned the screw.

She went on. " Lenny was all right. He was good to me as long as I was with him. *He* wouldn't have turned me into the street to starve."

" Who *has* turned you into the street ? " He could not disguise his exasperation.

Then he remembered. " Oh—your father."

" I don't mean Father. I mean the other one."

" There *was* another one ? And you expect me to take you back ? "

" I'm only *asking* you," she said. " Don't be so hard on me. I *had* to have someone when Lenny left me. He's been the only one since Lenny. And he was all right until he tired of me."

" Who's the brute you're talking about ? "

" He's a gentleman. That's all I can tell you."

" Sounds pretty high class. And where does this gentleman hang out ? "

" I oughtn't to tell you. He's a painter and he's awfully well known. Well—it's somewhere in the West End and we had a flat in Bloomsbury."

She answered his wonder. " I met him in Paris. He took me away from there and I've been with him all the time. There wasn't anybody else. I swear there wasn't— I swear."

" Oh, you needn't."

He got up and walked away.

" Ranny—don't go for the cab until I've told you everything."

" I'm *not* going. What more have you got to say ? "

" Don't look at me like that, as if you could murder me. You wouldn't if you knew how he's served me. He beat me, Ranny. He beat me with his hands and with his stick."

She rolled up the sleeves of her thin blouse.

" Look here—and here. That's what he was always doing to me. And I've got worse—bigger ones—on me breast and on me body."

" Good God——" The words came from him under his breath, and not even his instinct knew what he would say next.

He said—or rather some unknown power took hold of him and said it—" Why didn't you come to me before ? "

She hesitated.

" He never turned me out until last night."

Her pause gave him time to measure the significance of what she said.

" He didn't really tire of me till I got ill. I had pneumonia last spring. I nearly died of it and I've not been right since. That's how I got me cough. He couldn't stand it." She paused.

" I ought to have gone when he told me to. But I didn't. I was awfully gone on him.

" And—last night—we were to have gone to the theatre together ; but he'd been drinkin' and I said I wouldn't go with him. Then he swore at me and struck me, and said I might go by myself. And I went. And when I came home he shut the door on me and turned me into the street with nothing but the clothes on me back and what I had in me purse. And he said if I came back he'd do for me."

She got it out, the abominable history, in a succession of jerks, in a voice dulled to utter apathy.

And an intolerable pity held him silent before this beaten thing, although with every word she dragged him nearer to the ultimate, foreseen disaster.

She went on.

" I was scared to walk about the streets all night in these things. I always was more afraid of that than anything. Though *he* never would believe me when I said so. You don't know the names he called me. So I took a taxi and I went to the first hotel I could think of—the ' Thackeray.' But I hadn't enough money with me and they wouldn't take me in. Then I went and sat in the waiting-room at Euston Station till they closed. Then I sat outside on the platform and pretended to be waitin' for a train. *He* wouldn't believe me if I told him I'd spent the night in that station. But I did. And I got me death of cold. And in the morning me cough started, and they wouldn't take me in any of the shops because of it.

" I tried all morning, Starker's first. Then in the afternoon I went to Father and he wouldn't have me. He won't believe I haven't been bad, because of me things and me cough. I suppose he thinks I've got consumption or something. He saw me coming in at the gate and he turned me out straight. I didn't even get to the door."

" He couldn't——"

" He did—reelly, Ranny, he did. He said he'd washed his hands of me and I could go back to you. He said— No, I can't tell you what he said."

There was no need to tell. He knew.

She looked at him now, straight, for the first time.

" Ranny—he knows. He knows what we did."

" Did you tell him ? "

" Not me ! He'd guessed it. He'd guessed it all the

time. Trust *him*. And he taxed me with it. And I lied.
I wasn't goin' to have him thinkin' *that* of you."

" Of *me* ? "

" Yes—*you*." It was her first flash of feeling since she
began her tale. " It doesn't matter what he thinks of me.
I told him so."

" Well ? Then ? "

" Then I started lookin' for work again. Couldn't
get any. Then I came here. If you turn me out there'll
be nothing but the streets. If I was to get work nobody'll
keep me. I haven't properly got over that illness. I'm
so weak I couldn't stand to do anything long. There are
times when I can hardly hold myself together."

And still there was no feeling in her voice, and barely
the suggestion of appeal ; only the flat tones of the last
extremity.

" I've come here because I'm afraid of going to the
bad. I don't want to be bad—not reelly bad. But I'll
be driven to it if you turn me out."

It might have been a threat she held out to him but
that her voice lacked the passion of all menace. Passion
could not have served her better than her dull, unvibrating
statement of the fact.

" If you won't take me back——"

Her spent voice dropped dead on the last word and her
cough broke out again.

Ransome's next movement averted it. She revived
suddenly.

" Ranny—are you going for that cab ? "

He turned.

" No," he said. " You know I'm not."

" Then, what are you thinking of ? "

He was thinking, " I won't have Dossie and Stanny
sleeping with her. And I can't turn Mother out. So

there's no room for her. Yes, there is. I can get a camp-
bed and put it in the box-room. I shall be all right in
there, and she can have my room to herself."

No other arrangement seemed endurable or possible to
him.

And yet, while his flesh cried out in the agony of its
repulsion, it knew that in the years, the terrible, interminable years before them, it could not be as he had planned.
There would be a will stronger than his own will that would
not be frustrated.

And he told himself that he could have borne it if it
had not been for that.

There was a knocking at the door. The handle turned,
and through the slender opening which was all she dared
make, Mrs. Ransome spoke to her son.

" Ranny, do you know you've left the front door open ?
Who's that coughing ? " she said.

Neither of them answered.

" Hasn't Winny gone yet ? You shouldn't keep her
out so late, dear. It's time both of you were in bed."

At that he rose and went to her.

Presently they could be heard moving Stanny's little
cot into his grandmother's room.

That night Violet slept in Ransome's bed.

Ransome lay on the sofa in the front sitting-room. He
did not sleep, and at dawn he got up and looked out. The
rain had ceased. It was the beginning of a perfect day.

He remembered then that he had promised Winny to
walk with her to Wimbledon Common.

XXXII

" SHE'S ill. Fair gone to pieces. But the doctor says
she'll soon be all right again if we take care of her."

It was early evening of Sunday. They were going slowly
up the steep hill that winds, westwards and southwards,
towards the heights of Wimbledon.

He had just told her that Violet had come back.

" I couldn't in common decency turn her out."

In a long silence he struggled to find words for what
he had to say next. She saw him struggling and came to
his help.

" Ranny, you're going to take her back," she said.

" What must you think of me ? "

" Think of you ? I wouldn't have you different."
The whole spirit of her love for him was in those words.

She continued. " You see, dear, it comes to the same
thing. If you didn't take her back I couldn't marry you,
for it wouldn't be you. You'll have to take her."

" You talk as if I'd nobody but her to think of. Look
what she's making me do to you——"

" I'm strong enough to bear it and she isn't. She'll go
straight to the bad it we don't look after her."

" That's it. She said there was nothing but the streets
for her." He brooded. " If I was a rich man I could
divorce her and give her an allowance to live away. I
can't stand it, Winny, when I think of you."

" You needn't think of me, dear. It isn't as if I hadn't
known."

" How *could* you know ? "

" I knew all the time she'd come back—some day."

" Yes. But if Father hadn't died when he did we

should have been safe married. We missed it by a day. Mercier'd have married her two years ago. If I'd had thirty pounds then it couldn't have happened. But I was a damned fool. I should have thought of you *then*— I should have let everything else go and married you."

Slowly, drop by drop, he drank his misery. But she had savoured sorrow so far off that now that the cup was brought to her it had lost half its bitterness.

"You couldn't have done different, even then, dear. Don't worry about me. It's not as if I hadn't been happy with you. I've had you—reelly—Ranny, all these years."

But the happiness that by way of comfort she held out to him was the very dregs of Ranny's cup.

"That's it," he said. "I don't know how it's going to be now. She's the same, somehow, and yet different."

It was his way of expressing the fact that Violet's sufferings had given her a soul, and that this soul, this subtler and more inscrutable essence of her, would not necessarily be good. It might even be malignant. Most certainly it would be hostile. It would come between them.

"It's a good thing the children'll be at school now— out of her way."

"P'r'aps she's better—kinder, p'r'aps."

"I don't know about that, Winny. I'm afraid. Anyhow, it'll never be the same for you and me."

He paused, and then seeing suddenly the full extent of their calamity, he broke out.

"What'll you *do*, Winny?"

"I'll ask Mr. Randall if he'll take me on."

"You won't stay here?"

"No. Better not. I mustn't be too near, this time. That was the mistake I made before. And you've got your mother."

"And what have *you* got?" he cried fiercely.

"I've got plenty—all I've ever had. These things don't go away, dear."

They stood still, looking before them, with their unspoken misery in their eyes.

At their feet, down there, creeping low on the ground, spreading its packed roofs for miles over the land that had once been green fields, its red and purple smouldering and smoking in the autumn mist and sunset, there lay the Paradise of Little Clerks.

They turned and went slowly towards it down the hill.

THE END

WILLIAM BRENDON AND SON, LTD.
PRINTERS PLYMOUTH

Lightning Source UK Ltd.
Milton Keynes UK
UKOW04f0018160316

270220UK00001B/73/P